FIRST EMPEROR

EMPEROR

Tales from the Jade Room

Conrad Squires

Enjoy!
Conrad Squires
Dec. 20, 2016

Marshall Cavendish
Editions

Design by Bernard Go Kwang Meng

Published by Marshall Cavendish Editions
An imprint of Marshall Cavendish International
1 New Industrial Road, Singapore 536196

Other Marshall Cavendish Offices:
Marshall Cavendish Ltd. 5th Floor, 32–38 Saffron Hill, London EC1N 8FH, UK •
Marshall Cavendish Corporation. 99 White Plains Road, Tarrytown NY 10591-
9001, USA • Marshall Cavendish International (Thailand) Co Ltd. 253 Asoke,
12th Flr, Sukhumvit 21 Road, Klongtoey Nua, Wattana, Bangkok 10110, Thailand
• Marshall Cavendish (Malaysia) Sdn Bhd, Times Subang, Lot 46, Subang Hi-Tech
Industrial Park, Batu Tiga, 40000 Shah Alam, Selangor Darul Ehsan, Malaysia.

Marshall Cavendish is a trademark of Times Publishing Limited

National Library Board Singapore Cataloguing in Publication Data
Squires, Conrad.
First emperor : tales from the jade room / Conrad Squires. – Singapore :
Marshall Cavendish Editions, c2009.
p. cm.
ISBN-13 : 978-981-261-656-2

1. Qin shi huang, Emperor of China, 259-210 B.C. — Fiction.
2. China — History — Qin dynasty, 221-207 B.C. — Fiction. I. Title.

PS3619
813.6 — dc22   OCN276980011

Printed in Singapore by Craft Print International Ltd

For Mac, Andrea
and Bonnie

"You have to infer the whole dragon from the parts you can see and touch. Dragons are immense. I could explore the mountains, which are the top of its head. The dragon roams through space, so vast we feel that it is not even moving under us. In quarries you see the dragon's veins and muscles, the minerals, its teeth and bones. The stones, its bone marrow. The soil, its flesh. The plants and trees, its hairs. The thunder, its voice. The wind, its breathing. The lightning, its tongue. The red the lightning gives the world is strong and lucky—in blood, poppies, roses, rubies, the red feathers of birds, the red carp, the cherry tree, the peony, the line alongside the turtle's eyes and the mallards. In the spring when the dragon wakes, you can see its turnings in the rivers...The dragon lives in the sky, ocean, marshes and mountains. Its voice thunders and jingles like copper pans. It breathes fire and water. Sometimes it is one, sometimes many."

— From *The Woman Warrior* by Maxine Hong Kingston

"It was our job to conceal the human failings of the Emperor from the world outside, which was always ready to pull down a ruler who stumbled, like hounds on a wounded stag. In this we have always failed, but that never discourages our successors. And they will fail, too. They did not depend on us for strength or virtue in our duties of shielding the Emperor and keeping silent about his weaknesses. On the contrary—it was because we were considered so cowardly that we would be sure to be quiet for fear of punishment. I once heard a fellow eunuch say, 'If I tried to help someone, it would only be to his detriment.'"

— A eunuch speaks of his life.
From *Eunuchs and Castrati* by Piotr O. Scholz

A sculptor once made a magnificent teapot. Critics said, "But you can't pour tea from it!" The sculptor said, "You have missed the point. It is not a teapot. It is the *idea* of a teapot."

— Adaptation of a label from an exhibition of
Chinese teapots, Peabody Museum, Salem

Contents

Characters in This Novel   8
Ancestry of the First Emperor   13
Map of China in the Warring States Period   14
Map of the Ch'in Empire   15

PROLOGUE: Wonderful Things   16

BOOK ONE: THE INFANT
The Black Carriage   28
The Beginning   43
The Court Astrologer   61
Shen Neng's Journey   68
The Inhabitants of the Jade Room   72
The Gates of Hantan   79

Poems
Fu Hao of Shang   91
The Maker   92
A Royal Prince   93

BOOK TWO: THE KING
The Boys   96
How the Ch'in Came to Power   107
The Merchant Lu Pu-wei   113
The Late, Lamentable Lao Ai   120
A Rat in the Granary   129
The Assassins   137

Poems
The River Merchant's Letter to His Wife   151
Master K'ung and the Ancient Songs   152
The Power of the Moon   153

BOOK THREE: THE EMPEROR

The Last Great Battle 156
Mutations 165
Journey to the Otherworld 173
The Naked Mountain 188
The Emperor and the Immortals 193
The Unluckiest Man 205
The Homecoming 213

Poem

The Judgment of Wu Wei 228

BOOK FOUR: CHAOS

A Secret 234
Something Smells Like a Dead Fish 244
Plots in the Palace 248
Final Tales 256
The Journey to Mount Li 273

Poems

The Nomad Girl 282
The Journey of Baroness Hsu 283
Hills Rising above Clouds 284

AFTERWORDS

Chronology of the Reign of Ch'in Shih-huang-ti 286
The Real Life of Ssu-ma Ch'ien, the Grand Historian 288
For Further Reading 290
A Note to the Reader 297

About the Author 300

Characters in This Novel

Note to the reader: Those not entirely at home with Chinese names may find it difficult to keep track of who is who. This is not essential to follow the story, but you may find this guide to important characters of help, starting with the principal players. The ancestry of the First Emperor, in abridged version based mainly on the royal characters in this novel, is included for quick reference. The line would begin with his great-grandparents and run through to the Second and Third Emperors, where it would end.

PRINCIPAL CHARACTERS
Ch'in Shih-Huang-Ti
Known as Ying Cheng when he was young, ascended to the Ch'in throne as King Cheng at age thirteen, became First Emperor of the Ch'in Empire at thirty-seven

Ssu-Ma Ch'ien
Grand Historian, China's most famous. For information on his fascinating life, see the note at the back of this book.

The Eunuch Storytellers, Servants in the Ch'in Court
Thousands of eunuchs were required by the immense court of Ch'in to help keep the royal line as "pure" as it could be. Such an immense group, with extremely close access to the emperor, was powerful and well accustomed to organizing itself, likely on quasi-military lines. But there are no formal records of who did what or even the names of the highest-ranking eunuchs— a common vagueness among generally despised people. So the author has invented the names and somewhat plausible positions of the Eunuch Storytellers. The reader can be sure the

eunuchs (a) were fairly secure in their tasks, (b) were probably quite wealthy, and (c) had a great deal of time on their hands.

* Han Yin, Regulator of Entertainment in the Royal Palace
* Juan Chi, Chief Dispenser of Eunuch Punishments
* Wang Ts'ao, Major Domo of the Royal Palace
* Chia Tao, Major Domo of the Concubine Residences
* Tu Mu, Charioteer of the First Emperor
* Lo Yin, Chief Dresser of the First Emperor
* Meng Hao-jan, Principal Eunuch Trainer and Director of Eunuch Promotions

Inner Circle of the Ch'in Court

Key players

Lu Pu-wei, great merchant, Ch'in Regent and Prime Minister, "Uncle Lu" or "Second Father" to King Cheng—possibly also his real father, so the rumor goes

Li Ssu, Grand Counselor, enforcer of Legalism throughout the Ch'in Empire

Chao Kao, Chief Eunuch and Manager of Chariots

Other players

Wang Kuan, Prime Minister

Feng Ch'ieh, Chief Counselor

Meng Chia, Chamberlain

Note: All characters are historical figures except for those marked with an asterisk, which are fictitious. All characters are listed in order of appearance.

MAJOR CHARACTERS
Book One
Queen Dowager Hsuan a.k.a. Plum Blossom
Shen Neng, Secretary to the Queen Dowager
* Full Moons a.k.a. Sunshine, the wet nurse
Prince Tzu-ch'u, First Emperor's father, reigned briefly
  as King Chuang-hsiang of Ch'in Kingdom
* Chief Astrologer of the Ch'in Court
Lady Tzu-ch'u, rich girl turned courtesan turned consort
  turned Queen Dowager Hsia, First Emperor's mother

Book Two
Lao Ai, secret lover of Queen Dowager Hsia
Ching K'o, swordsman, assassin
Kao Chien-li a.k.a. Phat Kao, bosom pal of Ching K'o

Book Three
Prince Fu-su, Crown Prince of Ch'in Empire
* Mr Ten Thousand, a very unlucky peasant
Hsu Fu, Taoist priest who encouraged First Emperor
  in his pursuit of immortality
Ssu-ma Ts'ao, sister of Ssu-ma Ch'ien

Book Four
Hu-hai, Second Emperor
Tzu-ying, Third Emperor

SECONDARY CHARACTERS

Farmer Yang, modern character who found the warrior's
 head (really!)
King Chao-hsiang, First Emperor's great grandfather
Lord An-kuo, First Emperor's grandfather, reigned briefly
 as King Hsiao-wen of Ch'in Kingdom
Ssu-ma Tan, father of Ssu-ma Ch'ien
Lady Hua-yang, Number One Wife of Lord An-kuo
King Hsi, ruler of Yen State
Prince Tan, Crown Prince of Yen State
T'ien Kuang, sage of Yen State
Ch'in Wu-yang, Ching K'o's assistant
Hsia Wu-chu, First Emperor's physician
Scholar Lu, Taoist priest
Chen She, peasant, rebel general
Chang Han, Ch'in general who defected to a rebel camp
Hsiang Yu, aristocrat, rebel general from Ch'u State
Liu Pang, peasant, rebel leader, later Han Dynasty Emperor

Ch'in Generals
Key players
Meng Ao, tutor of both Ying Cheng and Ssu-ma Ch'ien
Wang Ch'ien, commander of empire-establishing battle
Meng T'ien, commander of northern frontier, builder
 of northern Great Wall
Fan Yu-ch'i, who defected to Yen State

Other players
Wang I
Lord Piao
Hsiang Yen

SCHOLAR CHARACTERS

Lord Shang Yang, principal proponent of Legalism
Ch'u Yuan, great and famous early poet two hundred years
  before period of the novel
K'ung Fu Tzu, Confucius
Hsun Tzu, Confucian philosopher
Han Fei, Li Ssu's major Legalist rival
Sun Tzu, author of the famous *The Art of War*

MYTHICAL CHARACTERS

Queen Mother of the West, believed to be the goddess of
  immortality
Kuan Yin, Goddess of Mercy
Yellow Emperor, said to be the grandfather of all things Chinese
Jade Emperor, Taoist ruler of Heaven, Man and Hell
Yen Ti, Red Emperor
Yao, Sage Ruler
Shun, Sage Ruler
Yu, Sage Ruler
Lady of the River Yangtze, revered as goddess of the great river
The Eight Immortals
Lord of the Dead
Duke of Thunder
Spirit of Lightning
Master of Wind
Master of Rain
Weather Watchers

Ancestry of the First Emperor (abridged)

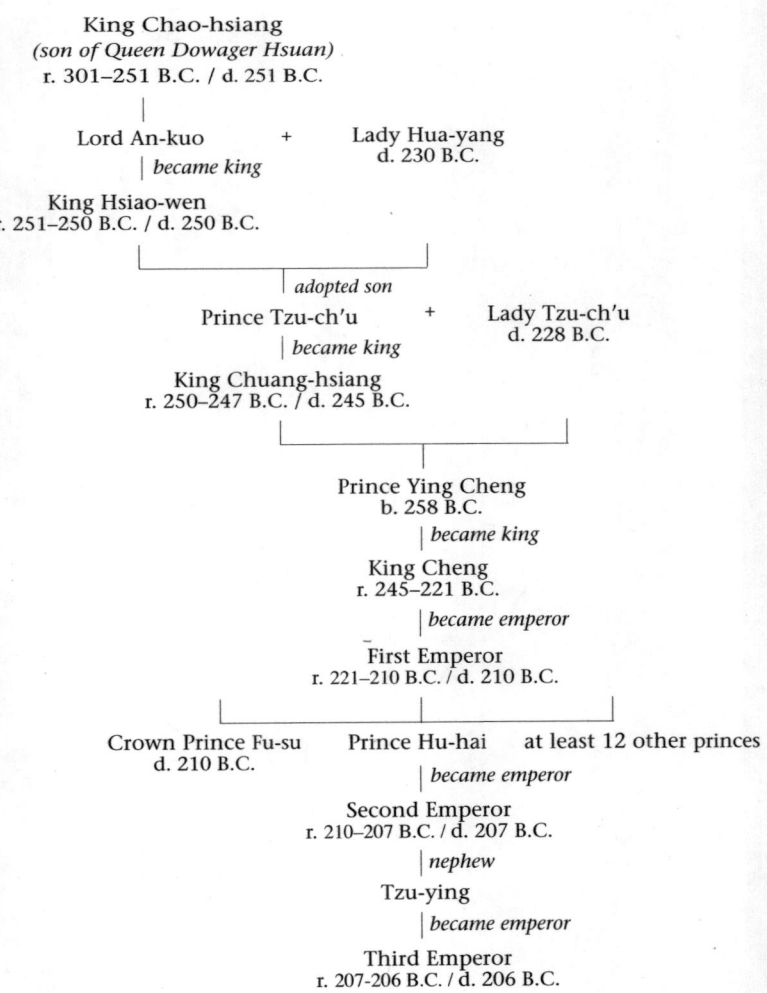

King Chao-hsiang
(son of Queen Dowager Hsuan)
r. 301–251 B.C. / d. 251 B.C.

Lord An-kuo + **Lady Hua-yang**
became king   d. 230 B.C.

King Hsiao-wen
r. 251–250 B.C. / d. 250 B.C.

adopted son
Prince Tzu-ch'u + **Lady Tzu-ch'u**
became king   d. 228 B.C.

King Chuang-hsiang
r. 250–247 B.C. / d. 245 B.C.

Prince Ying Cheng
b. 258 B.C.
became king

King Cheng
r. 245–221 B.C.
became emperor

First Emperor
r. 221–210 B.C. / d. 210 B.C.

Crown Prince Fu-su   **Prince Hu-hai**   at least 12 other princes
d. 210 B.C.   *became emperor*

Second Emperor
r. 210–207 B.C. / d. 207 B.C.
nephew

Tzu-ying
became emperor

Third Emperor
r. 207-206 B.C. / d. 206 B.C.

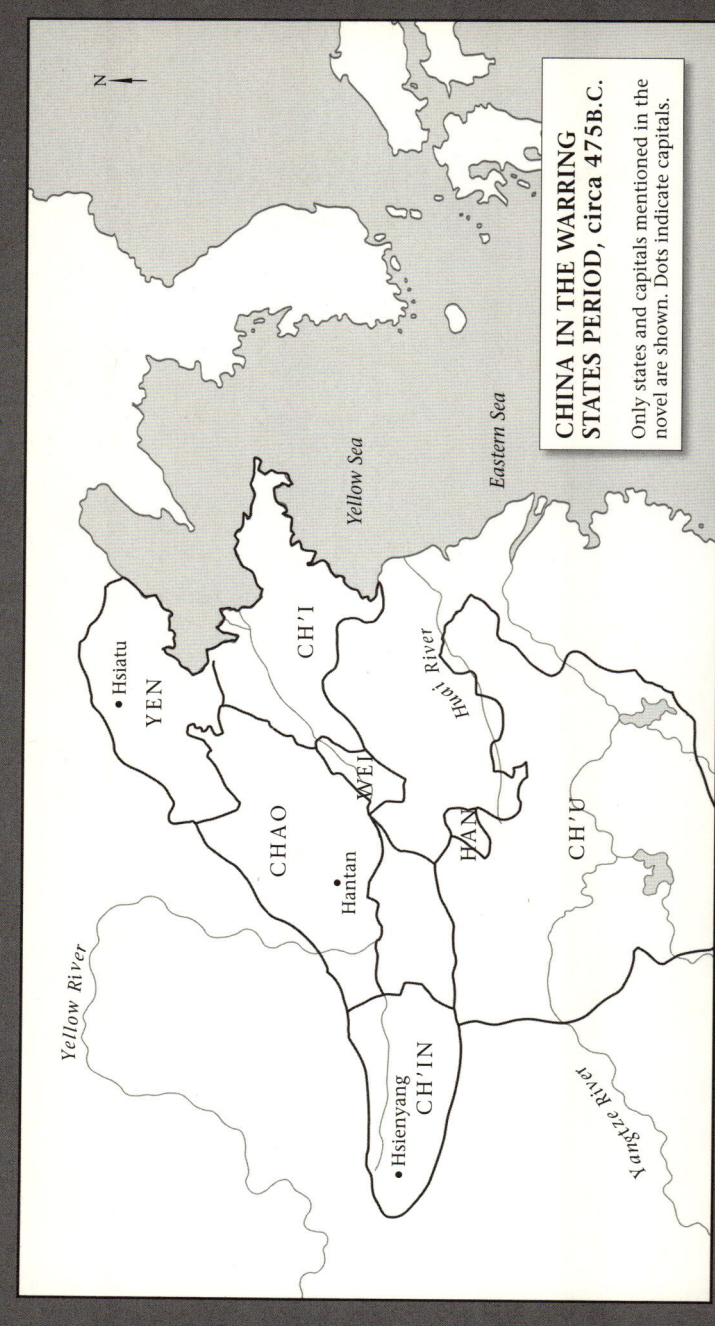

CHINA IN THE WARRING STATES PERIOD, circa 475 B.C.

Only states and capitals mentioned in the novel are shown. Dots indicate capitals.

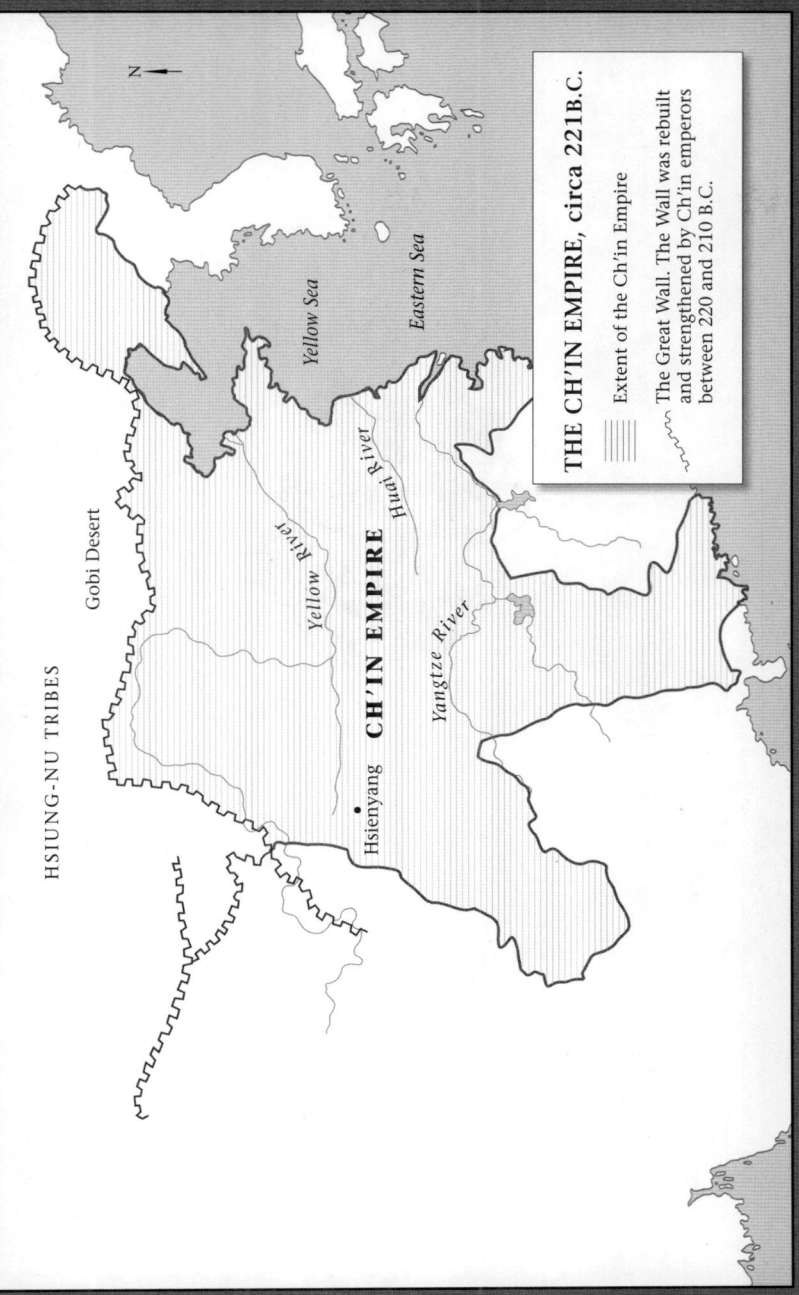

THE CH'IN EMPIRE, circa 221 B.C.

||||| Extent of the Ch'in Empire

〜〜 The Great Wall. The Wall was rebuilt
and strengthened by Ch'in emperors
between 220 and 210 B.C.

N ←

Yellow Sea

Eastern Sea

Gobi Desert

HSIUNG-NU TRIBES

Yellow River

Huai River

Yangtze River

CH'IN EMPIRE

Hsienyang

PROLOGUE

Wonderful Things

I. SEVEN THOUSAND CLAY SOLDIERS

Since every tale must begin somewhere, let this one begin with the groan of a rusty spade against something that was hidden in the earth a very long time ago—so long ago that China was not yet China. The spade belonged to a farmer, one Mr. Yang, who had come to his field in present-day Sha'anxi province to dig a well with neighbors early in the morning in summer, 1974. He was not expecting resistance in the loose fertile soil called loess in northern China until the *thunk* of the spade sent a painful shock from his toes to his head.

Numb but unfazed, he soon began to dig around the source of resistance, which proved to be a fiercely staring terracotta head, larger than his own, ending at the neck.

Farmer Yang took the head home. After diligent cleaning, he placed it on the family altar next to the portraits of his ancestors and worshipped it.

Yang hoped it would bring him luck, and it did—the wrong kind. Fearing that the head belonged to a demon who might come looking for it, his neighbors drove Yang and his family into the mountains south of the village. Then, not plagued by a need for consistency, they stuck the head on a pole above the village street to drive away the many other ghosts and demons that gather in small rural villages in China.

The head may have rebuffed ghosts, but as news of the find spread, it attracted large crowds of Chinese archaeologists and other scientists from the nearby city of Xi'an. Sinking exploratory pits all over Yang's field, they discovered that Farmer Yang and his neighbors had accidentally stumbled on one of the strangest and most important archaeological finds of the Twentieth Century: an underground army of seven thousand life-size terracotta warriors dated to the final years of the Third Century B.C.E. (Before the Common Era).

Drawn up for battle and in long tunnels originally roofed over with timbers, then hidden under dirt, the clay soldiers were on a mission to guard the man known as Ch'in Shih-huang-ti, the infamous First Emperor of the Ch'in Empire. ("Ch'in" is a name Westerners would alter to "China" centuries later).

The First Emperor was buried nearly a mile away under a man-made mountain of earth that once rose high as the Great Pyramid in Egypt. His burial mound lies south of the Wei River below a slope of Mount Li, whose veins were said to be rich with deposits of gold and jade. He was laid to rest not far from the tombs of his father, and in the vicinity of what was thought to be the tomb of the legendary Yellow Emperor, grandfather of all things Chinese.

As the excavation continued, it revealed generals and lesser officers, identifiable by clay "ribbons" on their backs and chests—charioteers, cavalrymen, archers, crossbowmen and foot-soldiers—an army manqué, safeguarding the First Emperor as he continued an afterlife that was held to be much like his earthly life—riding, hunting, governing, visiting his concubines, receiving tribute, et cetera.

No two of the seven thousand statues have the same face. Some scholars think the faces were modeled by the real Imperial Guard, but others believe the Guard would never have consented to have their souls stolen and immured in clay figures. Perhaps the artisans who created the soldiers used their own faces—many had signed their names on the backs of the statues. It's all conjecture, but it is hard to imagine the Guard saying to the fierce First Emperor, "No, you can't use our faces."

From 1974 to the present (that is, 2036), archaeologists have continued to uncover the soldiers while other scientists slowly closed in on the emperor's burial mound. Their discoveries have been astounding.

The First Emperor's empire was meant to last, in his words, "ten thousand generations." But just four years after his death, in 206 B.C., his empire lay in ruins, his huge palaces and legendary capital city of Hsienyang (near modern Xi'an) burned to the ground by a rebel army. His tomb at Mount Li did not survive the wrath of the enemy either. Arriving at the tomb site, the invaders tore off the tunnel roofs, stole the bronze weapons and burned the clay army all the way to the outer wall of the tomb, scattering thousands of pieces of stone armor.

Next, they penetrated the inner wall of the emperor's underground palace and the ghost-ridden imperial court, where there lay hundreds of skeletons and clay figures of long-robed, loose-sleeved court officials, agile acrobats, demure concubines and the ubiquitous peasant farmers. Many formerly living beings and creatures were buried with him, including craftsmen, officials, his beloved western pure-bred horses, rare birds and animals from the great park he had built near his palace, and, most sadly, the scores of princes and princesses who were, or would have been, his descendants. The First Emperor's successor, Hu-hai, had ordered them all to be buried alive. A multitude of wall paintings that might have spoken vividly of the First Emperor's life were destroyed by the torches of the invaders; now only faint traces of pigment remain.

The whole chaotic, gigantic mess—the underground courtyards, the toppled figures knocked over against each other, the portrait heads struck from thousands of clay shoulders—will take decades to sort out. That's appropriate: a near-contemporary of the First Emperor wrote that in addition to the artisans, at peak times 700,000 conscripts were employed to build the tomb over a period of more than thirty years.

II. THE HIDDEN CHAMBER

Inside the tomb a discovery even greater than the clay soldiers lay ahead.

Using new surveying, digging and measuring tools and minimally destructive methods of excavation, the scientists began to remove dirt from the main passageway that led to the First Emperor's burial chamber under the fifteen-storey mound.

The year was 2025, nearly fifty years after Farmer Yang's find. The scientists were excited to a man, because a preliminary sounding suggested quantities of mercury lay deep under the mound, giving them reason to hope that an early account of a huge map of China surrounded by a flowing sea of mercury might be correct.

When the passageway was cleared, scientists found splintery dry traces of the massive doors at the burial chamber's northern end. Working their way through the door area with care, they eagerly entered the chamber. Behind them the press pushed forward with cameras and microphones held high, eager to send the first view of the burial chamber to a fascinated world.

When the earth-filled chamber, longer than a football field, was finally cleared, there was disappointingly little to see. The vast room, with its great vaulted ceiling, reportedly once covered with precious stones to simulate a night sky, was vacant. Only naked blocks of gray stone were left, forming the floor on which the emperor's catafalque had rested (said to be on a bronze dragon's back). Broad grooves ran through the floor of the chamber, outlining what appeared to be a central island that corresponded roughly in shape to a map of the ancient kingdom of Ch'in. The scientists also found traces of mercury in the substrate but that merely seemed to confirm the early Chinese description of the chamber.

On the whole, the burial chamber was nothing to write home about—until a week later, when a scientist was taking a moment to catch his breath in the fetid air, with hands on hips and upper body bent over. In that very moment, his eyes spotted, at his feet, a small, circular-cut stone of a slightly different color from the larger stones. Judging that it could be an important find, he and his colleagues photographed it, x-rayed it and did everything modern science could do to figure out why it was there (short of trying to lift it, which they thought would destroy it).

Several weeks later, as the group of experts stood around the small, round stone trying to decide what to do, the same scientist lost patience. He kicked off a thermal slipper-boot, stepped forward and—unthinkable!—thrust the big toe of his right foot down hard on the stone! His large Chinese toe protruded from his black sock and a photographer took a picture of the toe just as it touched the stone. Later flashed out to the world, it became the best-known picture taken so far in this century.

At first, the only sound in the chamber was the collective gasp of every other scientist present; then a deep groan came from the stone floor, followed by a creaking and clanking of ancient pulleys. Finally, an entire six-foot section of the floor slid up reluctantly, leaving an opening below which everything was black.

The scientists uncovered a flight of steps leading to a small room below the burial chamber. The steps were directly below the area where the catafalque had stood. When the small room was cleared, the scientists noticed two things.

First, they found piles of tightly-stoppered, ochre-colored pottery vases, each one containing hundreds of rolled-up bamboo strips, individually about seven inches in length, and covered with writing. The scholars among the expert group soon realized they were looking at a huge quantity of books from the time of the First Emperor! Taking the appropriate precaution, the scientists later replaced the stoppers on the vases before moving all the vases to a laboratory for clinical conditioning.

The second subject conjured up a mystery.

Near the vases lay two unidentified skeletons, a large adult and a smaller figure, who was cradled in the right arm of the larger one. The skeletons showed no signs of violence. Puzzled as they were about their find, though generally not too surprised to discover skeletons in the First Emperor's tomb, the scientists accordingly removed them for examination and identification.

To date, there has yet to be an announcement of any findings related to these skeletons. The bamboo strips, however, could be read like a book, after nearly a year in the laboratory. The bundles were first unrolled, then preserved and photographed. They were intelligible to modern experts, having been written in small seal script, a simplification of earlier Chinese writing.

To the experts' astonishment, the bamboo strips were an apparently complete manuscript of the *Records of the Grand Historian*, widely-regarded as the most ambitious work of historial writing ever undertaken. The *Records* are the masterpiece of Ssu-ma Ch'ien, China's greatest historian. It's a description of the instructive deeds, both good and bad, of all the great ancestors, going back to a time we regard as mythical. His had been a most difficult task, undertaken in a time of ruthless repression. The First Emperor had murdered a large number of Confucian scholars and destroyed almost all the ancient written texts, a deed so un-Chinese that even today many Chinese people continue to slap on him the label "Burn books, Bury scholars!"

The immense work that is the *Records of the Grand Historian* is being scrutinized intensively today prior to scholarly publication. In the meantime, a second, separate group of bamboo strips, has caught the attention and interest of the Archaeological Institute of Shanghai. It has, in fact, honored me by asking me to select and translate the vivid and memorable material from them.

This second group of bamboo strips bore the ancient title, *Tales of the First Emperor*, which I have shortened to *First Emperor*. I have also added a subtitle, *Tales from the Jade Room*, since that was where most of the stories were apparently told.

The tales are accounts, exemplary in detail if not always trustworthy, of the life and times of the First Emperor. This collection was written by a calligrapher whom we believe to have been Ssu-ma Ch'ien himself.

The *Tales* tell us that he had served as the Recording Secretary of a small group of storytellers who were the First Emperor's highest-ranking eunuch servants—rich, powerful, and usually idle men who went about their work, unobserved but observant. Through the *Tales*, we learn what they saw and heard—what they *said* they saw and heard.*

The locale of the connected stories, which purport to begin around 260 B.C., is the westernmost of a group of quarrelsome states in present-day North China. These states were feudal remnants of the ancient empire of Chou, built on the ruins of the even more ancient empire of Shang, which in its turn replaced the legendary Hsia Dynasty. The states struggled endlessly for advantages, regularly uniting to pull down any king who gained too much power. For over three hundred years, these wars had become so frequent the Chinese call it the "time of Warring States."

The reader can, I am sure, imagine this evil period—a constantly boiling stew of everyday treachery, night marches, violent death and wars that had neither rules nor mercy. Throughout the period, the westernmost state, geographically protected and rich in grains, grew ever more powerful. Called Ch'in, it was seen by the other states as an uncultured frontier region.

Ch'in is where most of the tales take place. Ssu-ma Ch'ien wrote the tales in a colloquial prose quite different from the formal style of the *Records of the Grand Historian*. How and why

---

* Yet another discovery came to light. In one otherwise empty corner lay a small group of scrolls, modestly bundled together with a plain gray ribbon. The scrolls contained a collection of poems, also in Ssu-ma Ch'ien's hand. No one has known that he was a poet—and indeed these poems do not put him in the first rank, or perhaps even the third—but since most educated persons write poetry in China, it is reasonable to conclude that Ssu-ma Ch'ien was at least a closet poet. We later found a note about the poems among his other writings. Since the poems seemed connected to the narrative, if not directly, and appeared to illuminate certain of its aspects, we decided to include them throughout the book.

such a master as Ssu-ma Ch'ien would choose to record these airy, frequently humorous, often mendacious, stories the master himself will tell you.

III. NOTES ON THE STORIES

The scrolls I have chosen bear especially on the First Emperor's birth, life and death. Some are more trustworthy than others—actually, none are wholly trustworthy, but all are entertaining. The writing is so clear there is little need for explanatory notes, although I have provided modern dates from time to time, as well as a modern chronology of the events of the First Emperor's reign. This chronology appears at the back of the book.

It is our good fortune that Ssu-ma Ch'ien, ever the teacher, supplemented the tales with information whenever he thought it might help someone who was unfamiliar with his life and times. In the process, he has told his own remarkable and moving story.

Whenever I find an idiom that appears modern-sounding but mysterious, I have tried to substitute something intelligible from our own time. Also, because the modern Pinyin spelling of Chinese names and places in English looks strange to Western eyes, I have adopted the venerable Wade-Giles method of spelling.

Ssu-ma Ch'ien's eunuch storytellers offer contemporary versions of legends and the real events that shaped their time. But they also speak of their own friendships, fears and enmities, schemes and sorrows. In the final excerpts, we learn of chaos in the Ch'in Empire at the collapse of the dynasty. Invading armies rage over the land unchecked.

Like us, the storytellers did not wish to be forgotten. They were eager to speak and to be remembered, through Ssu-ma Ch'ien; a desire that now, two thousand two hundred years later, will at last be granted.

— Phillip Eccles, Translator

Postscript: What of Farmer Yang, driven into the mountains by the villagers? His was a novel fate!

As the terracotta warriors became a world-famous tourist site, museum walls rose around the three main excavation pits in which the soldiers were being restored and set upright in battle formation. Visitors, including some of the world's most famous leaders, naturally wanted to meet the man who had found the soldiers. And so, very soon, the authorities brought Yang and his family back down from the mountains and reinstated them in the village. We can only guess at the ensuing relationship between Yang and his neighbors!

In any case, as they got seriously into the trinket business, the villagers all grew wealthier than they could ever have dreamed. As a special treat for the hordes of tourists, the illiterate Farmer Yang was then taught to write his name in a swiftly running script, and for many years spent every day in the largest of the museums signing guidebooks for a fee.

I purchased one; I would like to tell you that Yang is a pleasant man, but I found him rather churlish. He refused to talk with me, or even look up, as he signed my book! Of course, his considerable age and somewhat tedious occupation may have something to do with his disposition.

About the Translator: Sir Phillip Eccles, K.C.I.B.E.F.F.R., is the J. J. Penworthy Professor of Ancient Chinese History at Oxford University and Distinguished Lecturer on Asiatic Languages at Cambridge College. He is the author of a large number of books and translations, and many scholarly articles on early China.

BOOK ONE
The Infant

The Black Carriage
Han Yin's Tale

(Translator's note: Han Yin, Regulator of Entertainment in the Royal Palace, is the leader of a group of eunuchs in the palace of Ch'in Shih-huang-ti, located in the ancient city of Hsienyang. The group meets every other Tuesday to tell each other stories of varying truthfulness about the life and times of the First Emperor, as he is called. Holding the jade *pi*-disk[1] speaker's scepter in his right hand (the custom among the storytellers), Han Yin is about to begin a story in the Jade Room, so called because the walls are jade green in color. Leaning comfortably on cushions lined up along the walls, eunuchs are listening. Now let us begin our story.)

* * * * * * * *

South of the village, said Han Yin, a thing that looked like a mole made of dust was flying across the plain. As it approached the village, it became a carriage of the old square-walled style, black as night, drawn by three troikas of horses harnessed in bronze, leather and silver. A squad of Ch'in State soldiers rode ahead, behind and beside the carriage, also in black, and armed with lances and short bows. Their bronze swords were rigidly held at the ready.

---

[1] A *pi*-disk is a circular disk, generally of jade, that has a hole in the center, frequently square

In a field just outside the village's stockade walls, a farmer and his wife were pushing and pulling a wooden plough, the muscles on the farmer's thin, bare back straining until they almost popped. Hearing frantic birds overhead, the couple saw dust rising and ran yelling for the gate, but two arrows from a soldier's bow killed them just as they crossed a brook. They tumbled into the water head-first and lay still, piles of rags pounded into the stream bed by the horses.

Other villagers were trying to pull the leather-hung gate shut when the soldiers smashed through, followed by the black carriage. The soldiers swung swords down on milling villagers, splitting heads from shoulders, cutting off protesting arms. Blood spread into pools on the hard earth.

Squatting on top of the carriage, reins in hand, the driver reached the largest building at the center of the compound. He leaned back and pulled the horses to a reluctant stop, neighing and stamping. The soldiers dismounted and went to the houses, slaughtering families and torching the huts. In minutes, all but one house was burning. The captain of the soldiers dismounted, throwing his reins to a subordinate. He walked rapidly to the carriage and knocked on the door with his sword handle.

"Majesty, your commands have been carried out."

Then he jumped to attention.

The carriage door opened, creaking. Also creaking faintly, a woman less than five feet tall, robed in mourning white that somehow seemed darker than the black uniforms of the soldiers, stepped slowly to the ground. Her hands and face were covered.

This was the Queen Dowager of Ch'in, mother of ruling King Chao-hsiang, great-great-grandmother of Ch'in Shih-huang-ti.

* * * * * * * *

"And her name is? What?!" shouted Juan Chi, feared Chief Dispenser of Eunuch Punishments, number two member of the group of eunuchs

*and a conversational rival of the speaker Han Yin for many years.
"All people in stories must have names! So we can remember them,
Han Yin!"*

*"Why, her name is—her name is—my goodness, I have forgotten,"
said Han Yin. "It has been so long since anyone called her anything
but 'Ma'am' or 'Your Majesty.' Even her son, the King, addressed her
as 'Cherished Venerable Mother,' a phrase he used because he knew
she hated to be called old. She was a powerful and useful ally; but
he wished at times that she would go ahead and die and join the
ancestors, so he could pray to them all without any actual responses,
especially from her."*

"Not good enough," said Juan Chi. "I must have a name."

*"Well, let me see. I recall that nearly a hundred years ago, when
she was a young princess of Ch'in, she was said to be so pretty a
familiar name for her among the girls of her court was 'Plum
Blossom.' Even though by the time of my story, she had no more sex
left than a yellow-spotted frog—a highly poisonous species, I might
add—I will call her 'Plum Blossom.' If I may continue?"*

* * * * * * * *

After the Queen Dowager, formerly known as Plum Blossom,
stepped down from the carriage, her secretary, my own great,
great uncle, the eunuch Shen Neng—may his body rest peacefully
in the earth and his soul take flight to heaven—followed.
As he did, he took care that the step did not creak, because no
one ever, for any reason, desired the Queen Dowager's critical
attention. This included her son, Chao-hsiang, King of Ch'in.

Behind him, with a great unavoidable creaking, came a large
woman brought on the journey for one reason: she had enormous
teats brimming with milk. As she stood on the stair, the carriage
groaned and appeared to kneel. Once she was safely down, the
carriage returned to its normal, well-balanced state. She mopped
her brow, though it was by no means a hot day.

"Bring them," commanded Queen Dowager Plum Blossom,

whose voice was like a rusty sword.

Soldiers entered the last house and returned to the Queen Dowager, half-carrying a shivering man and an equally frightened woman. The couple differed from the bodies scattered across the compound in two ways: one, they were still living, and two, they were unusually tall. The woman carried an infant.

"Kill him."

A soldier cut the throat of the man so swiftly, he sagged to the ground dead before he had time to look surprised.

"Here, child, to me," said the Queen Dowager in what was, for her, a gentle tone to the tall, young woman carrying the infant, who was trying to suckle one heaving, bare breast. The woman hardly noticed; she was thinking frantically, how can I save my child?

"When was your child born?"

"When the Great Dipper poured."

"Have you lain with anyone but your husband since you married?"

"No, Ma'am."

Trying unsuccessfully to get a grip on her right nipple, the infant began to cry.

A sleeve of the white robe twitched a command.

"Milk her."

Two soldiers came forward, one holding a basin. The other stripped off his heavily-padded, iron-studded gloves. In a movement surprisingly gentle, he took the young woman's exposed breast in his hands, warmed it, bent down to her breast and sucked at the leaking nipple in order to get a full stream of milk going. As the other soldier held up the pan to catch the milk, the first soldier directed her milk into the pan. When the stream ceased, he loosened her inner garment and did the same thing with her other breast. The milk was poured into a pottery bottle, which was sealed and placed in a brocade bag.

The young woman knew she would soon be dead, but habit took over and she burped the child, even though he had drunk only a little to that point.

"Is the child whole? Has he marks?"

"He is wh-whole, Ma'am. He has a mark like a tiger cub on his back. We said we must be c-careful with this baby, he carries the tiger, and tigers are untrustworthy."

Perhaps no harm will come to the baby.

"Give him to me."

The old woman took the infant and hid him in her white robes. She signaled for and received the brocade bag, turned and stepped up into the carriage, followed by Secretary Shen Neng and the wet nurse. Before the door closed, the young woman lay in the dust beside her husband.

Carriage and soldiers disappeared the same way they had come, going just as fast. By nightfall, ashes, wood chips and a few unburned bodies remained. When it was safely dark, dogs skulked back into the village and vultures came down to fight for scraps. The endless wind blew away what little debris was left. The earth was quiet again.

The dragons who lie coiled in the earth had many years of sleep before the great disturbance began and the world changed out of all recognition.

* * * * * * * *

Though not especially large, the baby had energy, hunger, and anger to announce. Its ceaseless cries spread out across the plain like a racing storm cloud, traveling hundreds of *li*[2] in all directions, insistent as a signal beacon. But more annoying!

The wet nurse and the Queen Dowager's eunuch clapped their hands over their ears; the coachman ground his teeth; the stout Ch'in-bred ponies, finest product of a nation of horse-breeders, rolled their eyes and tried to disgorge their hated bits—so upset by the crying they lost the rhythm of their

---

[2] *Li* is a Chinese unit of length equivalent to about one-third of a mile

compact, thirty-six-footed stride. It took all the coachman's skill with a whip to get their rhythm back. Nasty, senseless creatures, he thought, wishing for the thousandth time he'd chosen some other career.

Bouncing on their big, weapon-laden war saddles, the triple rows of the King's Guard exchanged irritated glances; some reached down to touch their free-swinging swords, infanticide in their hearts. Not that they would have dared.

And still the baby cried, sucking up energy from the earth, expelling it in great gusts. Only the Queen Dowager sat motionless, asleep or lost in thought. It was hard to tell, because the Queen Dowager always slept with her eyes open. One of her most frightening qualities was her trick of seeming not to notice anything, then snapping out a succinct command that was often the last thing the object of the command heard.

She reminds us of the late chief general Wang Mang, so terrifying because he was wall-eyed. Remember? When you stood at attention before him, waiting to find out what you had done wrong, one of his eyes would wander restlessly, on its own business, while the other stared at you unblinking. Then he would begin to dress you down savagely—or perhaps he was yelling at someone else on the other side of the room. No thanks to his wall-eye, no one could be sure who he was addressing!

It is also possible Queen Dowager Plum Blossom did not mind the baby's yowling as much as the others because she could not hear as well as when she was in her nineties. Age has some rewards.

Hours ago, the baby drank the last of the milk extracted from its late mother. The wet nurse repeatedly offered each of her white milk-depots, but the child persistently spit out her teats, once biting painfully around the edge of a huge purple nipple. The white flesh around the areola showed the marks of the four-month-old baby's sharp, new teeth and a circle of blood spots appeared on her breast.

The strong-willed baby cried for one whole day and the following night before he finally gave up and began to suck— and when he did, the nurse thought she would never get her nipples back; the suction was so fierce and prolonged. It was as if he wanted not just her milk, but all the considerable juice in her! When he finished, he let out an enormous, wet belch and went to sleep immediately, leaving her with a mess of white spit-up, something she was used to, though not in such majestic quantities.

As if to compensate for the storm inside the jouncing carriage, there was no cloud in the sky above the great world we call "All Under Heaven." It was a brilliant day.

Far to the south and west stood the great rampart home of the gods, highest of mountain ranges, where life was first breathed into the ancestors of man. Nearer, but still far beyond the reach of mortal man, were the mountains of the west, believed to be made of copper, iron and jade. Music can always be heard there, water spirits playing on stones. These mountains are thousands of leagues across, from east to west, Mount Rawtooth to Mount Everhigher. One especially tall mountain, Grammablossom, is so tall the Sun has to drive around it every day. Night comes much more slowly there, and once it has come, it is reluctant to leave.

Incredible creatures live in these mountains: four-winged serpents; great shaggy cloven-hooves; bears brown and bears black; there is even a high-flying kite with human feet whose meat is said to cure a goiter.

Mount Everhigher stops the onrush of the green Western Sea, which is fed by the Grandfather River. On its banks there lives a bird that looks like an owl but has green feathers, a reddish beak and a human tongue. This bird, called a parrot, is said to talk as well as any human, but that is nonsense—really, one can only swallow so much!

But we know all of that is the stuff of legends—the Western Mountains were far from the carriage and the soldiers, out of sight many times over.

The tiny company was now rolling relentlessly southeastward after being ferried across two rivers by riverboats belonging, like everything else in Ch'in, to the King. Now the travelers could see in the distance the mountains that mark the southern border of the upland kingdom of Ch'in. These mountains are like green teeth stuck in the gray-bone jaw of the loess plains; unscalable, they go almost straight up, narrowing at the top to what, if they really were teeth, would be the rending edge, if there was anything but empty sky to rend.

A few travelers who have taken this dangerous southern route have written that the mountains appear to rise and fall rapidly, as if they are chewing a great piece of red beef. A distinguished astrologer says the southern mountains are the plainest view available to us, the black-haired people, of a dragon at his dinner, masticating thoughtfully.

To the King's Guard, the mountains in a windless sky, yellow-green under the slow moving sun, were hostile and frightening—crazy, almost, even though the soldiers had passed through them more than once, driving south to surprise parties of interlopers from the state of Ch'u. They knew the passes. But sometimes, when he thought no one was looking, a soldier would shudder—a long, slow shake that started at the neck and traveled swiftly down to the square-booted toes.

As the third day of the journey ended, the baby fell asleep exhausted at a teat. His steady sucking had finally relaxed into a gentle, almost tender rhythm—as close as this baby will ever get to being tender!

His sucking and small mouth music sent a look of deep contentment into the wet nurse's eyes; she was a former courtesan, and much prettier than you might at first think. Besides all her many babies, now residing in the Royal Nursery to Care for the Progeny of Royal Wet Nurses, she has often known and liked well a man's warm insistent mouth at each of her breasts.

* * * * * * * *

"Oh, for heaven's sakes," said Chia Tao, Major Domo of the Concubine Residences, disgustedly. *"A Royal Nursery for the babies of wet nurses? What kind of idiots do you take us for, Han? You know perfectly well what happened to those..."*

"I think," said Han Yin quietly, *"that we can afford at this late date to allow one woman her dreams. Don't you, Chia Tao?"*

Essentially a kind man, Chia Tao nodded.

* * * * * * * *

Returning to his tale, Han Yin said, as night fell, camp was made efficiently and fires were lit. Before long, the wet nurse, the baby, the Queen Dowager's secretary, the coachman and all the soldiers not posted as guards were fast asleep. Only Queen Dowager Plum Blossom stared straight ahead, quite motionless as the blazing stars rolled on.

Above, the twelve zodiacal constellations that rule men's lives and days made their slow march: the dancing mouse, ruminating ox, striding tiger, nibbling rabbit, rain-bringing dragon, slithering snake, masculine horse, grass-eating sheep, skittering monkey, faithful watch dog, crowing rooster and snoring pig. All night long, the Jade Rabbit in the moon prepared its medicines.

The vast show went on and on, unwatched by anyone but the lonely guards. They looked up only to determine when their hours of sentry duty were over and they would be relieved, so they too could gather blankets around themselves, rest their heads against their saddles, and sleep. It was cold; fall frost was near.

Next day, the party made its way through more mountains. By midday, it reached a place near the western origins of the River Wei, just where the river becomes navigable. The carriage's wheels were removed and the carriage was placed intact into a shallow-draft sampan. In a separate boat, the Queen Dowager and her party, reduced now to secretary, baby, wet nurse and six trusted guards, went on by water.

The rest of the company was ordered to continue on horseback through a long, narrow pass, a dark crease in the mountains the carriage cannot negotiate. If all went according to plan, they would reach the Ch'in capital, Hsienyang, three days before the Queen Dowager's party arrived.

Mile by mile, the gentle Wei River broadened, fed by tributaries racing and tumbling down the steep slopes of the mountains and shining in the sun.

The Queen Dowager's party floated down to a village of fishermen and wheat and millet farmers, located two hundred *li* from Hsienyang. Here the black carriage was removed from the boat, completely dismantled and buried under a mound that immediately became the subject of local curiosity. In less than a generation, the tumulus over the carriage would become known as Queen Dowager's Hill, said to be occupied by spirits both propitious and unpropitious, a chancy sort of place that was fervently venerated by the peasants. Just before the party reentered the sampans, the unluckier two of the six soldiers accompanying the Queen Dowager had their throats slashed and were buried in armor with the carriage—appropriate sacrifices to the ancestors.

I expect they lie there still, faithfully waiting in the dust to be called to duty by the erstwhile Plum Blossom, who is also dust herself.

Something strange happened after the party disembarked and made camp for the day beside a river west of Hsienyang. At the Queen Dowager's command, the baby, who had by then grown passive as most of our relentlessly overfed Ch'in babies do, was brought to the fire. A soldier held the baby's left hand down on a straw mat, spreading his fingers apart. Another took a knife from his belt and cut off the first knuckle of the third finger of the child's left hand, immediately cauterizing it with a metal spear-tip heated in the fire.

This happened so swiftly the baby had no time to be surprised. But later, because the finger was aching, the entire camp paid dearly for the baby's discomfort. As the steersmen kept the sampans headed straight downstream, well clear of the slower-moving water along the banks, the party transporting the baby had an exceptionally unpleasant day of howling.

While the Queen Dowager's party was floating loudly downriver, the rest of the Guard was riding on through the high, narrow pass through the mountains. Their march was largely uneventful and relaxed; no one expected trouble at that point. But when they reached a particularly narrow path through the rock walls—so steep the path was in shadow—a chill held the hearts of the single file of cavalrymen, from the captain riding at the front to the most recent recruit leading water-carrying pack horses at the back. All talking ceased.

Just as they reached the narrowest, darkest point of the trail, they were attacked by a group of men hidden above them. The doomed soldiers never saw their killers; flights of whirring arrows fired by crossbows whined down, invariably finding the vulnerable points of their light armor. Horses fell, crushing riders, men slipped sighing out of their saddles, dead before they hit the ground. A few yells and it was over. After a brief wait, the ambushers clambered down the steep walls and cut the throats of the three soldiers still alive.

Following barked orders, the mysterious attackers buried the soldiers deeply, pounding earth over their corpses until no one but skilled trackers could have guessed that anyone had perished here.

This was abnormal for Ch'in soldiers; our military parties generally kill all their enemies and leave them on the open ground to be picked to pieces by kites and wolves, leaving bones to dry to dull ivory. Abnormal, too, in not taking the heads, because Ch'in soldiers must produce heads to receive their pay.

The clothing of the ambushers was strange. In most respects, it was about what you would see soldiers wearing in the streets of Ch'in's capital, Hsienyang: the rankers with their light clothing for mobility, tightly padded in the Ch'in manner with close-fitting caps or elaborately-coiled, long hair for skull protection, leather boots, pants, jackets and padded skirts; the officers with laminated decorated breastplates and tassels and ribbons indicating rank.

But the colors of the ambushers' clothing, though ochres and greens and blacks like those of Ch'in soldiers, were subtly different in their hues. And the belts were yellow, while the jackets carried brown patches of rank. If you were to guess whose soldiers they were from a distance, you might think they were Ch'in, but close up they would remind you more of soldiers from the enemy kingdom of Chao to the northeast.

Who were they, what were they doing here, and on such a mission?

Since no one now living will speak for them, I will tell you.

Their mission was assigned them by someone close to the Queen Dowager, acting through a highly-placed foreign person at the Ch'in court. This person, who may have been the then Minister of Justice, was in league with Lu Pu-wei, a thriving and ambitious merchant born in the state of Chao. He is someone you will hear a good deal more about presently. The soldiers' assignment was to eliminate all witnesses to the mission of the Black Carriage. Their odd clothing was intended as obfuscation, in case someone got away.

Their assignment completed, the ambushing soldiers rounded up their hidden horses and began the same journey through the pass the late King's Guardsmen had been following, guided by a map given them by the highly-placed foreign person I just mentioned.

But when they reached a second narrow place in the pass just twenty yards wide, a landslide buried them even more efficiently than they had buried the Ch'in soldiers. Whether this was a man-made accident or not, who can say.

While this mayhem took place, the Queen Dowager's journey homeward quieted down as the baby's pain subsided. He began to nurse as fiercely as before. Soon the party reached the city of

Hsienyang, near the juncture of the Wei and Ching rivers. When they arrived at the high-walled capital, an escort from the royal palace was waiting to bring the Queen Dowager from the river immediately into the presence of her son, the King. It is said he was extremely angry with her; but it is also said that he put her up to the journey, having been in on it from the beginning.

The Queen Dowager left a tiny party still on board the one sampan that was to continue the journey. This group included the wet nurse, the Queen Dowager's secretary, Shen Neng, and several soldiers—plus of course the baby, now a little traumatized by constant traveling, but still lively.

They went on at once, moving through the eastern mountains via the Hanou Pass, the only way out of Ch'in to the east. They went in relative safety, thanks to superb royal passes that were misleading about their names and their mission. The soldiers had discarded their uniforms, replacing them with worn peasant clothing. Leaving Ch'in, they traveled through its chief rival in those days, the kingdom of Wei, where the Wei River joins the immense, silty Yellow River. After a three-day journey on the great river, the small boat beached on a sandy shore, the dangerous eastern border of the state of Chao, whose relationship to Ch'in was permanent hostility. But thanks to a second set of beautifully forged Chao passes, the party was able to rent two carriages and move overland toward the Chao capital of Hantan, a two-day journey.

Hantan was a huge city at that time, virtually impregnable. Its thick, square walls rose twenty feet, high but not high enough to hide the earthen platforms on which the city's many splendid palaces rested.

* * * * * * * *

I must now digress briefly, Han Yin said.

At this time, there lived in Hantan an impoverished and little respected prince of Ch'in named Tzu-ch'u. Under house arrest in Chao, he was the child of the least and lowest concubines of the Crown Prince of Ch'in, Lord An-kuo. As such, he was seventeenth in line for the throne—so far from rule that he never even bothered to daydream about becoming King of Ch'in.

Tzu-ch'u was serving an apparent life sentence as a hostage. He had been sent to Chao to guarantee Ch'in's non-intervention in Chao's affairs, but the guarantee was obviously worthless because a year after Tzu-ch'u began his captivity, Ch'in invaded Chao twice, unsuccessfully each time. As a result, Prince Tzu-ch'u was no longer regarded by the King of Chao as a useful person.

Since Tzu-ch'u had been forgotten long ago by the Ch'in royal family, it sent no money to him. What a wretched situation he was in—poor, despised, far from the throne, and the son of the least favorite concubine of a crown prince! Tzu-ch'u did not even have women to soften his nights, other than the meanest sort. His life was indeed miserable, until his fortune turned, as Ssu-ma Ch'ien has written in the *Records of the Grand Historian*.

"Lu Pu-wei, a great merchant of Yangti, had come to Hantan on business. By traveling here and there, buying and selling cheap, Lu is known to have accumulated an enormous fortune amounting to thousands of catties in gold. He saw Tzu-ch'u and was moved to pity—that is said ironically—but he also said, thinking about the future, 'Here is a rare piece of goods to put in my warehouse!'"

We will say more about the lowly Tzu-ch'u and the wealthy merchant Lu Pu-wei presently, said Han Yin. But now I must take you back to a meeting that took place more than a month before the Black Carriage expedition to the high plateaus. The meeting was attended by just two people: Queen Dowager Plum Blossom and the Chief Astrologer of the Ch'in Court. As it happens, the...

* * * * * * * *

"Han Yin, there is no way all this could be true," said Juan Chi...
"and if it is true, how did you come to learn of it? The people you
speak of are all dead, except for the First Emperor, and who on earth
would be brave enough to speak of these things outside this room?"

Looking haughty, Han Yin said, "I know all these things because
Shen Neng, who as I have said was my great-great uncle, was
intimately involved. And he told me about this himself. Perhaps if
you'll let me finish?"

A somewhat sullen silence.

"Shall we pause for further refreshment, Juan Chi?" Han Yin
said. "A fine idea, I'd say."

"No, no—let us pause for mercy," said Juan Chi. "And please get
to the point! Who is that wretched baby and what in the hall of the
immortals has the infant got to do with Tzu-ch'u—we all know his
story, anyway."

"All right," said Han Yin. "We will continue the story in two
weeks. You can come back or not, just as you please, Juan Chi. Wake
up, everybody, time to go to bed!"

The Beginning
Ssu-Ma Ch'ien's Tale

During the preceding tale, it's possible you did not notice a small figure in a modest black robe hunched over a low writing desk, faithfully writing down every word. That was me. Black Robe's name—my name—is Ssu-ma Ch'ien. You may know me as the author of *Shih Chi* or *Records of the Grand Historian*, a summary of the history and thought of great men in times ancient and modern.

I think my personal story, too, is an interesting one, and this seems an appropriate moment to tell it. May these characters I write in the small seal script, the hand ordered by our First Emperor so all things should be written "correctly," flow swift and sure!

I was well-known, when I was still a whole man, as the Grand Historian, the seventh of my family to serve a ruler as the keeper of truth and a calendar expert. Scholars have been kind enough to say we were the keepers of the former ages, but that was when princes valued such knowledge—it would be death to imply any such thing today.

The *Records* are the great work of my life. These bundles of bamboo strips, *Tales of the First Emperor*, were composed for pleasure, but I think you will find them worthwhile. A folk proverb that is really a curse seems to sum it up—*May you live in interesting times*. Our times here in the Ch'in Empire have been far more than "interesting."

The baby in the story is Prince Ying Cheng, who went on to become First Emperor of the Ch'in Empire, otherwise known as Ch'in Shih-huang-ti. Cheng and I were boys together in Hsienyang, the capital of Ch'in. We were friends; at any rate, that's how he described our relationship. And I am glad he did because I'm pretty sure it's why I am alive.

I was a natural follower, a willing faller-in with all of Cheng's plans, which often involved making trouble for someone. He towered over me physically, especially when he was standing with his feet on either side of my head and I was lying flat on the ground, probably weeping from one of his bear-like cuffs. But he loved me; we both said so quite often, generally he first.

From an early age, I had a gift for writing. The eldest males in the family have long been historians here in Ch'in. My great-great grandfather was "imported" to the then western frontier state of Ch'in by the famous Lord Shang Yang, nearly a century ago, with many other scholars, engineers, bureaucrats and other useful people. Each eldest son was given the title of the Grand Historian of the King of Ch'in on the death of his father. Since I was the eldest son of the Grand Historian, that was my expectation.

Though we were friends in childhood, Cheng and I parted company when we were thirteen. His father died after a brief reign and Cheng became at first, the King of Ch'in. Still a minor, he was governed under a regency led by the former merchant Lu Pu-wei (whom he addressed as "Uncle Lu" and "Second Father"). I am sure that the restrictions on his power of the regency chafed young King Cheng from his first day. He overturned it when he was twenty-one, and got rid of Lu Pu-wei as soon as possible after that.

As I was to learn later, and later still when he was near death, he had kept an eye on me all along. Meanwhile, I continued my studies quietly. They had to do mostly with the calendar of rites and royal observances.

When I reached my majority, King Cheng deposed my father, Ssu-ma Tan, to father's great anger. Then the King made me the Grand Historian, with the primary responsibility of organizing the Cheng family rituals and ceremonies. Father could do nothing about his downfall officially, but he barely spoke to me after that, and moved his apartments as far as possible from mine in the family compound north of Hsienyang. I took no pleasure in being his successor, I can tell you. I would far rather have had his love and his wisdom, but I could do nothing about it—it was the King's wish. I consulted with the King daily for many years, following my appointment.

One day soon after I began to serve him, the King brought me to his water closet. Sitting on his toilet majestically, he said I was to record all things as truthfully as possible and on no account to become one more useless, flattering courtier.

"I am sick of the lying praises they all drop at my feet as if I were some sort of a god," King Cheng said, an angry look on his face. "I want someone near me whom I love and trust, an intimate not too frightened to be truthful, who will tell me what I need to hear, not what I would like to hear."

I nodded gravely and agreed to do what he asked. Of course I was lying: a man who believes a king when he asks for total candor is also asking for an early death. But I was lying with all the sincerity I could summon.

Bending forward, the King had himself wiped thoroughly by a eunuch kneeling behind him and rose from his chair, whereupon a second eunuch glided forward in the silly pigeon-toed walk eunuchs all have and received the royal soil from the first, removing it immediately. A fastidious man in those days, the King had his ass washed thoroughly and dried on a towel rushed forward by still another eunuch from another corner of the room. The King then stepped down three steps to my level—what an honor!—and embraced me painfully.

"I always did love you, you know. And I love the ancient learning, too, even if I have difficulty reading the old scripts. As long as I am King, which I hope will be forever, I will promote learning..."

More than two decades after that—when King Cheng had already become First Emperor—in the study of the large farmhouse I owned north of Hsienyang, I remembered that conversation, and much else.

I thought, too, of the famous poet Ch'u Yuan, a disregarded and dishonored counselor, standing by the Great River with a stone held to his chest, just before he jumped to his death in the angry current. And I remembered the venerated woman, Ts'ao O, of more recent times. Her father, a shaman who had lost the respect of his Prince, drowned himself on the fifth day of the fifth month, as Ch'u Yuan had, and she followed him faithfully into the Cave of Death. These persons I regard as superb examples of right behavior.

I spent my life around researching and bringing to light the traditional stories of these and many other heroes of former times, thinking them the only foundation on which honorable men can build. Then, in one ghastly month, I saw over four hundred Confucian scholars buried in sand and beheaded at First Emperor's command. And for what? For protesting the destruction of precious Confucian books, the sum of our ancient heritage, throughout the empire. Their surprised-looking heads rolled bleeding across the sand, turning it vermilion.

I took the injunction to be candid seriously, advising the Emperor more honestly about the wrong he had done than all his other advisors, even the bastard Li Ssu, who had supplanted Lu Pu-wei as Grand Counselor. I risked my life over this. I did not know how I was able to do it, because I am not a courageous man, but I realized that perhaps I was, after all, the Emperor's last honest voice, and that meant something!

Now, fully supported by the Emperor, Li Ssu had his way with the scholar class he hated. Seeing them as a hindrance to the fanatical obedience he believed the state demanded, he burned the ancient books, excepting only prognostication, agricultural and mechanical texts, and murdered scholars throughout the empire. The four hundred were only the start. This was an act more evil, in my opinion, than anything the Emperor ever did, including the savage burying-alive of the 400,000-man army of the state of Chao. I felt I had to say so in writing, whatever the consequence. As a scholar myself, I had to act, though I was terrified. If First Emperor were angry enough, I would be killed with all my family.

At the very least I would be thrust out to the outermost circle of advisors, the people without influence, one more faceless man among all the millions of black-haired people spreading across All Under Heaven, as we often called our empire. So I wrote a memorandum protesting these actions of books burning and scholars slaughtering.

As it happened, neither execution nor banishment took place. First Emperor merely cut my balls off.

But that is not the whole story. He offered me the choice between an honorable suicide that would leave my estates intact and heritable by my family, which would also be spared, or the utter humiliation of becoming a eunuch in his service.

In the interest of my family, and on behalf of my own reputation, I would have chosen suicide, except for one thing: I had not yet completed my life-work, the *Records of the Grand Historian*, though I felt I was within a year or two of finishing.

I was uncertain what to do. Thinking such a crisis in the life of his eldest son might bring us together and gain me the benefit of his wisdom, not to mention his blessing, I asked for my father's counsel. As we had scarcely spoken for years, I acted through my mother. His advice was crushing: instead of seeing me, he sent back the coldest possible message. I remember every word.

* * * * * * * *

Ssu-ma Ch'ien,
You conspired with the King to replace me, your father, before my work was done. It was as if you had committed patricide. Now you alone must face the consequences of your treachery. Decide whatever you like. Whether you live or die is nothing to me.

Ssu-ma Tan

* * * * * * * *

Not true! I never conspired against my father, whom I respected and loved more than anyone else. When the King chose me I could not have refused him. I was filled with bitterness and anger that was perhaps made even deeper by a feeling that he was right and I had somehow been unfilial—the worst crime. With nothing to live or die for, and no feeling that I was loved or respected by the man whose respect I wanted most, I decided the only thing that truly mattered, the only reason to live, was to complete the *Records of the Grand Historian.*

I decided to accept castration, to live, and to finish my work.

What I have written above, though true, puts the worst face on my actions. In my own defense, I would like to quote from a letter I wrote to a friend after I made my choice to be castrated so that I might live and finish my work:

"It was my hope, by a thorough comprehension of the workings of affairs divine and human, and a knowledge of the historical process, to create a philosophy of my own. Before my draft was completed, this disaster overtook me. It was my concern over my unfinished work that made me submit to the worst of all punishments without showing the rage I felt. When at last I shall have finished my book, I shall store it away in the archives to await the man who will understand it. When it finally becomes known in the world, I shall have paid the debt of my shame; nor will I regret a thousand deaths."

And so, disgraced, I left my beloved family of father, mother, sister, brother, wife and daughter behind to enter the high-walled world of the palace, the silent hell of the thousands of eunuch servants who are immured here for life. The Emperor's palace is served entirely by eunuchs. Apart from the Emperor, the royal wives, concubines and offspring, the eunuchs are the only ones who live in it. The blood security of the royal line—it must not be mixed with anyone else's blood—is crucial. So they are its permanent prisoners.

Each day, we have the daily spectacle of thousands of courtiers and soldiers waiting in long lines every morning to come in to work in the palace; then, in the evening, forming the same long lines to get out. But we eunuchs never come and never go; we are trapped for our wretched lives inside the high walls of the palace.

I will not bore you with the pain and anger I endured. Once finally recovered, I was made a servant in one of the lesser women's palaces in Hsienyang, assigned to the endless task of removing their night soil and driving it by oxcart to the Emperor's gardens each morning. I was not even able to obtain writing materials! For a long time the *Records*, my precious gift to the future, languished incomplete.

My heartfelt memorandum, and subsequent sacrifice, had accomplished nothing to help the scholars. Before the imperial carnage was finally over, thousands of scholars were killed, most buried alive. The greatest ancient treasures of our people, our books that were the heart of our civilization, were burned. Just a few copies of the *Thirteen Classics* were hidden here and there in ducal libraries. One set was kept in the Emperor's own library. So much for intervention.

The one thing I was thankful for is that the Emperor did not carry out his threatened punishment of our family, wiping them out to the third degree. Instead they continued to live quietly on the family estate, as they always had.

* * * * * * * *

After this climactic moment, I spent several years in the royal service, my life flowing peacefully as the laundry river behind the wall at the back of the palace. I attended to my take-out chore of the offal in the Women's Palace each morning and evening. Happily, the women of the palace were willing to accommodate themselves to a regular collection schedule, which minimized the time I had to spend doing it.

Then to my great surprise, someone unknown to me provided an inkstand, inks, brushes, writing materials and a lovely, small, red scholar's desk (all I have ever really asked of life). I was given access to my books and to the imperial library as well, so I was able—praise to the gods and ancestors who look down from Heaven—to finish the final books of my *Records*.

That labor took years more. After I was done, all that was left for me was to try to ensure their survival by hiding them; at the time I had no idea how to accomplish that. I decided to trust the fates and the Queen Mother of the West. Perhaps, honored by my sacrifice, she will arrange for a good outcome.

Not that I stopped writing; the habit was much too strong. I continued to write, often composing poems, one of my private pleasures. And so, especially in the long, unbusy afternoons, I went to my writing desk, or napped in a comfortable chair when I was not visited by the Goddess of Mercy, Kuan Yin, and therefore had nothing in my head to write about.

Few surprises came my way, which made it even more astonishing when a servant of Han Yin, Regulator of Entertainment in the Royal Palace, and one of the most powerful eunuchs in the palace, came to fetch me into the grand presence. He had a majestic house, a small palace, really, separate from the shacks of Eunuch City, as we called it, where most of us lived rather shabby lives, hidden among the shadows of the various palaces that composed the royal compound.

His house was attached to the walls of the Number One Wives' Palace, far grander than my Women's Palace, not far east of the Emperor's palace—an easy walk, really, especially since a convenient underground tunnel had recently been built connecting the two. (That was not unusual; all the palaces were now connected by secret covered passageways built by the Emperor, said to be increasingly fearful of assassins.)

Han Yin! As Regulator of Entertainment, his duties would have been prodigious if the Emperor had any interest in entertainment, but he had little. Especially in the early years of his reign, the Emperor labored at his desk day and night on the endless work of governing the Empire, insisting each night on reading a certain *poundage* of official documents before retiring.

The Empire was his personal toy and he insisted on total control. Because of his work habits, we were probably the dullest court of all time. This left the eunuch Han Yin with an enormous amount of time to dispose of. A former merchant, he owned estates all over the empire, and had thousands of servants, a retinue equal in number to those of some former Dukes of the Seven Kingdoms. He had the power to have someone strangled and dumped into the River of Sorrow with a snap of his fingers or a lifted eyebrow. Here today, gone tonight!

I am afraid of little, but I was nervous when servants brought me into his presence. He was a large man, but somehow not imposing—soft, really, as most of us eunuchs are. He sat cross-legged on a floor mat covering a raised platform along one wall of his study. He was facing away from me, head bent over whatever he was writing on the ebony desk in front of him. I guessed it was a memorandum, the mechanism by which all business gets done in the imperial palace. I also guessed it was bad news for someone, because official memoranda are very rarely about good news; I hoped it was not about me.

He wrote and I sat quietly, not daring to interrupt. I hate to interrupt anyone who is writing, anyway; concentration slips away so easily. Then he straightened up, turned and gave me three low-sitting bows, a full courtesy I had not expected. Despite an ache in my lower back brought about by wheeling cartloads of night soil through the rain to the Emperor's gardens, I returned his bow.

"Ssu-ma Ch'ien, I have of course read your *Shih Chi*, the *Records of the Grand Historian*, as far as you have gotten. They are our greatest surviving works of literature. It is a joy to me and a blessing to the empire that our esteemed First Emperor, the destructive bastard, has been unable or unwilling to destroy them along with everything else he so wantonly burned. Since much of your book deals with Ch'in and with him, his self-esteem must have got in the way."

Not true, as far as I knew. The *Records* are also banned now, and most likely will soon be burned, except for my draft and a few hidden copies I hope will stay that way.

But it was a deadly thing for Han Yin to say to me. I suspect it was an indication of trust. I guessed he was counting on "author's pride" becoming a basis for listening favorably to whatever was really on his mind. Of course he was right. I read my *Records* sometimes, and each time I do, I marvel at them, wondering how could I have known about this or that particular aspect of human behavior. How astute! What wisdom! What insight! Such praise from the outside for what I praise in my heart disposed me favorably toward him.

"But," said Han Yin, "I have a sense the *Records* are not yet completed. Is that so?"

Time to exchange trust for trust.

"That was so, sir, when I became a eunuch seven years ago. There was much work still to be done. But since then, thanks to the duties that left me much free time and a continuous supply of brushes, inks and bamboo strips provided by a benefactor whose name I do not know, I was able to finish the *Records*. They await the judgment of posterity. So I hope."

Han Yin began to smile, a frog-like smile that seemed to start at one ear and travel to the other. I felt a little shaky.

"Well, Ssu-ma Ch'ien, I am your benefactor. And if you will permit me, I will be your first reader of the concluding *Records*."

Overwhelmed, I shouted, "Of course you can! You are kind, sir," I said, going swiftly from timid to teary.

"No 'sirs' here, please," Han Yin said. "We are Confucians and of noble families. We are equals above and below the belt."

Too kind, I thought. And too true.

"I want you to follow me now," he said, unexpectedly.

Then he did the most extraordinary thing! He stood up, stretched briefly, then flung himself down on all fours and crawled straight under his writing table!

"Come on," he shouted, and disappeared.

I did so. Once under the table, I saw there was a curtained opening, barely my size—I am a small man, so the gods alone know how the larger Han Yin got through. I immediately crawled forward and pushed hard with my head and shoulders. I was entering an apparently windowless room, or would be entering it soon if my haunches would only follow. A cool breeze of fresh-smelling air came from somewhere.

Han Yin was kneeling in the center of the room lighting two lamps. As my eyes became accustomed to the dim light, I made out a profusion of multicolored mats, silken pillows, tables, chests, bottles of all shapes and sizes, many of jade, drinking cups, bronze ornaments, watercolors, calligraphy, all scattered across the floor and up against walls so milky green and translucent they seemed to be of pure jade—it was a fantasy, a room to escape to, dream in, tell stories in...

"Exactly," said Han Yin. "Tell stories is exactly what we do here—stories no one else in this present age must hear."

"Listen to me, Ssu-ma Ch'ien. I have a few trusted friends high in the Emperor's service. We all have plenty of time on our hands. For years we have been gathering at least every other week in this secret room. We can speak freely and say things that if overheard would bring death to us all in the outside world.

"For a long time we met to share the reports of our spies concerning the empire and to experience the pleasure of open, untrammeled conversation. What joy not to have to hew to the eunuch's lot: endlessly, tediously, bewailing our lacks, our inadequacies, our wretchedness

"But the meetings changed in nature. Where we once reported events and suspicions to the group, we began telling each other stories of varying lengths. Some of our stories were well-known, some were improvised; all were full of both truth and lies, like life. The one thing they had in common was the First Emperor.

"And," Han Yin said, looking modest, "we have gotten good at storytelling. It has become an obsession. Twice a month we gather, drink wine, sing, quarrel, tell jokes, eat, and challenge one another with our stories. No one attends to our comings and goings. Highly placed though we are, in the eyes of the palace we are just their silent servants—why would they be interested in us?"

Han Yin looked down at his hands, then up at me. I peered into his heavy-lidded eyes and realized I was looking at a genuinely happy man. Never mind his precious "business," his former masculinity, that he kept in a jar in his outer room as an object of veneration, a bringer of good fortune, and, especially, a necessary companion in the afterlife, when we all presumed we would be rendered whole again. In this beautiful green-hued room, all that seemed trivial.

"But why have you brought me here to tell me this?" I asked Han Yin. "I am a 'facts only' writer, a historian, straightforward as a thrown knife."

"I have brought you here," he said, pausing for effect, "because you may be 'facts only,' but you are also the best writer in what has become the Empire of Ch'in. No one can touch you."

This was true.

"We eunuchs know most things that happen in Hsienyang, and when word came of your reprehensible 'demotion,' we sorrowed at first as one would do when a huge oak is cut down in its prime. But one night one of our members, Wang Ts'ao the Tedious, as I like to tease him, even though he has been particularly kind and helpful to me in my career, had a remarkably imaginative idea. For him. Actually, for anybody."

"He said, 'Why don't we bring this fellow into our group to write down our stories? Of course no one can read them while old Live-Forever-or-so-He-Thinks is still around—but perhaps, if the stories are securely hidden, a future day will come when people will enjoy reading them as much as we enjoy telling them.

'And when they read them, they will know—that we eunuchs were here, that we may have been emasculated but we were also men of consequence, men with ideas and beliefs and an understanding of right and wrong.'

"We saw that Wang Ts'ao's idea was flawless, a great chance that had to be seized. We put it into action. And here you are. We hope you will write our stories, just as we tell them."

Doing this service for Han Yin and the other eunuchs was not optional. If I did not agree, enthusiastically, I would not be around long. And I had nothing better to do, anyway. So I said yes, of course, be glad to.

The following week, Han Yin asked me to join the group for further discussion. I will never forget that night. After scooting through the narrow opening under his desk into the Jade Room, I saw that it was now filled with a number of rather ponderous-looking men. I went to the one empty spot: clearly my designated place at a writing desk, where excellent brushes, inks and bamboo strips were waiting.

Han Yin spoke. "Let me be unusually straightforward, Ssuma Ch'ien. I would be glad if you would take this down. As you probably know, the Emperor has been going crazy. He is completely invisible to his people, and all because the court astrologers, a wretched lot of fakers, have told him to allow no one to see his face.

"They say it will increase his alloy of mortality, or some such ridiculous stuff! Certain he is a god, hoping desperately for immortality, he now drifts around in a hat with a heavy fringe that hides his face from view. Day or night he can be found in the huge, unfinished Epang Palace or any other of his eighty-some palaces. It is death to tell anyone where he is at any moment. But who really cares?

"Or, he boards a closed chariot and is driven along a secret tunnel out to his unfinished tomb at Mount Li, to review thousands of well-armed, life-size clay soldiers in their roofed tunnels. Imagine! An army of clay to protect him in the afterlife.

"What he will really need is protection from his successor, whoever that will be. The next emperor is going to want to grab all those ranks and files of bronze spears and swords and shields and crossbows and catapults and bows and arrows! What a colossal waste!"

The eunuchs around the room nodded vigorously.

"I have been told that sometime in the next two or three years he will go far to the south on a royal progress. These journeys have been ceremonial for the most part, but this time he will be going to a region to the south where there is constant fighting. And the enterprise will no doubt involve the entire court, thousands of us, his servants, and half the army. What sense does it make?

"Even here in Hsienyang, he's so afraid of assassins he hides in the middle of a huge army of living guards—you would have to kill a thousand soldiers to get within five hundred *li* of him! Who is afraid of someone who is afraid of everyone else? Even if he has life and death power. It wasn't this way before, but now, unlike Li Ssu, he's not using his power, he's just cowering in some corridor. I can hear the laughter and the plotting of rebellion in the south all the way from here inside the palace.

"But perhaps, Ssu-ma Ch'ien, I am straying from the point I meant to make," said Han Yin.

"Not at all," I responded. "I find this fascinating."

Ignoring my irony, Han Yin said, "Thank you. My point is this: the Empire is falling apart. Serious rebellions have begun in the south and in the east. The old feudal lords, moved here from Anyang at stunning expense—the idea being to remove them from their power bases—have put their heads together and are now working in concert for the first time. So the removal process, an idea that once seemed brilliant, has developed into something potentially disastrous. Well, we know that when and if they seize power, it won't last. They can't possibly stay allied. But by then, it will be too late to save those who now hold the Mandate of Heaven. The imperial bells are not merely out of tune, they're about to be stolen altogether!

"When the great disaster happens, whatever brings down the Emperor will certainly topple Li Ssu, too, who we think has softened disastrously in the last year or two. That leaves only the Chief Eunuch, Chao Kao, and he is—let us be charitable— not the most trustworthy of us half-men.

"If the palace goes down, will the palace servants survive? We senior officials of the 'Eunuch Empire,' and all the thousands of others who work for us, will not outlive the First Emperor. So in our view, we are already dead men. No one, absolutely no one, trusts us, and they are right not to. Denied our sexuality, unlike the long-departed hero Shen Neng, we have nothing to interest us but plotting. But we are still men, damn it, proud men at that, especially the group in this room. We are rich and, currently at least, powerful. We rose far.

"All along, we have had a secret weapon. We can stand still in a room full of high-ranking courtiers and senior officers, and they speak as if we are not even there. That makes us the best spies in All Under Heaven, even if we are only spying on our own behalf.

"That is why we began these meetings years ago. We have been meeting to share what we learn each day with each other ever since before King Cheng destroyed the other states and declared himself the First Emperor.

"Ssu-ma Ch'ien, I cannot begin to tell you how much palace business we have transacted in this room, how many times we have rescued one another just as we were standing on the brink of terrible missteps!"

Again there were fervent nods all around the room.

"But the serious gathering of intelligence is not really a meaningful activity any longer, if we are all to be destroyed, anyway. Oh, we need to keep tabs on things, of course; it would be foolish not to, and we are not fools. But we have asked you to meet with us and, we hope, to become our Recording Secretary in pursuit of another aim."

"Here in the Jade Room, besides intelligence and gossip, we have also entertained ourselves for years with stories of the kingdom and the empire. We now propose, with your help, to tell the story of the First Emperor's life from the inside.

"We don't undertake this altogether seriously, I should add. No one can or should ever attempt to compete with your *Records of the Grand Historian*, which even the Emperor cannot bring himself to destroy, there is so much truth in it—and, I must add, he reads your criticism of him, and his vanity is so great that he interprets it as praise! In any case, in my opinion, the *Records* will live forever."

Han Yin and I exchanged deep sitting bows.

"What we want to set down, with your inestimable help," said Han Yin in a highly official 'tone,' "are the greatest of the legends, fables and tales of the First Emperor, the stories told privately among us. We believe such stories will convey to the next residents of this world a sense of what it was like to be here, in this palace, during the rise and fall of one of the most powerful, brutal, but at times actually well-meaning men who ever lived."

We exchanged more sitting bows. A bit pompous, Han Yin, I thought to myself. In the interest of accuracy and completeness, I wrote this thought down:

"We believe our stories will complement and balance the *Records*, light where it is heavy, humorous where it is grim, free of 'moral tales' where yours is full of them. Our hopes are two: one, that you will not amend them even if you believe them inaccurate—we would like very much for you to use the exact words of the storytellers; and two, we hope that you will be good enough to associate our names with the individual stories. Then we too will have a place in history. We want," he said, his eyebrows nearly touching each other, such was his intensity, "the future to know that we were here, that we lived, and that in here in the 'Eunuch Empire,' we mattered."

An obvious difficulty occurred to me.

"But, Han Yin, if I write these stories you tell," I said, "how do you propose to save them when the Empire is destroyed? Look what the Emperor, who once described himself as a man of culture and a faithful keeper of the ritual sacrifices, has done to the Confucian *Annals* and other illustrious writings of the past. That which seemed guaranteed to last forever, the wisdom of the former ages, was gone in a few wretched bonfires, and the heads of the scholars whose job it was to preserve them rolled like kicking-balls across the sand. So what chance have we got to preserve a new Book of Fables?"

"Not a problem, Ssu-ma Ch'ien. We have devised a hiding place for your writings that is all but certain to be safe until an age of men clever enough to find them appears. That may be some time, it may be never. What matters is that the writings will be safe from the wolves of this age.

"So put your pen down. Just listen and I will tell you what we plan. We do not want this hiding place described anywhere until the one who will hide the Book of Fables is ready to do so. That will be the last record."

Han Yin told me what they wanted done, and how these writings would be preserved no matter what befell the Emperor. When he was done, I was convinced that the plan had a reasonable chance of success. And I felt enthusiastic about a writing project for the first time in a great while, even though I would be recording lightweight tales. But I had nothing else of consequence to do.

And perhaps the eunuchs would let me put in a poem or two among their tales from time to time! Unsigned, of course. My poems had always been private, for friends' eyes only, but I take some pride in them and find that I welcome a heaven-sent opportunity to publish them privately. So that is what I am planning to do. Enjoy them, please!

* * * * * * * *

So I joined the small group of eunuchs who spent many nights in the Jade Room. I was promoted to Master of Underthings in the Women's Palace, and soon brought to the Number One Wives' Palace, fulfilling the same function with a much finer array of Underthings. My duties were light—actually, they were almost nonexistent. Guided by Han Yin, who became my mentor and friend, and the other eunuchs, who also became friends, I began to accumulate estates secretly, as well as numerous concubines—I may not be whole, but neither am I a stone, and a woman's gentle hands are as soothing as they always were.

My freedom grew day by day and I dreamed that one day I would see my wife and daughter again, and that I might even retire far from the Emperor's palace.

So, twice each month, I crept under the scholar's desk in Han Yin's study, pushed aside a curtain, crawled through the passageway, popped through into the Jade Room and went to my small writing space in a corner. I wrote down, as nearly as I could in their own words, the eunuchs' stories, only adding comments here and there when it seemed necessary.

I have also tried to record some of the eunuchs' verbal fencing because, to me, their amiable bickering and jokes on each other were often more amusing than their stories.

The Court Astrologer
Han Yin's Tale

I was now working on my not very onerous duties—unless you count an occasional writer's cramp—of recording the stories of the eunuchs. The group was waiting, more or less eagerly, for their leader, Han Yin, Regulator of Entertainment in the Royal Palace, to resume his kidnapped baby tale.

Despite the carping of Juan Chi, Chief Dispenser of Eunuch Punishments, at the eunuchs' previous meeting—which may have been due more to the digestive problems that plague eunuchs constantly rather than any serious disagreement—the small group of high-ranking eunuchs gathered again in Han Yin's study on the appointed evening two weeks later.

They loved stories, especially Han Yin's, and were happy to have successfully concluded for yet another day the unspeakable duties placed upon them by the enormous royal family—unspeakable in the sense that the eunuchs never speak of them.

They were close friends. Long isolated from society and excluded from the normal everyday activities that occupy most people's hours, they formed deep friendships (and rivalries) with one another. And they were master plotters; making plots is rather like storytelling.

"And so?" said Juan Chi, "What is the outcome of this great 'baby' story you have been telling us, Han Yin?"

Han Yin cleared his throat.

"When we concluded abruptly two weeks ago, following

your rude interruption, Juan Chi, I was saying that it would be necessary to go back to four months before the 'great baby' appeared. Let us now do so."

The setting is the Palace of the Ancestors, inside the vast royal palace north of the Wei River where sits Hsienyang, capital of the Ch'in state.

Each day the Queen Dowager, formerly known as Plum Blossom, and the Chief Astrologer of the Ch'in Court spent an hour together, normally in the Small Throne Room, with no one other than her secretary in attendance. These were formal meetings, during which the Chief Astrologer knocked his head on the floor the requisite three times and then reached behind him for a scroll tied with gold braid. Unrolling the scroll, he related the current auspices concerning various activities in the Kingdom of Ch'in. These reports were drily edited versions of the same reports made in the previous hour to the King. For him the auspices are crucial, since they are tied directly to the King's main task of performing the rituals that keep the kingdom healthy and the Great Bells of Chou well tuned.

The Queen Dowager was bored with these pedestrian reports, but it was her nature to want to be on the inside in all matters concerning the kingdom, so she skipped her late morning nap each day and listened dutifully to crop forecasts, the peccadilloes of minor officials, omens for possible future journeys of the King, et cetera.

But on this day, the meeting of the burly, lisping Chief Astrologer and the tiny, white-robed Queen Dowager—she was in permanent mourning for her husband, the late king— in no way resembled the routine briefings both participants secretly loathed.

Because this meeting was at midnight.

And she had come to *him*. Not alone, either.

She had come to his tiny windowless study, accessible only through the vast and permanently bloody Room of the Auspices. She was acccompanied by her secretary, the eunuch Shen Neng of blessed memory. She had come at the request of the Chief Astrologer, who, though terrified of the possible consequences, had asked her to come at this hour. In his letter, delivered to her secretly, he said there was something that could only be seen in his quarters and that they should only speak at a time when none would observe her coming. Not that there ever is such a time in a royal palace. But let that be.

The Chief Astrologer was a man of great consequence in Ch'in. He was in charge of reading the auspices and assisting King Chao-hsiang to make the proper rituals to the ancestors so that all would be well in the kingdom each day. The Chief Astrologer's responsibility was always to be right, or if not right, at least to look as if he certainly would have been right, had the ancestral gods wished it. He was a big man, and he moved, spoke, and made love ponderously. His skin was thick as the bronze plating on an antique war chariot.

He had given much thought to how he should present the very unusual auspices of the day before—auspices modified slightly by a confidante well connected to someone of importance in a kingdom east of Ch'in. His first decision, acting on instinct, was to present them initially to Plum Blossom, the Queen Dowager, rather than to King Chao-hsiang, reversing the normal order. This seemed marginally safer to him, since her temper was less likely to flare than the King's. But he was almost equally afraid of the Queen Dowager, who might have his head struck off, or cause him to lose the gear that swung between his legs, with which he visited the willing if unexcited thighs of many a non-imperial concubine outside the palace every sixth night.

He had planned an elaborate and sure-to-please speech, with many references to the Yellow Emperor and other great predecessors, especially notable queens and duchesses, all the while leading up to the actual matter, which powerfully affected the future of the kingdom, very indirectly. Formality was the key, formality, and every euphemism he could think of. That was what he had planned, but when the tiny woman in white actually appeared in the doorway of his cramped study for the first time, he became so frightened he forgot all the excellent phrases he had spent the day crafting.

As she entered, followed by her secretary, the Chief Astrologer fell to the floor, missing his kneeling cushion, and began to knock his head on the stone, first the requisite three times, then for good measure three more, plus more, and then, although he was beginning to stun himself, several more...

WHACK!!!

The Queen Dowager drew her brass-bound fan and hit him on the back of the head with its business edge so hard that blood began to flow from his scalp into his thick, black hair. It mingled with the tears now pouring from his tear ducts, turning salt pink.

"Get on!" she shouted. "Stop banging your head and tell me what you have to tell me!"

Secretary Shen Neng was laughing, but oh so silently, behind her, just as we do each time we observe some new stupidity among our cherished masters.

"Your Grace, Ma'am, Mum, m-my Lady, I..."

WHACK!!!

A second blow, harder than the first. The Chief Astrologer disappeared inside his brocaded robe until all that could be seen was a pile of shaking clothes, spotted with blood and stained with tears. Quick-thinking, despite her 109 years, she saw that a somewhat gentler approach was required.

"Shen Neng," to her eunuch, "pick up this thing, sit him upright, and dry his disgusting face. Calm him down."

Shen Neng, still laughing silently, did so. They waited for calm.

Finally the Chief Astrologer, sensing no more imminent damage from the royal fan, got control of his breathing and began a highly unvarnished speech.

"Majesty, I have to tell you of two forecasts I made yesterday using the same beast. Neither is capable of being wrong."

"Your Grace will remember that Tzu-ch'u, forty-seventh grandson of the King and seventeenth son of the Crown Prince, Lord An-kuo, was sent to Hantan, the capital of Chao State, some years ago as a hostage. This son has had a child, a boy, by a concubine who comes from a noble family of the state. As Your Grace knows…"

The fan slipped quietly out from the place where the Queen Dowager's breasts used to be and began to rise.

"Well, never mind that," the Chief Astrologer said hastily. "Though he is so far down the line of possible royal inheritors, I regularly forecast the future course of his life, as I would for all the other princes of the kingdom. I was amazed to learn yesterday that by some combination of circumstances I cannot at present foresee, the son, whose name is Tzu-cheng, whose back carries a blemish shaped like a tiger, and who is missing a single knuckle of the third finger of his left hand, will one day ascend to the throne of Ch'in!"

This was enormously interesting to the Queen Dowager. Her blackbird eyes began to sparkle dangerously. The Chief Astrologer hurried on.

"Although I cannot see his path to the throne, I do see only too clearly his impact on this kingdom—he will destroy it through appallingly bad management of the armies of Ch'in. I know they are regarded as unbeatable here in the land of the mountains. But one day, he will stupidly invite the armies of our worst enemies to come safely through our mountain passes; once inside Ch'in, they will destroy everything we have built! Absolutely *every*thing!"

The Chief Astrologer's voice had become a wail.

"Go on."

"But Your Grace, I also learned in a reading of the same entrails that because of a conjunction of our most Kingdom-friendly stars, a second child was born, on the same day. He also has the mark of a tiger on his back, though not a missing finger knuckle. This birth took place in a barbarian village far to the west of Ch'in.

"If this child can be taken from its parents secretly and substituted for the first infant—without anyone's knowledge, including Prince Tzu-ch'u and his concubine—this child will grow up to be king. He will lead Ch'in to greater victories than any king has ever done, including all the greatest rulers of Chou and Shang Dynasties and, forgive me, those of your present, exalted, magnificent, all-wise son, King Chao-hsiang.

"In fact, this child will one day be emperor of all the lands between the seas! The world, Your Majesty! He will own everything in the world."

He lowered his head. The silence thickened like hot and sour soup as the Queen Dowager and the eunuch Shen Neng took time to digest the two remarkable prophecies.

"How should we accomplish this?" the Queen Dowager asked.

This was the difficult part. Feeling a knife of ice reach up to his heart and down to his bowels, the Chief Astrologer said, "Majesty, I do not know why, but the stars say you must go yourself, in secrecy, leading a troop of royal mounted guards, to the west to find this child. Here," reaching into his robe, "is a map I have drawn that will take you to the wretched village in which he and his parents live. You will know the parents because they are the tallest people in the village. You will know the child by the tiger mark on his back.

"Majesty, you will then return to Ch'in, but you will send your secretary, Shen Neng, and the child in secret to Hantan. There, Shen Neng will substitute one child for the other. No one, no one, must know of the exchange. This secret must remain with us.

"Also, Majesty, there is something more that you should know, but I cannot speak of it in the presence of anyone besides yourself, so I have written it down."

Casting a brief glance at Shen Neng, who as always was looking modest and innocuous, the Chief Astrologer reached behind him for an additional scroll and handed it to her.

Done. The Chief Astrologer began to shake uncontrollably. Without a word, the Queen Dowager and Shen Neng left the tiny study. When they reached her bedchamber, the Queen Dowager, being illiterate, gave the additional scroll and the map to Shen Neng. He read the scroll to her, which introduced the rich merchant, Lu Pu-wei, whom I mentioned earlier. Heads bent over both documents, they made their plans as the night rolled on toward morning.

Just before dawn, the Chief Astrologer was smothered with silken pillows in his bed by Shen Neng. Having long done good service for the kingdom, especially this night, this was a merciful death—a nice surprise, so to speak—which unfortunately was not extended to the various generations of his family then living. By the next day's end, they were slaughtered down to the last baby, hanger-on and servant, a slaughter that included all the concubines and even hundreds of harmless eunuch servants—so wasteful!

This was done to keep the secret and because the Chief Astrologer had not taken the auspices directly to the King, something the Queen Dowager remedied by breakfast, when the King was generally in a reasonable mood.

There is a saying that you do not discard the walnut shell until you are sure you have gotten all its meat. In their hurry to silence the Chief Astrologer, they made one miscalculation. He had also received a final message concerning the future, namely that the second child, after creating a vast empire, would take that empire straight to the same destruction the first child would have created. The only significant difference would be the scale of the crash—much, much larger.

The Chief Astrologer would never have willingly told Queen Dowager Plum Blossom, or King Chao-hsiang, this unpleasant fact, which would have sent him straight to a boiling oil-pot. But under torture, they might have got it out of him, and perhaps formulated a third plan to save the day. But at this late date, we cannot know.

Shen Neng's Journey
Han Yin's Tale

Picking up just where he ended the last meeting, Han Yin, Regulator of Entertainment in the Royal Palace, said, "Just before we told you about the late, unfortunate Chief Astrologer of our Ch'in State, we were describing a dangerous journey undertaken by an odd assortment of people, including a baby still on the teat. I wonder if any group was ever less suited to incognito travel."

Let us return to the journey of the eunuch Shen Neng, Secretary to the Queen Dowager, and his companions. First, there were the soldiers of the King's Guard, who were by now failing magnificently to disguise themselves in indescribably dirty robes. Then there was also, if you remember, a baby with a mark like a tiger on his back and a rapidly healing finger short of one knuckle on his left hand. And, of course, there was the memorably abundant wet nurse.

The miasma of depression, fatigue and constant hunger that is peasant life prevented villagers from staring, as the party made its way in two nondescript carriages across the highly unfriendly territory belonging to the state of Chao, Ch'in's current chief enemy. Against common sense, the carriages headed down rutted roads straight toward Chao's capital city, high-walled Hantan, which lay dangerously near the southern border, vulnerable to frequently invading Ch'in armies, and protected only by the aforementioned walls. Although Chao soldiers were everywhere, no one challenged the travelers; this in itself was suspicious.

During daylight hours, the baby was swaddled and tied on to the wet nurse, over, under, around or between her two large breasts; he was traveling comfortably. From his point of view, and hers, life was well organized—he was easily detachable for feeding, which he demanded frequently, he was a loud and willing burper, and if he wasn't eating or belching, he was mostly sound asleep and snoring loudly, dreaming the Jade Emperor alone knows what infantile dreams.

The wet nurse's familiar name was Sunshine, on account of her happy, open temperament, but owing to her huge breasts most people called her Full Moons. When she began her career as a concubine, having been sold into the profession at fourteen by affectionate but impoverished parents, she discovered almost immediately that she was exceptionally fertile. Indeed, there were certain men she remembered who barely had to look at her best features to create yet more offspring. Since she was constantly becoming pregnant, and magnificently endowed with tremendous milk depots, as she grew older she made the best of it by becoming a wet nurse, an occupation for which she had natural gifts.

It was not a complete blessing, however. Gradually the idea of having sexual intercourse with men for pleasure gave way to having sexual intercourse for having babies so she could maintain her milk supply at a reasonably constant level. As you will understand, this made her less attractive to men, though not much. By the time of our story, she no longer thought much about herself and her needs, or about men either. This was a pity, because at the time of our tale she was neither elderly nor unpleasant looking. She was merely monumental.

For those who do not know everything there is to know about eunuchs, you should be aware that Shen Neng was made a eunuch by courtesy of the Kind Cut, an excision that took the testicles but left the penis not only intact but capable of hardening at a touch or the blink of a lewd idea. Sadly, since

Shen Neng's time, the art of the Kind Cut has been lost.

(Mock groans from the listening eunuchs.)

Owing to constant bouncing together in the carriage by day, and by night of having a thin tent wall between them, Shen Neng had become ever more responsive to Full Moons, both above and below, if you understand me. And though the amorous looks he sent her way were not returned, they were certainly noticed by Full Moons. In her unique way, she reacted.

Once, as he looked on in the carriage, before re-wrapping the infant after a particularly onerous suckling, she took each white breast in her hands and palpated it slowly, rotating it first clockwise, then counterclockwise. As she did so she looked over the top, or tops, at Shen Neng, whose business under his robe was pointing straight up. After slow self-massage, she pinched and twisted each of her naked nipples gently to erection, wet her hands with her tongue, rubbed them together, then, with a slow, deep sigh, re-wrapped the baby in his package and strapped him back in between her re-covered pillow moons. Shen Neng understood this series of gestures. How can a woman so vast be so desirable, he thought rhetorically.

With poor Shen Neng in a more or less permanent state of excitement, the small party reached the end of the third day's journey toward the city of Hantan. The carriage came to rest near a small brook and the soldiers pitched three tents, a capacious one for Full Moons and the infant, a tiny one for Shen Neng, and one for themselves large enough for them to play various token games inside it. As is well known, soldiers, for whom money means little below the level of general, love to gamble even more than eunuchs do.

By the way, generals gamble, too; soldiers are their counters.

Late one night, when the moon was down and only a few stars were looking on, Shen Neng crept on all fours out of his tent past a winking fire and dozing guard. He slipped into Full Moons' tent, noted the baby sleeping peacefully in his night-cradle, and woke Full Moons by placing his right forefinger gently between her pink lips, which began sucking immediately, even before she woke up. When she did, she smiled and reached down to welcome and guide him into her damp crevasse that was fully as capacious as he was protuberant. A match made in heaven.

Two nights passed in this pleasant way. On the morning of the fourth day, after conferring with the soldiers, Shen Neng learned they were now just hours from Chao's capital city of Hantan. Shen Neng was brave, but now fear began to spread throughout his brain and body and down into his gut so that he could scarcely hold water. And then he couldn't.

So far he had used to perfection all of the vital information provided by the late Chief Astrologer as to how to locate, abduct and transport the baby. But their earlier adventures, which had seemed difficult at the time, now felt like a watercolor sketch of a quiet day on a still river.

His next task was to get into Hantan without being noticed, a near-impossible feat in time of war. Then he would have to substitute the baby Full Moons was nursing for the presumably cherished, precious only-child of Ch'in Prince Tzu-ch'u, the hostage, and his wife, Lady Tzu-ch'u, the former courtesan who came from a powerful Chao family. And to do this in such a way that they did not notice the replacement! As to how to carry out *this* part, the damned Chief Astrologer had provided not a single clue!

Shen Neng always prided himself on his resourcefulness and daring. But this was beyond belief! Forgotten now the dalliance in the carriage, the multiple consummations in the tent, limp, curled up his formerly lancelike member. His knees shook uncontrollably, his hands wrung each other constantly, his narrow, somewhat ratlike face darkened with fear.

Fearful passenger or not, the carriages rolled steadily along a major road in company with an ever growing stream of agricultural and mercantile traffic. By early afternoon, the destination was reached. The small party halted below the city walls of Hantan, frighteningly near the main gate.

And Shen Neng had no clue what to do next!

The Inhabitants of the Jade Room
Ssu-Ma Ch'ien's Tale

I think, reader, it is time for you to meet the storytellers who inhabit the Jade Room on these bi-weekly, tale-yarning occasions. But first, let us begin with a description of someone who is not here physically, though our lives all revolve around him: he is Ch'in Shih-huang-ti, First Emperor and first man of the empire. In all other respects he is here, because his destiny is the centerpiece of every eunuch story.

Here is a description of him I wrote some years ago in the *Records of the Grand Historian*. King Cheng, as he was then known, was in his early twenties:

"The King of Ch'in has a waspish nose, eyes like slits, a chicken breast, and a voice like a jackal. He is merciless, with the heart of a treacherous tiger or wolf. When in difficulties, he willingly humbles himself; when successful, he swallows men up without a scruple. I am a plain citizen in homespun clothing, yet he treats me as if I were his superior. Should he succeed in establishing his empire (as he certainly did!), we would all become his captives. There is no staying long with such a man."

That is our master. My eunuch friends here in the Jade Room know the First Emperor well; several serve the ruler personally. And they hold considerable power in the Forbidden City. Now, let us meet them.

In the farthest, darkest corner of the room, Han Yin sits

on his ebony scholar's platform, slightly higher than the rest. He is the Emperor's Regulator of Entertainment, a task of great responsibility had the Emperor retained any other interest besides the advice of his fleet of astrologers on how to become immortal. As things stand, the palace is hushed day and night—it is as much as your life is worth to sing one of the ancient ballads, or laugh, and this is a hardship for me because I am an uncontrollable giggler.

Han Yin rarely speaks, except when telling a story. His eyes are closed, but he hears everything, down to the least squeak of a hidden mouse; keen is the word for Han Yin, keen and below his genial surface, icy. You might not see that iciness until you had been around him for some time, but if there was some transgression on your part, you would soon feel his mind snapping shut on you.

For example. Foodstuffs are slid in to us on lacquer trays. The other day, a plate of fruit arrived with flies and even less savory creatures feasting on it. By the evening of the next day, the servant whose responsibility it was to provide edibles was no longer with us—I mean, no longer among the living. Our food will be fresh and clean hereafter.

Han Yin is past middle age, with snow on the roof, and rather a lot of roof above the snow, by which I mean that he is going bald. He is a large man, though you would perhaps not guess it, watching him collapsed in on himself as he sits, apparently dozing. He is our master and our master of ceremonies, choosing the speaker and the tale. No one ever questions his decisions, apart from Juan Chi, who is always ribbing him.

You have met me, Ssu-ma Ch'ien, former Grand Historian. I do not think I need much more introduction right now. I am of somewhat less than middle height, unusually dark-skinned and from childhood, a little overweight. I do not have many beliefs, but I value men who set a good example for their fellows and their descendants. And I have noticed that often, evil men fare well and good men fare badly. This has led me to question the wisdom of Heaven on occasion.

To Han Yin's right, incessantly bouncing off his mat to dispute this or that, is the ever-in-motion Chief Dispenser of Eunuch Punishments, Juan Chi.

Under his bluster is a man who has gained enormous power and uses it as ruthlessly as Han Yin does. And much oftener, for every day of Juan Chi's life includes one or more "dispensations of justice," as he calls them.

They may be as gentle as sentencing a first-time runaway eunuch to two months in prison and twenty blows of a bamboo whip, or, for a second offense, two months with a wooden frame around his neck. A third offense brings banishment, or more likely, beheading. Virtually everything else, from petty thievery on up, involves the loss of a limb, up to and including the one we have all lost. This empire of ours loves its punishments! If the Emperor and Grand Counselor Li Ssu have their way, the population would be noseless, earless and thumbless! One is careful around Juan Chi; he is a dog who will bite first and bark later, if at all. But I have learned a secret about him: underneath, he is a kindly man.

Only Han Yin seems unafraid of Juan Chi. Physically, I would not call Juan Chi ugly; I would call him very, very ugly. His features are irregular: he has a nose broken to the left long ago, and a cast in his right eye. His skin, rough as a plucked chicken, hangs in limp folds all over his body, lopping over visibly at the waist even under the loose robes he invariably wears. His feet smell abominably—it is interesting to note that whoever is to his right, which happens tonight to be the august and fastidious Wang Ts'ao, Major Domo of the Royal Palace, sits as far away from him as possible in this crowded room.

Nobody dares insult Juan Chi except for Han Yin, who teases him all the time with delicate, unanswerable comments.

There are bonds of affection between Han Yin and Juan Chi. Both were eunuchs from childhood, so they have known little else, and they have been long in the Emperor's service—since the early days of his kingship, when the king was just entering his teens. I am sure they have fought many battles together against the scholar class that infests the court. The scholars hate the eunuchs, who constantly try to undermine their court standing. This is a source of humor to me, as I am both a scholar and a eunuch. It seems especially ironic to me that when it comes to the Taoist canon, Juan Chi is a scholar himself. He is also a prodigious drinker and talker. As I said, he is quite a kind man at heart, one who does his duty but who also tries to execute the judgments handed down by the Office of Punishments in a moderate way. Often he takes risks to save people.

I mentioned Wang Ts'ao, Major Domo of the Royal Palace. Han Yin's description of him as being boring was facetious, because it is exactly what he is not.

Unlike most of us, Wang Ts'ao is physically beautiful, though in his fifties. He has a quick wit, a handsome face, a tall, graceful body. In conversation, Wang Ts'ao often causes the eyes of his fellows to brighten as a pretty, young woman passing under the window would. He is faintly perfumed at all times; it is such a joke to think of him being placed, doubtless by Han Yin, next to the abominable feet of Juan Chi!

Vain, he exercises regularly, uncommon among eunuchs. He has a good singing voice and is likely to chant his stories, accompanying himself on a small box-drum and sometimes a thirteen-string zither. He is animated and high-spirited, and has a prodigious memory. His physical presence is important in his job; as the Major Domo of the Royal Palace, he is officially the most prominent among us. Except for Chief Eunuch Chao Kao, whose far less prestigious and unglamorous official job is Manager of Chariots. Not that he sets foot in a chariot these days, palanquins being his preferred mode of travel.

Wang Ts'ao's palace tasks, involving so many wives, concubines, soldiers, courtiers and on occasion the Emperor himself, require great charm and discretion as well as a habit of command. All these things he has in abundance. I must say, he is a good fellow, too! I can easily see how he might appeal romantically to some. When his eyes are on me, I feel somewhat flustered!

A man with a high musical voice, Chia Tao, Major Domo of the Concubine Residences, sits at Wang Ts'ao's right. He holds the most dreadful position among us, doomed to be a nightly arbiter of cat fights that equal any feline battles in the fetid alleyways of our imperial city! There are between three and four thousand concubines in the palace—at the last official count five years ago, there were 3,615—but none are visited by the Emperor these days, so deeply immersed is he in the search for immortality. Lacking a clear hierarchy derived from imperial preferences, you can imagine the power struggles that take place—they outdistance anything you will find happening in the eunuchs' messes (we are organized along military lines).

The first thing to notice about Chia Tao is that he has deep, deep bags under his eyes, easily explained by the fact that for him a good night's sleep is impossible. Like Juan Chi, Chia Tao often becomes excited during his story-telling, but where Juan Chi rumbles, Chia Tao screeches. Also, he is gestural, to put it mildly. He is a frail man, who at times seems to disappear inside his rich clothing. He is always yawning. Unusually among us, he prefers men.

The burly man to Chia Tao's right is Tu Mu, the Emperor's Charioteer. To me, he does not look like a eunuch, even though he has been one since his youth and has been trained for service all his life in the military arts, especially mastering fractious warhorses, a job that takes both raw strength and skill.

As you might expect, Tu Mu is closely connected to Chao Kao, the Chief Eunuch—so closely it has always been assumed by Han Yin and the others that everything said in this room travels straight to Chao Kao. (It is our good fortune that Chao Kao permits this outlet, understanding that his senior eunuchs need to relax and speak freely at times.)

Tu Mu is the quietest of us. I remember only two occasions

on which he spoke at any length. His clothes are plain for a wealthy man—my eunuchs are wealthy men, and most own estates inside and outside the city (since they cannot leave the palace to go to the latter, they have managers for them). When we are not wearing our dull, black, short robes, trousers and headdresses, one would expect considerable finery. Some members are not above a little competition in the matter of colorful, elaborate dress, except for Tu Mu, who in other respects is pleasure-loving and quite wild at times. I call him "the soldier." In dress, he is plain as a pole.

Next to Tu Mu sits a personal servant of the Emperor, his Chief Dresser, Lo Yin, a man who laughs a great deal, but only behind his fan. The laughter rarely reaches his eyes.

He has an odd lump above his right ear, protruding from his thinning hair. It appears to be a bruise, discolored, but never gets better and never goes away. Perhaps it is refreshed daily by the Emperor?

Even in this room of humorists, Lo Yin is an exceptionally funny man, but his comments are always aimed at others, never at himself; and they cut, swift and deep. He could separate you from your head with a comment and you might not know it until you found yourself responding from the far corner of the room, where your head has come to rest. The last thing you might see would be your body sliding slowly down the wall, gathering speed as it plunges toward the grave.

Exceptionally ugly, like Juan Chi, Lo Yin is a marvelous storyteller, and I would not be surprised to learn—but I am sure I never will learn—that the Emperor chose him in order to hear his stories. Probably not much like the ones he tells here!

To Lo Yin's right, and Han Yin's left, for we have now toured the room, is a man with two responsible jobs. Meng Hao-jan is the Principal Trainer of Eunuchs and Director of Eunuch Promotions.

The latter title is more significant, as we are a truly vast hierarchy, really an army, with levels, levels and more levels.

As in the outside world, exceptional service generally leads to promotion, but not as swiftly as flattery.

Meng Hao-jan has a reputation as a hard worker and a firm, fair man. Men in this room have reached their present high rank, thanks to him. As far as I can tell, he never openly trades on his influence. Power unused is power preserved and respected.

Interesting to note that Meng Hao-jan and Lo Yin are the only two who came from humble origins. Many of the other eunuchs were "volunteered," so to speak, by aristocratic families who wished to get someone into the palace. Unfortunately, once their children became eunuchs, the families had even less contact with them than the parents of Taoist monks!

Meng Hao-jan was born a peasant in one of the southern prefectures, I forget which one. He has a reclusive nature. It has been hinted to me that he is an expert in poisons of all kinds, a remarkably useful skill in the court of Ch'in Shih-huang-ti, but I have no direct knowledge of this.

So here we are: the storytellers and their scholar-scribe, myself, hated by scholars, banned from worshipping before the spirit temples of our ancestors, harshly ruled by the feminine forces of the universe. No one will perform the required sacrificial rites for our souls after death. If one of us was to lose the jars containing our "Precious" that sit on shelves in our sleeping rooms, he would be born into the next world as a she-mule.

No doubt we are lacking in many respects, and we all fall short of manhood in the procreative sense. But here in the Jade Room, we are not lacking in friends.

The Gates of Hantan
Han Yin's Tale

"...So, my friends, that is how our dear, august First Emperor, child of the far west born to barbarian farmers, came as an infant to Hantan in the state of Chao. I believe that covers all the major points," Han Yin, Regulator of Entertainment in the Royal Palace, said to the eunuchs gathered in the Jade Room.

"The hell you say," shouted Han Yin's chief rival, Juan Chi, Chief Dispenser of Eunuch Punishments. "That's wrong twice! One, you didn't tell us how they substituted him for the other baby; two, there's no truth in it, not a word, Heaven's bells be my witnesses!"

"Well," said Han Yin, "as to that, I'll tell you how Shen Neng, who happens to be my grand-uncle on my mother's side, who is the source of this story and whom history will judge a true and rightful hero to all the eunuchs of the Ch'in era, successfully made the greatest baby substitution of all time! With help."

"Yes, yes," shouted all his listeners except for two who were too wine-soaked to speak. Even they nodded, eyes bulging.

"As to your other charge, that my story is food for hogs, you shall have your chance to tell your story next time, and then we will judge you as you now judge me."

"Of course, we all know you're going to be pitiful, Juan Chi," Han Yin added, "because your imagination really leaves a lot to be desired."

"In any case, Shen Neng has never been stuck for what to do

next," said Han Yin, after a brief pause, "not in his entire career. He was always notable for quick thinking and quicker action."

But now, Shen Neng was frozen in place, almost literally; he couldn't bring himself to put a slippered foot outside the carriage that he, the baby and the wet nurse, Full Moons, now occupied. All he could do was turn back to the embraces of Full Moons and hide himself, but she, alas, was occupied with nursing the baby, which didn't rule out fornication but eliminated foreplay. All things considered, he thought, it's like going into a dark closet and coming out again—hardly worth the bother!

Three days earlier, the small party had arrived at the massive city gate of fortresslike Hantan, wealthiest city in all of the ancient states. But by this time they were attracting unhealthy attention. The Ch'in soldiers, far from home and highly vulnerable, were getting restless; for them, restless equalled mean. Worse, they were forced to keep their weapons hidden. No soldier likes to have to hide the shining, lethal implements of his trade under dirty, old blankets. And though they didn't really mind being dirty, their clothes were also lousy, a state which wears on a soldier. Besides, people were yelling rude things at the two carriages, something that happens in Ch'in to this day.

Soon, Shen Neng thought unhappily, the Ch'in soldiers will start yelling back. Which would lead to discovery, as the rough Ch'in dialect is unlike the cultivated, multitoned lisping affected by the upper classes in Chao. The soldiers didn't speak like peasants either. On the rare occasions when a peasant grunts something or other, it is usually about food or fornication—but who cares how peasants sound?

On the fourth day, morning dawned disgustingly brightly. Shen Neng was standing irresolutely in the door of his carriage, when a barefoot, old man leading an immense water buffalo hobbled by. Shen Neng was paying no attention to him when the old man turned and swung his long goad across Shen Neng's face! The Queen Dowager's Secretary staggered back, his eyes blinded with tears, his right hand reaching inside his robe for his dagger.

"Take it easy, that was merely to get your attention in an unobtrusive manner! Also, I enjoyed it," the old man whispered loudly. "Before you use that short, sharp knife—Ch'in make, yes?—to cut me up, you should know I have instructions for you from a rich merchant who lives in Hantan."

Here it was at last, the signal for action! Dagger re-sheathed, sting of the ox-goad almost forgotten, Shen Neng bent down to listen to the old man's hoarse voice.

"His name is Lu Pu-wei and his home is on Jade Street—everyone knows it, he is the greatest merchant in the city. He orders you to enter the city, alone, at the time when crowds of people hurry in, just before the city gates are shut. Get yourself into the middle of the thickest part of the crowd and make yourself as nondescript as possible. The guards are tired at that hour, and there's a good chance your pass won't be asked for, or if it is, they'll just glance at it."

"Once you are safely inside the city, you must find Jade Street and ask directions to Mr. Lu's house. A blind beggar will assist you."

"I will do it, gladly," said a relieved Shen Neng. "But what about my friends here? I cannot just leave them. Can I?"

The old man laughed faintly, like the dying hiss of a kettle after the flame is out, and said, "Friends, eh? You can leave them here for the night. Mr. Lu has a group of thugs secretly watching to make sure no one comes near you. Two soldiers tried to last night, by the way. Didn't hear them, did you? No one will ever hear them again. Or see them again. They're bathing in the Yellow Spring today."

Shen Neng shuddered, recognising the euphemism for the journey of death, one that might have been his instead of the unfortunate soldiers.

The old man reversed his goad and gave the water buffalo, who was now asleep standing up, a series of thwacks that would be acutely painful to anything but a water buffalo. They were enough to get him ambling on again, and the old man disappeared in the swirling ebb and flow of the bazaar. It is hard to understand why people fear water buffaloes. Perhaps in the wild state they are not so dutiful.

Shen Neng went into the carriage and mounted Full Moons, not troubling to wake her. Then he ate two days' worth of food and took a nap until the sun began to roll swiftly down over the western edge of the world. He rose, brushed his hair, and said a happy goodbye to the infant and a voracious one to Full Moons. Something that felt like a plan to him was beginning at last.

The passage into the city was uneventful; soldiers called for his forged pass, but barely glanced at it—almost, it seemed to Shen Neng, as if they were part of a play merely acting the roles of guards. He was more right than he knew.

The city was familiar to Shen Neng, though he had never been in it. This is because the principles of city-building, traditional among the black-haired people from ancient times, are the same in all our states.

The basic idea is the protection of the ruler.

In the center of the northern quarter of the city, a massive rammed earth platform is the base from which rise palaces, temples and tombs. Earthen-walled, timber-framed, the palaces have roofs with beautiful glazed tiles that shone in the sun. The roofs are thick and heavy to keep out the cold; they are turned upward, often with dragon spouts at the ends, guarding the house from all evil and, as a practical matter, sending water down to gigantic cisterns. The main halls are on north-south axes with inner gates opening to the south. Courtyards, public and private, abound in both the palaces and the far smaller family compounds that surround the royal buildings.

The city is laid out like a chessboard, with the king at the center and top. A few pagodas stand here and there, carrying more dragons skyward. Ancient and modern temples are everywhere, though none are as large as the family temple of the ruler. Market streets alternate with narrow residential streets consisting of high walls and small, unwelcoming doors. Surrounding all of this are manned city walls, with frequent guard stations built into them. Beyond the walls lie the homes of craftsmen, and further out, the mostly scanty sheds of peasant farmers, who live with "one foot in their field," as the expression goes, meaning that the peasant is totally and permanently attached to his garden.

Large as Hantan was, it was fairly easy for Shen Neng to find his way. He asked directions once or twice—one person lied to him for pleasure, but another gave him a helpful response that put him on the right path.

Soon Shen Neng came to the Street of Jade, a relatively broad street two carriages in width, lined by the outer walls of large houses. The first man he encountered was able to tell Shen Neng exactly where to go, almost as if he had been waiting for him.

Coming to an entrance way set into the highest, most forbidding walls on the street, Shen Neng knocked loudly and the door opened immediately. He entered an outer courtyard. A huge gingko biloba tree stood at the center of the courtyard, casting seed and shade by day, across the well-swept pounded earth surface. By the interior wall, a small fountain bubbled and sang; an abandoned broom lay beside it. No one was near, not even the person who opened the door.

An inner moon door slid open noiselessly. Framed in it stood the most extraordinary person Shen Neng had ever seen. Nearly as round as tall—and not tall at all, scarcely more than a dwarf in height—the creature was dressed in silk, mock-dragon-infested green robes that in no way indicated his or her sex. No beard, no eyebrows, red lips, a completely bald head, tiny hands and feet. The dwarf merely looked at him. As the silence lengthened, Shen Neng grew frightened.

The Secretary knew the adage that he who makes the first offer in the marketplace has lost the bargain. But the silence was unbearable, and at last he said, "Excuse me, sir or madam, but I am Shen Neng. I have been bidden to enter the presence of the merchant Lu Pu-wei. Might you be he? Or can you tell me if he is within? If so, may I enter?"

Suddenly above him came crazy laughter, screaming giggles, cackles, cawings, hoots. Shen Neng looked up. Along the tops of the courtyard walls were monkeys from the south, many types and sizes, and it was they who were creating the din. Where did they come from? Why so silent up to now? Were they laughing at him?

He looked back toward the remarkable figure in the doorway, but it vanished through the still-open door. Trying to control his nerves, Shen Neng stepped forward and crossed into the inner threshold, leaving the monkeys behind. They immediately grew silent, shaking their heads and scratching in the rude places monkeys always seem to scratch first.

On the other side of the moon door, the house was dark. After a moment of adjustment, Shen Neng realized he was standing in a narrow corridor no more than four feet wide and six high, a virtual tunnel, that ran off as far as he could see both right and left. Clearly he was meant to walk through the tunnel, but which way? Suddenly a candle lamp flared far down to his right and he started toward it. But as soon as he began to walk in that direction, the candle went out. Total darkness. Nothing ventured, he thought. He drew his dagger, held it in front of him, and strode through the darkness. After perhaps sixty paces, the dagger arm ran into a cold, rough-surfaced wall—fortunately, he had been swinging his arms at the time and made first contact with them rather than his nose. A bruise or two, nothing.

Turning left by instinct, he looked down a corridor with a little more light and saw, at its end, a woman filling the corridor, roof to floor and side to side. Full Moons! He thought at first, but this woman was much taller and was holding an immense scimitar. It took all his boldness to walk toward her, but he managed it. As he approached, she pointed to her right with the scimitar. He turned down yet another corridor, at whose end was a tiny doorway bright with yellow light.

He barely managed to crawl through the door, scraping parts of his body on both sides, and popped into a room filled with light. Magnificent! Gorgeous carpets lay piled on top of each other on the floor and hung on the walls, paintings on silk fluttered mildly in a cool breeze coming from nowhere visible, oil lamps in braziers stood in ranks around the walls. There were desks, chairs, piles of books, and in one corner, what looked like piles of coins and jewels all mixed together, several feet deep.

"Do you like my house? And my favorite room?" A high voice said. "It is well protected, too, don't you think?"

The speaker was the small, round man he had seen first perfectly framed in the moon door. "I have everything I need here, including," the speaker said, pointing to one corner, "a scribe who keeps track of my winnings. I do not lose." A thin man sat at a high table, chained to a chair writing, never looking up.

"I had his legs broken," the round man said. "They were not needed. Likewise his tongue was removed. He sleeps on a pallet over there in the corner. I can't remember when he last saw daylight; I'm sure he can't either." The oblivious object of the round man's attention continued entering figures in the ledger.

"Have I the pleasure of addressing Mr. Lu Pu-wei?" Shen Neng asked.

"You do," said Mr. Lu. "And you are the eunuch Shen Neng, Secretary to the Queen Dowager of Ch'in. I admire your work, Shen Neng. All of it," he added, one eyebrowless brow arching meaningfully.

"Take a cup of wine with me, if you please."

The two men settled themselves on cushioned chairs, Mr. Lu on a higher chair. From an as-yet unnoticed door, a servant entered with a jug of wine and two cups. The servant filled the glasses, placed them on a table close at hand and withdrew, leaving the jug behind.

They toasted one another. It was the best wine Shen Neng had ever drunk—sweet and southern, lingering...They drank another cup, and another. What a fine man Mr. Lu is, he thought, as the broken-legged secretary goes on scratching in his ledger. There is nothing I would not do for such a man!

"That is true, Shen Neng."

Had he spoken aloud?!

Shen Neng found himself recounting the adventure with the infant, just as it happened, an account that required several more cups of wine. A terrible time they all had, but now it was all worthwhile because it had brought him to this remarkable, adorable man! Tears filled his eyes.

"I expect you're wondering what's next," Mr. Lu said.

The tears departed and Shen Neng's keenness returned at once. He sat straighter, though not altogether straight, in his chair.

"We have time to talk about that," Mr. Lu said. "First, would you like to see one of my fine, new toys? I traded a superb pair of western pure-bred horses, barbarian trained, for it, but it was well worth it. I would have doubled the price to get this."

He rang a small bell and a boy of perhaps fifteen entered the room, bowing low. He was carrying a large, round bronze bowl three feet across and two feet deep. In it, Shen Neng could see clear, still water. Rising up from the sides of the bowl, perfectly squaring the circle, were four peaked electrum handles gleaming golden in the dim light.

"Now watch," Mr. Lu said. "Watch and listen."

The boy dried his hands carefully on his shirt, freeing them of grease or moisture. Then he knelt before the bowl, first looking to Lu Pu-wei for permission to begin.

Holding his hands out flat over the two handles, he began to stroke the latter with his palms, slowly at first, then faster and faster.

For a while nothing happened. Then, a humming sound came from the bowl. As it rose in pitch, the water below each of the four nodes began to bubble, then spit, and then—

extraordinary!—it formed four perfect waves within the basin, waves that went nowhere but straight up and down!

Shen Neng had never seen such a thing. His eyes grew wider and wider, mimicking the boy's eyes, who was now looking up at the two men while he continued to move his hands so rapidly the motion had a stillness of its own.

Gradually, the boy's hands slowed and stopped. The hum quieted and the waves vanished, leaving the water perfectly still. Not a drop had been spilled outside the bowl. The boy bowed his head, Mr. Lu touched his shoulder, and the boy vanished as silently as he had come.

"It's called a spouting bowl," Lu Pu-wei said. "I have heard of only one other in All Under Heaven. This one, and the boy who can play it, is mine. Now the memory of it is yours, too."

Shen Neng was indescribably grateful. They drank another glass of wine, slowly this time. The things we men have seen!

"It comes from the Book of the Tao," Mr. Lu said. "The cosmic forces of the Universe. No man can truly control them. We can only wonder and try to learn."

Silence ensued.

"Well, well, let us get down to business," Lu Pu-wei said at last. "You know your charge? To substitute the baby without the parents knowing?"

Shen Neng must have looked very surprised because Lu Pu-wei went on to say, "You have not told me anything new, you know. There is no such thing as a secret in any palace, least of all the palace of the Ch'in, and I knew all about this long ago.

"Indeed, to a certain extent, I made it happen. One of your late Chief Astrologer's associates was in my pay. The forecasts concerning the two infants were true auguries, but the rest of it, the substitution of the infants, was my idea. By making Prince Tzu-ch'u and Lady Tzu-ch'u part of the plot to substitute one baby for the other, I gained a means by which I can control them forever. They would never dare admit to such a thing! I expect to profit by that, and my profit will be the Kingdom of Ch'in."

A shocked silence.

Mr. Lu waited.

More silence. Shen Neng was beginning to have a tremendous headache.

"All right, here's what is going to happen now," Lu Pu-wei said finally. "It's going to be easy. I want you to bring the carriage with the baby into the city when the gates first open. You won't have any trouble. Take the infant to this house"—and he handed Shen Neng an address—"bring the baby to the front door, well wrapped so people can't see it's a baby, and knock seven times. A tall, thin man will open the door. You just hand him the baby and clear out, your job is done.

"Afterward, stay here in Hantan. Come see me in a week. You're a useful man and I will have some work for you."

"But what about..."

"The wet nurse? Leave her with the soldiers. And don't worry about the soldiers. I have an errand I want them to do. She can fend for herself. A good wet nurse—as you well know—is a precious commodity."

Shen Neng, as always, did exactly as he was told. He found his way to Prince Tzu-ch'u's house, carrying the baby. Then he turned the baby over to the tall man who met him at the door. For him, that was the end of the matter.

Returning to Mr. Lu's mansion a week later, he waited at the front entrance, then was admitted and taken into Mr. Lu's employ, where he flourished, rising steadily until he was very near the top of the tree of the world—until Mr. Lu's disgrace, about which more will be said later. But by the time of Mr. Lu's downfall, Shen Neng was long since safely retired, with great wealth, to an obscure village far to the east of here, reasonably safe from royal vengeance. The village where I was born and raised, and first heard this story from my venerable grand-uncle Shen, I might add.

Sunshine, or Full Moons, or Ever-Ready, as Shen Neng

had begun to think of her, missed Shen Neng dreadfully for a week or so, but after that found full employment for both barrels in Hantan, serving wealthy and poor, relatively poor, with complete indifference and complete contentment. But she never had a better lover than Shen Neng the rest of her days.

The unfortunate Ch'in soldiers were sent on a long errand to the Yellow Spring. Their death journey began when their earth-lives ended, at the bottom of the Great River, throats slashed, bodies weighted with stones. They have not returned, though back in Ch'in their families remained hopeful for a long time. Soldiers seldom come home.

And that is the story of Ying Cheng's infancy. What? How was the substitution accomplished, you are asking? Frankly, I do not know. But I have three theories.

You may take your choice.

In the first, Lu Pu-wei, who had a powerful influence on the Ch'in Prince, Tzu-ch'u, and his wife, visited them the day the baby arrived in Hantan. After green tea served on a cool patio, Mr. Lu told them something like this:

"I have a favor to ask of you, but I do not have time or inclination to tell you exactly why I am asking it. It has become necessary to remove your infant and replace it with another one much like it, right down to the loud crying, the missing knuckle, and above all, the tiger marking on the back. I have had reports of the second infant, and I think on the whole you may find it somewhat more agreeable than your present one, who will of course be disposed of."

A wail rose from Lady Tzu-ch'u's lovely throat. "I will not, I will never, give up my very own baby!" she said loudly. The Prince, as was natural for him after years of life as a despised hostage, remained quiet, waiting to hear more.

"Nonetheless, madam, you will give up your baby, who is certainly going to be killed in any case. The difference is that if you do not cooperate in this small, umm, deception, you and your husband will also be killed. So you have your choice—

continue to live a comfortable life here, thanks to me. You will grant, Prince, life has been far more comfortable since I brought you together, will you not?"

The Prince grunted.

"So what is it to be?"

Another cup of tea and the thing was settled. We are practical people.

In my second theory, Lu Pu-wei had the couple killed and substituted another man and woman of similar appearance. Here, too, the essential part of the plan was that the first baby was killed. I am not entirely happy with this possibility, as it would have been likely to raise more questions among some people who knew the couple.

In my third theory, Lu Pu-wei had a powerful magician in his employ. The magician bewitched the couple in such a way that they readily accepted the substitution and lived happily together, more or less, ever after.

"One more thing," Han Yin added, "the Prince's wife, who was quite lovely and who, though from a noble family, had been a courtesan of astounding skills, was thought to have been Lu Pu-wei's lover long before he gave her to the admiring Prince. The final point in the story is that she was believed to be secretly pregnant when the Prince wed her, and that the child, which would have become the King of Ch'in and one day the real First Emperor of Ch'in (had he lived), was Lu Pu-wei's love child.

"This is perfectly plausible except for the 'love child' part. In the case of Mr. Lu, our late Regent and Prime Minister, love never had anything to do with his decisions and certainly not when compared to a mercantile opportunity like owning one's own prince.

"And now, it is time to say, 'Good night, my friends.'"

Fu Hao of Shang

First Consort of King Shang,
Lady General of the Army of Shang,
Revered Mistress of Anyang,
your second son places this holy cauldron
at your side. May its *t'ao t'ieh*[3] guard you
as you watch over the lords
and least creatures of our land.

You sit at King Shang's foot in heaven.
Your handmaidens comb your long hair,
unfold and perfume your peach silk gown.
Four white horses sleep near you.
Even night would not dare to assault
the mountain where you lie.

---

[3] *T'ao t'ieh* is the name given to a motif commonly found on ancient bronze
vessels of the Shang and Chou dynasties; the motif is said to depict a
fearsome, mythical animal figure.

The Maker

Fancy handles are the devil to cast.
You can't get pure metal any more.
As for a hardworking apprentice, forget it!

I have a nice design for a pot mold.
My father and granddad used it, so did I
until they said the king wanted something new.

So I put on little tigers here and there
and the king liked them. I put a bird on top
and the king liked that, too, but he said

"What happened to the tigers?" So now I put
birds and tigers on my pots, and today
I heard the king is asking about an elephant.

I would like to know what the gods want,
but they don't say. If you ask me, a bronze pot
in a burial pit is a dead waste of a pot.

A Royal Prince

Little duckling,
I combed your hair
and closed your eyes.
The palace still feels the rush
of your comings and goings,
the quick footsteps
that so often turned
the slow dance of the court
to helpless laughter.
It wasn't your destiny
to put on stiff robes of state.
Rumbling carts on the South Road
are not so heavy as my heart.
Dear son, since you must be buried
alone, I give you this small bronze
three-wheeled cart to play with.
Have a care for the wheels,
they aren't fastened well,
and the axle pins are sharp.

BOOK TWO

The King

The Boys
Ssu-Ma Ch'ien's Tale

The ritual by which a storyteller was chosen each evening was invariable. Han Yin, the Regulator of Entertainment in the Royal Palace, had a small, jade *pi*-disk of a green so light it appeared translucent. A leather lace could be passed through the hole in the disk to a similar hole in a small, carved, wooden speaker's scepter. Both disk and scepter had ancient markings that appear vaguely similar to our own writing.

As to the ritual, the moment the sounds of munching died away and were replaced with the gentle, occasional gurgle of a lifted wine cup, Han Yin would stand up, carefully, and sway toward the speaker he had chosen for the evening. He then handed the disk-scepter to the selected speaker, who kept it for the entire evening.

On this particular night, I was as usual preparing for my scribal tasks, wetting and stirring my inks and pointing my brushes; thus occupied, I was surprised when he stopped before me and handed me the speaker's scepter. My mouth fell open.

"There is a part of the First Emperor's life about which we are ignorant," said Han Yin, "and that is his childhood before he was crowned king at age thirteen. But you are not, Ssu-ma Ch'ien, having grown up with him here in the palace. We would be honored if you could tell us about his childhood. And your own," he added.

I sat for some moments, trying to think back on days that

now seem to have happened a long time ago, a lifetime separated from my life as an emasculated servant. I do not think I have spoken of my childhood in decades! But I have a good memory, and soon a few pictures came out of the dark.

"To be truthful—I know truth is an oddity in this room!—I don't remember much about myself and Ying Cheng as boys," I told the listeners.

"Certainly, he was a bully who used his physical size and special rank of heir to pound the rest of us into the ground at every opportunity. I was frightened of him, with reason—he was hell on birds and beetles, frogs, rabbits, and other boys, myself included. But I can offer you a few memories. If you don't mind, I would prefer to speak of myself in the third person."

Hearing no objections, I began.

* * * * * * * *

"In those days," Retired General Meng Ao told the small boys gathered around him for their classroom lessons, "Grandfather Dragon was asleep deep in the ground far to the southwest of here. His lair lay under the highest mountains in the world, even higher than the T'ienshan or the mountains of K'unlun, home of the Queen Mother of the West. The mountains I mean are so high and so very old they have no name at all. Some people believe that they were here before anything else was created."

The boys' eyes widened. No one said anything, not even Prince Cheng, who generally had an opinion on every topic.

"This was a long time ago, so long Grandfather Dragon was the only dragon in the world," continued the boys' teacher. "In fact, some think the Earth itself was his egg, the one he was born in. But that is just ghost-talk, none of the black-haired people ever believed that. We believe in dragons, though, for one good reason: we have seen them.

"Of all things under Heaven, I believe dragons are the most

interesting. They mean us well, most of the time, and we hold them in high regard. One moment a dragon can be tiny as an almond sweet, the next moment he can cover the sun with one wing."

"I can do that, too, with just my hand!" shouted Prince Cheng.

"A dragon can rise high like a puffball on the wind or slide through the Earth as fast as worms do. Indeed, many people think our beloved dragons are the Earth! Some of us think that," said Retired General Meng, slightly embarrassed by what for him was a display of emotion.

"Among us, there are people you might call specialists in dragons. For example, a 'wind and water' man. Who can tell me what a 'wind and water' man is?"

"I can," shouted Ssu-ma Ch'ien as Prince Cheng, always slower, glowered at him. "He's someone who tells you how to locate your house or bury a dead person."

"Exactly right," said the teacher. "He knows how fast the universe is changing. Moreover, he knows what range of mountains the nearest dragon is passing through and just how far he has gotten. He will have you build here, bury there, or dig your canal right over there, all according to the natural shape of the place and the plants that grow there. Follow his advice carefully and your family will have fame and good fortune for generations."

Saying this, he nodded at Prince Cheng, who inclined his head very slightly and sat straighter.

"But if you ignore a dragon's advice, there will be trouble ahead!

"There was once a general who was commanded to build a wall in the northwest to keep the horse-traders out of our empire. He did so. But late in life, he fell out of favor with the duke he served. Concluding his life in exile, the old general lamented, 'My family served Duke Wen's family for generations. If I had wished to rebel, with all the excellent soldiers I commanded, nothing could have been easier. But I would have died before I betrayed my Duke—what crime have I done under Heaven that my bell untuned and I lost favor with him? I shall die without fault or blemish!'

"The exiled general then became silent for a while, thinking about what he had just said. Finally he added, 'But that is not entirely true. I committed one crime for which I am answering now. In building the northern wall as my Duke commanded, I built ramparts and dug ditches longer than five hundred *li*. Doing this, I must have cut through the veins of Grandfather Dragon. That surely is my crime! And it is a crime for which the Duke rightly banished me from his presence and from the kingdom!'"

At this point, Retired General Meng paused to let the story sink in. Then, he urged of his charges, "Listen to me, children, and remember. Grandfather Dragon and his descendants are the great protectors of the black-haired race. We must respect them always, and never offend them.

"To this day, we believe a sky dragon chases both the Sun and the Moon at the time of our New Year. In every village, in every city, the people make dragons for luck using any materials handy—old clothes, discarded bits of wood, shells and shards. Each dragon is as long as the village or neighborhood can make it, and young athletes are chosen to be dragon dancers for the New Year's celebration. They practice for months—and so will you someday, because you fine boys will be dragon dancers, too. I am sure of that."

"I'm going to ride a dragon, a big one!" shouted Prince Cheng.

"Grandfather Dragon was alone for a long time, but then he had nine sons," the teacher continued calmly. "Where do you see them every day?"

"On the rooftops of our pagodas!" shouted the prince.

Retired General Meng said, "That's right. The first is the dragon of burden and he is used as a base for monuments. The second is a dragon of fantasy; he stands on the roof with his head looking up at the sky. The third is the loudmouth dragon, and you will often find him on our bronze-cast bells. The fourth is the strongest. He has a tiger's face..."

Prince Cheng looked up and smiled.

"...he guards the entrances of jails..."

"And the mountain passes into the state of Ch'in!" shouted the prince.

* * * * * * * *

Six brown monkeys sat in a row on the bank of China's Sorrow, the vast Yellow River, watching its waters weave snakelike coils around Ch'in and the states to the east, the remnant of the Eastern Chou Dynasty, the last empire in our land. It was unknown to the boys, though not to their teacher—Retired General Meng Ao, a scholar-soldier of the old type—who had been imported into the state of Ch'in together with many other gifted men, each drawn by promises of wealth but not always achieving it.

The 'monkeys' were Prince Cheng, his older brother and an ill-fated younger brother, Cheng-chou, who would later rebel disastrously against him, plus a boy whose name I have forgotten, Ssu-ma Ch'ien, and, always silent in the background, Chao Kao, the future Chief Eunuch.

Chao Kao was a servant who had been brought up in the palace because of a promise made to his father.

When Cheng's father, the present king, escaped from Hantan, the capital city of the state of Chao, Chao Kao's father, a servant, stood in the palace windows pretending to be the departing prince. This fooled the vengeful army of Chao and gave Cheng's father the chance to cross the river safely into Ch'in. Of course, when the imposture was discovered, Chao Kao's father was killed, but he had won a promise from the escaping prince that his son, taken along to Ch'in, would be raised in the palace and looked after. This the prince did—up to a point, as you will see later.

Among the boys, Chao Kao kept to the shadows, mostly trying to escape Cheng's notice. He rarely succeeded; Cheng beat him up regularly.

The boys were now on a several-day boat journey from their own Wei River, having paddled onto the vast Yellow River. It was time for one of their field lessons.

Both the boys and their elderly teacher had slept lightly and rose early, just after dawn, about the time songbirds and mountain-girls sing up the sun. Near where they sat, a hundred yards away or so, a long row of eighteen-oared boats had been pulled onto the bank. Multicolored, slim and misleadingly fragile-looking, the boats seem more like dragonflies than dragons, missing only the gossamer double wings. Their carved and upraised dragon heads, variously pugnacious, angry or smiling, identified them for what they were—Dragon Boats.

Later that day, they would be rowed by costumed oarsmen out into the current in a dangerous race that is very much like a battle. Their oars driving in unison to the beating of a wooden drum and a bronze gong struck by two men in turn standing amidships, the boats are steered by another man at a sweep at the stern. They constantly nose into each other, challenging for right of way and trying to snap their opponents' nearer bank of oars and tip rivals into the water—all the while ducking hundreds of stones and thousands of flowers thrown by the spectators who line the bank, trying to help their favorites by damaging their opponents. Unfortunately, the stones rain down on all the boats.

"The point of this mayhem," Teacher Meng had told the boys, "in which drownings are frequent, is to get good rain from the dragon next month during the rainy season—rain that does not flood the plains!"

At this early hour, the river was peaceful. A few fishermen were mending nets, and one mountain-song girl was sending her sorrows to the horizon, thanks to a voice that carried for miles. Otherwise, there was only this row of brown-robed boys and their brown-robed teacher.

While he was speaking to them, he was tying multicolored, silk ribbon charms to their forearms; this is insurance against being grabbed by souls of forgotten dead men that have wandered from their bodies, evil spirits from the river who may wish the boys ill. As a practical matter, it is a caution to avoid the sources of the noxious diseases that occur frequently in the fifth month when summer begins.

Meng Ao said, "Our proverb says 'the first month is good, the fifth month is evil,' and so we have believed since long before the days of our great-great-grandfathers in the years of the poet Ch'u Yuan, who wrote *The Great Summons of the Soul* that you have been reading."

Four heads, out of the six, nodded in unison. One boy, more nervous than the others, threw a leaf-wrapped triangular rice cake to the spirits of the dead who live in the river. A fat, green fish popped up to the surface and swallowed it in a single gulp.

"Ch'u Yuan, a counselor of the Duke of Ch'u, was exiled by the Ch'in after they conquered the state of Ch'u because he had written poems criticizing them. Taking a heavy stone and clasping it to his breast, he leaped into the River Milo on this very day and though many searched for his body, it was never found. We revere him for his honest, faithful council and count him a model for all who wish to serve their rulers well," said the teacher.

Several boys nodded, but a tall youngster shook his head angrily and said, "I do not understand, Retired General Meng, what he gained by killing himself? He only left his ruler prey to worse influences. It was stupid!"

Meng Ao turned to another boy, stockier in build, and asked, "How would you answer Prince Cheng, Ssu-ma?"

"I believe Ch'u Yuan wanted to set an example of what should be every advisor's duty, to tell the truth to his ruler as he understands it, and if he fails, at least to set an example to all others, both in his own time and in future days. That is what he did," said Ssu-ma Ch'ien, his eyes shining.

The taller boy jumped up, fists balled. "It's stupid to waste your life and so are you, Ssu-ma. You may be my best friend, but you will never be my counselor!"

He stripped off his robe, kicked off his clogs, and still wearing the silk ribbon charm on his right arm, jumped into the river—to swim, not drown. With each determined stroke, his strong, young back heaved into the increasing sunlight which illuminated the mark of the tiger on the back of his right shoulder.

Retired General Meng watched the boy, satisfied. He will be a strong king, he thought to himself. He is wrong about Ssu-ma—he will give him wise counsel all his life. He may not always take it, but if he is wise he will always respect it.

In these predictions, alas, he was less than half right.

* * * * * * * *

By the time Prince Cheng and Ssu-ma Ch'ien were eleven, just four boys were left in the group: Prince Cheng, Ssu-ma Ch'ien, Chao Kao, and a bigger, older boy whose name I still can't remember. Cheng-chou was now being taught by another teacher. And Retired General Meng Ao was no longer their sole tutor. He was often joined by Li Ssu, and occasionally even by the merchant Lu Pu-wei, whom Cheng called "Uncle Lu." But Meng was their teacher in all the weapons classes four mornings a week.

The boys began with wooden rods that were light and harmless, though occasionally painful, substitutes for swords. Basic positions were being taught to the boys. It was all gentlemanly, with elaborate salutes and much emphasis on assistance for the fallen—as if there were any of the chivalry of ancient days left after four hundred years of war with our neighbors.

One morning, Cheng and the bigger, older boy were hammering away at one another while I—while Ssu-ma Ch'ien —squatted looking on. The teacher stayed close to the boys, ready to jump in at the first sign of injury, especially to Cheng.

The larger boy was both stronger and quicker than Cheng, and probably more determined as well. Certainly he was braver. Cheng would cover up when he felt himself at the least disadvantage and the "sword"-play would stop at once. Even so, the bigger boy was getting the better of Prince Cheng. The latter tripped and went down twice; minute by minute he was growing more careless about his guard and swinging wildly.

The unthinkable happened. Just as Cheng dipped his staff to try to come up under the other boy's guard, the other boy launched a sweeping blow from the left that landed hard just above Cheng's right ear. The blow knocked him to the ground, stunned him, and left a long, red mark that rapidly became swollen as Ssu-ma Ch'ien watched, horrified, together with their teacher.

It seemed at first that it would be all right. Prince Cheng got up slowly, managing a smile; he bowed to the boy, who returned the bow, then embraced him. But the observant Ssu-ma Ch'ien noticed Cheng's hands were white on the boy's back, as if he was under tremendous pressure.

The swordplay was over. They had been having their lesson, as it was a comfortable day, outside by the river, in a rocky area. The boys gathered up their belongings and began to go back to the palace.

Prince Cheng lagged until he was five feet or more behind the bigger boy. Suddenly he snatched up a heavy stone and ran up to the boy. Using both hands, he smashed it into the back of the boy's head. The boy fell to the ground. When he was down, his eyes closed. Cheng then crashed the stone down on the boy's face, crushing the bones. The boy groaned once and died.

Cheng stood defiantly beside the dead boy, staring at the

teacher. Nothing happened. After a moment, the teacher asked Ssu-ma Ch'ien to go home, which he did, his thoughts whirling and crashing against each other. That night, and for many nights after that, he could not sleep. He had liked the other boy.

He never saw Prince Cheng after the incident, until a meeting over a decade later at which Cheng, now the King, told Ssu-ma Ch'ien he needed his counsel and asked him always to tell him the truth.

No one spoke of the other boy again.

* * * * * * * *

"Cheng was thirteen when his father died, possibly poisoned by the incredibly ancient Queen Dowager Plum Blossom," said Han Yin, adding to my narrative.

"Now Cheng was King; among the eunuchs who knew him the best, and feared him the most, he was already hard to serve! Big and mean by nature, he'd been a bully since childhood. Now he was a killer. But at age thirteen, king or not, he had nothing to say about how things were done—ruling the kingdom was at that time the job of the self-appointed Regent, the former merchant Lu Pu-wei.

"The Marquis of Wenhsin, as the wily old trader was now known, had created a huge estate with 100,000 serf families and was busy recruiting henchmen and gathering in scholars from all the states.

"Li Ssu, a young man rising fast, was Imperial Steward by this time—the palace eunuchs kept a close watch on him, you may be sure—and recently unretired General Wang Ch'ien. Wang Ch'ien, together with Lord Piao and Wang I, were the chief generals of the army, a busy bunch, carrying on the Ch'in tradition of putting down revolts, beating off attacks from the other states, and grabbing all the lands they can conquer, especially in the neighboring state of Han to the east."

Thank you, I said to Han Yin. I did not understand any of this at the time, of course. Whatever Cheng was like by then, I was still just a boy playing boys' games. The next time I saw King Cheng, he made me Grand Historian, replacing my father.

I passed the speaker's scepter back along the row of eunuchs to Han Yin and he tied it to the loop on his waistband.

My recollections of childhood were done and I was glad; they had stirred thoughts of my family—those of my silent father, especially—that I had been working hard to bury for a long, long time.

How the Ch'in Came to Power
Juan Chi's Tale

Since my second meeting in the Jade Room when I took up my brush as the storytellers' Recording Secretary, an argument has continued as to how much background our future readers will need to make sense of these stories.

Here's the argument: if the tales are hidden well enough to be safe, it will be a long time, perhaps even centuries, before they are found. "By then," says Juan Chi, formidable Chief Dispenser of Eunuch Punishments, "they will have forgotten who we are, where we came from, and so forth, and our stories will be just a bunch of monkey poop to them. So we need to offer them some background."

The counter-argument was succinct: history is boring.

But Juan Chi, as always, showed no signs of giving up. This evening, Han Yin, our leader, settled the matter. Nodding, he passed the jade *pi*-disk speaker's scepter to him and muttered, "All right, Juan Chi, tell your tale."

"I would like to take you far back in time," said Juan Chi, "to when we black-haired people received the most ancient gift of the Yellow River, that same waterway whose great northern arc encloses our homeland. The river gave us fertile soil, and we learned how to cultivate it in straight rows and grow the millet and rice that sustain us to this day.

"There are many legends of our beginnings. One sage says we all come from the cast-off skins of a woman constantly regenerating herself; another tells us that both Yin and Yang came from dark, formless gases; a third speaks of P'an Ku, whose dying body became the living earth and all its parts; a fourth says we are sprung from a chicken's egg, et cetera."

But the truth, said Juan Chi, is that no one is sure how *anything* got started. So let us begin instead with the revered demi-god, the Yellow Emperor, whom we call "Grandfather."

The trustworthy *Thirteen Classics* tell us the Yellow Emperor and his successor, Yen Ti, the Red Emperor, actually existed. The Yellow Emperor ruled the Central Plains and areas to the north and west, today the homeland of our Ch'in Kingdom. Subsequently, the Yellow Emperor gained dominance over the vast Yellow River Valley.

A few generations later, a leader named Yao became famous for compassionate, intelligent rule. In time, Yao abdicated to Shun, a multitalented farmer, who tamed elephants in the far south. Further on, Shun abdicated to Yu, who tamed floods and defeated the southern Miao tribes. At Yu's death, his son Ch'i seized power to found the Hsia, the first great imperial dynasty to rule the black-haired people.

Thus was born the age of the Sage Rulers. They created the models on which all rulers should pattern their rules of government (though few today follow the model).

But the ruler known as the Sage King Yu did more than control the floods that devastate our people. He divided his land into nine provinces, and had nine bronze vessels cast to represent them, symbols of power and prestige observed also by his son. When the Hsia dynasty finally fell, the nine *"ding,"* as the vessels are known, passed to Shang Dynasty and in turn to Chou Dynasty, when the last Shang emperor became too drunk to rule. We believe that as each dynasty inevitably weakens, the authority of heaven passes to a new, stronger power.

The Shang, a powerful clan that rose from peasant stock in the eastern thrust of the Yellow River, were the first to use bronze weapons. Slavery was a Shang institution; slaves were mainly prisoners-of-war. But one could move from slavery to freedom, and even seize power. Their priests, like ours, recorded the yield of the land, studied the stars, and tried to predict the annual rise and fall of the Yellow River. The king derived his power from his divine forebears. A "Supreme Ancestor" in Heaven controlled events on Earth, just as our Ancestor does today.

The Chou, who had lived to the west of the Ch'in homeland, defeated the Shang. The Chou realm included the Yellow River in the north and the Yangtze River and even farther south. The Chou Dynasty—which historians divided into two periods, the earlier being known as Western Chou—claimed the Mandate of Heaven, and the throne was the symbol of power for the Son of Heaven. The king was all-virtuous and wielded absolute political and religious power.

The decline of Western Chou, over some three hundred years, was named the Spring and Autumn Period after the *Spring and Autumn Annals* of the state of Lu, the chronicle of Master K'ung Fu Tzu's (Confucius) home state. Gradually, the feudal dukedoms of the empire became independent kingdoms, striving among themselves for power.

By the end of the Spring and Autumn Period, the balance of power came to favor two semi-barbarous states: Ch'in in the west and Ch'u in the south. But neither of them, nor any other single state, could dominate—like a wolf pack, the other states would unite to pull it down as soon as it became too powerful. This was a time of ruthless wars, subtle conspiracies, loyalty and treason.

In the Warring States period, following the Spring and Autumn, war became all-out. Conquerors put prisoners to death. Our soldiers of Ch'in have long received their pay only when they present the severed heads of their enemies. When towns were taken, whole populations were often put to the sword. Cannibal practices were revived—conquered enemies were thrown into boiling cauldrons to become human soup.

Ch'in was called "Land of the Horse-traders" by people in the ancient kingdoms, looking down their noses. The truth is that Ch'in was tougher and more daring than the Ancient States to the east of it. Here is a quotation about Ch'in from Ssu-ma Ch'ien's magnificent *Records of the Grand Historian*:

"The country of Ch'in was a state whose position alone predestined its victory. Rendered difficult of access by the girdle formed around it by the Yellow River and the mountains, it was suspended a thousand *li* above the rest of the empire. With twenty thousand men, it could hold back a million spearmen. The position of its territory was so advantageous that when it poured out its soldiers on other states, it was like a man emptying a jug of water from the top of a high house."

Inside steep mountain walls that provided near-invulnerability, the fief holders of Ch'in grew more independent and powerful year by year. They attracted political and military talent from the states to the east, rewarding these freelancers very well.

A crucial moment came when an important statesman named Lord Shang Yang, a principal exponent of Legalism, came to Ch'in. The bureaucracy was increased and centralized, and families and neighbors were set to spy on one another, with harsh punishments for wrongdoers and substantial rewards for informants. Ch'in became a highly organized state and the dominant power.

Legalism is a political philosophy that grew out of Confucianism. The significant difference between the two ideas is that followers of Confucius believed men were fundamentally good, and that, given instruction in right behavior, would behave like gentlemen, while Legalist proponents, most famous by Shang Yang, argued that human beings are evil by nature and can only be kept in line by swift, extreme punishment. This became the law of the land in Ch'in.

Between the prospects of rich booty and ruthless conscription, our Ch'in armies grew huge, sometimes numbering more than a million men. Our generals are capable and often brilliant men, drawn from the best talents throughout the ancient kingdoms. They have battering rams and superb heavy siege equipment. Ch'in soldiers were bow and arrow warriors, good in the saddle, riding light, fast horses. Officers gained posts by skill and bravery in battle. Fights to the death were expected, desertion or flight were cruelly punished, courage was rewarded generously.

The conquests of Ch'in Shih-huang-ti, who subjugated all the other states, are really the culmination of planning and strategic thinking that took centuries to develop. But it would be unwise to tell him that!

Because of the barbarous nomads to the north and the generally hostile states to the east, the only defense was constant vigilance on our long borders. That is why the idea of walls to guard passes or open stretches between the mountains developed and why a number of the ancient states ultimately had such walls.

Once able to withstand barbarian pressure from the north and west, Ch'in was free to advance on its feudal neighbors to the east and south. First, Ch'in was involved in successful wars with the former state of Chao to the northeast and with that of Ch'u to the south, leaving Ch'in in a position of great strength. But even then, a mere hundred years ago, Ch'in was not represented at the conferences held by other rulers.

* * * * * * * *

Because Juan Chi has a rather high nasal voice and a tendency to drone, several eunuchs were asleep by the end of his recitation. It took time to get everyone roused and on their way home through the secret entrance and Han Yin's lodgings.

While I was walking home, I remembered a recent rumor that General Meng T'ien, our tremendous commander of the northern frontier and builder of the northern Great Wall, is said to have invented the writing brush. That is nonsense, of course;

the blackhairs have always had writing brushes. He may have *improved* the writing brush; if he has, I wish he would let me know of it!

Next day, Juan Chi came to see me. Looking rather shy, especially for him, he asked me for my opinion, as a historian, of his summary. I said I found it interesting and well organized, as far as it went. What do you mean, as far as it went? he asked me, and I reminded him that I had just completed a hundred-bundle work on the same subject.

"Oh yes, I forgot," he said, blushing. "Of course." He left soon after.

The Merchant Lu Pu-Wei
Wang Ts'ao's Tale

"Even now, some friends sitting here believe that Regent and Prime Minister Lu Pu-wei was a great schemer and a villain," said Wang Ts'ao, the Major Domo of the Royal Palace, holding the jade *pi*-disk speaker's scepter in his beautifully formed hands.

"And that is true. But it is not the whole story. He was a merchant, but he wasn't a money-grubber. Think of his magnificent rise! He escaped from the highly *un*desirable merchant caste, which even eunuchs despise, to become one of the wealthiest men of our time. Then he served as Royal Tutor to Prince Cheng, the same time as he was Cheng's father's Assistant Chancellor. He was later made Regent and finally rose to be the Prime Minister of all Ch'in!"

By then, he was the most powerful man in the world. The boy-king who called him "Uncle Lu" and "Second Father" was dancing like a street puppet on his strings.

But just how did his phenomenal rise come about?

It happened because the moment Lu Pu-wei found a poor, abandoned prince of Ch'in, all but starving in enemy territory, he figured immediately that the prince might be the greatest merchandise he could ever acquire. Then, by moving the prince onto the throne of Ch'in, he rewrote our history.

Let me put one popular fable to rest. The notion that Prince Cheng was the result of an affair between Lu Pu-wei and the queen dowager, when she was a beautiful young courtesan, is a pile of ox dung. It's true our First Emperor really *is* a son of a bitch, but Lu did not father Cheng. I served him, so I know. Lu was never interested in sex with anything but boys. Or very young men.

Not that he was a saint—he certainly was not. Lu Pu-wei was a Legalist (since the Legalist philosopher Shang Yang's time a hundred years ago, everyone who counts in Ch'in has been a Legalist). The Legalists believe all men are bad by nature and can only be controlled by immediate, severe punishment for any transgression. Legalism also means, in our time, that the Emperor owns everybody and everything. One Emperor for all, and all for the Emperor!

But I never thought Lu was fully committed to the ideas of Legalism. As his Major Domo, I saw that he was actually a kind man, at least when kindness didn't affect his plans adversely. Of whom else in our blighted age can this be said? And he was generous, besides being acquisitive—his personal motto was practical and sound: *I judge a man by the size of the things he gives me.* However, his virtues were also his faults. Two qualities set him apart: he was a magician at weaving complex plots that often took years to bear fruit, and he had a compulsive need to be *seen* to be at the top.

That was what killed him, I think. As First Emperor said when he was still King Cheng: "There is only room for one king in the kingdom." Lu Pu-wei behaved as if *he* was king while the boy-king was growing up. He built a court greater than that of King Cheng's, artistically, intellectually. Cheng was bound to find a way to get rid of Lu. I am sure Lu knew that; perhaps it's why he lived so extravagantly. He may have known his time at the top would be brief.

Cheng, as emperor, is only supposed to speak to ordinary mortals through us, his closest household servants, and we are the only ones who are supposed to speak to him. But our Emperor made a joke of that rule every day. Unlike his younger sons, he was raised by soldiers, and he favors the rough speech and ways of a soldier to this day—not that he can't talk like a courtier when he has reason to. Old smooth-tongue! But until he fell under the spell of the damned astrologers, he went where he pleased, spoke to whomever he pleased, and did whatever he pleased. Now he spends much of his time each day at the ancestral sacrifices, in which he devoutly believes, but other than that, he follows no rules.

"That's the great thing about being emperor, I make my own rules," I've often heard him say that.

Lu Pu-wei was different. Not a talker. For a man who moved goods so freely, always looking for something good and trading it for something better, who spent money as if it was sand, he was parsimonious in his speech. Did you know he required silence from all around him, except when he wished to learn something?

I watched him every day, tiny on his massive scholar's platform, all but hidden behind an immense desk, writing and reading reports and directives. All I ever heard was the swish of the brush, the clatter of bamboo rolls being opened, and an occasional high-pitched groan—he had a serious bowel disorder. Apart from stomach trouble, nothing unplanned ever happened to Lu Pu-wei. Standing against the wall, waiting for something to happen, I thought at times I would go mad! But he did all he could to bring civilization to our frontier state of Ch'in—unlike the Emperor, who says, very forcefully, it is for the *world* to be like Ch'in, not the other way round.

That was the Lu Pu-wei I served.

Going back now to Han Yin's story of the baby prince, let us move forward a few years, to a time when our beloved and so very special emperor, Ch'in Shih-huang-ti, was about seven.

The same age as you, Ssu-ma Ch'ien, but you could not have met Cheng yet, as he and his parents were still in Hantan in the state of Chao, where his father was a hostage. A bad time. An enormous Ch'in army had crossed into Chao to destroy Hantan. The Chao army, furious because of the invasion and terrified by the doom that seemed to be waiting for them, wanted to kill Prince and Lady Tzu-ch'u and their son Cheng, and throw their bodies over the walls onto Ch'in spears.

It didn't happen, though, because as usual, Lu Pu-wei controlled the situation. By means of huge bribes, Lu successfully got Prince Tzu-ch'u out of the city across the border into Ch'in. A year later, he also arranged the escape of Lady Tzu-ch'u and young Cheng, the future emperor. Lu's reward was immediate. Once the family was united and safe, Lord An-kuo, the ruler of Ch'in at that time, asked Lu to become Prince Cheng's tutor, a job he was happy to accept.

Cheng's own father, Tzu-ch'u, became King when Lord An-kuo died after a rule of only one year. Tzu-ch'u made Lu Assistant Chancellor and ennobled him as the Marquis of Wenhsin, with an estate that included the revenues of 100,000 households in Henan and Loyang.

Tzu-ch'u's reign was almost as brief—just three years. When he died, the crown went to Cheng, aged thirteen. That's when he appointed Lu Chancellor and addressed him as "Uncle Lu" and "Second Father."

Great days for Mr. Lu! Eventually Lu Pu-wei became the Regent and Prime Minister. He had three thousand courtiers and ten times as many peasant farmers making him richer every day.

As I said, I was his Major Domo. Apart from the silence of his private office, Lu Pu-wei's court was breathtaking. What an eye for beauty! He valued intellectual beauty as well: scholars, poets and painters came to his court from all the ancient kingdoms, attracted by his generosity. They stayed like flies settling on a pool of honey. They were encouraged to speak their minds freely and debate policies with an openness that would have been highly treasonous at the hidebound Ch'in court in Hsienyang. The music was wonderful: musicians came from everywhere, especially the south, where the most famous drummers, singers and lutenists reside.

Here is an example of just how far from the hard-nosed

Legalist ideas Lu Pu-wei had gotten in his thinking. At the height of his regency, Lu asked each of his scholarly guests to record all that he knew. All the writings were put into an immense book. It took years. Believing this work covered all the knowledge in the world, Lu called it, without a shred of modesty or a nod of deference to the *Thirteen Classics*, "*The Annals of Master Lu.*" Because he had a merchant's heart, he had the work displayed at the gate of the main Hsienyang market, with a thousand pieces of gold hung above it. The gold was offered to anyone who could add or subtract a single word. Of course no one dared to. He was a magnificent self-promoter!

Lu Pu-wei's downfall was total, catastrophic.

He was implicated in a plot to depose King Cheng—"only room for one king in the kingdom." I doubt Lu actually *was* plotting, though, because it was clumsy and it failed—few things Lu did were failures. King Cheng wanted to execute Lu Pu-wei, but spared him on account of his services to his father and because Lu's many orators and proteges from all the Seven Kingdoms spoke up for him. I think the young king, new to power, was somewhat daunted. But Lu was exiled to his fief south of the Yellow River. He was not secure there. Just the opposite, because King Cheng was still thinking about him and certainly had spies at Lu's court. He should have pulled in his sails, but couldn't do it; in fact, so many envoys and visitors from other states came to see Lu Pu-wei that the King began to fear a second, probably more serious, revolt.

And that was fatal for Lu.

In the famous letter to Lu Pu-wei, you quoted in your *Records of the Grand Historian*, Ssu-ma Ch'ien, King Cheng wrote: "What have you done for Ch'in, sir, to deserve a fief of 100,000 households south of the river. What relation are you to Ch'in that you should be entitled 'Second Father'? Go south with your followers to Shu!"

Realizing disobedience would mean an extremely painful execution, most likely being sawed in half, Lu Pu-wei drank poison. His followers all died, too, and a court that had been the wonder of the world fell into deep and permanent darkness.

Then, because my skills were celebrated, I was brought here to serve the Emperor. I am wealthy and successful today, but believe me, this Emperor's court is dull as dust compared to Lu Pu-wei's court.

I often wondered why Lu did not have the boy-king killed and become king himself. We would have been a different Ch'in, not this murderous, inartistic, spy-ridden, bookless place. Why do you suppose Lu let the boy-king live? He could surely have had him killed in his early teens. It makes me wonder if I am wrong and that Cheng really was his illegitimate, natural son.

Then I remember that he liked boys, not women. Boys were his weakness. Perhaps that is why—well, we do not know what might go on between a boy-king and his "second father."

Anyway, so much for the regency of Lu Pu-wei. He accomplished something no one else has ever done, probably ever will do. Look back as far as you like through the annals of our ancestors, thousands of years, and you will not find one instance in which a man of the merchant class, so despised here in Ch'in, and even more despised in the older states to the east, put a man on a throne and, for a time, virtually shared that throne with him. It is unique. He made it look like the most natural, obvious thing!

What do we know about the origins of this exceptional man?

We know, *thanks to you, Ssu-ma Ch'ien—I bow*, that he was once a poor merchant of Yangti, a place I have never heard of and cannot find on any of our maps. But one is not born a merchant. He was born a dwarf. And there's a mystery, because in most households a child born as a dwarf would simply be discarded on the nearest hillside. I think he must have been born in a prosperous family, with a soft-hearted mother. Perhaps he was her first, maybe her only, surviving boy baby. I think she held tight to him when he was born; and a day or two later, when she was on her feet again, she and her husband probably had a huge fight over the infant, which she won.

If I am right, Lu grew up in a household filled with fine things. Given his small size, there was no possibility he would have been let out to play with other children—they would have stoned him to death. So from the time he learned to crawl and then to walk, young Lu Pu-wei was protected and constantly surrounded with the beauty that fills a rich home.

Many merchants, as we know, deal in the most awful junk, anything they can sell. Others speculate in foodstuffs. And others do—well, heaven knows what they do. But Lu had another motto, too: *Find something good and trade it for something better.* There are two parts to that statement. First, you have to know something good when you see it. Second, you have to know something better when you see it. With skill, you can always trade up. He must have acquired that skill early, perhaps indulged by a kind mother. And he had two other abilities: he was a courageous gambler—we have seen that!—and a superb, strategic thinker—we have seen that, too.

He had hundreds of trading agents throughout and far beyond the Seven Kingdoms. He had caravans that braved the deserts to the west. He had banks. He had huge storehouses full of treasures. He had a spider's brain and a spider's ability to spin a huge web. When he found Prince Tzu-ch'u on the luckiest day of his life, it was like finding a river of gold and he knew it. He daringly risked everything he had, converting thousands of items to catties of gold for bribes, gifts and princely living expenses.

I am sure his many businesses were even more successful after he became Marquis and Regent, with so much ready money at his disposal. If today our esteemed Emperor is the richest man in the world, it was not always so: once he had a rival who might have bested him if he had played his role better.

Gentlemen, I give you Lu Pu-wei, the little dwarf who loved beauty and was once a humble merchant from the city of Yangti.

The Late, Lamentable Lao Ai
Tu Mu's Tale

The pace of eating, never locust-like among the well-fed storytellers, slowed to a halt as they settled down for the evening's story, green wine bottles tipped over, peanut shells everywhere.

For once our leader Han Yin did not merely *look* asleep, he may actually have *been* asleep. Silence reached into every corner of the room; I waited at my writing desk, brush lifted but undipped in the ink bottle; I was still as a drawing of a scholar at his chores. A cough or two, a sneeze and a nervous giggle were swallowed by an increasingly unpalatable stillness.

"But what about me," came a high, thin wail, "when are you going to tell about me, Lao Ai, who was almost a king?"

The voice of a ghost, crushed to death between two millstones twenty-five years ago. We looked around at each other, assuming one of us spoke, and it may have been so, because several eunuchs were hiding their mouths behind their fans.

Han Yin stirred and said, "All right, Charioteer Tu Mu, bring forth Lao Ai. Try to remember you aren't driving the emperor's chariot tonight; take your time, for once; don't dash from the starting mark to the finish line as fast as you can." He then passed the jade *pi*-disk speaker's scepter to Tu Mu.

Unruffled, Tu Mu folded his fan and placed it to one side carefully. I could see he was slowly filling his shovel of a mouth with words when Chia Tao, the Major Domo of the Concubine

Residences, shouted, "But don't you dare leave out the beautiful Lady Tzu-ch'u, you old, cockless rooster! As the greatest of all concubines, I mean to make sure she gets her due tonight!"

Tu Mu nodded in agreement, reshuffled the story slightly in his mind, and began.

"Of course, my story really started with the unlimited ambitions of the unlamented exile, Lu Pu-wei, our former regent and prime minister," Tu Mu said. "He had the true merchant's great gift of always trading up, and unlike poor Lao Ai—"

"*Poor* Lao Ai," shrieked Lo Yin, the First Emperor's Chief Dresser, "a man hung like a team of stallions! We should all be so poor!"

"Shut up," Han Yin said succinctly, and Lo Yin bowed to him, but not deeply. "Sorry for the ignorant insensitive interruption, Tu Mu," said Han Yin, "please go on."

As I was saying—what was I saying?—oh, yes, unlike "poor" Lao Ai, Lu Pu-wei, the great merchant, nearly did become the King of Ch'in, said Tu Mu. That would have exceeded even his dream of power, I think.

Lu, whose third favorite saying was: *With enough money you can buy the heart of god*, moved among the Seven Kingdoms constantly before he came to the state of Ch'in.

When he was visiting the huge city of Hantan, capital of the state of Chao, he discovered a superb business opportunity. There was at this time a highly unfortunate man living an isolated life of poverty in Hantan. This man's name was Tzu-ch'u. He was the only son of the least favorite (among many candidates) concubines of Lord An-Kuo, the Crown Prince of Ch'in. That put Tzu-ch'u far down in the royal line of succession—seventeenth would be a good guess. As such, he was a board piece of very little worth to his grandfather, the King of Ch'in, who sent him to Chao with the offer that if he, the king, ever invaded Chao, that state might execute Tzu-ch'u.

"Wait a minute," said Han Yin. "This is familiar. Haven't we heard it before?"

"Yes, of course," Tu Mu said, "but you don't know where I'm going with it. It won't end up the same way."

Unhappily for Tzu-ch'u, the King of Ch'in forgot his promise immediately and proceeded to invade Chao. Seeing that Tzu-ch'u was utterly worthless as a hostage, Chao might have executed him. But the truth is, it wasn't even worth that much bother. The state of Chao had other invasions to deal with. It virtually forgot Tzu-ch'u, leaving him in a situation of near starvation in Hantan.

Lu Pu-wei had spies everywhere. One told him about Tzu-ch'u and his sorry situation. The Spider, as I call him, hatched a magnificent plan, of which the first step was a visit to Prince Tzu-ch'u. Lu gave him some money and said to him, "I know how to enlarge your gate for you!" He convinced the Prince that, against reason, he might nonetheless be able to set him on the throne of Ch'in one day.

Lu gathered a fortune in gold and took it to Ch'in, where he arranged for himself, a visit to Crown Prince Lord An-kuo and his consort, Lady Hua-yang. Lu cultivated the Lady assiduously during many more visits that always included rich gifts.

"Since you are childless," said Lu to Lady Hua-yang during one of these visits, "if Lord An-Kuo dies before you, you will be entirely at the mercy of the inferior consorts, who are both numerous and fecund. Because they have already borne eighty sons or more to Lord An-Kuo, you can count on them to be merciless toward you, Lady Hua-yang. They hate you because you are the Crown Prince's favorite wife. In all likelihood, they will poison you straightaway."

During increasingly intimate meetings with Lady Hua-yang, Lu began to praise the obscure Tzu-ch'u, the son of the least and lowest of all concubines of Lord An-Kuo. He actually told Lady Hua-yang that Tzu-ch'u, who had never even seen Lord An-Kuo, missed him enormously and wept night and day for his father!

With skillful prompting from Lu, who suggested she would be able to walk on the backs of all the other consorts if she would sponsor this son of a lowly mother, Lady Hua-yang went to her husband, Lord An-Kuo. She said she had decided to adopt the young man who had shown, according to Lu, such admirable filial piety. She asked Lord An-kuo to make Tzu-ch'u his heir and he did so. He had a jade tally engraved, naming Tzu-ch'u as his successor. Then he broke it, keeping half the tally and giving the other half to Lady Hua-yang. This decision was kept secret, of course.

Had the state of Chao known its despised hostage from Ch'in was now actually the crown prince in waiting, imagine what they might have done with that!

Returning to Hantan, capital of Chao, Lu continued to look after Tzu-ch'u, improving his circumstances wonderfully and often drinking with him. During one of these drinking bouts, Tzu-ch'u saw an extraordinarily beautiful woman from a noble family in Chao. Her name was Chao-chi, or daughter of Chao. Unfortunately, her notoriously wanton ways had forced her high-ranking family to abandon her; she became a courtesan, exceptionally skilled at dancing and several related arts.

They were drinking the exceptionally heady wine Lu was famous for keeping in his wine cabinet. After any number of glasses, Tzu-ch'u stumbled up to a standing position and grabbed Chao-chi rudely by the breasts—though he later said he merely wanted to touch her pretty shoulder, but missed. The two tumbled to the floor together in a tangle. One grapple led to another and soon they made love roughly on the floor, with Lu Pu-wei looking on and probably saluting them by doing to himself what we used to be able to do to ourselves. Remember?

Next day, Tzu-ch'u came to the gate of Lu's palace and gained entry. He went to tiny Lu Pu-wei in his huge office and said, without preamble, "I must have Chao-chi! I want to wed her!"

What he didn't know as he made this request was that Chao-chi had been Lu's lover and was pregnant with his baby, the future King Cheng, our beloved emperor.

And by the way, Wang Ts'ao, this wasn't the first or last time a man who liked men better ever got a baby on a pretty concubine.

Lu Pu-wei may have been angered by the loss of Chao-chi, but I am certain that when he thought about it, he could see a huge advantage for himself in giving Chao-chi to a likely future king of Ch'in! In any case, happy or not, he agreed, and Tzu-ch'u took his courtesan home that day, a grand prize for boorishness if ever there was one!

Were they happy? Who knows! Most likely not. I suppose it depended on how many men Chao-chi permitted to occupy the pass between her lovely dancer's legs. In any case, she had her baby in due course.

Unaware of these developments, murderous old King Chao-hsiang of Ch'in laid siege to Hantan, unsuccessfully, though not without causing the usual plague, starvation, families eating other families' sons, et cetera. But now that Tzu-ch'u was so much more prosperous, and the Ch'in army was nearing Hantan, the soldiers of Chao wanted to kill Tzu Ch'u and loot his palatial home. Lu, always resourceful, bribed the soldiers and escaped to the besieging Ch'in army, taking Tzu-ch'u with him. Later, Lady Tzu-ch'u and her young son, Cheng, were transported safely to the Ch'in capital of Hsienyang. Her escape was enabled by Lu and her own family, which had not after all wholly abandoned her, especially now that she was wed to a prince.

"Where do I come in?!" came a high voice far down the line of listening eunuchs. "What about me?!" Fans snapped open around the circle.

"Be still, I'm just giving you the background," said Tu Mu. "I'm getting to you, Lao Ai, man with a millwheel around your member!"

Giggles from the storytellers.

Time passed, bringing the usual sorrows and joys, Tu Mu

continued. To no one's grief, King Chao-hsiang of Ch'in died in the fiftieth year of his reign. He was a great king and conqueror, cruel, cunning and personally repellent, who defeated many neighboring kingdoms. He would have been remembered forever had it not been for the far greater exploits of Cheng, his great grandson, that lay just ahead.

At King Chao-hsiang's death, his son, Lord An-Kuo, became King Hsiao-wen of Ch'in, but died almost right away, and Tzu-ch'u, the once forlorn hostage in the enemy city of Hantan, succeeded him as King Chuang-hsiang. And he too died not long after that. Hmmm...

And so, at the age of thirteen, Cheng—the baby you claim was substituted for, Han Yin—became King of Ch'in. And his wanton mother became Queen Dowager Hsia. She might wisely have chosen to settle down into a matronly mode, but, being still a young woman, she simply resumed—if it had ever been discontinued—her love affair with Lu Pu-wei. Also, in her separate palace south of the Wei River, she contrived to sleep with every other man she could get her legs around. She was something special!

As we have been told, times were good for Lu Pu-wei. Together, Lu and the Queen Dowager ran the kingdom to suit themselves for eight fat years. Until Lao Ai's stupidity brought them all down.

But perhaps it was just Lu outsmarting himself. Have you noticed that once a clever man has got the best of everyone around him, he seems to go after himself? That may have been the case with Lu Pu-wei.

During these eight comfortable, enriching years, as he and the Queen Dowager gathered ever more wealth and power— and King Cheng continued to think of himself as a boy who needed a wise "uncle" to guide him in all matters—eunuchs who knew them believed Lu thought the Queen Dowager was out of control. Ever one to put down a vessel the moment he had drunk all it had to offer, Lu set about thinking of possible ways to disgrace her. As usual, he found a gem—a gem named Lao Ai.

Lao Ai was a clever peasant who had grown up living like an animal in mountains far south of Ch'in—a land so remote that people once thought it would never come under the control of the black-haired people. They were wrong, but at that time no civilized person went south. No one knows when or why Lao, an exceptionally handsome man, left the mountains and came north, crossed the rivers, made it through the passes, and entered Ch'in. His obvious goal, like so many others who have come here—including most of us—was to make his fortune.

From puberty on, Lao was honey to women. He was a gifted actor, though without formal training, and that talent served him well, too. But his greatest talent was the exceptional size of his "Precious"—it was said that having stroked his Precious erect, he could walk around naked with a millwheel around it! Think of that, my keyless friends!

I don't believe that story, by the way, not that I wouldn't like to, given my own lack in that area, but I just don't. Maybe from time to time, he put a large wooden ring around it, of the type that slows ejaculation and paraded around naked wearing the ring. A form of boasting. What is certain is that he was horse-hung, to put it crudely. It was also certain that if Queen Dowager Hsia heard of this exceptional man, she would want to see it, and put it through its paces.

That's what Lu Pu-wei must have figured. He sent Lao Ai to be a servant in the palace of the Queen Dowager. My guess is that next, someone arranged for her to see Lao Ai in the bath or in some other situation in which he was naked and likely to be erect, for example, watching concubines kissing each other in all their various entrances and exits.

Anyway, the plan worked. He immediately became the love of the Queen Dowager's life, able to fill her as no other man had ever done.

But while her having sex with a future king was basically

all right with Lu Pu-wei, entering into a lifelong liaison with a man who did not serve Lu Pu-wei's ends was not all right at all. The Queen Dowager, knowing this, and believing she needed to conceal the affair from Lu at all costs, arranged a fake castration.

"Oldest trick in the world!" Groans from the listeners.

"Well, I can't help that, it's what happened," said Tu Mu. "Thereafter, Lao Ai practiced and put on public view his new persona, that of a mincing, high-voiced, fraidy-cat eunuch of the *worst* type..."

"Now just a moment...!" exclaimed one of the storytellers.

She and Lao Ai were married secretly by a Taoist priest, who was sent to the netherworld after the ceremony by Lao Ai personally. His remains were carted out of the palace and the city in a closed carriage, taken to the eastern mountains and burned. Then the ashes were buried. The happy, faithful, secret marriage could begin.

Lao Ai got two sons on the Queen Dowager. They were hidden in her servants' quarters for several years. All was well, so to speak. Because he was a cunning man, Lao Ai contrived to penetrate and join the partnership of power that was Lu Pu-wei and the Queen Dowager. The trio gathered more and more of the reins of government into their hands.

All might have gone well, but Lao Ai, not the brightest star in the sky, soon overreached himself. He plotted to overthrow King Cheng. He subverted a large fraction of the King's Guard but one of its members went to King Cheng, who was now twenty years old and eager to take the reins. The plot failed miserably. Lao Ai was crushed between two millstones, as I mentioned earlier, and his two sons were beaten to death in a sack and thrown into the Wei River.

King Cheng also learned from informers about all of Lu Pu-wei's machinations, from his first dealings with Cheng's father, Tzu-ch'u. He wasn't told that Lu Pu-wei might have been his own father—who would have dared tell him that?! He could not have Lu Pu-wei killed because he wielded too much power, but he did remove him from the prime minister's position and exiled him to his estate at Wenhsin. There, a short time later, on a written suggestion from King Cheng, Lu Pu-wei took his own life—that was a way to keep his family from being killed, as he thought, but it did not turn out that way; the King had them all killed, down to the last mewing infant.

The Queen Dowager was another matter. Whatever his paternity, King Cheng was indisputably her son and it would have been unthinkable to have her killed or to cut off her—and therefore his—personal avenue to the ancestors. The rites that protect the kingdom would have been befouled for all time by such a matricide! So he sent her to her country palace, ordering her to stay there and live the pure life of a nun. We have all known such nuns.

Lao Ai, what shall we say of him? He had a unique claim on our attention, we who keep our businesses in jars, hoping against hope that we will be reunited in the afterlife. He had a large enough sexual apparatus, history tells us, for several men—which makes him an immortal symbol of the great and tragic injustice of life along the Way!

We eunuchs feel quite strongly about this.

A Rat in the Granary
Juan Chi's Tale

"Juan Chi, the jade *pi*-disk speaker's scepter is yours tonight. Tell us about the worst man you know," said Han Yin, unsuccessfully suppressing a smile because he knew quite well whom Juan Chi would choose. We all did, even a newcomer like myself.

I have told you we were all a little frightened of Juan Chi, the Chief Dispenser of Eunuch Punishments. Frightened, but not terrified, because we also knew that Juan Chi was a reasonably kind man. This was in spite of his truly awful job, which involved daily executions of eunuchs in the palaces, endless floggings, hourly lopping off of ears, fingers, toes and tongues, not to mention gouging out of eyes, as well as brandings. In fact, about the only things safe among the eunuchs from Juan Chi and his merry men were our genitalia, and that is because they are bottled up and shelved in our bedrooms for safekeeping until hoped-for reunions in the afterlife.

Cruel punishments were the daily outcome of the wicked Legalist philosophy, which dictated swift and overwhelming punishment of the person being penalised, and of everyone afterward who had anything to do with him.

At great risk, Juan Chi often reduced the severity of punishment for offenders. At times, he even released someone who had been proven guilty as charged. (In the empire of Ch'in, if you are charged you are guilty.) In doing so, he accepted the possibility that if found out he might be given the same punishment. I wonder if any of us other than Juan Chi would be brave enough to do that?

I believe, given the chance, Juan Chi would have been still more lenient. In tending toward mercy, he was at all not like Grand Counselor Li Ssu, who used the Legalist practices of his predecessors to build an empire of terror. To Li Ssu, there was no difference between kindness and stupidity. You punish to control and that is all there is to it—spare the punishment, lose control. The punishments of palace eunuchs may have been less harsh than those in the rest of the empire, especially in the rebellious south, but they were carried out under the nose of Li Ssu, so to speak. And Li Ssu had a very sharp nose.

In fact, said Juan Chi, the worst man I know, Li Ssu, is both relentless and ruthless. Apart from serving Ch'in Shih-huang-ti, whose life was like bread buttered on both sides, Li Ssu did not care about anyone but himself and his family, especially his cherished, eldest son, Li Yu. He hounded people to death without compassion. As a prosecutor-judge in the early days of his service in Ch'in, Li Ssu may have been the basis for the story about the First Emperor's famous "red dog," the one who knew what people were thinking and invariably told the Emperor what he sniffed out.

Recently, Juan Chi continued, our friend Wang Ts'ao entertained us by imagining what Lu Pu-wei might have been like as a boy. I should like to do the same for Li Ssu.

Boyhood happened a long time ago for Li Ssu. He never had a boyhood, not as we think of one. As a child he was on his own, barely surviving daily on some of the cruelest streets of the ancient city of Shangch'ai in the southern state of Ch'u. One day he was hunting for rats, his only meat, when he was grabbed and carried off bodily by the servant of a wealthy merchant to the residence of the merchant. There he was washed, fed, and sent to the man's bedchamber.

This merchant had been watching Li Ssu on the street from a passing palanquin. Even under nine years of dirt, collected in the alleys between the meanest wooden shacks of the city's poorest quarter, Li's features were beautiful, chiseled fine by daily hunger, and his bare brown hands and feet were long, slender and graceful. The merchant, like Mr. Lu, had an eye for beauty.

Li Ssu knew what he was wanted for. Although the merchant was a new face to him, it was not his first time in a rich man's bed, or his twentieth. In the bedchamber, ridiculously overdecorated with silk hangings, he made love to the merchant in a way that thoroughly satisfied the man, for whom erections no longer came easily, or really, at all—his concubines had a soft life!

The knowledgeable, young Li Ssu pleased the man so much he was given a small room of his own near the back of the merchant's business office so he could provide rapid service. He even had a sleeping mat, the first he had known. That night, as he went to sleep, full of food and well content, he heard the steady bell-tone of a caged cricket in the master's study. "Good luck for me," he thought briefly, and fell asleep, dreaming of roasted rats.

To this point, his chances of survival had not been good. But Heaven favored Li Ssu, and over time his desperate wars with the rats gradually seemed like fading nightmares. From what I know of his life, especially since he came to Ch'in, I think he was never entirely rid of the rats he had once killed for food. Perhaps their desperate fight to survive and their endless hunger have overshadowed his entire career.

What happens to child prostitutes in the streets of our cities is not something we care to dwell on; many of us have been there.

For beautiful, young Li Ssu, things turned out far better than most street children. Besides being energetic and skilled at his sex-craft, he was a quick-minded, funny, pretty, entertaining boy. The merchant became exceedingly fond of him, teaching him the merchant's business. Eventually, he adopted the boy.

From the gutter to prosperity and promise, just for licking

another man's privates! I swear, it makes me nostalgic for the days when my "Precious" was something other than a wall decoration!

Nods in the room.

As Li Ssu grew to be a young man apparently destined for a merchant's life, the practice of "hired pens," that is, advisors, was flourishing among the Seven Kingdoms. Innumerable men, distinguished for cleverness and unscrupulousness, began to leave their native countries in droves to serve rulers elsewhere. Fortunes were made by those who could give persuasive advice to kings and dukes and marquises, especially when the advisor provided plausible reasons to do what the ruler wanted to do anyway (usually to gain an advantage over a neighboring country). The rewards were excellent, but it was a risky business; you could lose a great deal by offering the wrong memo at the wrong time. Li Ssu listened to stories of such men and the rewards they reaped, and decided to become one.

But you could not simply go into business for yourself as a counselor. You needed training, guidance and especially the endorsement of a well-known sage. Li Ssu knew this. His great chance came when he learned that the great Confucian teacher of rational cause and effect, Hsun Tzu, was accepting students. Li Ssu left his befriender and would-be adoptive father without a word or glance. The only possible sign of "filial devotion" anyone ever saw from Li Ssu was a reverse one: his later single-minded effort to expel all merchants from Ch'in out into the darkness of the world beyond our borders.

Using his personal attractiveness as a weapon, the young Li Ssu began his studies, which were essentially to forget about the Tao and the Mandate of Heaven nonsense, and watch what people actually do—and if they are not doing what you want them to do, show them vigorously, with examples, how to improve. Li Ssu took these lessons as sacred text.

"Discard the notion that people ever get better," I heard him say on many occasions. "If they transgress, punish them immediately, savagely, publicly. Make the transgressor and his family to the third degree examples for others not to follow—oil them, light them up like flaming torches and post them high in the public square. Then do the same thing to somebody else the next day. Even the dogs will get your meaning eventually."

The rats were truly a lifelong *motif* for him. I have been told that when Li Ssu was a student with Hsun Tzu, he saw rats in a lavatory in which he was about to relieve himself; they were eating dung, but ran away when he came near. But in the granary where he worked, he saw that the granary rats ate well; indeed, they were not afraid of anything and never ran away, but simply sat there staring. The most savage cats did not frighten them.

Li Ssu drew a famous lesson from this: Talent or lack of talent is not the point—what matters is where you place yourself.

When ready, Li Ssu made for Ch'in as so many other scholars and soldiers and adventurers were doing—because there was advancement to be gained and money to be made in Ch'in! And he struck gold immediately. Lu Pu-wei, as he had welcomed many other talented men to Ch'in, greeted Li Ssu and put him to work leading a cadre of secret bribers and assassins whose task was to visit other rulers and bribe them with gold, if bribable, to serve Ch'in's interests; or, if unbribable, to stab them with hidden short swords. Pleasant work for a bright young man with a nose like a rat!

This was right after Cheng's father had died and Cheng became King at thirteen, which meant Regent Lu Pu-wei was in firm control. Li Ssu served Lu faithfully as it was in his interest to do so, but when King Cheng as a young man exiled Lu Pu-wei to his estates and then forced him to commit suicide, Li Ssu immediately set about serving the King even more faithfully.

He had a near miss at the start.

Ch'in was xenophobic at times, and this was one of them. Li Ssu's name was on a list of foreign advisors to be expelled, but he sent a letter to King Cheng outlining the many benefits and treasures Ch'in had obtained from beyond its borders, as a result of the knowledge and talents of counselors like himself. King Cheng accepted Li Ssu's argument and promoted him to Chief Justice. When Cheng's conquests were complete and the Ch'in empire was created, he advanced him again and again, eventually making him his Grand Counselor, the equivalent of Lu Pu-wei's old job.

I did not mention Han Fei, Li Ssu's one intellectual Legalist rival, who also studied with Hsun Tzu when he and Li Ssu were young. They were friends then.

One day Han Fei arrived in Ch'in, nominally on a mission from his own state of Han but really looking for a better job. Han Fei's arguments amounted to these two points: Don't give the masses what they want; and people don't think, they only obey. They can't govern themselves. To which thoughts Li Ssu heartily subscribed, of course. Sensing a potential rival—the King had heard of Han Fei and said, after reading his writings, "How far might I not go with such a man?!"—Li Ssu treated Han Fei warmly as a friend but then secretly threw him in prison and murdered him, or persuaded him to commit suicide!

To this day, I think of our Emperor and Li Ssu in this way. Earth and Heaven, as we are told, are divided into female and male principles, just as coins have two sides. Well, I think of our Emperor as one side of a coin and Li Ssu as the other.

Ch'in Shih-huang-ti is a dreamer and a warrior and, it need hardly be said, a man of raging, limitless ambition. His hunger is for the ownership of All Under Heaven, and one day, Heaven itself.

Li Ssu, on the other hand, is devious, a planner and an organizer. He loves the pleasures of this earth, they are his unremitting hunger, and so he lives a life that in its grandeur is modeled dangerously closely to the life of the Emperor.

Li Ssu wants order in the empire at any price—you can say that he is either the finest flower, or rottenest fruit, depending on your metaphorical preference, of the poisonous tree of Legalism. Every day the bodies are piled up in every village and city square; night and day the roads are choked with noseless, earless, tongueless men—not to mention missing limbs. Just as Li Ssu promised.

In fact, the maimings have become so common one almost forgets what a whole human being looks like!

In any case, King Cheng seized the great Ch'in army, the superb tool inherited from his ancestors, and used it to make an empire of black-haired people greater than anything that had come before it. It stretched from the wastelands to the west, the jungles to the south, the high, dry plains to the north, and the magical sea to the east, with all its monsters and demons. With Li Ssu's invaluable help and guidance, King Cheng had himself named First Emperor at age thirty-seven.

After that, to a point, the Emperor worked extremely hard at governing. He was said to keep reading official documents every night until they reached a certain weight on a scale! But he constantly had vicious, overwhelming headaches. A year or two after becoming Emperor, he began to be distracted by court magicians' promises of immortality because he was terrified of dying. His grip on the reins loosened slowly and he left more and more of the work to others. Eventually, Li Ssu was largely left to govern Ch'in as he saw fit—and he knew he was fit to govern!

Li Ssu was busy as one of the Sage Emperors. By his own account, he created the provinces, prefectures and commanderies, carving them out of the old boundaries of the ancient states. He ended the dukes' and princes' domination of their lands, moving them to Hsienyang, where he could watch them, in scores of thousands. He built thousand-mile roads and canals, simplified our writing, and doubtless did much more I have forgotten.

Along the way, brothers, said Juan Chi, Li Ssu and our Chief Eunuch, our beloved Chao Kao, who has given each of us here so much preferment, formed an alliance: Chao Kao would manage the palaces and Li Ssu would manage the empire. It has been a good arrangement so long as you don't mind the groans of the people, which are faint here inside the imperial walls.

Juan Chi, Chief Dispenser of Eunuch Punishments, sat looking down at his mat for a long time.

Then he said, "It may surprise you to know that I was a musician at one time, playing the *erh hu*[4]. I had good fingers and I found beauty in its sad sounds. That might have become my career, but to my great shame, Li Ssu found his way to something in me that to this day I do not find in myself—perhaps it is that I do not mind death and do not feel pain, especially when it is someone else's.

"He recruited me and trained me in the secret service he calls the Judicial Police. If it was my neck or someone else's, I always thought it might as well be someone else's. I did well, I suppose, by his standards, but in recent years I have begun more and more to feel the pain that I daily inflict on others. I have wept the same tears as my victims. My job has become unhealthy for me. I suppose I will have to kill myself one day. Not that that will make amends, of course. But it will gain me a good, long sleep at last, something I greatly desire.

"Perhaps Li Ssu, or the human remnant inside him, still dreams of rats in the night; I dream of Li Ssu."

---

[4] The *erh hu* is a two-stringed, bowed Chinese musical instrument sometimes known in the West as a Chinese two-string fiddle.

The Assassins
Chia Tao's Tale

"This is my favorite story for one reason: it's the closest our Beloved Leader ever came to getting killed," said Chia Tao, Major Domo of the Concubine Residences. "Just one more little twitch of a smile from the Lord of the Dead and he would have been a ghost for certain."

"As my story begins, King Cheng, aged thirty-one and fully in the saddle, is happily double-crossing, warring, hostage-poisoning, betraying and assassinating his way to a roll-up of the older states to the east of his beloved Ch'in Kingdom. The truth is he's getting much too large for the lace-adorned underpants of any mere king. He's starting to think about something larger in the way of underclothing—emperor-sized, for instance."

What a splendid time he's having! Every day is a vicious man's dream come true. Every day brings fresh rewards: a new, surprising and creative death for an old enemy, somebody's army destroyed, a new bauble. Every day he has more land to mark MINE on the silk map of the future Ch'in empire he sleeps under. Makes a fellow look forward to jumping off the concubine and out of the bed in the morning!

But even a king—even *this* king—has his bad days and it is time to tell about one of King Cheng's worst days.

King Cheng's bad day actually began a year or two earlier, in the feudal state of Yen, northeast of Ch'in. Yen was a skinny state formed by mountains on two sides. It was bounded on the north by Yen's keep-out-the-barbarians wall and on the east by the Yellow Sea. Its high-walled capital city, Hsiatu, is a famously beautiful place filled with gardens, palaces and temples—a pleasure to walk about if it weren't for the thieves and pickpockets on every street corner.

Overall, Yen was a prosperous state, laxly guarded and intensively farmed—best farmland in the Middle Kingdom except for Ch'in itself. Fed by the waters of hundreds of irrigation canals, its steeply-terraced farms of rich, yellow earth grow crop after crop of millet every year. Yen's rulers, to hear them tell it, were faithful to the principles of the old, wandering scholar-knight, Confucius, but they also admitted to a healthy dash of Lao Tzu-like belief in magic—nobody goes anywhere or does anything significant without first reading the dragon bones. Or any other set of omens handy. It's deep in the nature of the black-haired people to embrace *any* set of beliefs—who knows, the rhinoceros horn worshippers could be right! Heaven knows they're potent!

At this moment, the kingdom of Yen was peaceful but nervous. Its king, Hsi, had watched Ch'in overwhelm other kingdoms, first the powerful Ch'u far to the south, then destroy Chao and Ch'i on Yen's southern and southeastern borders, respectively. The Ch'in armies were now a scant hundred miles south of Yen. Once they were down, Wei and Han could not last long.

Here comes the Tiger of Ch'in, a friendly smile on his face: "Nice day, neighbor!" Keeps you on your toes, having a tiger striding around outside your bamboo fence!

King Hsi of Yen had an admirable son, Crown Prince Tan, a bright young man who was usually better informed about matters of state than his father. Especially when it came to King Cheng. He and Cheng had been boyhood friends in Chao, where they were both hostages.

But their friendship ended long ago, before Cheng inherited the crown of Ch'in at thirteen. Soon after that fatal moment, the boy-king demanded that the state of Yen send Prince Tan—age seven, who had just got safely home to Yen—to be a hostage in Ch'in as guarantee of good behavior on the part of King Hsi. Which King Hsi did. He didn't miss the Crown Prince much, anyway, since the latter had lived far from Yen most of his young life. The King of Yen thought, if I give this Cheng what he wants, he'll be satisfied and never ask for anything else.

Alas, once he had Prince Tan hostage, King Cheng treated him without honor—so badly that one dark night, after a final belly-full of stale bread, whippings, and slimy drinking water, Tan managed to slip out of his miserable quarters in Ch'in's capital city, Hsienyang, and escaped to Yen. Imagine how cheerfully the pot of ever-boiling oil in the throne room bubbled next day when King Cheng heard about the escape. How would you like to bring a Tiger news like that?

So that's how things stood. Ch'in the Tiger was pussyfooting ever closer to Yen as King Cheng sought any excuse to cross his million-man army over the border of this lush land of Yen. It touches the ocean! Somewhere in that vast ocean, King Cheng fervently believed, live the Eight Immortals—he wanted to meet these special people and learn their secret.

An excuse for a quarrel with Yen came along right away. One of King Cheng's three top generals, Fan Yu-ch'i, having fallen prey to the intrigues of his other two top generals, lost favor with King Cheng and escaped to Yen, where Prince Tan, an old acquaintance, offered him refuge. Very offensive behavior, befriending a king's enemy.

The Prince's counselors, unhappy about his offer of refuge, said to him, "You are putting meat in the path of the Tiger."

The King of Yen, a rash sort when he wasn't being cowardly, wanted to carry the war to Cheng's immense army, not far away. But the counselors, acting on the principle that you never know who'll be employing you tomorrow, said, "That would be like trying to pluck a scale from a dragon's back."

All the counselors agreed it would be smarter to dump

General Fan over the defensive wall to the north to fend for himself among the barbarian horsemen that range like wolves along the northern border.

However, unwilling to desert an old friend in a tight spot, Prince Tan disagreed vehemently, and he carried the day, even though the royal counselors asked, "Are you willing to sacrifice your country for one individual?"

Well, sure.

About this time, an unusually talented man named Ching K'o arrived in the state of Yen. This Ching had many talents: he was a student of the classics, a good drinker, a skilled fornicator, a keen swordsman. Small, wiry, quick and mean, he was also known to be a capable man with a dagger—he'd sought at one time to study daggermanship under the greatest dagger master of the time, but that worthy champion sent him packing because Ching K'o was neither famous nor known to him.

Arriving in Yen, Ching met a man named Kao Chien-li, a well-known dog-butcher and harp player. With similar interests on many fronts, they became friends right away and shared a carefree life while Ching was waiting for employment. Every day they'd sleep late, get up and go down to the main city market to drink, sing—Kao played, Ching sang—womanize and carouse until after midnight, when servants would come with wheelbarrows and cart them home. Kao had plenty of helpers to do the dog roundups and the butchering, so he had lots of time off, too.

On the rare days when he wasn't pursuing pleasure, Ching made friends with worthy men throughout the city. One new friend was the well-known sage T'ien Kuang, who held no office.

Prince Tan and T'ien Kuang were old friends. Finding the negativity of his counselors unhelpful, the Prince went out alone one afternoon. He headed straight for T'ien Kuang, who lived in a modest but lovely house with a moon gate and a quiet interior garden nestled against the west wall of the palace. T'ien greeted him warmly and Prince Tan knelt and bowed three times. Addressing T'ien as Master, Prince Tan asked T'ien how he could destroy Ch'in's power.

"You should talk to Ching K'o," said T'ien.

"Who?"

"Ching K'o. He's a stranger in town, a very talented man and a gifted assassin. A genius with a knife. You'll find him living with Kao Chien-li, the dog-butcher and harp player. Don't be deceived if you find Ching drunk—right now he's a dagger without a sheath, just rusting until someone like yourself picks him up and makes use of him."

Prince Tan was dubious, but T'ien Kuang was a man of virtue. The Prince agreed to talk with Ching, and left T'ien, after many more bows and thanks. He asked the elderly whitebeard to tell no one of their secret conversation.

After Prince Tan departed, T'ien Kuang went to Ching K'o at once and told him to go to the Prince and offer his services. Then he said, "The Prince warned me not to talk about this; saying that shows he does not trust me. Please tell him I am now dead, to prove that I will not talk." And he cut his own throat.

Shaken, Ching K'o went to the Prince. The latter, who had loved the old man, bowed twice to Ching K'o, then advanced toward him on his knees, crying copiously.

"He didn't need to *die* to show me he was faithful!"

Ching K'o sat down, whereupon the Prince moved off his mat, bowed his head to the floor and said, "Honored Ching K'o, I need a courageous man to go to King Cheng and offer him a bait so large he will have to take it, the greedy bastard. The man will then be close enough to King Cheng to stab him to death.

"Whoever replaces Cheng is sure to fall out with his subjects very soon. After that we can make an alliance of states to defeat Ch'in. This is my heart's desire!

"Will you consider participation in my plan? I have a major role in mind for you, Mr. Ching."

Ching K'o sat silent for a long time before replying. Then he said, "I am a man of little worth—I fear I cannot accomplish a major mission."

But the Prince moved closer, bowing again and again, and Ching K'o at last accepted his appeal—no small thing, since it meant certain death. Get in, that's hard; get the job done, that's very hard; get out again—never.

Prince Tan was so excited by Ching's acceptance he nearly wet his mat. "May the Lady of the River, who dwells on a misty mountain by the Yangtze, bless you, honored sir! I will ever call you friend. Now, what do you need to get started?"

"I need a more detailed plan," Ching K'o admitted candidly. "And may I have a nice house near your palace while we're planning? I know of a good house that has just become available."

"Of course, of course, nothing too good for a hero of Yen! A fine mansion, food from the Great Ocean, pheasant, a bed of ivory...and how about some finely carved carriages, clothing laced with gold, these jewels from the Far West, concubines...?"

"That would be nice," Ching K'o replied to every offer.

There was a difference of opinion about the starting date. Prince Tan, an impatient youth, had been hoping it would be next week, or at most, the week after. Ching's thoughts ran along different lines—maybe, for example, towards the end of the Year of the Rat, next time it came round, a decade from now? Surely there's no rush.

Meanwhile, Ch'in was on the march again. The chief general of the Army to the East, Wang Ch'ien, defeated Chao, destroying its 400,000-man army down to the last bowman. General Wang then marched to the southern border of Yen.

Thus threatened, Prince Tan went to see Ching K'o again, finding him in the marketplace singing with Kao. He explained the military situation to him, pointing out that the stakes had been raised, and action was required *now*. Whereupon Ching K'o said, "Honored Prince, I am frankly having second thoughts about undertaking this task. I am not feeling all that heroic these days."

At this, the Prince waxed a little wroth—all right, he was very wroth—and told Ching K'o to start packing and be under way by Tuesday or find himself boiled in oil here at home in Yen on Wednesday with a *lot* of disrespect to follow, instead of getting boiled in oil in Ch'in after assassinating Cheng and being worshipped as a hero thereafter—every place but Ch'in, of course.

The alternatives didn't look very different to Ching, except for their effect on the length of his future life. So he agreed to pack up at once.

But first he said to Prince Tan, "Unless I take some proof of goodwill, the king of Ch'in will not let me approach him. May I remind you that he is eager to get his escaped General Fan back—in fact, he's offered one thousand catties of gold and a fief of ten thousand families for the capture of General Fan, in whole or in pieces."

"Prince, if I might have General Fan's head and the map of Tukang (a rich district in Yen) to take with me, I know that King Cheng will welcome me and I can carry out your assassination plan. I will roll up my favorite dagger, Little Bite"—which he now revealed, a beauty, with a jeweled hilt perfectly fitted to Ching's hand and an extremely keen, slightly curved blade, sharp on both sides, with a hint of discoloration along the edges that was a deadly poison—"in the map and go for King Cheng at the right moment."

Loyal Prince Tan refused to have Fan killed. That made it necessary for Ching to visit Fan Yu-ch'i, who was settling into a peaceful, and thanks to the Prince, prosperous middle age.

Ching K'o told General Fan that King Cheng had already killed Fan's parents and all his relatives for three generations and, adding injury to insult, had offered a substantial reward for Fan's head, any condition, no questions asked. This wasn't strictly true—actually, none of it was even slightly true—but

Ching was always a man to employ a profitable lie when an occasion called for it.

"So," he told the General, now weeping copiously and so hard indeed that his stomach was heaving painfully, "I see you are enraged by these infamously evil deeds of King Cheng toward the most loyal of all his generals—former generals. If you would like to avenge your parents' deaths, and of *course* you would, I have a superb plan.

"It's really very simple. If I could take your head to Cheng in a box, I know that he would welcome me, likely even embrace me. When I am close enough, I will seize his sleeve with one hand and stab him through the heart with my dagger"—which he now showed the general—"I call it 'Little Bite,' nice, isn't it? So, will you help by granting me this one request?"

The old General agreed to the plan. He immediately bared his arm, shouting, "This is the chance I have been waiting for! Revenge!" He grabbed his short sword off the wall and lunged forward onto it awkwardly, plunging it deep in his belly. In a few minutes he was dead, though not without many suitable groans.

Prince Tan lamented when he learned of the General's death, but what's done is done, and only a fool fails to take advantage of a helpful turn of circumstance. He had the corpse decapitated. The General's head was salted and put into a nicely, and thoroughly, scented sandalwood box, velvet-lined, general's-head-size.

Ching K'o would have gladly delayed further. In fact, he is said to have tried hard to save himself and buy more time by hiding in an empty oil jar behind the palace. But the Prince's snuffling lion dogs found him and the old threat of boiling oil was wheeled out again, this time really bubbling, and he was persuaded to get under way.

For an assistant on the journey, he chose a young killer named Ch'in Wu-yang, a big man with a face and body like an ox—in contrast to Ching, who was slight and weaselly-looking.

This Wu-yang was somebody whom everyone else, including Prince Tan, was terrified of, and with good reason, since none of Wu-yang's many relatives were alive at this time, all having met with exactly the same unfortunate accident involving a canal and various lost body parts.

On the day of departure, the Prince and the few advisors who knew the plan went with Ching K'o and Ch'in Wu-yang to the River I to sacrifice to the gods. Ching K'o sang a plaintive song, accompanied by his pal, the dog-butcher, Kao Chien-li. Everyone was in tears, especially Ching K'o! Next Ching K'o chanted: "The wind is wailing, cold the River I, and a hero sets forth, never to return."

He sang one last song, a martial air, and looked around for possible gratuities. Hearing no coins clink into his upturned hat, he sighed and climbed into a wagon with Ch'in Wu-yang. They drove off, taking the long southern loop *well* to the south of Ch'in general Wang's waiting army.

It's a long way from the western tip of Yen to Hsienyang, King Cheng's capital in southern Ch'in—a long, long way. Let's skip the many difficulties and dangers Ching K'o and Ch'in Wu-yang faced together, the thousand bribes required to get past a hundred watchtowers, local brigands, dishonest ferrymen—it's a tradition, ferrymen among us blackhairs are supposed to be dishonest—the herds of horses they wore out, the nights they slept outside in the rain, and so forth, the little box in the back bumping along, quietly, one hopes. It would be nice to report that they bonded on the journey, but they didn't. Ching snored and Ch'in smelled.

Let's pick up the story just as Ching K'o has greased enough palms to get to the greasiest palm in the entire Kingdom of Ch'in, the right hand belonging to the eunuch Meng Chia, the King's Chamberlain at that time. His price to get Ching K'o into the throne room for an audience with the king was no less than a thousand catties of gold, the size of the reward for the General's head. Worth every catty, Ching K'o said to Wu-yang later.

Meng Chia reported to King Cheng: "Your Majesty, I have met with an emissary of the King of Yen, who trembles at the mention of your name and begs, no grovels, to become your subject. He hopes that he will have the honor of sending you as much tribute as possible on a regular basis, perhaps even bi-monthly.

"As a sign of his goodwill and earnest desire to grovel, he has sent his personal emissary to you, one Ching K'o, a trusted scholar. Ching carries the head of Fan Yu-ch'i in a sealed casket, together with the map of Tukang, the treasurehouse of Yen. Ching K'o awaits your majesty's pleasure."

The principal palace of King Cheng at Hsienyang at that time, in the eighteenth year of his reign, was extremely modest compared to his two hundred and eighty later palaces, being a mere third of a mile long on each of its sides. But it had one interesting feature, an invention that came out of Cheng's very reasonable fear that everyone in the world hated him and would do just about anything to get at him and tear him to pieces and then probably eat the pieces: the palace was constructed in a maze form so no one who did not have a diagram could hope to find his way either to the Throne Room, where the king held state, or to the exit, which was unmarked but very well guarded. But the throne room itself wasn't well guarded, as you'll see.

After a suitable pause of two months, a reception was prepared for Ching K'o. Can't rush these things, King Cheng was a busy man! At the appointed hour, Ching entered the throne room, bowing deeply every other step, carrying the sealed box and shaking it to produce promising little thumps from time to time to whet the King's appetite.

The lout Ch'in Wu-yang followed Ching K'o at an appropriate distance of five paces, carrying the case in which the special map was rolled up, with the dagger, Little Bite, at its heart. Seeing King Cheng on his throne, "brave" Wu-yang began to tremble uncontrollably, his knees suddenly extremely rubbery, but Ching K'o merely laughed pleasantly and apologized for him.

"Please forgive my ignorant servant, Your Majesty. He is a rough, country fellow from the far north and I believe he is overawed by his first sight of Your Majesty," said Ching K'o.

"As of course I am, too," he added hastily.

He paused, and when the King lifted one hand, palm down, Ching lifted the box, opened its catch, and pulled the head of General Fan out by its long, lustrous hair. It was very well preserved, artistically, one might say. The corpse handlers had worked its lips into a gentle smile, also leaving the eyes open so it appeared to be smiling an affectionate hello at King Cheng, who smiled back at his deceased enemy and relaxed visibly inside his heavy, gold-weighted robes.

Next, the treasure! Unable to control his greed, King Cheng stepped down from his throne and rapidly crossed the marble floor to where Wu-yang was standing with the map case. "Give it to me!" he roared. "Give it to me *now*!"

Ching K'o took the map and began to unroll it carefully, feigning calm until he reached the hiding place of his jeweled dagger. In one swift motion, he ripped it out and, jumping across the small space remaining between himself and King Cheng, grabbed the right sleeve of the king's brocaded gown— but the king leaped back in alarm and the gold-embroidered sleeve tore off!

Ching flung the useless sleeve away and ran after the king, who tried to hide behind one of the throne room's many dragon-engraved pillars, meanwhile trying to get his long sword out of its scabbard. Damn, stuck!

His ministers were stuck, too, rooted in their places with open-mouthed, staring-eyed astonishment. Because of the king's suspicious nature, they could not bear arms in his presence. To make matters worse, the royal guards in the courtyard just outside were forbidden to enter unless the king called them— and he was too panicked to remember to call them.

What a scene! One of the most famous moments in the history of Ch'in. The ministers, up and moving at last, raced toward Ching K'o to try to pull him down with their bare hands. The king's trusted physician, Hsia Wu-chu, quicker off the mark, yanked out his bag of herbs, intending to beat the assassin Ching K'o over the head.

King Cheng the Brave was running around and around a pillar, still trying to draw his sword. Finally, he pulled it out and aimed a backwards blow at Ching K'o, striking him on the left leg, which shattered. Now it was Ching K'o's turn to be desperate, as the tide turned against him. He threw "Little Bite" at King Cheng, hoping to break the king's skin, which would kill him, as the blade carried deadly poison. But the dagger hit and stuck in the thin, bronze sheath that covered the wooden pillar!

Seriously injured, Ching K'o slipped to the floor, leaning his back against the pillar as he slid down it slowly. King Cheng, braver by the minute, struck him with his sword, eight times. Eight gaping wounds, blood everywhere!

Just before taking a one-way passage to the underworld, Ching was supposed to have said, "I failed because I tried to take you alive and because I was determined to force you to agree to Prince Tan's demands."

In keeping with our policy of scrupulous truthfulness, said Chia Tao, it is my duty to tell you that another school of historians claims Ching really said: "I have failed to kill you, for the very reason that I did not *wish* to! I wanted to talk peace with you, as my prince desired." The idea behind this reputed statement was that he thereby saved face for his lord. But King Cheng was more interested in acquiring heads than saving faces!

In my opinion, said Chia Tao, both statements are ridiculous. Everybody knows Ching K'o tried like a demon from hell to kill the king, but failed when the brocade sleeve of the king's robe tore off. Just as everybody knows King Cheng, no warrior (an understatement), ran like a rabbit and hid behind a pillar. He only got brave when Ching K'o became defenseless.

As you might imagine, King Cheng got angry once he stopped shaking and feeling nauseous. Crawling back to his throne, he gathered his thoughts and then gave his physician a nice reward. After sentencing Ch'in Wu-yang, the accomplice, to boil in oil, he also punished a number of his ministers in the same way for being slow off the mark. The royal guard didn't fare well either, although heaven knows it wasn't their fault. But nothing can ever be King Cheng's fault.

He attacked Yen right after that—how lucky the Ch'in Army of the East was already on Yen's border! The King of Yen, a profound political thinker, had his son Prince Tan killed by yet another assassin and sent *his* head to King Cheng, but the king was unmollified. The war went on for five years until Yen was destroyed and every member of the royal family and all their servants, and the families of all their servants, and the pets of all the families of all their servants, and—oh, you get the picture—were exterminated.

King Cheng would become First Emperor the following year, but that is another story.

There is a tail to this tale, though, Juan Chi told the storytellers. Remember the dog-butcher, Kao Chien-li? Ching K'o's friend? He was the kind of person who knew when to lay low. When the awful news about Ching K'o got back to Yen, Kao changed his name and became a waiter newly arrived from the far south, living under the ridiculous name of Phat.

His waiting went on a few years, until one day, as Phat Kao sat listening to someone playing the harp with other waiters, he began to comment negatively on the music. The other waiters, tattle-tales to a man, told the master of the tavern, "This man understands music."

Phat was ordered by his master to strum the harp in the tavern. The dinner guests loved his playing and offered him wine. Having missed his old life dreadfully, Kao decided it was time to come out of hiding. He began playing for a living again, under his own name.

His skills were so great that word of his playing very soon reached the First Emperor (the former King Cheng), a music lover who was personally all thumbs, as we learned when we saw him try to draw his sword.

The First Emperor sent for Kao and made him Court Musician. Someone informed on Kao, saying he had been a close friend of Ching K'o, but the First Emperor liked his playing so well, he said, "This is just another crazy musician. He's harmless. Oh, let's be safe, though. Blind him."

As time went by, he found Kao's music very soothing and constantly asked Kao to sit closer to him when he was playing.

Like Ching K'o, Kao had an assassination plan. It was vaguely similar to Ching Ko's. Biding his time as he moved closer to the First Emperor, he prepared by weighting the thick end of his harp with a great deal of lead. When he was finally close enough to bash out the First Emperor's brains with his harp, he stood up and raised it to strike, but, probably because the weight of the lead threw him off, he missed the First Emperor by a mile and hit himself on the left kneecap. Oooow—unfortunate!

Fool me once, more fool me, try to fool me twice, more fool you! The First Emperor had Kao put to death at once, whacked by his own harp, and he never again allowed the follower of any former prince near him. So in the long term, the bad day planned by Ching K'o turned out nicely for the future First Emperor, Ch'in Shih-huang-ti, after all.

Most days did, said Chia Tao.

The River-Merchant's Letter
to His Wife

My lady of sixteen springs
I shall be at Chofusa
when the last leaves touch the earth
    by the high gate of Hsienyang.

If I come there first I will wait
and will hope you come to me soon.

I have seen stars in the black river.
When we crossed them, they ran away
    as the golden fish in our pond
    flee from your slender fingers.

When I come home
I will clear the moss from the stones
    beside our gate.
Moss does not grow on the clay banks
    of the great Yellow River.

Sweet eyes, little wind of the bells,
I hear your voice above the time-ringing
    in the Shanglin Gardens.

Though the river is full of danger,
    I will come home.

I pray you meet me
in the valley of Chofusa
before winter snow falls,
wetting the green roofs of Anyang.

Master K'ung and the Ancient Songs

"There were more than three thousand ancient songs,
but Confucius rejected those that were repetitious
and retained those that had moral value..."
— *from* Records of the Grand Historian

I have heard it said one time
a citizen of Cheng called
to my student Tzu-kung,

"There is a man at East Gate
...lost as a stray dog he looks!"
Tzu-kung knew at once it was me.

A gentleman loses standing
by dressing incorrectly.
Therefore dress is important.

A gentleman can't change
his looks. Therefore,
looks are unimportant.

It's true, I am like a stray dog,
that is certainly true.
Oh, Ssu-ma, you missed the point.

For such an ugly man as I,
anything beautiful has moral value.
I saved all the songs I could.

The Power of the Moon

There is an ancient painting
of a poet drunk on rice wine
in a garden under a white moon.

His friends have all fallen asleep
or departed. He has fallen on his knees
by the brook in the garden.

He sees his own eyes
shining up at him, sees twigs
in his hair, laughs and laughs.

The season is early fall.
A few leaves are leaning against
the garden's bamboo fence.

BOOK THREE
The Emperor

The Last Great Battle
Tu Mu's Tale

After the eunuchs had gathered, eaten, indulged in the invariable belching competition, settled down and begun to digest their substantial dinners, Han Yin opened his drooping eyes and looked down the line of distinguished eunuchs at me, the humble Recording Secretary of the group, where I sat in a corner hunched over my writing materials.

He said, "Ssu-ma Ch'ien, we are enjoying your faithful renderings of our tales. Is there something in particular you, with your long historian's nose, might wish one of us to talk about? Something not mentioned already?"

I knew what I wanted to know. "Tu Mu," I said, looking down at the massive First Emperor's Charioteer, please tell me about the last battle with our greatest rival, the southern state of Ch'u. The one that led straight to the Ch'in Empire. I believe you were there."

"Well of course I was there, you foolish man," Tu Mu responded angrily. "That was my job!"

"I'm sorry," he said to me, in a room that was suddenly quiet. "You are definitely not a foolish man. But you are right, I was always there, at every major battle, though well back and out of harm's way. To keep the king safe, you understand. I stood beside King Cheng and did the real work of managing the horses while he pretended to.

"Our job—his job—was to allow his steadfast presence to

hearten our troops. Not that those head-hunters ever looked backwards when the blood was up! But by the time the Ch'in army was charging, it really wasn't him any more; it was his double standing beside me. He would certainly have left, quietly. As you know," the Charioteer said, smiling a little, "the First Emperor is a tremendous coward."

His straight back stiff against the wall, he drew his knees into the vicinity of his chin and closed his eyes, putting himself back at the scene of the battle. Finally, he began, and he did not open his eyes again until he was done speaking.

"It was General Wang Ch'ien's greatest battle, and that is saying something," he said, finally. There was a pause. When Tu Mu spoke next, his voice sounded far away and he seemed barely conscious of us, the hidden lamps, and the steady green glow they gave to the entire Jade Room.

Some people believe our present leading general, Meng T'ien, has become a greater general than Wang Ch'ien. But they were not there with us on the far side of the Wu Pass, camped on the lush southern plains of Ch'u.

The battle was a masterpiece. Wang Ch'ien borrowed an idea from Sun Tzu's book of military strategies and tactics, and mixed it with Ch'in's "straight ahead, no prisoners" approach. It was the greatest military feat I ever saw or hope to see, but it was spoiled at the end by a cowardly and cruel decision.

This was in the twenty-third year of King Cheng's reign (222 B.C.). The year before, the King had made a bad mistake: he had allowed an inferior general to persuade him that he could successfully invade powerful Ch'u with a small, fast-moving force. The general, who was a fool, succeeded at first, driving far to the south and actually capturing the king of Ch'u. Triumphant King Cheng went all the way to Ch'u's capital city of Ying, far south of the Yellow River, to lord it over his new territory.

But soon after his visit, there was an uprising at the River Huai led by a general of Ch'u named Hsiang Yen. The same foolish Ch'in general who thought he had pacified the kingdom was defeated by the still-deadly Ch'u army with its back against a cliff wall and nothing to lose. Sun Tzu, the great Ch'i general and author of *The Art of War*, rightly said you must never press your enemy until they are in such a desperate position they can only fight their way out alive, or die standing.

In any case, the Ch'u army was famous for having a sharp sting—I saw them slaughter our boys in many other battles and I can tell you that was true! And it was certainly true this time—they broke through our lines in a dozen places and then turned where they stood, flanking the outnumbered Ch'in army. It was a disaster, a rout!

It could not be tolerated. A short time later, King Cheng went, on foot in plain robes, through the streets of Hsienyang to Wang Ch'ien's home where he was living in retirement. Cheng was always able to humble himself when it served his purposes. The King urged the great general to unretire, command the Ch'in armies, drive south and deliver a death blow to Ch'u, the only real rival Ch'in had left.

Wang, the old warhorse, agreed readily. But he said, "Your Majesty, I have two requests to make. One, I will need 600,000 men, not one spearman less. Two, if you please, I would like my rewards now, not later. I am fighting for them, anyway. If I win, I will enjoy them. If I lose, you can have my head, assuming it is still available and not sitting on a pike staff in Ch'u's capital city, Ying."

King Cheng did not like that part of the bargain—he had said, "Wang Ch'ien, if you succeed, you do not ever have to worry. I will take care of you,"—and it galled him that for Wang Ch'ien, that wasn't good enough. But he had no choice, and rewarded Wang Ch'ien appropriately at once.

The other part, the size of the army, he agreed to readily, knowing it was achievable. Recruitment and, where necessary, conscription was carried out throughout Ch'in; soon the army was 600,000-strong. Wang Ch'ien drilled them ruthlessly, executing officers of troops who were in his view not serious enough about following orders. Before long, everyone had the message. Besides, our soldiers knew the pickings would be good in Ch'u!

Everything was ready. We set out from Hsienyang, taking two days to cross the Wei, and drove south at once.

King Cheng rode beside me in the royal chariot, which bristled with dagger-axes and spears. He was tall and magnificent in war armor that never felt a blade, carrying a dagger-axe that never bit an enemy's neck, wearing a splendid dragon-hilted, short sword that never stabbed upward to the heart. I must say, though untouched and virginal, he was also splendid! You would have sworn he was a hero.

We were near the head of our vast parade, more than a day's march from one end to the other, sharing the lead with a chariot carrying General Wang—who, being an actual soldier, sat in a very comfortable camp chair except when he wanted to impress the foot soldiers by marching with them.

Ahead of us, behind us, on either side of us, were innumerable companies of soldiers whose duty was to keep any suddenly appearing enemy crossbowmen more than a bolt-length—about two-thirds of a *li*—from King Cheng.

He enjoyed the whole business. War and the rituals are the only real business of a king. Besides, he was in about as much danger as he would have been on his knees during his daily communications with the ancestors and Heaven in the major temple of the palace, or hunting small birds with his own little bow in the immense Shanglin Gardens. Lack of danger, I have always felt, helps one feel brave.

He really looked extremely good.

Messengers rode to General Wang constantly, reporting this or that local attack by units of the Ch'u army, who, though the main body was still far to the south, were beginning to test our perimeters.

The sound of a marching army, which you might expect

would be that of a rhythmic tramp, tramp, is actually much more chaotic. The closest I can come in my mind is that it was like a thousand crowded beehives, a high and constant hum, or perhaps the sound of a horde of locusts simultaneously chewing and playing their violins.

Clouds of dust rose everywhere, turning the sky to a kind of yellow even on bright days, as scores of foraging units rode out to gather up Ch'u millet, rice, cattle and other foodstuffs, loot, rape and set fire to villages, et cetera, et cetera. It is an enterprise like no other. Perhaps only men can truly appreciate this marching men from horizon to horizon, the rumble and clank of weapons, all in a kind of endless thundering.

We were on the march for weeks, every day like the one before, constant punishments, exercise, drill work with the weapons, until one day we reached a rising point of land to see, across a valley north of the Ch'u capital of Ying, an army of what seemed to be nearly equal size. It was a sight to behold! The Ch'u banners flying proudly, that same hum of bees or crunch of locusts. There was a feeling of a tournament about it; the two armies were like brothers come to try a wrestling fall or two.

Two days earlier, King Cheng had quietly departed—quietly for him—with enough men to keep him safe.

He left behind one of his doubles, an equally tall man who looked something like him until you came up close and saw that he had a constant tremor in his arms and legs, and his eyes would not lock on yours. He had been hidden in one of the supply wagons the whole time, and came to the King's chariot in the darkest hours of the early morning. We said nothing to one another. What was there to say? The next day he took the King's usual place in the chariot. People close to us knew that the King had gone home, but from a distance the illusion was quite successful, I have been told.

General Wang ordered the army to make camp, a strongly fortified camp that would not be vulnerable to the enemy army across the valley. Then he held a council with his senior captains and commanders.

Of course I was not present at that council, but I had a friend among the commanders, an old war dog who had served with my father, the general, in the state of Chao years ago. My father, thankfully, had picked the right time to go over to Ch'in, just before the Chao army was annihilated. We had some time on our hands, and he told me General Wang's orders.

The army was to behave as no effective army ever does in the field, to play games, such as throwing arrows into jars, gamble, dance, sing and pretend to drink massively—anyone caught really drinking would have had his throat cut on the spot—and generally to behave like fools, but always safely inside our fortifications.

This pretence was carried out in plain view of the enemy; it went on for days. But all the while the men were fully armed under their black robes, just waiting for the unison beat of the great Ch'in war drum and its thousand brothers on the chariots. Up close, you could see the tension on the faces, hear the quiet voices and the terse sentences when the men were not pretending to sing drunken soldiers' songs that never made it into K'ung Fu Tzu's *Book of Songs*. None of it suggested a festival! But from a distance, like the King's double, the illusion was complete.

The idea, my friend told me, was to watch for signs of relaxation in the Ch'u camp. General Wang thought that when they saw what we were doing, they would think "Those men behave like fools on holiday." They already felt they were a better fighting force than we, having beaten a Ch'in army less than a year earlier. Now, thought General Wang, they will begin to feel contempt for us—and start to relax.

It took more than a week, but our hidden forward observers began to see signs the enemy was losing discipline. Their guards were not as alert, their drilling lessened every day, there was some drinking, and so on.

General Wang waited like a drawn bow. One pre-dawn morning, when our camp fires were still lit and the men were pretending to be asleep in the tents, he commanded the Ch'in army to assemble quickly and move toward the Ch'u army as quietly as possible.

No drums, no flutes, no banners, no war songs, no keening women. Six hundred thousand men, marching heel and pointed toe in the square step, the terrifying Ch'in march to battle. The earth was shaking, but not a sound anywhere—well, that's not really true, but there was amazingly little sound, so little you could almost hear the gurgle of Ch'u soldiers as their forward posts went down, their throats cut, before they could sound an alarm.

The surprise could not be total, of course. They heard us coming. But the loss of discipline, of readiness, was fatal. They could not get into defense formations in time.

On command, the Ch'in army began to run, the chariots of the officers rolled, groaning forward faster and faster, the horses shaking and neighing in the traces, nostrils flaring, desperate to go to full stride of thirty feet or more. Now, at last, the Ch'in stone war drums began to beat on their rumbling war chariots, the bowmen and crossbowmen knelt and stood, knelt and stood, sending round after round of deadly bolts into the huge enemy camp—right up to the moment our spearmen and swordmen crashed through the flimsy wood of their stockade and fell on the disorganized Ch'u.

The immense Ch'in army was like a giant ball rolling across the plain. It was not aimed at any *part* of the Ch'u army, it rolled up the hill and crashed into the entire Ch'u army, engulfing it. As the Ch'u soldiers began to scream and turn their backs to run, our archers drowned them in a nightmare hail of arrows and bolts—a whining no one who heard will ever forget. No one left the field that day.

I held my horses firm, several hundred yards behind the bowmen. Beside me, shaking with fright but of course in no danger whatever, the King's double stood. Our job, his especially, was simply to be there, to be visible, to be alive.

And then, in an instant, he was not alive. Tens of thousands of Ch'in crossbow bolts and arrows whined through the darkness toward the enemy, but one, probably aimed by an assassin who was never apprehended, whirred back to us.

My god, I thought, if he falls we could lose the victory that is almost ours, and I would lose a great deal more than that!

Swiftly I reacted. While he was still falling, I reached down and grabbed some spare harness. Then I pushed my shoulder into him, leaning forward to prop him up. I used the harness to weave him into a standing position. When he was finally secure, I shook uncontrollably for a moment—seemed longer— and took my place beside him as before. The difference was, he was no longer shaking.

I turned my attention back to the battle. All this took only moments, but I could see that the flight had become general and the Ch'in army was after the fleeing Ch'u so fiercely they were like wolves—pikes and dagger-axes raised, swords swinging, slashing—indeed, they were so hard on the enemies' heels many of the Ch'in soldiers were taking Ch'in arrows in their backs. But that was routine for the Ch'in. No shields, no wounded, no mercy.

They caught them all, though it took days. They cut every Ch'u soldier, footman, spearman, officer, into many pieces, often not bothering to kill them first. They left them there, neither in Heaven nor Earth. Just empty wanderers, forever crying for home.

General Wang had fifty-five wagon-loads of unassorted body parts made up and rolled down to Ying with the message that the soldiers of Ch'u had decided to come home. You could hear the cries of women for miles. Then he burned the city to ashes.

For the second time that night in the Jade Room, there was a silence.

Tu Mu opened his eyes; he was weeping.

"It was a great battle," he said. "And it was a desecration—not the first time such a thing happened, certainly. But I was there and I saw it. It was wrong; it was shameful, it was cowardly.

"They should have been buried with honor. They were warriors."

Mutations
Lo Yin's Tale

Tonight the jade *pi*-disc speaker's scepter went to Lo Yin, Chief Dresser of the First Emperor.

"As one of the relatively few members of this distinguished group—cough, cough—who have truly mastered the skill of reading, I propose to begin by quoting you at some length, Ssu-ma Ch'ien. I apologize for this, but I simply do not know a better place to start my story," Lo Yin mumbled. As usual, he spoke through his nose.

He picked up a familiar bamboo scroll, unfolded it, and held it out as far from his eyes as possible. Then he cleared his throat like a bawling ox, took a long drink of perfumed wine, and began speaking with reasonable clarity for a man with a stub of a tongue.

Chao Kao, the Chief Eunuch, removed Lo Yin's tongue when he became the Emperor's personal dresser, believing it would be more difficult for a speechless Lo Yin to pass along inappropriate or embarrassing remarks that might fall from the Emperor's lips. Luckily for Lo Yin, Juan Chi, who as Chief Dispenser of Eunuch Punishments oversaw the tongue removal, was a close friend and left Lo Yin with just enough tongue to speak intelligibly. As a result, virtually all of the Emperor's inappropriate or embarrassing remarks, which happened virtually every time he spoke, were passed on and shared widely.

The ancient wars that had gone on for centuries were now

over at last, said Lo Yin.

Over a period of twenty years, by subversion, assassination and if necessary invasion, King Cheng had crushed the last of his enemies—and in the land of All Under Heaven, nothing left standing now opposed him. He was the most absolute ruler and the richest man who ever lived. Accordingly, it was time for a new title. I quote from his speech just as you have it in your *Records of the Grand Historian*, Ssu-ma Ch'ien:

"In the twenty-fourth year of unremitting war, betrayal, assassination, head-hunting and so forth (221 B.C.), I, King Cheng, son of King Chuang-hsiang (the former Prince Tzu-ch'u), am now in control of the entire land. Insignificant as I am, I have raised troops to punish the rebellious princes. Thanks to the sacred power of our ancestors, all six kings of the ancient kingdoms have been chastised as they deserved, so that at last the empire is pacified.

"Now unless we create a new title, how can we record our achievements for posterity? Pray discuss the question of an imperial title."

Have you noticed how faithfully the tail of a comet follows the head? Present and fawning on this occasion were Prime Minister Wang Kuan, Chief Counselor Feng Ch'ieh and Chief Justice Li Ssu, a man on his way up. They happily agreed with the king that not even the Five Emperors of ancient times could match his exploits. For the only truly appropriate title, they referred even further back in historial beliefs, to the days when heaven had its Heavenly Sovereign, earth had its Earthly Sovereign, and ruling over them both was a deity called the Supreme Sovereign. They felt that "Supreme Sovereign" would cause the royal bells to ring loud enough to be heard by all of creation.

But King Cheng felt that using the title "Supreme Sovereign" was spreading honey on the bread a little too thickly. Furthermore, he did not wish to risk offending any of his fellow deities. So he said the counselors ought to address him, more modestly, as August Emperor, and only after his death, refer to him forever as First Emperor, Ch'in Shih-huang-ti.

An edict was issued to this effect at once, and our beloved king left kingship behind in favor of emperor-ship. All hail Ch'in Shih-huang-ti, Sovereign Emperor! Thus began the dreaded Power of Water, the terrible reign of the color black, and the paramount, though usually inauspicious, number six.

Our First Emperor had had enough of war and intrigue, and desired stability. Advisors suggested that he should govern by creating new sub-states with rulers from his own clan who would report to him. He rejected this suggestion, saying that as soon as they were safely away from the capital, they would start plotting against him. Instead, at Li Ssu's urging, he created thirty-six provinces, each with a governor, an army commander and an inspector to watch each other and the population, and to make sure the strict Ch'in laws were enforced by exceptionally strict punishments under the code of Legalism.

Li Ssu directed an enormous relocation program in which thousands of principal families from all of the six ancient kingdoms were moved from their power bases, the feudal lands, directly to Hsienyang, where they were to live pleasantly and ineffectually ever after in pleasure palaces thoughtfully built for them by the Emperor. He gave them all soft lives. It was like smothering them with silk pillows and it was a brilliant, though flawed, idea that worked very well, for a while.

That was how the new Ch'in Empire, the Middle Kingdom, All Under Heaven, call it what you will, began, led by a master of war and treason, the Emperor, and under him but constantly growing in power, a master of keeping the black-haired people under his large, merciless thumb, Li Ssu.

This was about a year after I became the king's hand-man— sorry, the First Emperor's—personal dresser. I have been closer to him than anyone, closer to him each day than I am to you now here in the Jade Room. I know his daily habits, needs and moods, especially the latter—I had to or I would not remain in his service, or even be alive.

Because of his vitality and sheer size, First Emperor seemed larger than his majestic robes at first—they fit physically, of course, but no matter how gorgeous they were, they were never what you noticed about him. A general once called him a ratlike man; if so, he was a giant rat! Many called him the Tiger of Ch'in. I always thought that was a much better description: powerful, sly, treacherous, deadly.

Deadly! When his brother, a general leading a Ch'in army against the state of Chao, rebelled and died fighting Cheng, his brother's officers and soldiers were executed to the last man; then, at Cheng's orders, their corpses were mutilated so they would not be whole men in the afterlife. Including his own brother! Makes me shudder! That's when I slipped off to make sure my "Precious" is safe in its green bottle on a high shelf.

After he was invested as First Emperor, his robes became even more splendid—silver and gold thread, dragons rising out of vast oceans, sashes crusted over with precious stones. It was unbelievable at times. It took me and my assistants an hour or more to dress him, not counting washups, beard combing, sex relief, and nail ornamentation

But then, the First Emperor changed. I don't know exactly when the change began but I came to feel he was shrinking in his imperial robes. His disposition was as nasty, arbitrary and vengeful as ever, but now he grew petty, which was unlike him. Having laid waste to everything in sight, being without a single rival, his concerns moved from the consolidation of an empire to personal matters.

He spent more time with his favorite concubines at first, and that was unusual for him because he had never shown much interest in fornication before. The ladies, who had complained bitterly about the infrequency of his visits, now complained about his excessive interest in them, his violence, his crudeness.... Nothing satisfies them!

And that wasn't all that changed. He was still profoundly

attentive to his imperial duties as the intercessor, the man who prayed to the august ancestors in Heaven on behalf of the Ch'in Empire. Early every morning he went, attended by two Confucian scholars *and* two Taoist priests (to be on the safe side) to the Hall of the Sacred Rites, where he spent hours on his knees, deep in conversation with spirits no one else could hear. Then came a long day of court, scores of imperial judgments, a brief, light supper—he was always a moderate eater—and after that, he regularly read at least twenty-seven pounds of imperial documents weighed hourly until the requisite poundage was reached—signing, rejecting, proposing and disposing, raising some in rank, executing others, reviewing massive public works projects, et cetera. Finally, he climbed up into the huge imperial bed, where, no surprise, he often had one of his headaches and lay groaning in agony, sometimes for hours.

Those *were* his habits. They aren't now. Back then, no one was in doubt about who was making the decisions up to the point when he became Emperor, and for some time thereafter— he was. Li Ssu had no doubt who was boss, fawning on him to an extent that embarrassed even me, the finest fawner in the Jade Room. Later—I don't know.

First Emperor became disinterested in all but the largest projects—his tomb, of course, located south of the river, where scores of thousands of men had been at work ever since he became king at thirteen. The immense palace at Epang, also south of the Wei. The Shanglin Imperial Gardens, a kind of model Taoist wilderness that he hoped would attract Immortals (!) he could converse with; he created it as you or I might create a butterfly garden. The huge network of carefully graded, hardened imperial roads; heaven knows he traveled them often in his occasional "progresses" to demonstrate his power—and especially, to show that he was alive—to all and sundry in the world outside the palace. And there were the hundreds of miles of canals great and small.

Apart from these, he only seemed really interested in

completing the northern wall defenses. The rammed earth Great Wall was no engineer's proposal, by the way: an astrologer had told him he needed to do it, so he could use it to bring the northern tribes under control. I don't think his engineers believed it was possible even after they had completed it.

But much of that happened early in the imperial reign when his interest in governing was still at its peak. As his desire to live forever grew, he gradually lost interest in most of his projects. I blame the useless crowd of lying magicians who came pouring into the imperial court mostly from the eastern states of Ch'i and Yen, them and their constant yammering about immortality! It seemed immortality was his only interest. Otherwise, he was apathetic most of the time, except when a courtesan who was servicing him got a feeble rise. When the astrologers and magicians had his ear, you could see something new in his eyes. I swear it looked like fear.

My regular station was, and still is, outside his door. I will never speak of it anywhere but here, but I heard him sobbing at night, many times. What does he have to cry about?! He owns everything in the world.

I think he is just ridiculously afraid of dying. In the years after we became an empire, I saw him gradually give much of his power to now Prime Minister Li Ssu, who took control of everything that mattered. These days Li Ssu outdoes himself in cruelty, silently assented to by the Emperor.

One day, a sage named Shun Yu-yueh rose at a banquet to question the government of the Empire, saying it was no longer modeled on antiquity and therefore could not last. Seeing the Emperor seething under this criticism, Li Ssu immediately declared that the entire scholar class was like Shun Yu-yueh, and they all did great harm by giving people information that made them discontented. The *Thirteen Classics* were to be burned, except for those on medicine, prognostication and agriculture—plus your own *Records of the Grand Historian*, Ssu-ma Ch'ien—to keep the black-haired people in docile ignorance. The bamboo bundles with the wisdom of seventy generations were thrown into bonfires! And all the books *were* destroyed, leaving only a precious few in the royal library.

Now, said Li Ssu, history begins with Ch'in Shih-huang-ti. There can be no destructive ideas, no dissent; examples from the past can never be quoted to undermine the present.

In the following year, something even worse happened. I am no friend of the scholars, but I believe what happened to them was a great crime. Using a temper tantrum of the Emperor over scholarly ineptness and cowardice, Li Ssu argued that the lot of them were traitors, spreading lies throughout the empire. He pressed on to bury alive or behead hundreds of scholars, discrediting the entire scholarly class, whose stock in trade was remembering and recommending better times and better ways of doing things—clear criticism of the present. This murderous destruction terrified the few remaining people who could think, and left Li Ssu free to raise taxes and enforce ever harsher laws, which he did, while living a personal life of drunken revelry.

I was in the court on an errand when the first group of scholars was thrown into a cauldron of boiling oil, turning red one at a time, like lobsters. Except for their screams, the court was utterly silent. No one dared say a word. Finally, there was one sage left, a very ancient man. Waving off the soldiers, he walked with great dignity to the cauldron and flung himself into it.

I wept. Who could help it? I also hid my eyes in my sleeve. There is hearsay that the Emperor had saved this old man for his bravery, but I was there; the Emperor just sat on his throne listening to the initial shrieks and staring as the now-silent flesh parted from the bones of a wise and brave, old man. The Emperor is truly a pig of a man, brothers.

Today Li Ssu scarcely bothers to inform the Emperor of what he is doing—he just does whatever he likes and passes decrees to the Emperor, who stamps them with his seal like a zombie—no real thought, just drifting. And things are getting worse. No one is safe. The palaces rise in Hsienyang by the hundred; people are moved here, there and everywhere to uproot them; constant uprisings are put down with ever-greater brutality. I tell you, friends, the world is in chaos.

Of course this was not news to me, Ssu-ma Chi'en! Protesting this royal insanity was how I came to lose my posterity!

One of the worst things, Lo Yin continued, was the Emperor's exiling of his eldest son, Prince Fu-su, a man of honor and probity, to the northern wall, and the service of General Meng T'ien whom you mentioned, Tu Mu.

The Prince was sent there for protesting Li Ssu's murderous attack on the scholar class. He had the temerity to suggest to his father that the end of the scholar class would lead to unrest everywhere in the empire. I fear that with him far away in the north, Li Ssu will gather even more power into his own hands. We will miss Prince Fu-su a great deal, depend on it. He was a moderate man and an educated man, for a prince. Prince Fu-su's younger brother, Hu-hai, is scarcely worth mentioning; under the tutelage of Chao Kao, he is already ruined and dissipated, and he is still in his early teens!

No one here will forget that when the Emperor decided some of us were spying on him for Li Ssu, he had a hundred of us killed—just like that. What kind of man kills his faithful servants?

As for the Emperor today, I serve him. But I no longer marvel at him. I think half his heart is missing.

Lo Yin sighed a long and shallow sigh, and said, "I believe I am finished, Han Yin. My tongue is quite sore."

"Superbly done, Lo Yin. We understood every word," said Han Yin.

Journey to the Otherworld
Chia Tao's Tale

Earlier, I described the unusual entrance to the Jade Room, but your memory may need refreshing.

First, you get down on your hands and knees, then you go under the carved, wooden scholar's writing desk in Han Yin's study; next, you part a thick wall curtain and crawl forward five feet through a passageway in the wall toward dim, green lamp light; as the passage narrows, you reach a place in which you must force yourself through a truly tiny entrance into the Jade Room itself. This last part is a real push, I can tell you, even for a small man like me!

In truth, it's not easy for any of us portly men. I have always thought that it may have been created as something of a joke by our leader, Han Yin. Except for gaunt Juan Chi, the Chief Dispenser of Eunuch Punishments, none of us eunuchs are what you would call slim. Rich food and lazy lives take care of that. One is plumper than the rest, though. Chia Tao, Major Domo of the Concubine Residences, though frail in appearance, has a pyramidal structure: as he goes downward toward his knees, he gets wider and wider.

His unusual shape may explain why Chia Tao has a unique way to enter the Jade Room: he backs in. It is interesting to watch. First, much huffing as he translates from vertical to all fours; then a scuffling as he negotiates the underside of the writing desk; next a scritching like a gigantic mouse as he backs into the passageway. Presently one of his large feet (often in a dirty sock) appears, followed eventually by the other. Kicking of feet and groaning in the passage. Finally, with an audible pop, his posterior pushes through after his legs; then we hear even more groaning. Now, Chia Tao's substantial middle—Han Yin once told me that while Chia Tao was talking one day, he, Han Yin, began to look at Chia Tao's middle, and imagined he was looking at the entire world—enters the Jade Room. This is followed by Chia Tao's belly, touching the floor, Chia Tao's smaller chest, narrower shoulders, and finally the sweating head and red face of Chia Tao himself—another triumphant passage!

"Why backwards," I asked him once.

"If I am ever permanently stuck in there I want the outside world to remember my face, not my bottom," he answered.

On this night, we could see, almost from the moment his feet appeared, that Chia Tao was agitated; and when his face finally presented itself, it was unusually pale. He crawled directly to the nearest open space along the wall, gathered pillows around himself and sat hugging two pinkish pillows to his chest, saying not a word.

"Are you all right, Chia Tao?" Han Yin asked.

"All right? All right? I suppose I am."

He mopped his brow, which looked clammy. "Do you believe in ghosts?" he asked us all, looking from face to face.

We all nodded; though as it happens, I do not.

"Good. Then perhaps you won't mind so much. Because... because...I think I am a ghost myself," said Chia Tao.

Without a word, Han Yin reached over and handed him the jade *pi*-disk speaker's scepter.

It was last night, he began. I had waded into an awful row in the Concubine Residences right after dinner—it was a stupid quarrel over one girl's stolen bath oil or something, and the fur was flying, I can tell you! Since I am the only man around, they always expect me to settle these things. I waded in and got royally scratched for my trouble. And bruised.

When things calmed down at last, I lumbered off to my house behind the Residences, feeling quite depressed by my rotten concubine-ridden life.

When I got there, the front door lamp, normally lit at dusk, was dark; that was a surprise as my butler always lights it for me. He knows I am often at work making peace in the Concubine Residences of an evening because after supper, when it is clear the Emperor is not coming—again—they get terribly distressed and ornery. Since it was evening, I had to enter my courtyard by feel. I was swearing to myself—it had been an awful day—and my mood wasn't helped by tripping over something and falling hard on the pave-stones.

I reached the moon door but couldn't find the latch for the longest time. Where are my servants? I shouted, but got no answer. When I finally opened the door, it was even darker inside than it had been in the courtyard. It was perfectly black, so black I could not see my fingers a foot from my eyes. I know my house well, of course; it's the only place I'm free of the wretched caterwauling of the concubines, so I strode confidently—but slowly—across the hall floor toward the main stairway.

Behind me there was the most tremendous crash!

I couldn't move, just stood shaking. Then, in front of me, a little to my left, one of the oil lamps in a wall-sconce lit. By itself. Strangest thing I ever saw, to that point.

It wasn't much of a light, though. My front hall, normally so cheery, was all gloom and shadows, deep wells of darkness everywhere. I turned around and saw that one of the pair of enormous man-high vases flanking the inside of my front door had fallen to the floor, shattering into tiny pieces. It was a pile of rubble. I suppose it's a measure of how distressed I was that I never stopped to wonder how a vase you can't even lift had tipped over on its own, or how once it had fallen, its three-inch walls had broken open like an old paper wasps' nest and scattered on the ground. I went over to it, timidly, as you can imagine!

And found a book. It must have been inside the vase.

It wasn't like any book I'd seen before. I don't even know how I knew it was a book! No bamboo slips for pages, no ribbons, no sewn silk sheets. I knelt beside it and examined it. There were two thin boards, covered by leather and dyed dark red. The two boards were held together by a spine of the same material, perhaps three inches thick. On the cover of the book were some symbols in gold that were meaningless to me, though I felt I ought to know what they meant. Between the two boards were white sheets of a thin material, piled one on top of another. When I finally was able to pick up the book, they were attached to the spine, perhaps sewn to it.

I was on my knees, holding the strange book, peeking at its insides but really afraid to open it, if in fact it would open. It began to shake, a little at first, but soon so violently I felt as if I was about to be thrown by a horse! Naturally I dropped it and it fell open right to the middle.

As I stared at it, I thought, crazily, that the book was staring back.

At first the two sheets facing each other at the middle were blank. Then lines began to appear, slowly, on the sheets. As I watched, they became a picture! First it was just lines, then shades of gray and black filled in until I realized I was looking at a drawing of the huge inner courtyard of the Epang Palace! There wasn't a bit of light on the sheets, so I have no idea how I could see it, but I could; it was as if I had cat's eyes.

Suddenly it wasn't a drawing any more, it was the courtyard itself. And I was in it.

There was no one in the courtyard—which of us has ever seen it that way?—until at the far end I saw a figure coming down the steps of the gigantic Temple of Supreme Harmony. Just one, and he was wearing the same black robes of Ch'in that I was.

Brothers, it was like a dream. But it *was* no dream. I could feel the bricks under my feet. He did not seem to be walking, nor did I, yet we were coming toward each other. As we did, I felt myself getting smaller as he got larger, until he was many times taller than a man. I knew I was in the presence of a god, or demon, or some creature I could not identify.

And if you can believe it, I was not afraid!

"I am the Lord of the Dead," he said, when we were face to face—or rather his kneecap to my face. I found myself staring up at him. He was green jade, everything; the skin of his hands, or rather, claws, ending in foot-long steel blades; the scales of his neck; his flat face with two nostril holes but no nose, two eyebrows but only one eye, and ears that were folded wings. For several feet around him, the courtyard appeared to be on fire—but there was no heat!

I fell to my knees, rendering myself even smaller. It seemed appropriate. I reached forward and touched his ankle, also green. "I–I'm very glad to make your acquaintance, my Lord. This is then, *T'ien*, Heaven? And you are Huang Ti, the God Emperor?"

A sheet of dark fire roared across the whole huge courtyard. "No, you jackass! This is the Otherworld! And I am the Lord of the Dead, exactly as I said."

"My apologies, sir. But, sir," I whispered, "why am I here? I was fine recently."

"Because you are dead!" he roared down at me. His breath was bad.

I was one huge shiver.

He seemed to soften. I don't know how else to put it. Everything sagged a bit and a soft rain began, putting out the fire.

"But look," the Lord of the Dead said, becoming jovial, which was much more frightening, "I don't wish us to get off on the wrong foot. The fact is you are welcome here in our little Otherworld shadowland, Chia Tao. Your reputation precedes you. You have dealt nobly and sternly with Ch'in Shih-huang-ti's thousands of concubines for many years, never failing to flail when needed, and keeping them reasonably under control and actually happy from time to time, not that anyone cares about that. Everyone knows you have the worst job in the Palace of the Living, and you do it faithfully and nobly. We dead salute you!"

Would you believe it, he gave me a very grave and respectful three salutations! With each bow, I felt myself growing, until by the time the last one was done, I was actually the same size as the Lord of the Dead. Nearly the same size.

"Now let us talk business face to face and eye to eyes," said the Lord of the Dead, though I must admit I could still hardly look at him; he was so ugly.

"Now that you are here with us—for good, so to speak—we want to reward you for your faithful work in the Upper World of the land between the seas. And," I could have sworn he looked a little embarrassed, "we have an opening we need to fill as soon as possible. In my opinion, given your work background and your 'skill set,'" a phrase unfamiliar to me, "we believe you are the ideal candidate."

"Before I offer you the job officially, however," said my Lord, "I wonder if you would be interested in making a tour of the Otherworld with me?"

I said I would.

"Then take my hand–oh, sorry," he said, as one of his knife-like fingers sliced the first two knuckles off every finger of my right hand, leaving only my thumb intact, "I am always forgetting about that. Never mind, we'll toughen you up soon. You'll never miss them. Just walk around to my back and grab my robe, tightly...All right, are you holding on? Both hands? Oh, sorry, I forgot again. Just do your best."

"Did it *hurt*?" shouted Tu Mu.

"Are you out of your *mind*?" Chia Tao replied. "Of course it hurt! It hurt like seven devils—almost enough to distract me from what came next!"

Ulp! We went straight up so fast my head was spinning. When I could open my eyes again, I saw that his ears had unfolded into two immense, feathered wings that were now beating hard on either side of me.

The dark world was fleeing from us, palace, city and all, first a dot then not even there. I thought I saw the Great Wall for a moment, but soon it too was gone. The earth was curving at the ends like a bow being drawn; it got rounder and rounder. The most astonishing thing as we continued to sail outward: it turned into a small, round child's ball, mostly blue with splotches of green and brown here and there, and a lot of fuzzy white. And it was spinning!

I looked up and the moon was getting bigger and bigger above us. We were headed straight for it and it didn't look half as happy as the Jade Rabbit you see from home, I can tell you! I thought we'd crash, but we didn't—we took a horrific right turn and flapped all the way around the gigantic moon, twice, and then started to come down again.

The moon disappeared, the earth got larger and became one long curve again, like the bow once it has released its bolt. There was more and more blue below us. I could see white caps, waves, surf, even boats—but not like any I ever saw, no sails, just long, black things. I couldn't imagine how they could move. Then a green lady standing in the water was waving to us, and beyond her, tall buildings, tallest I ever saw, hundreds and hundreds of feet high, not a dragon-spout or green roof tile anywhere, and then–*whump*, the Lord of the Dead landed on a hard pavement in front of buildings that made me feel tiny again.

"Are we near the Great Wall, sir?" I asked him.

"No," he said, carefully folding up his ears, "this is the capital of Otherworld. It is going to be your home from now on. I looked up at the buildings and they looked down at me, with cold disapproval, I felt.

"So what do you think of Otherworld?" he asked me, and as soon as I got my breath back, I offered a timid, 'It's nice.'

"Nice! Well, yes. It is nice," he said. "And now about that job offer."

"I won't beat the broom with you. We would like you to become our new Supreme Director of the Ministry of Weather. You will have a princely rank, far above that of a mere major domo; your sexual apparatus will be fully restored to you; and your job will be to make sure the laws about distributing clouds and rain are carried out to the letter. You will have the full resources of our largest Bureau at your command. How does that sound, Chia Tao?"

Incredible! I could barely croak an assent. No more concubines!

"All right, let's get to work. We have some revising to do on you."

He snapped his fingers and a group of demons came rushing out of a large, pillared building behind us. Before I could react, they pulled the skin off my body, hung it on a hanger, and replaced it with a two-tone, dragonish armor plate, adding a very long and powerful tail that almost pulled me over.

Was it painful? Yes it was! It hurt like—like—oh, I can't describe it, like when he cut my fingers off. But the amazing thing is, the pain was over instantly, the moment they had zipped up the dragon-skin.

My arms got longer and more leglike and my legs got shorter and then I found that being on all fours was comfortable to me. Looking down between my legs, I saw an immense penis had been added, too, though I don't know just when that happened. I just looked at it and it became erect—you could pound earth for the Great Wall with a stick like that!

"Do your lightning, Supreme Director."

I had no idea what he meant, so he threw a demon at me. Instead of ducking like any sane former human, I looked hard at the demon and two bolts of lightning roared out of my eyes and incinerated him while he was still in the air!

"Good work, Supreme Director. You are a fast learner. Now I would like you to meet your principal assistants."

Four interesting specimens popped out of nowhere and stood at attention in front of me. I will take some pains to describe them for you accurately, but it is difficult, because just like weather, they kept changing color and shape.

The first and foremost of my associates-to-be was the Ancestor, or Spirit, or Duke, of Thunder—he answers to all those titles. At this particular moment, he too was quite batlike. His wings were leathery, his feet were clawed and he had an eagle's beak set in a monkey's face. Or perhaps the other way around. In his two hands, which hung far down from his wings, he had a steel chisel, for cutting hearts out, and a hammer, for beating on an enormous drum he wears on his head to create the thunder sound that kills everyone who comes too close. He seemed exceptionally unpleasant to me, even for a demon, but as I worked with him in the Bureau of Weather in the next few months, I learned that he was good-hearted, even sentimental. He loved firecrackers.

Next to him was a weeping woman I am sure some of you would regard as beautiful. As I watched her, a more or less continuous puddle grew at her feet, and I realized she was the likely source of all that blue water the Lord of the Dead had carried me over. But the tears were merely because she was sad, for a reason I could never get at.

I asked what her job was.

"Sir, I am the Spirit of Lightning, the female principle," she said melodiously. "Years and years ago I flew up to *T'ien*, Heaven, and stole a ray of light there, just one. As punishment, the Sky God sentenced me to fly after the Duke of Thunder and release the ray of light every time he is about to strike his drum. Then I have to fly after it and go and catch it again. It gives me such headaches, you can't imagine!"

Taking a long time to materialize was an old man wearing a blue cap and carrying a sack that had something lively bulging at the bottom. A real peasant, dirty, bare feet and all! I was about to pass on to someone more interesting, but I looked in his eyes and saw something, a hint of a head full of jokes, perhaps, so I stopped and asked what he did.

"Honored Supreme Director, I am the Master of Wind and have for a long time had the pleasure of carrying a bag of wind, or as you might say, a windbag. My job is to release winds at propitious and appropriate moments that harry and chivvy the Spirits of Thunder and Lightning in the directions they are required to go—some call me the Whip of Heaven. I also uproot things and blow over things every chance I get," he said, eyes sparkling. I could see that as old as he looked, and doubtless was, he did not feel old inside. A good way to be.

My final principal associate was the Master of Rain, dressed in yellow scale-armor, similar but inferior to my own golden-green and diamond-studded skin-armor. He had a tail like me, but tail for tail, I had him beat. He too was wearing a blue cap. He told me his work was to stand on a cloud—directed by the Master of Wind, of course—and pour water on the earth from his watering-can. This last looked like a joke; it was small as a child's toy, but he told me it could never be emptied as it was constantly re-supplied from the oceans.

He lives in some set of mountains or other, I was not familiar with them. Maybe the Cat's Hills? He added that they were in all respects except size and shape identical to our earthly K'unlun range.

The Master of Rain had two special abilities, it turned out: he could walk through water without getting wet and through fire without being burned.

"I should like to meet your First Emperor one day," he said, "and show him what water can really do. The Yellow River, your 'River of Sorrow,' gives you just a taste—the great Ch'in Shih-huang-ti will rue the day he claimed to rule the Power of Water!"

If I can arrange that meeting, I will do it gladly, I thought.

Stumbling down the steps of the large, stone building behind us—stone, mind you!—next came four harassed-looking young men, all in trousers and some sort of white-colored shirts with short sleeves so that one could see their disgusting, hairy arms.

All were carrying huge bundles of white sheets, dropping them constantly and tripping on each other as they bent to pick them up. They seemed completely distracted and not at all aware of my presence, so I asked the Lord of the Dead who they were.

"They are not mere flunkies, though they do look like sheep, don't they?" he said. "They bear a heavy responsibility. Their difficult jobs are to check on the weather constantly and make sure after the fact it happens that it was what you ordered. As you may know, weather is constantly getting out of hand"—here the lords and ladies of thunder and lightning and the masters of wind and rain looked uncomfortable—"so the work of these young men is never done. Fortunately, they are dead, so they need no sleep."

"What are they called?" I asked. "What is their job title?"

"They are the Weather Watchers," he said. "It's not an easy job, as I said, and they are wrong much too often. It is *extremely* irritating," he said, raising his voice.

"Anyway, would you like to see your offices?"

We went into the tallest building, signed a large open book, entering the time, date and purpose of our visit at the request of a bored-looking man in gray. That done, we entered a small room with sliding doors—very crowded, it was!—that began to shake in a terrifying manner as soon as the doors closed. When we finally exited, we were somewhere else altogether.

"This is the Bureau of Weather," the Lord of the Dead said proudly. We passed through any number of identical featureless rooms, all filled with scribes leaning forward over some sort of writing machines so close their noses were nearly touching them. They reminded me of ants, and I said so. No one said anything, but I could see it was not a popular comment among my aides, the Weather Watchers.

"And here is your Office."

It was beautiful! Two of the walls were completely transparent so I could look out at an enormous vast city and beyond the buildings to the blue water and the lady who had waved at us when we flew in. A wooden rectangle, ten times the largest I have ever seen, stood at one end of the room. Behind it was something you could lean back in or spin around in—I know it is hard to believe, but I did both things as often as possible.

"And this is your Desk. I am sorry, you don't know what this 'Desk' means, do you?" he said.

I nodded.

"Simple. You go to that device behind it, which is called a chair. You sit on the chair. Thereafter you do as little as possible."

"So, once again, welcome," the Lord of the Dead resumed. "And now, get to work. There's a backlog. By the way, if you're curious, there is no salary, there are no healthcare benefits, there are no vacations; in fact, there is no time off at all, it's a twenty-four-seven job. Weather takes no holidays."

"But," he said, his tone softening, "in case things should slow down a little, you do have one benefit: all the former humans you can eat. A cart comes around, you'll hear its bell. But don't stop working to chew. And be careful: some of them have been on the cart a while and are gamey."

That said, he vanished, and my associates drifted back to their various offices without so much as a "glad to have you with us, boss." I was alone. And I had no idea what I was to do!

I sat down and began to play with my chair.

Pretty soon—I think it was pretty soon—I noticed a large, black button on my desktop. I pushed it and behind me a large part of the wooden wall disappeared, replaced with what I had to assume was a large map of the Otherworld. At the very moment I worked that out, a drawer of the desk opened. In it was a huge jumble of pieces of metal with words on them: RAIN, CYCLONE, HIGH PRESSURE, LOW PRESSURE, EARTHQUAKE, FLOOD, CATASTROPHE, SNOW, TORNADO, MUDSLIDE, FOREST FIRE, EXTREMELY WINDY, UTTERLY DESTROYED, MILLIONS DEAD...there was more, but that's all I remember.

I knew these were clues but I didn't feel any farther along, until I saw a white button, so I pushed that and in through quite a low door, maybe a foot high, walked a cat wearing glasses. When she reached me,, she took them off and I saw she was beautiful.

"Can you help me?" I asked.

"Of course I can," she answered, "but I won't."

"Let me put it another way. Would you like me to step on you?"

She began to purr, undoubtedly signifying great fear. "What you do with those metal pieces is you grab a bunch of them, get up, walk over to the wall map and stick them on it. That's tomorrow's weather. So tired," she yawned, showing fangs some demons would kill for, "I will take a nap now."

She strolled across the desk to a far corner just out of my reach, curled up and went to sleep at once. I did what she told me, grabbed some pieces at random, took them to the map and placed them randomly on it. Wherever I put one, it stuck fast. When I had used up all the pieces, a sign lit up above the map. The sign read, "Tomorrow's weather has been decided. The Duke of Thunder, the Lady of Lighting and the Masters of Wind and Rain await their orders."

I went to the door of my office and yelled for them. When I turned around they were already inside the room behind me.

"I wish you wouldn't do that!" I said. "Here is tomorrow's weather."

They studied the map for a moment, wrote notes in ink on their palms, and left, grumbling.

That's *it*? I thought. That's all *I* do?

There was no day or night here, as I told you, but I did have something they called a twenty-four-hour wristwatch on one of my scaly forelegs, so I set its alarm for twenty-four hours later, and went through the same tedious activity.

Days, weeks, months, eons went by, always exactly the same.

The only thing that relieved the monotony was the arrival of the meat cart every long once in a while. I did just as the

Lord of the Dead had advised; I tried to exercise some care and certainly chewed every bite twenty times or more, but even so, some of the humans were very rank, one or two even requiring regurgitation, which of course was lucky for them, as it led to rebirth. They were all extremely noisy. If that was the highlight of my day, just imagine how bored I was.

One day as I was heading toward the map with my bundle of weather, I slipped on something—I will never know what—and fell backward, slamming my head hard against the desk. I saw stars, the first I'd seen in a long time, then everything was quiet and dark—well, it was always dark, but now it was darker, if you know what I mean—and I can't remember a thing after that.

That is, until this morning, when I felt as if I was drowning in a cold waterfall. Someone had dumped a pail of cold water on me! I looked up and saw my servants staring down. If I didn't know better, I would swear they were laughing! I got up on my hind feet, my head pounding. One of the vases by the door had fallen in the night, I could see blood on some of the pieces. My blood, I knew by instinct. My forehead, my ears, my neck were all awash in blood. People were scurrying here and there, bringing towels, more water, urging me to come and lie down, sir, et cetera, et cetera. Which I did at once, because I still had a horrendous headache.

By evening, I felt somewhat better. So I came here. You could say it was a dream, but brothers, I tell you, it was real! I'm sure I was there, in the Otherworld. I've been away a long time, have I not?

Lying just for the joke of it, we assured him that he had.

And my skin—it's still dragon-plate, I know! With that, he lifted his robe until we could see his well-filled, gray-white belly. "It's all plated, right?" he asked.

A joke's a joke, but—no, we said, it's just your regular, huge belly.

"Yes, but..." he said, lifting it with both hands. "Isn't it a little green? Don't you think?"

No, we said. And your arms are arms and you have two eyes and you look perfectly normal. This made him look very disappointed. But there is one thing you still have, we said.

"You still have dragon's breath!"

After the laughter died down, Juan Chi said, "There's one thing I don't understand, Chia Tao."

"What's that?"

"Aren't we supposed to be telling stories about the First Emperor? Isn't that the point of this whole business? What on earth has this ghost story of yours got to do with Ch'in Shih-huang-ti?"

"Oh, that," said Chia Tao. "I forgot. Every day when I went to make the map of tomorrow's weather, I would find the place where Hsienyang, our capital city, would be and I would put the words VIOLENT THUNDERSTORMS over it. I figured one day I'd be sure to get him.

"I guess not."

The Naked Mountain
Han Yin's Tale

"Persons like us whose testicles are 'lost, strayed or stolen' are likely to have a reduced view of human potential," said Han Yin, the Regulator of Entertainment in the Royal Palace.

"We are not optimistic people. But others make up for our sour views, and in his brutal way, the First Emperor is one of them, never more than when he is searching for personal immortality. He thinks he can do everything!

"But that's *him*! Who should *we* follow? Confucius, of course! Old K'ung Fu Tzu! That's the life for us eunuchs!" Han Yin continued, jade *pi*-disk speaker's scepter in hand.

"Everything like clockwork, nothing mysterious, just 'do the right thing' all day long.

"And all night, too," he added. "Respect for the past, respect for the ruler, blah, blah, blah..."

Everyone ate thoughtfully.

"But our dear Emperor 'Tao' as we call him, since he is not merely on the Way but is the Way (to hear him tell it) is something else again."

Everyone grunted thoughtfully.

"Remember when he cut down all those trees on the mountain that belonged to that minor goddess, the Lady of the River Yangtze? He left that mountain bare as a baby's bottom and destroyed her beautiful temple to teach her a lesson for flooding and preventing him from crossing the river! He took the axe to the first tree himself! Of course he got tired immediately, and left the rest of the forest to us thousands of servants, courtiers and soldiers to finish the job of 'shaving' her mountain.

"By the end of the day, he was exhilarated and feeling even more consequential than usual, and for once he didn't have a headache, so he spent several hours explaining the universe to his secretaries and servants. As it happens, I had the fanning duty. I remember every word he said! I wrote it down that same evening.

"This is what our beloved Emperor said in my hearing on that particular day."

Since the Lady of the River caused this storm, keeping me from crossing her river, I ordered her hillside forests cut down. Let her live there cold and naked!

I, the Ruler of the World, faithfully keep the rituals that placate Heaven and soothe the ancient families. But as to my own faith, that is nonsense! Let me tell you what I believe.

The universe has no beginning, and it will never end. There is no natural realm, no supernatural realm. The universe has just three elements: Heaven, Earth and Man. We worship Heaven; it is powerful but not manlike. Our Shang ancestors thought that it was manlike and they called it Shang Ti, the First, but that ridiculous belief died long ago. There is only T'ien, Heaven.

The law governing all things is Tao, the Way. I learned this in my youth.

The Way consists of two forces, Yang and Yin. Yang is sun, light, warmth, male. Yang is me. Yin is the moon, dark, cold, female, a drifter. Sometimes one is more powerful, sometimes the other. When Man acts against the Way, things get out of balance and trouble comes. As it happens, I actually contain both male and female. In fact, I am the Way, indistinguishable from its essence. If I do something, there is no doubt it is the Way. The imperial bells are never out of tune. I am the one who says if they are in tune or not, and I say they are never out of tune.

Many spiritual beings dwell in natural phenomena, like our disrespectful Lady of the Yangtze River here. And isn't this a day she will never forget?! Some live in stars, some in rivers, some in woods. Likewise, ancestral spirits, on whose goodwill most men depend, and to whom I sacrifice on behalf of the entire Empire and all the black-haired people, are always with us. But I do not depend on them, I command them.

Each man has a soul, each soul has two parts. When you die, as you surely will, though I will not, one part of you sinks into Earth. It can return as a capricious, malevolent, untrustworthy ghost. Such demonic ghosts can take possession of humans. The other part of the soul rises into Heaven or joins the ancestral spirits and the spirits of place. All spirits disintegrate after a time, crumbling into the universe, but meanwhile they influence affairs.

As undisputed Ruler of All Under Heaven, I deal with both Heaven and Earth on behalf of mankind. But every man living also copes with spiritual forces according to his strength and gifts.

The Black-haired People engage in divination, make sacrificial offerings, use charms and amulets, communicate with spirits, and especially, propitiate their own particular ancestral spirits, their most likely sources of good luck and protection. The universe is not a friendly place for you, and only a fool denies the need of magic on the journey. So men follow many different cults. Some use geomancers, with their 'wind-and-water' readings, and their science of harmony. And all consult the great and ancient diviners' handbook in considering their actions. I myself do nothing without a favorable trigram—but of course, my diviners read the dragon bones exactly as I wish them to!

So everything has its place and should stay in it. I do not think much of absolutes, good and evil, and all that. I am rational. I am also absolute—the only absolute, in fact.

Confucius said human beings are moral beings, capable of living on a higher plane than animals. I have observed that this holds true for me, but no one else is capable of it. Of course I live on a higher plane than all other humans. Rules, manners, courtesy, loyalty, compassion are not necessary for me. The Empire's entire function, *indeed, Heaven's function, Earth's function, is to do my whim.*

My Grand Counselor, Li Ssu, is the chief advocate of the philosophy called Legalism. He says every man must serve the state and that is necessary because I, the Emperor, must be all-powerful. He has complete powers to enforce this throughout my Empire, a power I gave to him. When he rises too far, thinks too much of himself and his own fortunes, I will take back the power. That is certain to happen one day.

I have been told of a great fish in the southern seas that I must kill—that its evil spirit is separating me from the Eight Immortals. I am on my way to kill it now, with a crossbow that fires arrows one after another so fast they seem one flight.

"What an idiot," said Han Yin, to responsive nods all around the Jade Room. "So touchingly naive, so crazy one almost feels sympathetic to him. And getting crazier every day—hiding in dark palace-to-palace tunnels, coming to meals naked. I almost feel as if I will miss him when he's gone—and if he keeps stuffing himself at every meal, it won't be long!"

Several of the eunuchs stopped eating, briefly.

"You know," said Han Yin, "it wasn't long after the 'Great Unification' of the Empire and his ascent to emperor-hood that he began to be obsessed with immortality. It couldn't have been more than two years. He tried to communicate with the Immortals and get them to give him the Elixir of Life. I am certain he expects to join them one day."

* * * * * * * *

(Translator's note: All the bamboo strips were in perfect condition when they were removed with enormous care from the pottery jars in which they were sealed twenty-two hundred years ago. This one especially significant bundle of bamboo strips, unfortunately, accidentally dropped into an acid bath in the laboratory where the bundles were being unrolled. There followed a desperate, heroic effort at retrieval from the bath, during which a lab technician seriously burned her hands. Sadly, much of the bundle was destroyed, leaving only this fragment. I felt that it was important to include it, even incomplete, because as far as we know, it is the only place in which the First Emperor speaks for himself—even the speech in the *Records of the Grand Historian*, in which the soon-to-be emperor decides on his future title, is thought to be a set-piece, created by Ssuma Ch'ien to express the sentiments he thought logical for the occasion. So here we have, brief and tantalizing, what are apparently the words of Ch'in Shih-huang-ti himself, speaking to us out of the darkness and dust of twenty-two hundred years. Of course, one must assume that devious, old Han Yin is telling the truth!)

The Emperor and the Immortals
Meng Hao-Jan's Tale

Tonight, feeling the desire for a preamble, Han Yin, our highly-regarded leader, said, "Most of us here have at least some education. That education, plus our talents for plotting, spying, undercutting and all-around treachery, are what have led us to the august positions we hold in the 'Empire of the Eunuchs.'

"Not that it is *officially* our empire, of course. But we are getting closer. I am sure we all hope for a future in which eunuchs are running the imperium, especially our brilliant Chief Eunuch, Chao Kao, who talks openly of a time when his hand will hold the whip and he will drive the empire, instead of managing the First Emperor's brigade of chariots. But as each dismal day brings more executions throughout the empire, it is harder than ever to imagine a day in which we are on top.

"There is no real reason to think Chao Kao will be better than First Emperor, or Li Ssu, who runs everything the Emperor doesn't. Indeed, Chao Kao may be even more poisonous than our present leaders. He is gifted in that direction..."

"For heaven's sakes, get to some sort of point," Juan Chi said wearily, "if there is one, which I doubt. Or pass the jade *pi*-disk speaker's scepter TO SOMEONE ELSE!"

"All right, all right!!" said Han Yin, with equal vehemence. "Just setting a scene! I was about to say that this august group—all but you, Juan Chi, god knows where *you* came from, pal—consists of some Confucians and some Taoists. We have our differences, but we also all believe a little in just about everything.

"We agree that the Emperor started going crazy early, probably at some time after Ching K'o's attempt on his life when he was still King. It didn't happen overnight. But since he became Emperor, he grew crazier and tried to repave the Way with his own wishes. First and foremost, he wishes not to die. Ridiculous, of course.

"He even sent his dear, oldest son, Prince Fu-su, north to command the Wall under General Meng T'ien, and why? Not because he is an able administrator, or because the Prince strongly protested boiling or decapitating all those scholars.

"I think it is because the Prince's keen, youthful face makes the First Emperor feel like an old prune starting to fall in. That's not good if you're a dreadful coward and what you're afraid of most is the exact thing happening to you..."

Sensing he's had his time setting the scene, Han Yin ended by saying, "Meng Hao-jan, tell us something we do not know," and passed the speaker's scepter to the Principal Eunuch Trainer and Director of Eunuch Promotions.

* * * * * * * *

Without further ado, Meng Hao-jan began his tale.

The First Emperor woke up one night and through blurry eyes, noticed that the lamps were smoking in their sconces and casting strange shadows on the wall—elephant-eating snakes, monster whales, demons, horrid ghosts. Disembodied heads reminded him of the scholars' heads he had enjoyed kicking around a royal courtyard with the imperial guard a month or two ago.

I am completely alone, he said to himself, self-pity rising from his toes through his entire body. And when it is my time to die, I will be even more alone.

Hearing his voice, the fifty guards outside his bedchamber

stirred as if a breeze had come down the corridor; but nobody dared go in to him—it was as much as one's life was worth to intrude on the presumably sleeping emperor!

Nobody looks at me, ever, he thought, not even my women when they are servicing me! Actually, especially not them. Only that one time when I gathered three of my officers and we dressed in monk's robes and went out into my city. A beggar came up to me, looked up, and ran away screaming! I would have spared him, but the officers were afraid that he might tell people who he had seen—they cut him down before he had run fifty feet. And then those brigands, those assassins came...!

Unable to finish the thought, he stared across the room. He could see the piles of daily documents for review next day—the unromantic business of managing an empire, such headaches they caused him! You have no idea what I suffer on your behalf, my people, he thought. No idea. Then he climbed back into the royal bed and went to sleep until very bad dreams woke him up again.

"Is this going anywhere, Meng Hao-jan? I find it boring so far," said Juan Chi, grumpy as always. Several other storytellers nodded in agreement.

"Well then," said Meng Hao-jan. "Here's a fairy tale for you."

* * * * * * * *

Once there lived an emperor, a reasonable man by his own account. It was reasonable, said the emperor, that being emperor he should be able to do whatever he wanted to do.

This emperor, who is of course completely fictional, was fortunate beyond the dreams of men; the fact is that he owned all the things of this world, and the world as well. He had conquered the Seven Ancient States "as a silkworm devours the mulberry leaf."

He had been a dutiful son, despite cynics' persistent whispered questions about both his paternity and his maternity.

He always gave proper reverence to Heaven and Earth, the basis of life, and carefully observed the ancestral precepts, recognizing the latter as the basis of order. He also presided over sacrifices made daily to seven generations of ancestors, whether or not they were his by blood.

This emperor had a red dog as big as a cow. The bureaucrats were terrified of it because it had a nose that could smell and report bad officials to the emperor. He declared this dog a Minister of the Third Rank.

The long, one-way journey to the Yellow Spring was what the emperor feared most. He was not frightened of war, because in war, other men did the dying. Nor was he concerned about the mass deaths of the conscripts, who were carrying out the public works projects that were on a scale attempted by no one since the Yellow Emperor, if then. But, as he was someone who really did not believe in life after death, thoughts of ceasing altogether unnerved him.

Imagine then how exciting it was when he arrived on his first imperial progress in the ancient kingdoms to the north and east—his latest conquests—and found a widespread belief in sympathetic magic incorporated into the Tao. The fundamental purpose of this magic was to placate evil spirits and invoke benevolent spirits; for example, drops of sweat, shed by a sorcerer dancing, were said to induce rain. I know, I know, it's silly, but the emperor was fascinated.

"Bring me the most famous magicians, technicians and adepts of these kingdoms," the emperor told his military leaders.

He did not wish to appear gullible, but he had heard rumors of a certain elixir made from herbs that would prevent both the sky-soul and the earth-soul from leaving the body and returning to their respective homes. He was eager to know the magicians from the ancient kingdoms who boasted of alchemy among their many skills.

As soon as it was known that that was what the emperor wished to hear, it turned out *all* the magicians were dedicated alchemists, and had in fact spent their entire lives studying *just such herbs* as the very ones the emperor was interested in. What a surprise!

This emperor was a man of limited imagination. How could a man who achieved so much possibly have a limited imagination? I will tell you how. He was a one-thing-at-a-time thinker. Ever since his boyhood, much of it spent as a boy-king restless under the thumb of a regent, the ancestors constantly whispered their one desire into his ear: *restore the ancient empire.*

He thought of little else during the decades it took to achieve the task the ancestors set him. That accomplished, the next need was to revise the social order, make powerless vassals of the old feudal lords, and thereby create a proper balance in the empire so it would last. He approached this work too with almost fanatical intensity.

But making an empire work was not as much fun as creating an empire. So, to relax from the daily drudgery of empire management, he tried actual thinking. His first, and worst, thought: having created All Under Heaven, he was going to have to leave it to others. The devil with that, he whispered to himself in the imperial bed, where only the concubines, who are never believed about any silly thing they say, could hear him muttering.

What luck to find this new possibility of living forever! In response to the emperor's wishes, both spoken and unspoken, plots and designs began to be spun, new enterprises hatched.

Another reason the emperor was afraid of dying was that there had already been three nearly successful attempts to kill him. Desperate to see if the people were behind him, the emperor, disguised as a peasant, went outside the palace at Lanchih with a mere four armed guards, also disguised as peasants. A group of brigands, who did not recognize the emperor but were interested in any money he and his guards might be carrying, tried to kill them. Of course they had no chance against the imperial guardsmen and were killed. In a panic, the emperor ordered a general search of the entire countryside for more brigands, but found none. A few peasant farmers were executed and several towns were exterminated down to the last cat.

These attempts on his life increased the emperor's sense of his human frailty. The emperor gathered hundreds of magicians and attached them to his court, which already had an army of soothsayers, scholars, et cetera. In the end, these charlatans actually outnumbered everyone else at the court except for the eunuch servants and the imperial guard. A swarm of locusts, carousing all night.

During his next imperial progress, the emperor journeyed along the shores of the Eastern Sea, offering sacrifices to the sacred mountains and rivers and the major gods and goddesses of the places he visited. From the terrace at Lanyeh, the emperor looked across the ocean for the first time, wondering what lay beyond. A magician told him that somewhere beyond the horizon lay three islands; on one of these islands, spirits drank from a wine-fountain made of jade, rendering themselves immortal. The emperor sighed a great sigh and decided that it was reasonable that he should live forever. It's well worth the effort, because my people need me, he thought.

He climbed—was carried up, actually—the sacred mountains of T'aishan to commune with spirits who lived there. He also erected a tall, stone boundary-pillar filled with his exploits. On his way down Mount T'ai, he was caught in a storm and took shelter under a tree. The friendly, thick-branched tree was named a Minister of the Fifth Rank on the spot.

On his way back to the capital at Hsienyang, he stopped at Pangcheng, fasted for a few hours, purified himself ritually, and sacrificed at a shrine. He had hoped to recover a famous bronze tripod of the ancient Chou Empire that had been lost in the nearby River Ssu. But a thousand divers found nothing, if you don't count watery graves.

Throughout his reign, he made a number of these journeys to every part of the empire, even the most intractable and barbarous far to the south; and everywhere he erected pillars praising his own accomplishments. He did not need others to do it for him! Not that he lacked for sycophants—what is a court for, what are concubines for, and what are eunuchs for, for that matter? But I digress.

The emperor returned to Hsienyang, to which thousands of noble families were already being transported from every quarter of the compass. These families were forced to say farewell to their feudal revenues and live on the emperor's dole—which was substantial—in hundreds of palaces being constructed day and night by a conscript labor force of previously unimaginable dimensions. The racket was unbearable!

I should mention there are three types of immortals: celestial immortals, corpse-free immortals, and earthly immortals. The emperor would have settled for any one of these forms, as long as he could stay in control of the empire.

A group of Taoist priests, led by a rascal named Hsu Fu, presented a memorandum to the emperor. Not bothering to name the source of their information, they grew more specific about the three islands: each was a fairy island, and they were named P'englai, Fangchang and Yingchou. On these islands, a number of immortals lived, constantly replenished by the aforementioned jade fountain. The proposition Hsu Fu put forward was that if the emperor would equip a fleet, Hsu Fu would sail for the islands and return with the secret of immortality.

He was truthful about returning—he did come back, saying that he had met with an immortal who told him that the emperor's gifts were much too cheap. Hsu Fu asked him what he desired, which turned out to be three thousand handsome youths and beautiful maidens and many more precious gifts than the first fleet carried. Hsu Fu also reported that magical herbs were to be found on P'englai, but that enormous, angry whales harassed and drove off his boats. He said that if he could return with archers armed with repeating crossbows, the whales could be killed, thus removing that obstacle. He was granted these requests as well.

Soon the second, much larger, expedition sailed away with a great ringing of gongs and sounding of bells. Red flags and cheering peasants were everywhere. Its hundred ships dipped down under the horizon—and were never seen again. Rumors persist that they did make landfall eventually, and founded a kingdom; no one really knows.

Discouraged but not defeated, the emperor turned next to a man known to us only as Scholar Lu from the Ch'in province of Yen. This man went in a different direction; he journeyed to the western mountains to search for a Taoist adept known as Kao Hsienmai, who he said had become a *ti hsien*, an earthly immortal whose body was imperishable. Kao, explained Scholar Lu, had swallowed magic blossoms and was now happily living forever, in a tomb. Unfortunately, Scholar Lu never found Kao—too well hidden, I expect. He returned to the court and reported that the search for immortals and magic herbs and fungi had come to nothing. He also advised the emperor to change his sleeping quarters secretly every night in order to avoid evil spirits.

Scholar Lu said, "For subjects to know their sovereign's whereabouts detracts from his divinity. A pure being cannot be wet by water or burned by fire. He rides on clouds and endures as long as heaven and earth. If Your Majesty will not let his whereabouts be known, we shall be able to obtain the herb of immortality."

"I wish to be a pure being," replied the emperor. He ordered Hsienyang's two hundred and eighty or more imperial palaces and pavilions to be connected by causeways and covered-walkways, and furnished with hangings, bells, drums and concubines. Only his chief ministers knew where he slept, and it would have been death for them if they were to reveal his sleeping place.

As the emperor became obsessed with immortality, he left

more and more of the day-to-day management of the empire to his chief ministers, led by Li Ssu, now the Grand Counselor— oh, sorry, someone like Li Ssu, this is a fairy tale, of course. In any case, the ministers ruled even more harshly than their emperor. Working on his immortality, the emperor ordered the court scholars to write poems about immortals and pure beings; these were set to music and played wherever he went.

One year, a shooting star fell to earth and changed to a stone. On it, someone inscribed: "After the Emperor's death, the land will be divided." No one admitted to creating the inscription, so all the unfortunates who lived in the vicinity of the stone were executed and the stone was ground to dust.

One autumn, an envoy from the emperor, traveling east of Hsienyang, was stopped at Huayin by a man with a jade disk who said, "Please give this for me to the Lord of Haochi." He added, "This year the Primal Dragon will die." When the envoy asked him what he meant, the man vanished. The envoy presented the disk to the emperor and told him what happened. After some time, the emperor said, "These mountain spirits can only see a year ahead." As he rose to leave the council chamber, he turned to the court and said, "The Primal Dragon means first among men."

The Imperial Treasurer was ordered to examine the jade. The Treasurer discovered it was the very same disk that had been dropped in the waters of the Yangtze when the emperor attempted to cross it years before. Everyone was amazed.

Common sense suggested these strange occurrences were omens of disasters to come, but that was not how the emperor's huge oracular staff interpreted them. After a few days in council, they returned to the emperor and with straight faces told him that the finding of the jade disk was extremely favorable; that therefore, the mountain spirit's comments should be ignored.

They added that this was an opportune time for another massive removal of the hereditary families from their feudal estates, whose revenues were the true source of their remaining power. Accordingly, thirty thousand more families of the old aristocracy of Chou Empire were removed from their castles and palaces, and brought to Hsienyang to live with others under the royal thumb—comfortably, to be sure, but also utterly dependent on him.

The other good auspice was that the moment was well suited to yet another royal progress through the empire, this time to the far south. Accordingly, all was made ready and eventually the emperor set forth.

"And that, my brothers, is as far as I can trace the fairy tale of the Emperor and the Immortals."

"Wait a minute, Meng Hao-jan!" shouted someone over the general babble of outrage in the Jade Room. "That is no kind of a story at all—you have to have an ending!"

"Must I? Well then, I will finish it myself. I will tell you what sort of outcome I would wish for the kind of man who just three years ago murdered over a hundred of our dear comrades. And for what? All because he thought that one of them might have warned Li Ssu, that he, the Emperor, was becoming jealous of the size of Li Ssu's retinue.

"When the Emperor went to Li Ssu's principal palace, he discovered the latter's retinue had been cut way down. Returning to his own palace, the Emperor said, 'Someone has been telling tales.' He killed the lot of them, strangled his closest companions, just to warn us not to talk about his business.

"I call that unkind—even if they were merely his servants! Just as we are. So here is what I think happened to the emperor in the fairy tale."

* * * * * * * *

When the emperor woke up, sweating and swearing, his head still pounding, a cock was crowing. The light in the east was just beginning to compete with the ever-burning lamps in the Temple of the Ancestors.

He sat on the edge of his high bed for a while, swinging his feet as he had done on the banks of the sleepy Wei River when he was a boy. The headache had not gone away. He pressed his thumbs deeply into his eye sockets to try to squeeze the pain out, but it only became worse. His mouth was dry and his arms and legs were aching.

"I'm sick!" he shouted. "Damn it, I'm sick! Get my physicians in here!"

Everything was perfectly still. Even the cock was silent now.

Where was his dresser? Where the hell were his slippers?

He dropped down off the high bed, nearly falling to the floor.

"You people will pay for this!" he shouted, heading for the massive doors. He swung them open. There, standing like statues, so still they might indeed have *been* statues, were his Inner Guard, his Grand Counselor, his Chief Eunuch, his Principal Wife, countless courtiers and beyond them—rank on rank of soldiers, an army of defenders, bronze weapons gleaming. As far as he could see, and it seemed as if he could see farther than he ever before, the army stretched out. Every last man had his back to him, completely ignoring him. Unheard-of! Unforgivable!

No sound or movement. The silence was terrifying. He looked back into the royal bedchamber. It had grown larger somehow. Silver rivers were flowing in the floor—the great rivers of Ch'in. Rising a foot or more above the swift rivers, the marble floor was formed in the shape of a huge map of the empire—his Empire.

This was his burial chamber! And the figures surrounding the chamber were not living humans, they were painted statues.

All around the edges of the empire, dead, naked concubines lay head-to-foot in open invitation, their eyes staring. Their bare feet and heads were touching. Strung together like bait fish on a ring, he thought.

He stepped across a small, marble bridge that had just risen over the nearest of the rivers and crossed into his new Empire.

As he did so, his bed began to change: its color, formerly the black of the state of Ch'in, gradually turned to gold; the shape changed, too. There was a huge figure of a swimming dragon and on the dragon's back was a golden box, highly carved with imperial symbols and verses. He recognized it all; it was his catafalque, meant to carry him into the world of the dead.

He was drawn toward it; as he stepped forward, the lid of the box rose slowly. He stepped onto one of the dragon's front legs and heaved himself inside the box, which was quite comfortable with linens and pillows. He composed himself carefully.

As the lid came down and darkness embraced him, he thought, why, this is it—I *did* achieve immortality, after all. Of a sort. Which means there will be more than enough time to think about that, lying here in the dark. Already his folded hands were cooling against his chest.

The Unluckiest Man
Meng Hao-Jan's Tale

The eunuchs were restless tonight. Noting the direction of the jade *pi*-disk speaker's scepter, there was a little wave of discontent as fans snapped, cups were overturned, and so forth. But no one said anything much aloud about the story that appeared to be in the cards tonight—one they'd all heard before—until the most suspicious among us spoke.

"Oh, no, Meng Hao-jan!" Tu Mu, the First Emperor's Charioteer, said. "You aren't going to tell *that* old story, are you?"

"I don't know why not," huffed the Principal Eunuch Trainer and Director of Eunuch Promotions. "It may be old to us, but if someone in the future hasn't heard it, it will be brand new. And you must admit it's funny. You *must* have laughed the first time you heard it?"

A disrespectful silence ensued. Mistaking silence for surrender, Meng Hao-jan went on.

"You'll remember that early in our First Emperor's reign, I think it was his third year..."

"Fourth," muttered Chia Tao.

"Third or fourth year. There was some minor trouble with our northern bad neighbors, the Hsiung-nu..."

"Some neighbors!"

"Will you let me tell it?!"

"Anyway, they rode down and wiped out a few blackhair villages. Or maybe it was half the northern frontier and all of the northwestern frontier, right out to the mountains of the moon, that got wiped out together with a few million blackhairs. How would I know?"

Ordinarily, no one here in Hsienyang, certainly not the First Emperor, would be serious about a few hundred or even million blackhairs flayed, skinned or vice versa. But the recent incursion of the barbarous Hsiung-nu into his domain reminded him of the *big project* he hadn't yet put in motion, owing to preoccupations with empire-wide canal network, extended post roads, new currency, everlasting Epang Palace and tomb building, relocation of the feudal lords, and so on and so forth.

I mean *The* Wall, of course. The six-thousand-mile wall. The wall that is a chariot wide and running from the eastern ocean across the western desert to the impassable mountains. The one that would include rebuilt remnants of the ancient kingdom walls to become one HUGE wall, that would keep the Hsiung-nu out of the Empire forever.

Not that a wall could stop them by itself.

The Emperor planned to garrison the forts built into it every thousand *li* or so, along the way. If any big attacks started, the soldiers could get word of the attack to reinforcements in a hurry. It didn't ever work very well, of course, because the Hsiung-nu immediately did the obvious: any time they wanted to cross the Wall, they'd start by killing everyone in the three or four garrisons who might have got wind of the crossing. And I do mean *got wind of*—a large gathering of Hsiung-nu in any one place creates a truly terrible smell.

That was the plan for the Wall. The Emperor set it going right away. He put his most famous general, Meng T'ien, in charge. He then sent his oldest son, Fu-su, the Crown Prince, into exile in Meng T'ien's service—his punishment for writing a memo protesting the Emperor's burning of the sacred books.

Once the general arrived and his surveyors had mapped the route of the wall—what a job that must have been, all those mountains, valleys, rivers, deserts—Li Ssu sent recruiters to all prefectures to tear 500,000 men from the 500,000 bosoms of their wives, sweethearts, mothers and others, and marched them north to extreme cold, bad rations, hard labor, no healers, diseases of all kinds. Most were dead by the end of the project, anyway, dead and buried in the wall—world's longest cemetery, it's been called. But if you are thinking about costs, in the Ch'in Empire, it is cheaper to conscript 100,000 peasants than it is to save the lives of the workers you have by treating them decently and giving them proper food, shelter and medicines.

That's what our First Emperor thinks.

From first to last, the big worry was the dragons sleeping in the northern earth (all but a few who live in the sky, the water or fire).

General Meng had many Taoist sorcerers and other filthy shamans to tell him how to build the wall in a way that wouldn't cut through the bones of some dozing firebreather and bring ruin on the Empire. But the sorcerers, even the best of them were mere men, not gods or immortals. They seldom got it right. For example, there is a place where the wall bows out for miles. The story is that a dragon stopped to rest there and fell asleep with his shoulder against it, pushing it into a huge curve.

Anyway, the Emperor was sure some disastrous misstep would happen as the builders raced across the top of our world, pounding earth into a wall shape. He worried night and day about this, neglecting his ceremonial duties. Then he had a great, a supreme First Emperor type of idea. Actually, I'll bet the idea wasn't his, except in the sense that everything in the Empire is his, including ideas. I suspect it bubbled up through Li Ssu in one way or another, like most ideas.

Off went an edict by post-horse from the palace up the northern fast road to General Meng. After the normal ceremonial bric-a-brac, it boiled down to this: Meng, you are to sacrifice ten thousand men, one every *li*, to propitiate the sleeping dragons.

Snacks, you might call them.

General Meng is tough. I don't think many things give him qualms. He's killed fleets of men and sent hordes of others to their deaths. Building the Wall was causing a lot of deaths, and he agreed—it was necessary. But this directive did not sit well with him. Killing some poor bastard via beheading every *li* of the way across our immense northern frontier, just for ceremony—it was too much.

There had to be a way to comply that didn't require mass murder. And, because Meng is smart, he thought of one. First, he sent riders to all the hundreds of labor camps along the route of the wall with instructions to find, without saying why, a man with a very particular name.

From a camp far west of General Meng's headquarters came word of success. They found the man, brought him back and presented him to the general. It would be foolish to think this man, a peasant from Shu, far to the south, expected anything good to come of his selection. That's the lesson we've all had drummed into us all our lives: power never means you well, so just try to keep it from noticing you. Hunker down. Too late for this man, though, so when the poor peasant stood in front of General Meng in his huge tent, his knees were knocking together audibly.

How astonishing! The general rose to his feet, took the poor, blubbering man by the hand and led him to a seat in a fur-lined chair to his left. His mouth was open almost to the floor!

Meng and his right-hand companion, the Crown Prince, fed the peasant excellent food and lots of it, though not so much as to make him retch at the change from his daily ration of a few spoons of rice and a bone to gnaw on. I doubt he was any less frightened, but he began to relax as the wine and the fire warmed him.

After the supper, General Meng said, "Now, sir, I am told that your name is Mr. Ten Thousand. A fortunate name! You have the honor to serve the Empire in a way that will save thousands of lives."

Gods! thought Mr. Ten Thousand. It's worse than I imagined! He tried to leap to his feet and run away, but his feet, drugged with wine like the rest of him, were not taking messages.

General Meng explained: "I have received a command from the Emperor that in order to keep the dragons friendly and at peace, we are to sacrifice and bury one man every *li* of our journey to the place where the wall will end. That journey is ten thousand *li*.

"I esteem and praise the Emperor in all things, but in this case, I felt the command was wasteful on three counts: one, it is somewhat cruel; two, the dragons are asleep and if we wake one by cutting across his spine, all hell will break loose, anyway, sacrifice or no sacrifice; and three, I will not *waste* ten thousand men, no matter what the Emperor wants.

"So this is where you come in, Mr. Ten Thousand."

There is no way to convey the impact of these words on Mr. Ten Thousand, even in his drugged state. I'm for it, he thought, looking up through the general's tent hole toward the distant moon. I'll never see another dawn. That was correct.

To comply with the Emperor's edict, Mr. Ten Thousand was killed that night, but mercifully, tenderly. Then the soldiers cut his body into small pieces. Exceedingly small pieces. So that today, there is not a single *li* of the entire journey along the wall in which a piece of Mr. Ten Thousand is not buried, guarding us all. And not one dragon ever woke up. That we know about.

* * * * * * * *

From time to time, I stopped writing to look around at the faces of my fellow eunuchs to see how they were receiving this hairy camel of a story. Most were impassive and some were asleep, but Lo Yin, the First Emperor's Chief Dresser, had been looking more upset by the minute. Now Lo Yin's face screwed up tightly and then opened like a huge, bright orange peony in the spring.

"And that's all the Great Wall means to you, Meng Hao-jan?" Lo Yin shrieked. "Some sort of stupid joke?"

"I am from a small village in the far south," Lo Yin said, "deep in the hottest regions of Shu. Although I was traded north years ago, I have tried to keep in touch with my adopted family via the imperial couriers.

"Just last year, a thousand soldiers swept through my homeland and snatched up all the men. They brought them north, nearly naked, and drove them onto the Wall to ram the earth into place. Since then I have not heard from one member of my family. I believe that when winter came in the north, my father, my uncles, and my brothers all froze to death. And I am sure the remnant of my family not taken north starved to death with no males left to work in the rice paddies. Take away the farmers, don't expect a harvest.

"So, Meng Hao-jan, my family *is* that wall. I pray to it—what else should I pray to? And I do not like your joke!"

Drawing himself up to his full height seated, which was about a foot higher on the wall than Lo Yin, Meng Hao-jan said, "Well, if I felt like apologizing I certainly would do so, Lo Yin, but I see no reason to apologize to an ignorant, southern barbarian like yourself."

At this point, with my two companions staring angrily at each other, Han Yin took over as he generally does.

"Brothers, let us be reasonable," he said, "we are a family, after all, and surely reasonable eunuchs can differ without swordplay ensuing."

"Besides," he said to Meng Hao-jan, "you know that in a quarrel of arms between you and Lo Yin, he would certainly lose. Since we already know the outcome, why make a trial of it?"

His fan, which had been waggling in a monitory manner, disappeared into his black robe. Deep breaths around the room.

"But I am curious," said Han Yin, "if we leave aside joke-telling and tales of personal loss ascribed to the Great Wall, what do we, who haven't seen it, really know about it, beyond the fact that it is a slammed gate in the hungry faces of our northern enemies, the covetous, barbarous Hsiung-nu?"

"But I have seen the Wall," said Wang Ts'ao, the Major Domo of the Royal Palace, "I spent a winter there serving the Crown Prince. The Emperor, alternating between rage at his eldest son and fatherly concern for his well-being—he loved him best among all his offspring—sent me to look after him, to make sure he dressed properly, ate well and so forth. So while looking after the Prince, I saw a great deal of the Great Wall.

"They say along the wall that some workers escaped into the western mountains and live there to this day," continued Wang Ts'ao.

"I can well believe that! There has been so much superstitious nonsense told about that wall. Peasants believe the Emperor has been building it personally with a Magic Whip that can stop the Yellow River from flowing, a Magic Spade that can dig a *li* of earth at a time, Magic Boots that can step over clouds and a Magic Horse that can fly over mountains. They say the Great Wall goes on forever, round and round the Empire, and the First Emperor will never stop building it to keep our enemies out. It's all nonsense, but the Wall is not. It is real.

"When I served the Crown Prince, we hunted north of the Wall sometimes, riding behind Meng T'ien and the Crown Prince on their beautiful, black, western pure-bred horses; the river water was clear and drinkable, but we had to break the ice most mornings; we had to wear furs in the mornings, too, even when it was summer; in winter we made tea out of doors from melted snow.

"Fish and game are abundant. There is a desert to the west in which nothing lives, certainly not the poor peasants who had to work on the Wall there. The desert is blazing hot, so hot clothing catches fire sometimes and people burn to death.

"Weather conditions are terrible all along the wall, changing almost *li* by *li*. It was almost impossible to reach some workers' camps with food. Convoys constantly headed north, but not enough of them reached the workers with their loads of grain. Sandstorms blinded eyes in the summer, gales brought frozen snow in the winter.

"The watchtowers along the Wall were thirty feet high. Sentries could give alarm by lighting signal fires, by means of trumpets and gongs. The larger garrison towers could hold up to two hundred men with armor and weapons. It was said in the army that when you were sent north to a garrison, it was for life. Many wrote poems of sorrow at the loss of all contact with their friends and families.

"I believe the Great Wall is the most important thing the Emperor has done for the black-haired people, that it has been worth the lives it cost. Now the watchtowers are garrisoned, the Wall has brought our northern enemies nearly to a standstill, freeing the bulk of the Ch'in armies to go to the south, even to the southern ocean, and make us a truly unified empire.

"That is what the Tiger has done, there is no disputing it.

"I have been told that at the furthest end of the Wall, where the western mountains begin to cut the sky with their ragged peaks, the Emperor has erected a stele that says the Great Wall is "the most warlike barrier in the world." It took twelve years, and at least a million lives. And it was worth it.

"I believe the Great Wall will keep this dynasty safe and in its central place between Heaven and Earth for thousands of years," Wang Ts'ao concluded.

Around the room, I saw heads nodding in agreement. Meng Hao-jan was nodding with the rest.

The Homecoming
Ssu-Ma Ch'ien's Tale

When I decided to accept my castration and live so I could finish my *Records of the Grand Historian*, instead of choosing the honorable death of a suicide, I knew the wound would hurt. I was desperately afraid of it.

I also guessed I would not have a comfortable day for the rest of my life—which wasn't likely to be long, either, because few of us "crows," as the outside world calls us, have normal lifespans. I knew, too, that I would be immured for life here in the Emperor's abode, cut off from friends, family and clan.

And the physical pain *was* severe—although I barely remember the cut now, drugged and drunk as I was. It hurt in a thudding sort of way, as if a pine tree had fallen on me. Afterwards, of course, it hurt more, and has gone on hurting, especially in damp weather and moments of misery. That pain has subsided, though, as did the pain of lost friends once I began to make friends among the palace eunuchs. But the loss of my family, that is another matter. That pain has never ceased to trouble and sadden me. Tears that flow easily do not wash it away. It is the hopelessness of being cut off from one's family. At times I feel I might better have died. At times I think finishing the *Records* was not worth it.

I have had such feelings for several years.

But my life has not been all darkness. I became friends with the storytellers over time; indeed, they were a family to me, especially Chia Tao, the Major Domo of the Concubine Residences, the funniest man among us, who has been like a brother to me. I found conversation with him endlessly delightful, with sudden twists and turns and leaps like a small, agile goldfish; he was full of sunlight for a man with such a dreadful job. Cheerfulness is a precious commodity among us eunuchs. Also, his humor was wicked and I do love a bit of scurrilous gossip! After many visits back and forth—my residence and his were nearby—he invited me to join his mess and take meals with him on a regular basis.

"Ssu-ma Ch'ien, what is it with you today? You look sadder than a mule in a stone quarry," Chia Tao said, his eyes unusually serious.

I took my time answering. Finally I said, "Chia Tao, I have had no contact with anyone in my family since the day they cut my "Precious" off. You would think the family bonds would have frayed and broken after all this time, but they have tightened around me like wet leather strings when they dry. I especially miss my father, who turned his back on me even before I made my choice. My friend, I feel much pain!"

I thought he might have some joke for me, but instead he asked if I would like to be in touch with them. Would I?! I jumped to my feet.

"Relax! It's time for you to learn a secret not many know about among all the thousands of eunuchs in the palace," he said. "I want you to meet me back right here, in the mess, just when you hear the drums for the first watch."

This was at the morning meal. I do not remember how I passed the day. I was so excited.

At the first watch, we met again. He took me along a circuitous path, down alleyways between the scores of larger houses and smaller huts that seemed to grow against the palace walls. Lanterns were lit here and there, but for the most part it was dark, with a few dogs barking.

After an hour of confusing twists and turns, we reached the

looming darkness of the high outer wall that separated us from the world; against it huddled a smaller shape, coal-black in the starless night.

We found our way to a low, unlit doorway and Chia Tao pulled it back. The door creaked so loudly I thought people must hear, but everything was quiet.

Once my eyes got used to the darkness inside, I saw hundreds of baskets of charcoal, on the floor, on tables, stacked up on shelves—enough to light the cooking fires and hearths of the Concubine Residences, I thought.

Chia Tao said, "Exactly. This is one day's supply of charcoal for Their Royal Pains. In the morning, it will be taken by servants everywhere it is needed; in early evening, the baskets will be brought back here, empty, and immediately refilled."

"Refilled from where," I asked, "there's no gate near here I know of."

"I'll show you," he said, and guided me to the back of the storehouse. We went through another creaking door, walked down a passageway and came to a second door. He lifted a bar and swung it open—same sort of creak—and then we stepped into a room that as far as I could tell was identical to the one we had just been in.

"But wait a minute—the wall—we must have come through it!" I exclaimed.

"Exactly!"

"Well then, that means—we're outside the palace!"

"I always said that you were a smart man, for a eunuch."

I stood still for a moment. This door here meant we could come and go from the palaces as we pleased! Of course, we would run a huge risk...

"Every one of our brothers knows of this door. Those of us with family or friends outside often make use of this passage," said Chia Tao.

"What's more, Chao Kao, the Chief Eunuch, winks at it, for those who are on his good side. Of course, if Li Ssu knew

there was a rathole like this, that would be another matter—
our heads and limbs would be traveling north, east, south
and west! But he doesn't know. As far as we know.

"It doesn't do to linger here. I think that's about enough for
tonight—we ought to go back. As we go, I want you to find some
way, you being a clever fellow, Ssu-ma Ch'ien, to memorize your
route to the charcoal houses. Write nothing down.

"By the way, as you probably guessed, a gang of charcoal-
sellers come to the outside storehouse each day with their baskets
of charcoal and leave them in this room. Nine eunuchs bring
the full baskets inside the palace and bring out the empties. The
whole thing is repeated next day."

I did as he suggested, counting steps to each left turn or
right turn, taking note of every dim landmark I would be able to
remember. It's not so hard if you're a trained observer.

Back at the mess, Chia Tao explained to me that the charcoal
houses were not just a means of coming and going from the
palace in secret; they also functioned as a mail drop, in which
written messages could be rolled up and passed from one side
to the other, and delivered—"We pay a lot for that service, too,"
said Chia Tao—"but I don't know what we would do without
it. You cannot spend your whole life locked inside high walls of
rammed earth and stone. It would make you even crazier than
we are!"

I said a very warm and grateful good night to Chia Tao, actually
embracing him, something that was intensely embarrassing for
him. I resolved to do it at every opportunity.

That night I decided to try to contact my family as soon as
possible. Chia Tao would tell me how to sign up for the postal
service, I knew. I would write to someone. But who? Perhaps my
younger brother, Han?

I went to sleep a different man than when I had risen that
morning. A man with hope.

* * * * * * * *

Having arranged for the delivery of messages via the charcoal houses with the help of Chia Tao, I took up my brush and unfolded and pinned down a panel of silk on my writing desk late one afternoon, when my duties concerning the royal wives' underthings were completed for the day.

It was a clear, cool day and the late fall sun was slanting in through crossing clouds. I sat for some time licking my brush to a fine point and wondering what I ought to say to my brother, with whom I had not seen or spoken for so many years. Here is my much-blotted letter.

Dear Brother,

I am still alive. And I have finished the Records. The days pass. I do useful, though boring, work here in the palace, and am not without companions.

Our family turned its back on me seven years ago when I chose to become a eunuch so I could finish my work. I understand. If it had been you, brother, perhaps I might have done the same. How can one know? What matters to me is I have never ceased to love you all, brother, mother, sister, my dear wife and my beautiful daughter.

Above all, I continue to reverence our father, whose anger on being deposed as the Grand Historian by the Emperor in my favor I ignored at the time, being young and stupid, but now understand. No one understands better than I do now how powerful is the urge to complete the work your entire life has prepared you for. But you cannot change what has happened, you can only express sorrow, as I do. I beg his forgiveness, and yours, and every member of the Ssu-ma family.

I pray at a family shrine each night. I pray that I will hear from you someday, even see you, before my body enters the earth and my soul goes to heaven.

Your brother, Ssu-ma Ch'ien

I spoiled three silks with tears writing this letter.

The next day, I arranged for the letter to be taken to our family estate some miles to the north of Hsienyang, where I believed my brother and my entire family still resided.

* * * * * * * *

Weeks went by, with no response. One morning, I thought I heard a slight noise at my door. I shrugged on a robe and went to open it. On the threshold, I found a small roll of silk, tied with a scarlet ribbon. I could hear my heart pounding. When I bent down to pick up the letter, it sounded as if someone was beating a stone drum! Stumbling in my haste, I brought it inside to my desk and sat for a long time before opening it.

Dear Brother Ch'ien,

We received your letter and have been talking about what to do ever since—I am very sorry for the delay. The letter is being brought to the Emperor's palace by your elder, teenage grandson—yes, you have not one, but two, grandsons now! This is your sister, Ts'ao.

And I have news that I know will distress you very much indeed. I am very sorry to have to tell you that after you were castrated and disappeared into the imperial palace, our brother Han could not bear to live. A month after you left, he hung himself from a rafter in the major barn. We mourned him two years. I must also tell you that at that time, the family blamed you for his death in addition to your own—for you were dead to us and remained so, a ghost who does not visit even in dreams, these seven years. But we were not taught by our father for nothing, Ssu-ma Ch'ien. Even in the silence of not speaking your name, we understood the importance of your work and the reasons for your choice.

Though we never talked of it, I think that in our ways we honored your choice. And time changes the way one looks at things. I came to feel it was Han's weakness, not your doing, that led him to take his own life. And I am sure that your wife Hsuan has similar, perhaps even stronger, feelings.

We live the lives that are given to us. The seasons came and went, and I would say the family healed in some degree. Until your letter arrived. It had the force of a lightning bolt! We all read it, many times, and many family members could not say your name enough. It was like a healing rain or an auspicious birth. We hope you will continue to write to us and so cross this bridge of silence. Perhaps someday you can even come to the estate if that is ever permitted! Your two grandsons are fine boys and your daughter is a wonderful mother, though your wife Hsuan has aged. Of course so have I!

Your loving sister, Ts'ao

I have no way to tell all the thoughts and feelings that fled through my mind as I read and re-read this letter.

I have had two dreams in my life, to write the records of former times, and to be an honored member of my family. The first was granted to me, but emasculated and imprisoned here in the palace I had given up the second. You know when a dream is denied you, it turns hard and brittle and is like a jade dagger in your soul. Hardness and hate grow around it. Now much of this hate, directed toward the Emperor, the author of my disgrace, ebbed away by the next sunrise. I felt almost whole again!

The question was what to do next. My heart told me to run for the charcoal houses on the next dark night and flee this revolting palace forever. But we blackhairs prize common sense, and common sense told me that course would get me killed and nothing would be served by it.

I decided I would continue to correspond with my sister, and try to find out all I could about the family, including my wife and daughter. Perhaps one day I would see father again, and ask for his blessing. I was not optimistic about that though—she had not mentioned him—and I felt if there was any good news in that quarter, she would have told me. So, I began the first of many letters to my sister, and even as I wrote I was already anxious for a response. My good sister!

* * * * * * * *

Visiting the ancestral home seemed so simple the way you put it, dear sister!

My heart jumped like a shining carp in an imperial pond when I read her encouraging words. But I am cursed with a practical nature; the difficulties came marching at me in rows and ranks like the Ch'in Empire army.

If the difficulties of leaving the Hsin Palace and getting safely past the Epang Palace to the north could be negotiated, and re-negotiated on my return, there were many other obstacles. There was the matter of crossing the covered walkway across the Wei River. That is an imperial road, seldom used by commoners. And if I should get that far, there was still the major south gate into Hsienyang; maybe I could get through that, but maybe I couldn't. However loosely guarded it may be these days, I had no doubt that it was guarded, just as the north gate would be. Something was bound to go wrong!

I puzzled for days, then decided to bring it to the Jade Room and the storytellers. We spent the best part of an evening discussing it, and by the time we were done my wise-headed friends helped me make a plan. It would take daring, but at least it had a chance of success.

May Heaven bless them all.

* * * * * * * *

We waited for that time of month when the Jade Rabbit in the moon has hidden itself in Ch'ang O's bosom—that is, it was very dark.

It was also early autumn, not yet shivering cold but with an edge to the air that made one bring out extra garments. I put away my regular short, black coat and longer, black robe, black shoes and servant's hat, and put on the most ordinary robes in my cabinet. I do not bother with mirrors but was sure I looked very ordinary, though comfortably warm, by the time I was done. Then I slipped out of the Wives' Palace, and moved down through the alleys and byways to the inner charcoal house. I entered and waited for several hours, coughing constantly because of the charcoal-dust, which hung in the air though the baskets were empty.

The door to the world outside the Hsin Palace creaked open. A small group of very nondescript men came in, carrying baskets full of charcoal; they saw me, I am sure, but paid no attention to me, merely hoisting the previous day's empty baskets onto their shoulders and carrying them into the alleyway, where I could hear the heavy snuffle and sneeze of oxen. The last worker in came toward me.

"Grandfather, it is me," he whispered. My elder grandson! "Quickly, climb into one of the baskets."

I did so and he immediately threw a heavy, ill-smelling cloth over me so that I could see nothing. After a few moments, the other men re-entered the charcoal house.

My basket was picked up roughly by two grunting men. One I assumed was my teenage grandson—he was the one who did not curse at the extra weight. Swaying in a way that made me nauseous, the basket was hauled across the floor and through the doorway, not without banging and more cursing. Another walk of twenty feet or so and I was swung first one way, then, much more vigorously, the other way up onto one of the carts, which tipped, creaking. I really must try to eat less. More baskets followed, burying me in a swiftly rising pile.

Beside the cart, near my head, my grandson whispered, "Sir, I will be driving this cart. We will follow the main road at the west side of the Shanglin Gardens north to the covered walkway and use it to cross the Wei. Then our group of oxcarts—there are twenty-one of us—will enter the main gate to Hsienyang. Inside, we will go to the charcoal-sellers district with the others so as not to attract any attention. The rest of the carts will stop there, but we will go on north through the unguarded gateway out the north road to our family estate. That will happen tonight; tomorrow night, we will repeat the process in reverse and bring you back to the palace.

"You must not smother if you can help it, or cough or sneeze, and do not talk either to yourself or to me, for that matter. And *relax*, Honored Grandfather, you will be safe."

None of his charges proved easy, especially not smothering or sneezing, though I must say I did not feel conversational! I will never again warm myself by a brazier's charcoal fire, no matter how cold I get!

It was a rough, slow journey.

The walls of the bridge over the Wei magnified and echoed the great clomping oxen hoofbeats. I was shaking in fear so hard that the basket was rattling when we were challenged at the main gate by the Ch'in soldiers. But their inspection must have been cursory because we were moved on right away. It seemed interminable, all the same. We passed through the north gate as well. At a point when I was really getting desperate to get out, the cart stopped and my grandson began to remove the baskets covering my own. It was a bright dawn. Finally, he snatched off the wretched cloth and said, "Honored Grandfather Ssu-ma Ch'ien!! Here is your home place!"

So beautiful! The last harvest of millet was in; the land stretched out flat and brown and warm on every side as far as I could see! No fetid city air to breathe, nothing to push me down or silence me! I stood up and shouted, loudly as I could—though it was probably a croak after all that charcoal-dust—"HOME! I'M HOME!"

Then, despite the wondrous and welcoming ambience, I had a great fit of coughing, producing yellow phlegm. My grandson gave me a bottle of water to drink, which I drank with more pleasure than any wine I've ever had.

* * * * * * * *

I climbed down from the cart, rearranged my clothing and brushed myself off as best as I could. Next, I stretched my cramped arms, my legs that were almost numb and my very tired back. Then, I climbed up on the cart beside my grandson, who was looking happy and rightly proud of himself. I put my arm around him and gave him a good, hard hug. He took up his ox-goad and persuaded our two oxen to resume their slow but steady pace. Down the road we went.

Little changes in this fertile country with few trees and no hills. It is all about growing food. To me, especially when I think of all the millions of people who are alive because of what we grow, this is the most beautiful place under heaven. I began to hum loudly, until I noticed that my grandson was struggling to keep his hands at his sides and not clap them over his ears.

We were nearly twenty *li* from our family estate, so it was a journey of several hours. Here and there, the landscape yielded up a peasant's home or two. Finally, with the noon sun directly overhead, I caught sight of the family home in the distance, approaching slowly in the distance.

Our compound has belonged to us for five generations, counting my daughter and my grandsons. It is a large but not an elaborate dwelling, rising three storeys, with an outer wall, a large courtyard and garden, an inner wall protecting a much smaller private courtyard, this last surrounded on three sides by three tiers of apartments.

The family shrine to the ancestors is in a room of its own on the first floor; next to it is my father's study, where I hoped he was sitting, prepared for my return. Other rooms on the first floor included a major storage area for foodstuff, a room for dining, common rooms, and the bedroom of my honored father and mother; the rest of us had smaller rooms on the upper two floors.

Even though the 'palace style' in these days of Hsienyang's glory is to paint every wall some distressingly bright color and cover the walls with ornamentation, paintings of dragons and phoenixes, et cetera, the Ssu-ma compound is, I am glad to say, old-fashioned country plain. It is cream and brown and white, with green-tiled roofs and just a few open-mouthed dragons here and there, emptying rainwater into the cisterns buried in the earth. The constant songs of crickets in cages compete with animal sounds from the barns behind the compound night and day. A bell is struck to announce the time; a smaller bell summons the family for important meetings, or festivals, or major meals together.

This is my home; it looks as if it belongs in this land, and it does. As do I.

I cannot describe for you my mixture of feelings as our cart slowly drew toward the entrance to the compound. Besides, I do not want to rain tears all over my bamboo slips and spoil them when recalling the events of my visit. Therefore I will keep my story plain.

About two *li* from the house, the peasants who farmed the Ssu-ma estates and contributed to our livelihood (in addition to our earnings as horologers and historians for the royal court) lined both sides of the road. Many had rakes or hoes and were holding them upright as if they were weapons. Their children stood beside them, as did their wives and sweethearts. I began to recognize faces here and there, including some who had played with me as an infant and told me stories before I reached the age when I was shipped off to court to study with, and play with, the future emperor.

I felt I should wave, but I could not bring myself to do it, perhaps because I could not read their faces. They were impassive and silent as if I was passing through a dream.

Two household servants, eunuchs both, whom I remembered very well, held open the main gate to the outer courtyard. One of them loved me as a child; I was not so sure about the other one, who had been cruel to me once. I looked into their eyes, something we do not do often, and for the first time I thought this was not a dream, this was my home. The one who loved me was smiling, but not with his mouth. My eyes smiled back, in return.

* * * * * * * *

My grandson drove the cart across the large courtyard to the moon door to the family's smaller inner courtyard. There he helped me get down, my bones creaking loudly as the cart. I stopped at the doorway, fearful, but he took me firmly by the elbow and led me into my family home.

A fountain was splashing at the center of the courtyard, and the crickets were singing as always, but otherwise it was silent. I looked up at the balconies of the second and third floors; they were filled with a score or more of my relatives, aunts, uncles, cousins and some I did not know. My first impulse was to wave my arms to them, but they seemed so impassive! Not a sound, not a gesture, of welcome or anything else. They just stared. I looked back for a moment or two, and then I had to look down.

My grandson still had my elbow and was gripping it tightly. Now he led me down the courtyard a little way and we entered the largest common room; like all the other rooms, it was doorless, of course. There is no such thing as privacy in a Ch'in home, great or small. We stepped up a stair and went inside.

My sister was standing there, touching her hair, which had become gray. Otherwise she was just the same, slim and lovely, her eyes shining. She walked toward me and I had just time to note that she still limped from when a cow had kicked her foot when we were small—then she was in my arms. Her shoulders were shaking; mine, too.

We talked—oh, I do not remember all we talked about. After a while she gestured toward a chair and I sat down. She left the common room for a few moments that seemed like forever, and returned with my dear mother. I jumped to my feet and embraced her, then led her to the chair. We did not speak. She sat and I knelt by her and put my head in her lap, as I used to do a long time ago, for her to stroke my hair and sing to me when I was upset.

This was the pattern of the day. By ones and twos and threes, my sister brought in all the people in the world most dear to me. We did not say a great deal; there was not so much to be said, after all. People would come for a while and take my hands, or embrace me, and leave, replaced by others whom I loved. After a while they too would glide away again, some sobbing, others not able to stop smiling.

My sister left the common room one more time. When she returned she brought my daughter, now a mother twice over herself. She and her husband and my younger grandson came and knelt by me as I had knelt by my honored mother. We said much, or rather, I listened to them talk about their dreams and hopes, but I think I will not share that with you, posterity.

While we were still gathered there, I looked up and my lady wife was standing just inside the common room. She was perfectly still, as lovely as I remembered her—I have never had a day of captivity in the palace when I have not desperately missed her touch, her voice, the imprint of her body on mine as we lay together, her shadow in the dark, and I never will—and tears were flowing down her beautiful cheeks, dripping from her chin onto her robes.

Then she raised one hand to her mouth and whirled out of my sight.

I threw my arms around my kneeling daughter and did my best to draw her right into my body. After what was either a long time or no time at all, my sister returned.

She said, "Ssu-ma Ch'ien, it is time for you to see your father."

We walked a little way down through the courtyard and entered his study, just as we had done hundreds of times when we were children. So far from being forbidden then, even when he was working he would always stop and welcome us and talk with us.

Now he sat still, old and doll-like in his chair, though his eyes were as bright and keen as I remembered. We knelt before him. After a very long time, he put one hand on each of us, much as I had done with my own child.

I could feel a kind of a blessing in his thin, white fingers.

My sister had said he had not spoken, other than a necessary word or two, ever since I left; he had become even more silent, if possible, after my brother killed himself. But now he spoke.

He told me he did not lay my brother's death at my door, adding that my brother had been like a stiff tree unable to bend with a wind. He did not add, or choose to add, that the wind was a wind of shame at my disgrace. He paused and then he said what I most wanted to hear: that he honored my decision to live as a eunuch so I could complete the *Records of the Grand Historian* he himself had begun so long ago.

He said, "The work is everything, son. You did right."

Later, we had a great feast in the inner courtyard, with music and much laughter and dancing. It lasted for hours, well into the night, and then it was time to go.

As the oxcart rumbled through the outer courtyard, I looked back up at the second floor to the window of our room. My wife was there, looking out. A nearby candle illuminated her face. As we rolled away, I kept watching her until the window went dark.

The return journey was also tedious and uncomfortable. Arriving at the palace near the end of a long night, in the darkest hour, I washed myself and lay down on my pallet. Sleep healed some of my wounds, at least until morning.

The Judgment of Wu Wei

Stone sits not more still
than Wu Wei, kneeling before his judge.
"Your Worship," he says,

"I kneel before you, guilty.
Do you with me what you will.
I deserve *all* the Five Punishments."

Impressed by Wu Wei's sense
of personal responsibility, the judge
grants the right of further speech.

"But if I might make one small request,"
says Wu Wei, "do not tear the life
from this right hand of mine.

"Whip me, scourge me, stand me
in the market. Write all my crimes
on a halter and hang it on my neck.

"Brand me, if you will.
But, I beg you, sir,
spare this right hand.

"Look how its five fingers gaily
wave—like the five grains, hemp,
millet, rice, wheat, pulse.

"Was it not written
by Hsun Tzu, the ancient one:
'The axe must not enter the forest!'

"Then the five grains will not fail,
the people will surely have
abundant food in every season.

"To me my five fingers seem like
the five elements: water, fire,
wood, metal and earth.

"Think of the catastrophes
that would follow if these five
elements are out of balance.

"Seas would become mountains,
seasons would tumble out of sequence,
even heaven and earth would get mixed!

"Who could wish such a fate?
I beg you, learned sir,
spare this right hand!

"In dreams I wear the five planets,
Venus, Jupiter, Mercury, Mars
and Saturn on the fingers of my hand.

"The stars ride through the black night
looking for Chang Heng,
who named them.

"In the veins of this fine hand
flow all five metals: gold, silver,
copper, lead and iron.

"Majestic sir, only
think of the treasures lost
if this hand were to die?

"These fingers are fast and deadly,
too, as kiss of centipede, scorpion,
spider, toad and the viper that secretes

"the five poisons Chang Tao-ling
mixed to create the Elixir of Life.
Oh, what a disaster that would be!

"Once a necromancer painted
my nails with the five colors:
red for joy, yellow for empire,

"white for mourning, black
for our beloved state of Ch'in
—and the criminal green.

"Thus protected, how could one
fail to thrive? See the paint traces
in the moons of my nails?

"Sir, spare this right hand
and I will sacrifice the five beasts:
ox, goat, pig, dog and fowl!

"With these fingers I have tasted
all the five tastes—salty, bitter,
sour, sweet, fiery...

"With these fingers I have sent
nourishment to the five viscera:
liver, heart, lungs, kidneys

"and spleen, our earthly sources
of love, propriety, righteousness,
wisdom and good faith.

"This energetic, supple hand
has truly served the gods—O my Judge,
please spare this hand!"

The judge can't speak a word.
He sees the waving grains,
tastes the sweet elixir of life.

There can be only one verdict—full
pardon. And when Wu Wei dies
many years later, honored by all,

his right hand is severed and bronzed.
It is said to be venerated by the great
Wu clan unto the present day.

BOOK FOUR
Chaos

A Secret
Ssu-Ma Ch'ien's Tale

"Ssu-ma Ch'ien, I am going to tell you a story no one knows,"
Han Yin said to me one warm, spring afternoon, as we were
sitting alone in his teahouse.

"Well, almost no one.

"Li Ssu knows, of course," he said, "and Chao Kao, the Chief
Eunuch. General Wang Mang. All the storytellers know. The
wives know. Some of the concubines, which means they all
know. A few astrologers—most of the court astrologers, actually.
Oh, really, everyone knows of it. But maybe you don't. Anyway,
it's not the kind of thing you are supposed to talk about. But it's
hard to resist talking about it!"

Actually, I too knew what he was about to tell me. You can
read the tale and decide for yourself whether Han Yin's secret is
a true one or not. Then I'll tell you what I know.

"It happened in that crazy time when a sorcerer persuaded
the First Emperor to commission a fleet and fill it with thousands
of beautiful youths of both sexes.

"You know the practice of 'doubling' for the Emperor,
finding a lookalike, grooming him and dressing him like the
Emperor and bringing him forward on those occasions when
it might be dangerous for the Emperor to be present—or when
he wants a day off from being Emperor. Our beloved ruler has
a stable of such doubles, one or two of whom look enough like
him so that from even a little way off you would swear you were

looking at the man himself.

"Several months ago, a rumor began to go around that Ch'in Shih-huang-ti had died and been replaced by his lieutenants with one of these lookalikes. That since the deception had worked from the start, they were determined to continue with it as long as possible. It was to their great advantage, of course, to replace an authentic madman—let us admit it, our Emperor has become as crazy as anyone in the world—with a puppet.

"Well, rumors are wispy things and that one would have died away except that, soon after it was circulating, the Emperor began to appear in public less and less. There were a few court appearances, when he came to the court nearly alone and composed himself on the high throne before anyone else was admitted. Then again, up there on that throne, it would be very hard to tell if it was First Emperor or a double. His nightly palace-to-palace scampers became even more secretive, too. We began to think perhaps he really was dead.

"At present, many of us are not sure that we have a living emperor. Li Ssu is doing all the business of the state. We wonder how long this can go on," said Han Yin.

* * * * * * * *

I happen to know there is at least some truth in Han Yin's story. I had risen rapidly through the eunuch bureaucracy with absolutely no effort on my part. I was now serving as Director of Undergarments in the Palace of the Number One Wives, which also, rather sadly, means the oldest, most wrinkled and therefore least visited wives.

As the wives I served got older, their undergarments became more fantastic—multilayered silks with vaguely pornographic paintings on the inner layers, jewels in the oddest places, unexpected gaps or suggestive holes just where you would perhaps least wish to find them among these wives. Among the concubines, it was the opposite; the older concubines lived in extremely comfortable and total seclusion. Their undergarments were designed for warmth, comfort, friendliness to the touch, full coverage, et cetera. Something to do with expectations versus comfort, no doubt.

My apartments were spacious and well appointed, and I was ably served by young men who pleased me, if in no other way, by being uniformly handsome and obsequious to a degree you might find repellent. They suited me.

All my creature comforts were met, if not all my desires. My duties were light. I found copying down all the nonsense spoken by the eunuchs in their chamber an agreeable and entertaining task, once I had got over my historian's ardent desire to correct their mistakes. Some of what they say, I feel they actually believe; and much else is pure fantasy, whether planned out in advance or created on the spur of the moment. Grown men they all are, men of considerable gravity, quite conscious of their august positions among the servants of the Emperor. But they are also most entertainingly silly. Besides, I had long since finished my own work, the *Records of the Grand Historian*, and apart from an occasional poem, I had little else to do but look forward to the bi-weekly evenings in the hidden Jade Room listening to the storytellers.

So, with everything going well at last, naturally I was sleeping badly. Such is the irony of life!

I tried a number of things: massage by naked maidens walking up and down light-footed on my back; harpists and singers; sleeping draughts. Nothing worked for long. A wall candle would gutter out and I would start up from my bed, fully alert, onto my feet, trying to remember who and where I was. Then I would remember, and on some occasions, I am ashamed to say, I would weep. I missed my family even more now and my one visit felt like a wound. But I was afraid to try again, both for myself and my grandson, who was taking a big risk for me. I might sit an hour or more before the urge to lie down again would come over me; then the process would repeat itself an hour later. Long nights!

One night, I was sitting disconsolately in my bedroom, my mind meandering along the forks of past decisions, when my curtains were parted abruptly. It was Wang Ts'ao, Major Domo of the Royal Palace, in his black robes. He was looking grim. Beside him was a eunuch I knew who served in the Emperor's guard, looking splendid and extremely irascible in the red robes of his service. For a moment I thought I was having a nightmare, but when I rubbed my eyes and opened them again, both the eunuchs were still there.

Wang Ts'ao said, "Ssu-ma Ch'ien, you have been summoned. Dress in your formal robes and come with us immediately."

I did so.

I was marched—there is no other word—by the soldier at a brisk pace across several courtyards and through various halls, with Wang Ts'ao trailing behind. I could hear him puffing, and it was a satisfaction to me to realize I was more fit than he was.

I had never learned my way around the First Emperor's palaces, so I was completely lost by the time we reached our destination: a small, plain room with a single, low desk, a mat, and an entire wall full of bamboo strips densely populated with characters. Even when I was Grand Historian, I never saw so many official memoranda in one place!

A man sat on the mat. I could not see eyes, downcast under severe eyebrows, but his nose looked as if it could cut paper, and I thought him a bird of prey—like one of the great eagles that flies in the far north. The sleeves of his silk robe, which was gray, were tied back so he could write more quickly without staining himself. As a writer, I have tried that trick but it does not seem to work for me; most of my ideas seem to be up my sleeve and the sight of my naked arm invariably distracts me from the sentence I am constructing.

Clearly aware that I was standing over him, he continued to write for a moment, I suppose, to impress me. Presently he said, "You are Ssu-ma Ch'ien?"

I agreed.

"I am Chao Kao, the Chief Eunuch. His Imperial Majesty wishes to see you. Now."

My jaw fell open. I had never seen the terrifying Chao Kao before—he was really quite ordinary-looking, birdlike qualities apart—and the Emperor and I had last spoken with one another privately, outside the main courtroom, in his water closet soon after he made me Grand Historian. That was over twenty years ago.

"You are to be blindfolded, because as you may be aware, no one is permitted to know where the Emperor sleeps. Except for one or two of us," he said, looking down at his fingernails with some satisfaction, I thought. They were well-trimmed—the nails and fingers of a writer, I thought.

I was blindfolded and marched out into the night, between two soldiers this time, at an even faster pace. We went down three flights of stairs, the soldiers more or less carrying me between them. The air was stale, which made me think we were in one of the palaces' innumerable and connecting, underground corridors.

After a walk that felt like a mile or more—try walking a mile blindfolded—we stopped and began to climb stairs toward noticeably fresher air.

We came through massive doors that creaked as they swung open, and stepped into what felt like a large space. I imagined I heard breathing on all sides, but at a considerable distance, and I thought to myself, crossbowmen, their iron bolts probably aimed at my heart. I had just time to imagine what it might feel like to have a thousand armor-piercing darts of steel pass through my body more or less simultaneously—it would certainly require a clean-up job!—when the soldiers on either side halted suddenly. So swift was their motion I was thrown forward against their hard-muscled arms; so violent was the impact my own arms ached for a week afterwards.

I think it was at this moment I decided that the evening was not going to have a fatal outcome. They took the blindfold off and I was marched across the floor of a huge hall until we came to a small area fronted by brocade curtains.

We stood still for a moment or two, then there was a kind of a double hiss in front of me as curtains were parted and I was propelled forward another fifteen paces. The soldiers released me and I got used to balancing again.

The room was not pitch dark, though it seemed so at first. I was aware of dim shapes, especially a large rectangle, waist-high, straight ahead. There were lamps, too, but they must have been indirect; I was aware of steadily glowing light but I could not find the source.

The rectangle was a bed. I was in a bedchamber!

But it was not a bed like any I had seen before. It was draped in white, with no curtains or other hangings. It was much more like—no, it *was*—a bier, of the kind you might place a body on, to lie in state before burial.

In fact, there was a body on it, lying flat on its back, hands folded over its stomach. A decorated cloth lay across its eyes, one end hanging down into a basin of steaming water. The feet were bare and quite unattractive.

This is strange, I thought.

Had I been summoned to record the death of our beloved Ch'in Shih-huang-ti? No, that made no sense. Am I to be sent to heaven or hell along with him, perhaps in the guise of his only friend? Not that I was, but he might once have thought so, on those sweet, summer mornings when he was happily pounding me into the ground.

The answer: none of the above.

I noticed that the body was breathing, though shallowly. One finger, visibly crooked, was raised in a gesture to me to come closer—which was hard for me to do, very hard indeed, because there was this dreadful odor around the body. But I did it.

"Ssu-ma," came a wheezing croak, "I am glad to see you again. Or I would be if I could see you. But I daren't take this damned thing off."

"Give me your hand," the voice said, and the right hand, more of a claw, reached in my direction. Responding was extremely difficult, but I steeled myself and reached out to take his hand.

I would like to tell you whether the hand was warm or cold, but I cannot: I was astonished by its thinness and livid color, the color of old lead or bronze before it begins to turn green. His skin was bumpy; where it was bare, it looked like the skin of a dead chicken!

"Ssu-ma, my old friend," said the croaking voice. "I have thought so often of the wonderful times we had together as boys before I became King of Ch'in. How are you, my friend?"

How am I? How am I? With or without castration, I thought. You son of a bitch!

I was not tempted to speak these thoughts aloud.

"I am well, Your Highness. It is good to see you, too," I lied. It was horrible to see him. He had been a big boy, a big king, and a huge emperor in his immense imperial robes—but now, in pajamas, he seemed so small. I am not large, but if he were not already flat I am sure I could have flattened him! For a moment, I dared to think about that. Then I thought about the crossbows.

"Ssu-ma, will you grant me a favor? For the sake of our friendship long ago, will you call me Cheng as you did then?"

"Certainly, your Maj–Cheng," I said. And strangely, I found myself remembering that we *had* had good times, many, in the days before Cheng became king and, seeing his chance, had decided to be the second coming of the Yellow Emperor—His Semi-Sacredness, Han Yin calls him.

Something about holding hands, which we still were doing, may soften the heart.

"It is good to see you, Cheng," I said, realizing that I may have been the first, non-inner circle person in decades to speak to Ch'in Shih-huang-ti.

"I have terrible headaches, Ssu-ma," Cheng said. "I read into the night—I used to read reports from all over the empire, but now I read treatises on magic. For years I was able to read twelve hours a day, but now I read for an hour or two and everything begins to go red, then dark, and I get terrible chills and I feel as if an earthquake is happening inside me..." He shuddered.

"Can't the doctors help you?" I asked. "What do they say you should do?"

"Every kind of thing. They have me doing such stupid things I don't even want to talk about it. In the end, the only thing that helps at all is just to lie here like this in a dark room and try to be quiet. I had a tame nightingale once, but it died..."

"I'm sorry," I said.

"No, I am sorry, Ssu-ma," said Cheng. "I have always wanted to tell you how sorry I was that I had to call for the loss of your–your–your..."

"Manhood?"

"Yes. But I will tell you something you may not know. Li Ssu was determined to have you killed as an example to our critical scholars. He said one death at that time might save a larger number of deaths later. But for the sake of our friendship, I couldn't let him do it. I ordered the castration and he had to agree to it. He will not cross me openly."

I could have guessed that, but I didn't care to dwell on it.

The Emperor—what was left of him—said, "Now they just hide me away, Li Ssu and Chao Kao. Every night they bundle me up in a pile of blankets and bring me to one of the palaces. I don't even know where I am. By day, they are the only ones who talk to me—I cannot even speak directly to the soothsayers and magicians now.

"What is happening in the empire, Ssu-ma? What are they doing in my name?"

Here was a golden opportunity to renew my entreaties for law tempered with mercy, for a reduction of the tax burdens that left the peasants, now freehold farmers, far worse off than they were when they were peasants on the great estates that used to govern the land. These so-called freehold farmers were starving even after a good harvest!

I could beg for an end to the century-old barbarous custom of promoting soldiers and officers in the Ch'in armies according to the number of enemy heads they brought back from battle. This was a custom that continued even after Ch'in's principal enemies had knuckled under as provinces of the empire, a practice that rendered the profession of innocent bystander an extremely dangerous one.

I could tell him that General Meng T'ien and Crown Prince Fu-su, now at work extending the Great Wall, were eager to put an end to the deaths of hundreds of thousands of conscripts in an enterprise that may yet prove ineffective at keeping the northern hordes out. Indeed, it may attract them south!

I could have said a great deal, especially since there were brush-fire rebellions almost everywhere in the empire now, and above all in the unsubjugated rebellious south.

What I actually said was, "Your Majesty, the great family of black-haired people, your children, bless and pray for you every day. The granaries are full, the great canals are running smoothly, the highways are open and safe, the whole land is at peace. The bells of empire are in tune, Heaven is pleased, and your ancestors are smiling down on you. Things could not be better."

I couldn't see the edges of the room and I had an idea that wasn't accidental. Sometimes you can actually hear people listening.

Ch'in Shih-huang-ti's shrunken stomach seemed to relax as he drew in a breath.

"I am so glad to hear it, even if, as I suspect, it is not true. I am not a stupid man, Ssu-ma. I took a savage instrument in my hands and used it to force a peace—the peace of the dead. That was not what was in my heart to do. I listened as you did to the stories of our ancestors, and I remembered how the Chou of the west guarded the passes and protected the Shang kingdom until the Shang grew so weak and dissolute that it was necessary for the Chou to climb to the throne. Heaven demanded it. Growing up in the same land as the Chou homeland, charged by the Chou themselves with the task of protecting the empire five hundred years and more ago, I could see that only a similar power could end the interminable wars among the Seven Kingdoms. The weapon was there, and I–I used it.

"And we have done much since then, a very great deal, to bring order and permanence to the land."

The bells of Heaven and of Hell know that is true!

"But I have thought about my sons; I cannot imagine that they will carry on the great work I have begun. I sent the best of my sons, Prince Fu-su, a man of integrity and judgment, north to die. I was misled into thinking I could rule forever. The shamans of the east told me immortality was within reach. And if I were truly immortal, I thought, we could finish all of our work and it would last forever. So I gave all my effort, all my strength, to living forever."

There was a long silence, followed by a shallow sigh.

"But I see now it was all lies, Ssu-ma. There is no such thing as immortality. There are no gods, no heaven. There is no Tao. There is only the slow corruption of the body. As you see."

"Your Majesty, all these years...why did you send for me now?"

"I loved my first wife, Ssu-ma. I loved my tutor. At one time I loved my 'uncle,' Lu Pu-wei, who was good to me. And, thinking over my life, I realized that though I was not good to you, I loved you, too. You were—perhaps still are—an honest friend. And you are the last friend I will ever have. I wanted to say goodbye to you."

I felt a little pressure from his thin hand. I returned it.

"It is the same for me, Cheng," I said quietly.

I stood there for a while until the soldiers came to blindfold me and return me to my apartments. I am certain that Chao Kao and Li Ssu heard every word we spoke.

They are poisoning the poor bastard.

Something Smells Like a Dead Fish
Ssu-Ma Ch'ien's Tale

(Translator's note: A few feet from the mass of bundled bamboo records in the room below the emperor's burial vault, archaeologists found a small, separate group of bundles. Remnants of different colored ribbons—green, rather than the imperial Ch'in black, had been used to tie these. When translated, the prose was different, too, much less polished, with clear signs of having been hastily written, with very abrupt stops and starts. The entries strongly resembled notes of the kind one might make in a journal, and so these bundles proved to be: Ssu-ma Ch'ien's fragmented record of the last days of the huge Ch'in empire, written after the eunuchs had stopped meeting. The balance of Book Four is offered here undated, just as he wrote them twenty-two hundred years ago. Breaks in the manuscripts are marked by asterisks.)

* * * * * * * *

A great deal has happened in the Empire of Ch'in in the months since my night visit to our very sick First Emperor. It is necessary for me to tell you the story directly as all the storytellers are away on a journey that proved more fateful than anyone could have imagined.

One evening in the Jade Room, Han Yin told us that a new imperial progress, the first in years, and the first one to the dangerous, southern edge of the Empire, had been scheduled recently. He had learned this from a well-placed astrologer of his acquaintance at the Court. It was all done in haste, Han Yin said, and it felt suspicious to him, the more so because he was convinced the actual Emperor was dead. Why would Chao Kao and Li Ssu take the crazy chance of bringing a double of the Emperor, really only fit for long-distance viewing, into sustained close contact with so many people who knew the Emperor?

As to the matter of the double, I knew better, as I have told you. The Emperor was still alive, barely. I did not understand why Chao Kao and Li Ssu granted the dying emperor's request to see me, his boyhood friend, but I was certain it would be best to tell no one about it, especially about my suspicion that he was being poisoned. Though I felt friendly with every one of the storytellers, I was not inclined to trust them or anyone else totally. But when I heard Han Yin say he felt suspicious, I felt ten times more so. I immediately thought the Chief Eunuch and the Grand Counselor were planning this royal progress so they could get the Emperor as far from the capital, and the main Ch'in army, as possible, to make it easier to do away with him.

But then, Han Yin surprised me.

He said, "This is going to be a much more substantial progress than any of the past imperial tours. The entire court will be making the journey, and a substantial detachment of soldiers. There will be some twenty thousand people in tow, including most of us. Not you, though, Ssu-ma Ch'ien. The point of the parade is to pound it into the thick heads of the southern tribes and their petty princes that they are well and truly under the thumb of the Emperor, and they'd better get used to it and settle down!"

Much tapping of fans and grunting of assents. I don't know if it will surprise you to learn this, but though these eunuchs are cynical, they are also patriotic. Since their own fortunes rise or fall with the rise or fall of the empire, it's logical to be patriotic.

The day after Han Yin's announcement, word of the imperial progress became public. Immediately, life in Hsienyang turned upside down, what with planning, provisioning, packing, polishing, et cetera. A gang of a few thousand peasants and their few belongings can make a mess of our roads, so you can imagine what an Emperor, his Court, and his army can do! It took from autumn well into muddy spring to get everything properly organized and onto a line of carts and chariots and livestock. But the day finally came; as I watched from a window, I saw a line of marching men and wagons that must have stretched out more than thirty *li*. When the tail end finally passed over the horizon, Hsienyang was quiet; but of course fighting broke out among the women left behind in the Concubine Residences, just as it always does.

For a few weeks, there was relative quiet, and the official reports of the progress that reached us were few and routine. Then I received a secret memorandum from Meng Hao-jan that was a true thunderbolt! I am adding it to the text of this report to you, posterity.

ROYAL EUNUCH MENG HAO-JAN TO ROYAL EUNUCH SSU-MA CH'IEN

No matter what information you may receive about this, here's what really happened at Pingtai in the Year of the Tiger, year eleven of the reign of the mighty Ch'in Shih-huang-ti! And afterward.

Think about this, dear friend, you who remain so collected at all times! We were in the traveling palace, the "royal progress" of all time, a thousand miles south of Hsienyang, when our Beloved Master over-ate one day. After dinner he complained of cramps and bloating, and by next morning he was gone—dead—poof! like a puffball or a fan snapping shut. What were we to do?! It was hot as Hades, I can tell you, and I am sure that you have heard how Ch'u is this time of year!

A dilemma! Hu-hai, the Emperor's currently favored younger child, a real lazy idiot, was traveling with us. His older brother, Fu-

su, the Emperor's heir and the only son who could have taken charge, was on the Great Wall. We did not know where to turn. All we knew for certain was that we were in great danger. If the locals found out the Emperor was dead, the chances are we soon would be, too.

And so seven of us, led by Chao Kao, the Chief Eunuch, met secretly and made a plan. Among the seven are also Li Ssu and Prince Hu-hai.

According to plan, at nightfall of the very morning of this death, we carried the coffin, a plain one, to a carriage escorted by yours truly and others. We then regularly brought food to the carriage, as well as official reports, eating the former and tearing the latter to pieces, and we consistently issued imperial orders just as if they were coming from First Emperor.

But, we ran into real trouble! The weather grew still hotter and the litter began to stink to heaven! With a thousand miles to go before we were home and safe, clever Chao Kao had an answer that nearly worked—well, it did work, but you would not have enjoyed the last few hundred li of the journey.

To allay suspicions about the smell, Chao Kao had several cart loads of salt fish brought in around the royal litter, the pretext being the Emperor had a raging taste for fish. What a sight! The venerated, late 'God-Emperor of All Under Heaven,' stinking to heaven, surrounded by creaking fish carts, all smelling worse every day. But the people who turned out to see the Emperor pass by never said anything— they offered all due reverence. Nothing like a five-hundred-man horse guard, weapons out and at the ready, I always say!

The rest you know, or soon will know, Ssu-ma Ch'ien. When our royal progress passes through the great gateway at Hsienyang, everyone in the world will know Ch'in Shih-huang-ti is dead. He tried so hard not to die!

Your loving friend, Meng Hao-jan

An ignominious, ridiculous end to Cheng's life. So much accomplished, so much destroyed. What did his life change? What on earth will happen now?

Plots in the Palace
Ssu-Ma Ch'ien's Tale

Events in Hsienyang are happening too swiftly for the storytellers to keep up, leaving me to report to you on what I see and hear.

Li Ssu's famous "granary rats"—much of the royal court—scurry for their lives. No one knows which way safety lies; really, there is no safety when the men at the top are playing a game of chance for power and you are one of the tokens in the game.

People are racing around like fleas in a peasant's blanket. And I am no exception! I have no idea what's going on in the palace. For a while I thought I did, since I was trained to recognize patterns in the movement of the stars and lives of men, but now I too am scurrying about, trying to escape attention. So much easier to sort the threads of the past! All one can think about is staying ahead of the executioner's saw.

Two nights ago, I had a late visit from a very distressed Tu Mu, First Emperor's Charioteer. Normally a self-possessed, quiet man, he was barely coherent when he arrived.

After a few cups of wine that disappeared down his gullet, he began to tell me a very different story about the Emperor's death from the one Meng Hao-jan sent me. Sadly, Tu Mu's tale was far more plausible.

Tu Mu began by telling me that our small circle of old friends contains a smaller circle secretly sworn to serve Chao Kao to the death. We are all loyal—Chao Kao is the unquestioned leader of the royal eunuchs and his slightest whim is carried out as if it were law. But he has a plotter's instincts, and plotters require confidantes. Tu Mu said there were three and he was one. He refused to name the others.

"Why tell me this?" I asked Tu Mu.

"Because I am not comfortable with what we did and what we are doing now," Tu Mu said. "I had no qualms at the time—the Sky God and Heaven are far away and do not seem interested in our doings, and Master K'ung has been dead for a long time. Besides, I want the future people to have a true account of these wretched times. It may help them understand us."

First, said Tu Mu, you should know the Emperor did not die of stomach distress, even if that's what most of the court thinks—or says it thinks.

He died on Chao Kao's orders. Hinted orders. To give him credit, Chao Kao did not look happy. He called me into his tent and dismissed his servants. He was holding an imperial edict in his hands.

"This is a summons from the Emperor to Prince Fu-su," he said. "He wants him to come here at once, with General Meng T'ien and a large force. It can only mean one thing," Chao Kao said, "he means to make Fu-su his heir. The Emperor cannot live much longer and when he dies, Fu-su will take charge. That will be the end of us, Tu Mu. What should we do about this?"

Sir, you are in charge of sending letters and sealed orders, I told him. I think we must begin by destroying that edict.

"But then what?"

It was rhetorical. He did not have to say more. I am not a fool.

We killed the Emperor in his sleeping chariot—I did, myself, shoving a whole fish into his mouth and holding his nostrils shut. It was nothing; he was so weak from months of slow poisoning he could barely stand, much less fight me off. When he was quiet, I climbed down from the royal chariot and went to see Chao Kao. A guard stopped me.

While I waited outside Chao Kao's tent, Li Ssu arrived with

the royal jade half-disk and the imperial seal, followed by his secretary. Li Ssu was so agitated I don't think he even saw me. He and the secretary went in at once and were inside the tent for a full turn of a glass. Once I heard shouting—you must know, Ssu-ma, that the two men hate each other—and when Li Ssu finally came out, his face was darker than the hot and cloudy, southern summer night. But he no longer was carrying the jade half-disk, I noticed.

I then asked to see Chao Kao to report to him on the status of the First Emperor. Thereafter I returned to my tent to sleep; it had after all been a long day. I was, however, woken before dawn by a messenger summoning me to Chao Kao's tent. When I got there, my two friends and one other co-conspirator were waiting inside.

Without any preamble, a somewhat flustered Chao Kao said, "Friends, the Emperor is dead by Tu Mu's right hand. But you are the only ones who will ever know this. When it is time to announce the Emperor's demise, we will say he died of a stomach disorder.

"I have staked our lives on the ascendance of the Emperor's younger son, Hu-hai, to the Imperial Throne. Li Ssu has thrown in his lot with us and forged an imperial decree that is supposed to be from the Emperor. In it he names Hu-hai, his youngest son, as his successor. He will be recognized as Erh Shih-huang-ti, Second Emperor. But we have business to do in the north before we can announce the Emperor's death. If Fu-su and his ally, General Meng T'ien, contest the succession, which they are certain to do since Fu-su is the Emperor's eldest son, they will undoubtedly prevail. And if they do—you can depend on this," he said, looking at each of us in turn, "we will not outlive them."

We shuddered.

"Li Ssu offered a brilliant alternative, to which I added one or two modest suggestions," Chao Kao said. "He has also drafted a second edict, commanding Fu-su and Meng T'ien both to commit suicide for some trifling offense. Fu-su is certain to do it, and Meng T'ien, as a man of honor, will have to follow him. When we have word from the northern wall that they are dead, our way to the throne—because Hu-hai is my toy, a lazy, greedy creature who knows only what I have taught him—will be clear.

"So, a dangerous time, but we can turn it to great profit if we keep our heads. What I must know from you is this: are you with me?"

He turned to each of us and we swore to serve him to the end. When we were done swearing, I heard crossbows being disarmed on the other side of the tent walls.

The rest I think you know, Ssu-ma Ch'ien, Tu Mu said.

Almost.

I rode north with the co-conspirator, who, as messenger, was official bearer of the false edict to Fu-su and Meng T'ien, said Tu Mu. Nominally his servant, I was actually in command of the journey, even if I had to wait in a separate quarter while the co-conspirator served the edict. When he returned from his meeting with the Prince and the General, he reported to me what happened.

"When I arrived with the imperial edict, Fu-su at once began to prepare to kill himself. But General Meng T'ien, the old fox, pleaded with him. He talked about the huge responsibility the Emperor had given Fu-su, overseeing hundreds of thousands of conscripts on the Wall and a major arm of the Ch'in army.

"Meng T'ien said, 'This messenger is just one man, Fu-su. How can you know it is not a trick, even though he carries the royal jade disk? Please send a message to your father asking him to confirm the command. Ask him something only you and he could possibly know about. When word returns there will be time to decide what to do. But please do not kill yourself now!'"

"I will never forget Fu-su's response: 'When a father gives a son a command, it must be obeyed.' Confucian, honorable, vulnerable to trickery to the last! He retired to an inner apartment and killed himself. Within that same hour, General Meng T'ien killed himself as well."

When I hurried back to Li Ssu and Chao Kao with this news, Tu Mu said, they released the second imperial edict naming brainless Hu-hai as the Emperor's choice of a successor.

After a few days, now being close to Hsienyang and on the safety of the major imperial road to the south, they judged they could safely announce the Emperor's death. Oh what a weeping and wailing and gnashing of teeth! My goodness. You would have thought everyone's favorite pet cricket had died.

Hu-hai's first imperial decree was that the First Emperor's wives and concubines were to join him on the journey to the underworld. For hundreds of years, there had been few human sacrifices to dead rulers. The emperor of the new age took thousands of people into the dark with him.

Hu-hai's second edict named Chao Kao his Palace Chamberlain, the position closest to the ruler.

Tu Mu drained a cup of wine, vomited into a basin, and sat back gray-faced. I think he was waiting for my comment. But my first reaction was, what difference does this revelation make? None I can see. We sat in silence for a time; then he left.

* * * * * * * *

I have many sources of information inside and outside the palace. Inside, the world of the new emperor was constricting rapidly. His ministers and principal advisors were barred from his presence, by Chao Kao, no doubt. Even Li Ssu, perhaps the only man alive who could be said to have an intimate relationship with the late emperor, could no longer gain access to Hu-hai. And his memoranda, which had served him so well, and had been such deadly weapons for decades, were now sent to Chao Kao for reading and commentary. I am sure they did not reach the Second Emperor.

A grim day came when Hu-hai ordered all his remaining brothers, and all their families, executed. They were charged with conspiracy. Ten princesses were forced to hang themselves. Most of the palace attendants, except Chao Kao's coterie, were killed or exiled. And every one of Hu-hai's personal servants were replaced by men hand-picked by Chao Kao.

Hard on the heels of those orders came an edict condemning most of the old emperor's counselors. Their crime, I have been told, was insufficient respect for Chao Kao, because he was born a servant!—all but Li Ssu, for whom Chao Kao had something special in mind. I will write of that in a moment.

* * * * * * * *

The palace is filled with disgusting debauchery as the worst elements among us take their cue from Hu-hai, the "Emperor of Pleasure," as he is known. He is said to be drunk all day and serviced by women all night, just lying in sloth. Someone said he is a bad judge of character, having none of his own, and I judge that to be true. In our histories, we read that all families of rulers decline, generation by generation, until the Mandate of Heaven is withdrawn. We seem to have skipped a number of generations to get to Hu-hai!

* * * * * * * *

My grandson sends me letters reporting that the world beyond the Ch'in Empire passes is also in turmoil.

Summons to military duty with no end-point, corvees for forced labor that are in reality death sentences to work on the Epang Palace, the great empire-wide spiderweb of canals and roads, and always the Wall, leaving fields untended for want of laborers. He tells me there are peasant revolts everywhere, which by themselves would be not much more than nuisances, but they are matched by rebellion among the frontier guards, especially in the proud former kingdom of Ch'u.

And of course there is much plotting among the ancient, supplanted noble families, whom Cheng moved to Hsienyang but left intact. What seemed brilliant when he did it now seems asinine because they, with all their wealth, are together in one place! With an unlimited capability of causing harm. It now begins to look as if there is a fire on the land that will not be put out, at least not by this dynasty.

* * * * * * * *

Li Ssu has come to an end.

His was the most remarkable career of our time. He rose from bastard child to scholar to spy and ultimately became Grand Counselor of Ch'in. He was the late emperor's second, some might say, better, self, taking on more and more of the management of the empire as the emperor grew more and more obsessed with magic and immortality. In his time he possessed riches and estates second only to those of the emperor himself, of whom it was said that the known world was his estate. Cold-hearted and evil though I well knew him to be, Li Ssu was said to be a devoted father of many sons. One of them was the means of his downfall.

Here is how it happened.

First, Chao Kao isolated Hu-hai, especially from Li Ssu. It is not hard to imagine the lies he told the Second Emperor about Li Ssu. Throne memoranda in Hu-hai's name blaming Li Ssu for this and that began to come from the imperial secretariat. Then, Chao Kao saw his opportunity to destroy Li Ssu, and like a predatory cat, pounced.

Li Ssu's favorite son was the prefect of a town that came under attack by a peasant leader with native genius for military matters, the southerner Chen She. Li's son was able to escape, but the town was overwhelmed by Chen She's men. Chao Kao made it known that Li Ssu's son had collaborated with Chen

She secretly—the charge was nonsense, of course. Chen She would have had Chao's head on a pole instantly if Chen could have captured him—but Li Ssu was summoned to the Office of Law Enforcement and tortured until he confessed, as any of us would have done. Li Ssu and his son and all their living relatives, more than three hundred, were sentenced to death.

* * * * * * * *

The day appointed for the execution was dark, the sky covered with clouds. Li Ssu's relatives knelt on the public execution ground. Three observation towers had been erected, one for Second Emperor, one for Chao Kao, and one for the late emperor's ministers who remained alive. There were few left, but I am sure Chao Kao felt that the execution would encourage them to work even harder at their daily tasks.

Li Ssu and his son were brought to the center of the square. They wept and embraced one another, remembering with regret that they had spent many good times together, and now there were to be no more. Then they were separated, and each was stripped naked and sawed in two.

Afterwards, soldiers made their way among the ranks of Li Ssu's relatives, stabbing the men and strangling the women, who were not thought worthy of steel. The mass of bodies was loaded onto carts and dumped into the Yellow River, which fortunately was near flood height and swift-moving at the time. And so the body and spirit of Li Ssu left the kingdom of the living.

Now Chao Kao is in control. But of what? For how long?

Final Tales

Ssu-Ma Ch'ien's Tale

Since I have farther to go from my quarters on the north side of the great central courtyard to reach Han Yin's quarters than most of the storytellers, I am often last to arrive.

Tonight, late as usual, I took a deep breath, knelt down, crawled under his carved scholars' table and went through the narrow opening to the Jade Room. The crawl space has become a tight squeeze. I often hear the storytellers laughing when I grunt with the strain. Tonight, as I gathered myself in order to pop through, my belly seemed to be almost touching the floor. But though I groaned and moaned as usual, there was no laughter from the Jade Room.

First Emperor made black the color of his empire, so boring black is the color of our daily uniforms. But as I looked around in the rose-orange light of the long-burning lamps, every one of my storytellers was dressed in white, the color of mourning, from head to foot. The floor was covered with white-dyed bearskin rugs and white blankets covered the walls. The tables were white, the dishes were white. Only the food was its usual natural color.

On a table at the center stood two pottery bottles, narrow-necked and slim, one white, one black—a far cry from the score or more of multicolored wine bottles usually scattered around the room in easy reach of eager hands and thirsty throats.

Seated around the room, looking far from relaxed, my

storytellers were for once utterly silent. No one nodded to me.

One man was missing, the fierce but secretly kindhearted Juan Chi, Chief Dispenser of Eunuch Punishments. His normal place beside Han Yin was vacant. The room felt huge with his absence.

Juan Chi's disappearance and the strangeness of the scene ripped my normal, cheerful babble from my mouth. They were all waiting for something and I decided it would be wise to join them. I crept to my writing desk, opened my ink bottle, wet and pointed my best, round writing brush, dipped it in the ink, re-pointed it, and waited.

"Dear friends, my companions for so many years, and, if I may say, brothers," said Han Yin, "we have today lost one of our best, Juan Chi, breathing and unusually cheerful when I encountered him this morning, dead before dinner. He was cut down as he exercised, by Chao Kao's private army of thugs. After they beheaded him, his body was dumped into the ever-flowing river. His surprised head, I am sad to say, graces a pole among the hundreds of other heads that line the inner court of the palace. Like them, it will sit until it rots away. We will be forced to go past it every day from now on. And there is not one thing any of us can do about it. Certainly not protest to Chao Kao—that would earn the protestor the same fate."

It is not our nature to weep and wail, at least not the males of our race, though I have seen enough tears on the faces of moaning women to float an armada of immortality seekers. What we do naturally is laugh, though often we laugh when nothing is funny. Nervousness, I suppose, or wanting to hide what we are really feeling. No one was laughing tonight, though, or crying either.

Silence. More silence.

Finally, Meng Hao-jan made a little huffing sound and said, "Let's speak frankly, Han Yin. We all know that three of us cast the dragon stalks and decided to support Chao Kao in everything he does—everything—which now includes this atrocious murder of a man we loved and admired. And there is worse coming. They—for I am not one of them—will undoubtedly survive the housecleaning ahead as Chao Kao goes about ensuring that only people utterly loyal to him get to go on breathing. People who have proved themselves by doing who knows what despicable deeds. As I said, these three will prosper in the reign of Chao Kao, if by some chance he succeeds in stealing an empire. The rest of us will not. In fact, given the suddenness of Juan Chi's departure, I doubt whether the rest of us have many days left."

"So here we are," said Meng Hao-jan. "What next?"

"I have a suggestion," said Wang Ts'ao. In the lamplight, he seemed handsomer than ever. As always, he spoke quietly with his eyes downcast, "I have no desire to know the names of Chao Kao's confederates in this room. We are all brothers or we are nothing. I suggest we begin the evening with a single toast to Juan Chi. Each of us can choose the white wine bottle or the black one. The rest will not watch you as you make your choice. Then let us carry on as we always do, enjoying one another's company, both here and in the Region of the Yellow Spring, should we be fortunate enough to remain together."

There was a rustle of assenting fans around the circle. One by one, by rank and by age, the storytellers crept forward, wine dishes in hand. True to Wang Ts'ao's suggestion, no one watched the others as they made their choice of wine. But, though I was pretending to look down at my writing table, I did watch as each of the eunuchs poured himself ruby-colored wine from the white bottle and returned to his seat.

I was last. When it was my turn, I too reached for the white bottle but Han Yin's fan snapped open sharply, making me jump.

"Do not take offense, Ssu-ma Ch'ien. You have been a good companion and a good friend. But I want you to drink the toast from the other bottle. You have a journey to make that must be separate from ours."

I did so. We lifted our cups.

Wang Ts'ao said, "Friends, a good journey for Juan Chi, the

kindest executioner I have known."

"Good journey, dear friend," rang through the room and echoed in the silence that followed as we drained our cups. For me, it is still echoing.

* * * * * * * *

"Now, my friends, I propose we get to our storytelling," said Han Yin, "we do not have all night!

"Our present lives began here in the palace in the service of the First Emperor. We have worked hard and well. We are successful men, wealthy and powerful by the world's standards. But the world within the walls is our world—the world outside we have no part in. So by our traditions, the past is dead to us. We never speak of it and consider it rude to talk of our origins. Worse, to ask about them.

"But this is a special night. If you are willing, I would like to suggest that we tell our own stories tonight, adding them to those we have told about the First Emperor. We are," said Han Yin, "as entitled to our lives as any whole man outside the Forbidden City. And I also suggest that our esteemed friend and companion Ssu-ma Ch'ien record these tales of ourselves among the mass of material he has written about the Emperor. I for one want to be remembered. Besides, it will be easier for posterity to understand these times of ours if posterity knows who is telling these tales."

I bowed deeply over my writing desk.

"Perhaps," here a slight twitch of Han Yin's eyes, slightly reminiscent of a smile, took place, "we might allow ourselves the same privilege of fantasizing and, let us say, exaggerating, that we have done in telling tales of the Emperor. Indeed, if you wish to do something other than tell your own story, you may do so. Only let whatever you say be something that brings us a little closer together by evening's end. We have a journey ahead."

"Will you begin, Meng Hao-jan?

Meng Hao-Jan

Meng Hao-jan, Principal Eunuch Trainer and Director of Eunuch Promotions, looked down and said a few quiet words to himself before he began.

My story, he said, is not the usual thing you will probably hear from this splendid group. Far from any rich man's house, much less a palace, I was born in a rice paddy twenty *li* from Ying, the capital city of what was then the troublesome southern state of Ch'u.

The harvest was going on at the time. I have been told my mother, who like all the villagers, was cutting and bundling the grain when she felt a pang or two, then popped me out onto a hillock with nothing more than a quiet grunt. She rested a few minutes, dried me off, swaddled me in the shirt she ripped off her own back, tied me around her so I could get at a teat when I cared to—which I am sure was immediately—and hurried on to catch up with and pass the gleaners so she could continue cutting down the rice.

They tell me she never put down her sickle. An ill omen, as far as I am concerned.

My childhood is too tedious to mention. Like bear cubs, my brothers and sisters were. We were always hungry and we fought over every scrap of food thrown our way. Our mother and father were working all the time, every waking minute. They got no rest, ever. I cannot even begin to imagine how they summoned up the strength for the frequent fucking they must have done to get all of us. I don't like to think about that.

We played, I suppose. I had a little dog I thought was a friend, but one winter, with nothing left to eat, we ate him.

When I was eleven or so—I really don't know for certain—our father gathered up all but the two strongest boys, tied us together securely and threw us into a cart. He pulled the cart to the city, which none of us had ever seen, of course, and brought us inside the city wall.

You know the rest of this banal story, I am sure. We were

sold to the cutters. They rubbed us up erect—I remember that was pleasant—then cut off our highly stimulated penises. Such howling you never heard! Well, you have, of course. After that it was the usual thing: they treated the wounds, and were not unkind to us as we were healthy, young and valuable to them, and brought us to recover in a large room with pallets all over the floor. We spent some weeks there, being brought out for exercise and play in the courtyard. In short, we got well.

One by one, we were taken away to service in various places. One day, a tall man gathered me and we rode to what was then the state of Ch'in, to the world here inside the passes.

I knew nothing, I was no one. The gods, if any, gave me a good brain and a pleasant face. Older men in service looked after me, and I gradually moved up through the ranks to my present position. I have known no other life, experienced no other joys, or sorrows, than I have known here.

That is my story. I'm afraid it is very boring, and I apologize if I have put you to sleep!

No, no, nothing of the sort, we all said.

"Thank you, Meng," Han Yin said. "Nothing you or anyone else here is willing to tell us about your past lives before you were born into this brotherhood can possibly be dull to us!"

They exchanged deep, seated bows.

"And now, Tu Mu, give us a tale of your origins, please. We all know your tremendous skill with arms, and have admired your majestic and warlike squatting on the war-coach of the late emperor as you guide his spirited black horses, the greatest six in the empire, through their superb multiple gaits in the Inner Courtyard. How many times each of us has wished the Emperor himself was aboard, going off to war, perhaps to die a splendid death in battle—who could possibly wish for more than that? But as we all know, he was an utter coward, and would never go into battle under any circumstances. *What's an army for, if not to protect me?* That was his motto. So it seemed to me your position as First Emperor's Charioteer may have been the safest in the empire.

"We also know that from time to time people have called you 'Tu Mu the Lesser,' though I must admit I have no idea why that is so. Enlighten us."

Looking a little put out, and as always, a little self-conscious at being the center of attention, Tu Mu began his tale.

Tu Mu

What you say is true. I know behind my back I am called the Lesser. No shame in that—I bear the name of my late father, a man few people seem to have heard of these days.

He was a great man in his time, a general in command of a major army of the ancient state of Chao. You may remember that army, especially you gentlemen born and raised in Ch'in. It was the 400,000-strong army that tried to defend the city of Hantan against the Ch'in horde and were buried alive to the last man. And my father was nearly among them. But I am ahead of myself.

As general, my father spent many years patrolling Chao's own northern wall, trying to keep the Hsiung-nu barbarians from riding down out of the north, burning villages, raping women and stealing horses. It was hard, lonely and undoubtedly dangerous work, but there was one compensation.

In a counter-raid across the border, my father captured a number of women and children and brought them south for slave labor. One of them managed something a little better for herself: she was remarkably beautiful, especially for the flat-nosed Hsiung-nu, and gifted with a lively sexual imagination, I believe; she became my father's favorite concubine.

Which is how I came to be.

I was one of many sons of my father, but he favored me from the start, giving me his name.

I was raised in the army, maybe the only place I could have been treated as an equal, not being of pure Han stock. A man among men is an old expression and believe me, I was treated like a man long before I was one. My toys were weapons, my schools were battlefields. I could ride and drive horses almost before I could walk. The skills I learned before I was ten years old are the skills with which I served the late emperor, nothing more, nothing less.

The Hsiung-nu came raiding one day, while my father was away on the eastern end of the wall. A foul-smelling rider snatched me up and threw me across his horse before I could find a sword. A quick sortie, a little booty, including me, and back they went, leaving only dead bodies behind them, one of whom was my mother.

We rode north across plains with no features to help me remember the way home. Finally we came to their camp, hundreds of smoky yurts hung with skins. To my great surprise, the Hsiung-nu warrior simply dropped me at an opening in one of the dwellings. I was home.

They treated me well. Indeed, they treat all their children well if you don't count the girls, seen by the Hsiung-nu as a necessary part of the furniture of life. Outside the walls of this palace, are our people different?

After a few fights, some of which I won and some I lost, I was accepted as part of the clan. I already had a little of their language, full of grunts and whistles, from my mother, and that was a help. I can speak their speech well to this day, even if my memory is not what it was back then—but much good it does the Emperor's Charioteer to be able to speak to a Hsiung-nu warrior!

I already knew how to drive a chariot, but now I learned to ride horses Hsiung-nu style, bareback. They could slip on and off their horses at full gallop and spear or shoot game on the dead run.

Perhaps many youngsters would, at twelve, have felt their old lives slipping away and would just let them go, becoming "of the clan" all the more deeply for having arrived late to the barbarian way of life. But for whatever reason, I wasn't one of them. I think it was because I was a general's son and had pride in, felt part of, his command. Even if I was only half-Han, the blackhair heritage was who I was and who I remained. I always planned to get home if I could.

My chance came when I was sixteen and first taken on a raiding party to the south. I deliberately lagged behind the other riders who were all intent on the way ahead. When we were well inside Chao, I was already far back, almost out of sight, and slipped down into a glade. My horse and I found a good hiding place and stayed quiet for a day or two. I don't know that the Hsiung-nu warriors even missed me, battle-crazed as they were, until they were well on their way home and it was much too late to turn back to recapture one youngster.

I made my way back to Hantan and found it in ruins. I learned my father had gone over to the Ch'in army at a crucial moment. In fact, his defection may have led to the Chao defeat. Four years had gone by; it seems like nothing now, but then it was a quarter of my life. I was bereft, with no means of making a living apart from my martial skills, and no chance of joining the Ch'in army, which apart from welcoming useful turncoat generals was the sole property of men born and raised in Ch'in.

No employment, no food. Near starvation, I sold my posterity as many of you did, for a livelihood as a servant. With a horde of other recent eunuchs, I was brought here to the palace. My fighting skills were observed and noted, and one day I found myself selected as a part of the king's guard. I had, I will say quite immodestly, acquired great skill with horses, and that led directly to my service as a charioteer.

Eventually, since I was the best horseman in the palace, I was chosen to drive the king's chariot. I will not say it has been the best life I could have made for myself, but it has had its moments!

"Thank you, Tu Mu...Lo Yin," said Han Yin, "what have you to say to your messmates?"

Hard to understand, as always, because of his stub of a tongue, Lo Yin, the Emperor's Chief Dresser, grinned broadly. He coughed several times into his fan, set it aside, and began to mumble.

Lo Yin

I must have been an exceptionally ugly baby, perhaps even more ugly than I am now, with my crooked nose and my "moomf, moomf" speech.

In any case, on the meadow of a hillside deep in the far south principality of Shu—a stretch normally reserved for exposing girl babies—a boy baby was placed one night. It was me, doubtlessly screaming my lungs out. A passing hermit named Han Shan who lived in the pine forest far above the meadow heard me. This is the story he told me, of course, as I have no recollection of any of it.

Hearing the loud cries, he knew at once that it must be a boy baby who was yelling so much, a gander among geese. He negotiated his way among the little bundles until he came to me and on a whim, he picked me up and took me to his cabin, where no one else ever came.

I must tell you that I have no idea why he picked me up. My guess today is that he was a lonely man—a problem for hermits, you know—and he might have thought I would make a good pet. I expect I did.

He spent most of his waking hours with me, teaching me to read and write so early in my life I cannot remember being illiterate. Interesting, isn't it, that we are all literate? I would say that as a class, eunuchs are among the dumbest, least educated people in the Ch'in Empire. Yet here we are, quick-witted, one and all. Is it any wonder that we have received preferment in the royal service?

I do not include you, Chia Tao. You got here by the luck of the dumb.

In any case, I grew up alone, for the most part, until the

hermit died while carrying a heavy bundle of wood to the cabin. If he had only let me help out sometimes...!

I came down the mountain after I buried the hermit and was fortunate enough to find a family that was willing to adopt me, despite my ugliness. And though they later sold me to the cock-choppers as a practical matter, I bear them no grudges because for some years at least, I was loved and embraced by the joy of family life. So that's how I got here. And like everyone else in this room, I did well, even if it is rising to my august task of putting the undergarments on a fat, balding, dyspeptic, boring maniac. They took my tongue to keep me from telling imperial secrets, but if you can understand me—Lo Yin said, speaking very slowly and for him, distinctly—CAN YOU UNDERSTAND ME? We nodded.

But that precaution failed. One of the things you learn when you work intimately with a tyrant is that the men around him are invariably inferior men. I exclude Li Ssu from that, but I decidedly do not exclude Chao Kao! His success depends on one thing only: like the Emperor, he is utterly single-minded.

Friends, he said (I thought perhaps his eyes looked a little moist, but it may have been the candlelight. In any case, Lo Yin would be the last man in the world to cry over anything whatsoever), I began here in this room—it is my father and mother, and you are my brothers. If, as rumor has it, one can take but one memory to the Yellow Spring, it will be the memory of you here in our beautiful Jade Room.

I'm done.

A long silence.

Finally Han Yin said, "Thank you, Lo Yin, your feelings are reciprocated by every man here. We will hear next from Wang Ts'ao, our dear Major Domo of the Royal Palaces; and then from Chia Tao, Major Domo of the Concubine Residences."

"End of the line as usual," said Chia Tao. "Go ahead, friend Wang."

Wang Ts'ao

Like Chao Kao, I am a 'natural,' not castrated but incapable of reproduction. I have the business the rest of you lack, but it just doesn't do anything whole men would see as dangerous.

This makes me a rarity in our service and, of course, gave me a huge leg up for promotions because I have never known a time when I was not of this service. And, modesty aside, I was a bright lad and have been an intelligent and hard-working man all my adult life. That is why I manage all the tens of thousands of tasks carried out by thousands of eunuchs under my command, and not just here in the major palace but in all the many palaces occupied by the late emperor, especially during the last few dark years. That was when he scurried secretly from palace to palace with hordes of retainers, courtiers and soldiers, in that order, scrambling along right after him. What a ridiculous life he—we—have led!

It was not just the soothsayers and necromancers that rattled the emperor into hiding away like that, you know. The gods had a hand in it.

After the emperor cut down all the trees on the mountain that was home to the Lady of the River, leaving her homeless, she fled west in a silver chariot drawn by yellow eagles—far, far to the west, in fact, to the Jade Mountain, home of the Queen Mother of the West. She burst through the doors of her Mother's palace without any ceremony, raced to the throne, and fell weeping into the Mother's capacious dwelling—it is said to be so large that at times Moon and Sun sleep in it together.

Naturally, the Queen Mother of the West asked her beloved daughter what the matter was. It is that dreadful Ch'in Shih-huang-ti, she replied, between sobs. He has destroyed my home in a fit of pique and all because he lost a bit of jade!

Since Jade Mountain is composed entirely of jade, that was hardly impressive to the Queen Mother. What shall we do to him? she asked.

Well, said the Lady of the River, I have heard that he stays up every night studying letters and documents, governing his kingdom. Can we do something simple, like give him terrible headaches every night so that he cannot sleep?

Done, said the Queen.

And I have been told that he is a terrible coward as well, said the Lady. Could we make him even more terrified of death than he is already?

He trembles day and night, said the Queen Mother. He will never have a happy day for the remainder of his life.

The Lady was mollified and the Queen was pleased at having been able to pay back an insult to her favorite daughter. They had a little wine—the gods can drink wine twenty-four hours a day, you know, and never become nauseous—and then they began a game of tiles with two other goddesses that as far as I know is going on yet.

So when the magicians went to work on our late emperor, they did not have the former blustering, murderous bully to work with. All that was left was a spineless, much weakened coward, only able to show rare flashes of his former imperious self.

Apart from having to move the entire court every night, which was a pain, I was very pleased. I will tell you truly, I always hated him.

"Thank you, Wang Ts'ao. Well said. I believe you speak for us all, and I for one believe every syllable of your story."

"And now, Chia Tao, I confess that I am eager to hear about your past."

Chia Tao

To start with, unlike most of the rest of you, I never did like women. Especially girls! I was much more interested in young men. Still am, for that matter, in my dreams. In the old days, when I had my business, Tu Mu, you would really have turned my head!

At which Tu Mu actually dropped his head and brought his

fan up so that it rested in front of his face like the roof of a shack. But I could see his ears were red. The rest of us were laughing—a great relief in a night that did not have the usual quota of jokes and laughter.

Not that I can do anything about any urges now, said Chia Tao. Well, if I'm to be honest with you now—although honestly, I don't know why I should be, as nobody else is—I never could. I was frail, not very well—have had a terrible cough all my life, as you know. And though not outstandingly ugly as, say, Lo Yin is—"I like that!"—sorry, Lo Yin, I thought you were asleep because your eye was wandering again. Well, anyway, I certainly was no beauty.

It was my bad fortune as a child and youth to live in a large house in Pengcheng belonging to a wealthy family—my family—that consisted almost entirely of women.

I had seven older sisters, all of whom would have been exposed if my father had not been so tender-hearted. They saw me, especially the younger girls, as a sort of living doll, I suppose. They dressed me in the most ridiculous clothing, miniature versions of the kinds of dresses you put on your daughters when you want young men to notice them so you can arrange marriages and get them out of your hair. They even played at binding my feet, but fortunately my mother put a stop to that, or I would be the proud owner of a couple of golden lotuses where my feet should be! They taught me how to sing, to dance, all the womanly arts.

Frankly, it was awful. It was worse than being beaten.

Then one day, the family received some bad news. A Ch'in army arrived and tore our whole city apart, killing most adults, enslaving others, and bringing quantities of children back to Ch'in for training as servants. I was such a child, and was castrated not long after I arrived in Hsienyang. I never saw my parents or any of my sisters again, and I feel sad about that to this day. There were one or two who had treated me kindly. I had loved them.

That's my story, such as it is. I know it's dull. What I would really like to tell you about is life in the concubine residences.

I know I complain about it endlessly, but it's really just the right sort of place for a fellow like me, someone with no interest in women. Their continual fighting by day, the disgusting stench of thousands of over-perfumed bodies, the noisy rutting at night—most of them have never been within twenty *li* of an emperor, so of course they turn to each other, the squabbles, the constant intrigues—tell me, what part of my present life would you like to hear about most?

No, no, that's fine, that's good, we shouted. Your early life is fascinating and sufficient—we've learned so much about you, thank you, thank you—various voices rose in protest and eyes rolled toward the ceiling.

"And you, Ssu-ma Ch'ien? In this time with us, your quiet, steady presence has made us esteem you," Han Yin said after the babble died down. "What would you like to tell us about your life as a whole man?"

Ssu-Ma Ch'ien

As you know, my friends, I have transcribed your tales as you told them to me. Such work keeps a clerk busy and gives little time to have feelings of his own, apart from wishing the ache in the fingers of his brush hand would go away! So I haven't reflected on what you, my brothers, have been saying, just getting it down. But I feel constricted now, as if there was a sort of poison sack around my heart. I do not know what to say to you. Please give me a moment.

My friends, I think you know my story better than I know yours. I was a fully grown man, with a profession and a family. I had been on the good side of King Cheng for a long time, and prospered. There were even rumors that I would receive the title and estates of a marquis, rich land with many peasants to produce more than ample food.

But of course, it all changed when I had an attack of

conscience just at a time in life when most of us begin to put away such things in favor of comfort and security. I wrote a memorandum of protest to the king, and he gave me a choice: exile, suicide or emasculation. Since either of the first two choices would have ended in the confiscation of my lands and thrown my family into beggary—and still worse, would have left my history of our times incomplete—I chose emasculation. For the rest, you have known me here and no doubt made up your minds about me.

What I want to say is that your courage, your gaiety and your talents for fellowship have breathed the life back into me. I was a lost hulk without feelings when I entered the service of the Emperor. All I had then was an utter determination to finish my *Records of the Grand Historian*, the kind of determination a dog will show when he is guarding a bone.

What you have done for me is beyond words. It has been, it is, a joy to be alive again, a joy to know men like you. And you are not half-men, you are the wholest men I know. If I have a family, it is you. I am more grateful than I can express in words.

* * * * * * * *

Once I was finished, I seemed to have no life left.

I could have said no more even if I had wanted to, being completely choked up. The storytellers were just blurs in my eyes. But presently, they began to tap their fans on the floor, loud and long.

When it was quiet, Han Yin, in the gentlest way, said it was time for me to leave. They would be staying on.

As I looked back a final time before crawling into the passageway, they were reaching for each others' hands. Every man present had drunk from the white bottle, allies and spies alike. No one was speaking.

Quiet as it then was, the Jade Room was not as still as the stars that shone in the clear sky above the great central courtyard of the Forbidden City. This palace of a dead emperor. He was gone; all the imperatives of life in his service were gone, too, the rules we hated and counted on. What more could be taken away? What next?

My slippers crunched lightly on new snow and old ice. A long walk lay ahead.

* * * * * * * *

At home, I turned and turned on my mat, warm enough but unable to sleep.

I knew they would not be found until morning, perhaps not right away even then. Perhaps the odor of the corpses would give them away. Because the passageway was not known to Han Yin's servants, the wall would have to be broken through, probably damaging one or another of the corpses in that undignified process. And these, both the murderers and those who had remained faithful, were my dearest, perhaps my only, friends! These supposedly weak and timid eunuchs had all chosen to die as friends, not to live as betrayers. I couldn't stop thinking about them—sleep simply would not begin. Finally, I got up, lit a lamp and began to write. Poetry, I think.

When I looked up from my writing desk again, the black of pre-dawn night was gone and the air outside was actually visible, not the clarity of daylight but a pearly gray that softened everything I could see, the patterns of the walkways, the dragons on the roofs, a servant hurrying past with a lantern. Though I could not see the flakes yet, I knew it was snowing gently.

I sat looking into the nothingness for some time, then stumbled off to make a pot of tea.

The Journey to Mount Li
Ssu-Ma Ch'ien's Tale

The useless, sodden Second Emperor Hu-hai is now nearly invisible to his court, sealed off by the order of Chao Kao except for brief, silent appearances once a week. I am told that his days and nights are spent in alcoholic stupor, and he is ministered to constantly by well-instructed courtesans. His apartments are heated to the point of being nearly unbearable; he is said to be comatose most of the time.

Of course the Chamberlain, Chao Kao, is emperor in all but name.

His list of those to be executed is posted in the court each morning. Many who read it do so trembling, but others find its essential insanity very humorous. Minus the stability, such as it was, of his closest allies—the eunuchs who took poison with their brothers—Chao Kao careens from suspicion to suspicion like a boulder roaring down a mountain, and wherever his eye stops, death lights its fires. He had most of Hu-hai's older brothers killed; those who survived only managed to do so because they were out of reach. And he also had on his conscience, if any, the tragic death of the ten royal princesses who were forced to hang themselves. Their deaths may have been gentle by comparison with most of the murders done by Chao Kao's assassins, but they aren't so pretty when one sees the bulging eyes and bursting tongue of a lovely fourteen-year-old girl as she slowly strangles to death.

And he has gone further. He has killed virtually all the palace servants except for those whom he knows to be loyal to himself; and that number thins each day as he finds or imagines some new reason for mistrust. Many ministers, too, are dead or exiled, and those who remain are stringless marionettes.

Chao Kao is entirely focused on the world inside the palace, with the result that the chaos around the throne is reflected by chaos throughout the empire. The Confucian scholars are reportedly making their presence felt among the ancient families once more, prophesying that the Ch'in Empire is tottering. In fact, it is worse than that.

I hear that a number of military leaders, peasants and aristocrats from the ancient families are gathering new armies throughout the empire, and are said to be slowly converging on the land between the passes. With our armies leaderless, what will stop them from entering Ch'in?

* * * * * * * *

When one compares great villains, a few gold threads appear among the masses of dark ones.

The late Li Ssu seems almost benevolent compared with the relentless darkness that is Chao Kao. Li Ssu, who carried the political philosophy of Legalism further than anyone else ever had, who caused the unjust death of millions of people, who— perhaps this is least forgivable—encouraged Ch'in Shih-huang-ti in every mad idea so that he, Li Ssu, could take the reins of empire in hand more firmly.

But Li Ssu nonetheless had at least some sense of the welfare of the state. After all, he simplified our written scripts (with great benefit to me!), unified weights and measures, created a great network of roadways that were used for commerce as well as military travel, organized the building of the Great Wall. And of course, much more.

In his last months, when he must have felt completely hopeless, he sent memorandum after memorandum to Hu-hai urging moderation and conscientious rule. Wasted, of course, because none of Li Ssu's advice ever reached Hu-hai. All were intercepted by Chao Kao, who as far as I can tell, has no waking idea that goes beyond personal aggrandizement. He is utterly merciless and his cruelty is exceeded only by his treachery. So Li Ssu does not look quite so bad, compared to Chao Kao. But no one is weeping over his demise.

* * * * * * * *

Now Chao Kao is the only power in Ch'in. But he is far from satisfied.

One day recently, he gathered the remains of the Emperor's court in the Grand Hall. Hu-hai was present, looking lost and tiny on the high imperial throne.

"Your Majesty, I have procured for your zoo a rare beast, a miniature horse from the Great Desert to the West," shouted Chao Kao. "Bring it in, please," he said to an attendant.

Through bleary eyes, Hu-hai looked at the beast that was then led in and began laughing right away. "Chao Kao, that is a spotted deer, an ordinary deer!"

"No, Your Majesty, it is a tiny horse! Is it not a horse?" Chao Kao called out to the nobles and counselors in the Hall, every one hand-picked by him, of course. They assented enthusiastically.

Hu-hai began to distrust his own eyes, which by now were none too trustworthy. As he entered a palanquin preparatory to leaving the court, he was seen to be shaking his head. When he was gone from the Hall, everyone roared with laughter.

* * * * * * * *

A moment of relative quiet in the empire came when, after all Ch'in's generals had been killed or forced to commit suicide, a tax man, one Chang Han, gathered the remnants of the Ch'in's army and destroyed the first of the rebel generals, Chen She, as well as other rebels in many parts of the empire.

But all too soon the army of a new rebel, an aristocrat from the former state of Ch'u named Hsiang Yu, met the previously successful Ch'in general, Chang Han, and defeated him soundly, though Chang Han was able to escape with a few subordinates. He returned to Hsienyang, and Chao Kao immediately sent him a forged letter from Hu-hai ordering him to commit suicide. But Chang Han was in touch with a close friend who served Hsiang Yu, who urged him to flee the capital and join forces with Hsiang. This he did, leaving the capital of Ch'in all but defenseless.

Chao Kao has secretly agreed to surrender to yet another rebel leader, a peasant named Liu Pang, who was coming through the passes unopposed with tens of thousands of soldiers. Who knows if that rumor is true or not? We are in limbo. This cannot possibly go on.

* * * * * * * *

The useless disaster of a puppet emperor, Erh Shih-huang-ti, otherwise known to all as the wastrel Hu-hai, youngest son of the real emperor, is dead, a suicide either by his own hand, or the 'mercy' of a concubine, or, who knows, the jeweled dagger of Chao Kao himself.

Chao Kao pretended bandits had gotten inside the palace and sent his soldiers to the court, ostensibly to protect the emperor but in fact to kill him. The story goes that Hu-hai could not face them and killed himself. Whether that is true or not, what difference does it make?

Following the Second Emperor's death, Chao Kao ordered all surviving ministers and princes to come to the Grand Hall of the palace. His intention was to proclaim himself emperor. He and his bodyguard, a few hundred men, went there, but when they got there, they were met by utter silence. No one had come; all were hiding in their homes and palaces. Chao Kao, for the first time, I think, lost his nerve and retired to his apartments to try to think what to do.

* * * * * * * *

Chao Kao has issued a proclamation that Tzu-ying, a nephew of Hu-hai's, has a legitimate claim to the throne of Ch'in and should therefore be proclaimed Third Emperor. He also declared that Hu-hai was a tyrant not worthy of burial in the imperial ancestral tomb. That much, at least, was truthful; few have been less worthy of any honor than Hu-hai!

Chao Kao sent a messenger with a memorandum about the accession to Tzu-ying and instructed him to abstain from meat for five days prior to being crowned. The messenger also carried the imperial seal. My informant was of the opinion that Chao Kao's secret plan was to kill Tzu-ying when he came to the palace for the coronation.

But the plan failed dismally. Claiming illness, Tzu-ying begged Chao Kao to come to him instead, and when he did—how foolish!—soldiers loyal to the imperial family cut Chao Kao into small pieces. I cannot imagine that Chao Kao would ever have done such a stupid thing if my friends, the Storytellers, who served him well, had been alive to advise him.

The fear and hatred of Chao Kao was so great that Ch'in cavalrymen were given bags, each containing one piece of Chao Kao, and commanded to ride out of Hsienyang in all directions for at least three days, then bury the pieces in hidden places.

The day after Chao Kao's death, Tzu-ying became Third Emperor. He made a brave start, refusing to take revenge on Chao Kao's followers, and rescinding the order forbidding Hu-hai to be buried in the royal tombs, as, whatever his faults, he had been, indeed, the "Son of Heaven." The cynic in me wishes to add that Hu-hai had to have been the "Son of Heaven," in order for Tzu-ying to be one.

In any case, I don't believe Tzu-ying will occupy the throne for long. In the woods and hills of Ch'in, there are tigers.

* * * * * * * *

I was right. The one-time peasant turned general named Liu Pang did attack Hsienyang, having joined forces with the aristocrat, Hsiang Yu. And Tzu-ying, the Third Emperor, lost his nerve. In a cowardly effort to save his life, Tzu-ying dressed himself as a commoner and rode out in a plain carriage to beg Liu Pang for a chance to surrender. He carried the imperial seal and signal tally in his hands and had tied a silk cord around his throat, betokening servitude. How pathetic!

The self-styled Duke of P'ei, Liu Pang, who had come toward Hsienyang through the unguarded Wu Pass, accepted Tzu-ying's surrender. But when Hsiang Yu, who commands the larger army, caught up with Liu Pang, he immediately beheaded Tzu-ying.

The empire Ch'in Shih-huang-ti had said would last forever was blown out like a taper in the wind, leaving only darkness behind.

I am sure that Hsienyang will not survive the rebel army's arrival. A bloodthirsty man, for all of his ancient, ostensibly noble lineage, Hsiang Yu and his men are sure to loot the city and burn it to the ground. If Liu Pang doesn't get there first.

Perhaps the lost armies of Hantan, the 400,000 men who were buried alive by the order of the First Emperor's grandfather, are laughing in hell today. The balls I used to have are itching.

* * * * * * * *

North of Hsienyang
Before dawn a few days ago, the older of my grandsons and I left the imperial palace and came north once again to the country estate of my ancestors.

The palace gates and the city gates were wide open; there were no guards to check passes. No one was here to greet us. The family and the servants have fled to Hsienyang, I think, even though I believe it has become the least safe place in the world, with the enemy armies of Hsiang Yu and Liu Pang headed toward it through the great pass no longer defended by Ch'in. They will burn everything in their path—for warmth, if for no other reason, because the Ch'in winter is already freezing and bitter.

This will be the final entry in my journal here at the Ssu-ma estate. When my grandson and I have to leave here, we will not be running to the city. As soon as I finish these final notes, we will go to Mount Li, to the First Emperor's tomb. My grandson keeps watch for signs of smoke in the distance.

* * * * * * * *

They are coming! There are fires on the hills.

We have packed an oxcart with the *Records of the Grand Historian* and the *Tales of the First Emperor*. A fragile burden indeed—hundreds of bundled strips of bamboo, each bundle secured with silk. An ox hitched to the cart stands waiting just beyond the moon door of my scholar's garden; it is bare and brown now, like death, but unlike us, it may bloom again.

We will drive the cart on the back road to Mount Li, where Han Yin and my other friends long ago arranged a safe hiding place for our documents and for us. Once there, the boy and I are to go on a longer journey.

I had asked him not to come with me—not that there is any safety anywhere now—but he refuses to leave my side. I have the deepest feelings of guilt and sadness about him, the more so since he has been of enormous help to me in these past two years. With my consent, he undertook to do some work on the manuscript, checking facts and offering suggestions here and there about the writing. To my great surprise—though it should not have been a surprise—I see he has a considerable gift as a historian, especially for one not yet twenty! That gift can never flower now. I am so sad that he has not had his chance to make a name for himself or to contribute to the work of remembering the past. For me, my soul yearns upward, my flesh longs for earth. I have done my work.

If Kuan Yin, the Goddess of Mercy, smiles, these tales of the rise and fall of an emperor will not be found for a long time. All of us, conquerors and kings, peasants and slaves, eunuchs, wives and concubines, will be dust. The contentions of the present age that are burning all across the vast plains and mountains of the empire of Ch'in will lie drowned and forgotten in the river of time.

We hear war drums on the wind. Time we were going.

* * * * * * *

This is my final entry.

We have completed our journey, entering the mausoleum with our scrolls, down a long, well-hidden secret passage that begins far south of the burial mound. The passage, barely large enough to crawl down—so like the entryway to the Jade Room—leads to a secret room hidden underneath the emperor's catafalque.

No man still alive has ever seen his burial chamber, as all the workers were killed, but I have been told the catafalque lies on a bronze dragon's back that rests in turn at the center of an island shaped like the empire of Ch'in. It is said to be surrounded by ever-flowing rivers of mercury. The roof is set with precious stones made to shine like stars in the night sky. On the floor of the huge burial chamber, an underground replica of Hsienyang spreads out, the palaces, of course, not the hovels.

Beyond the dead city stand thousands of clay soldiers, armed with bronze weapons and ready to repel enemies in the underworld and die again for the emperor. Their presence is doubtless a great comfort to my boyhood friend, Prince Cheng. He could always convince himself of anything; conjuring an army of clay to life would be nothing for him. I wonder how his soldiers will fare when a real army finds them? Not well, I think.

Cheng began many great projects, but rarely finished any— not the Great Wall, not his search for the Immortals, not even his beloved Epang Palace. So, as the scholars always said, the Mandate of Heaven was removed from him. He did not serve his people well and they rebelled. Near death, he trusted two men, Li Ssu and Chao Kao, to install his eldest son as the next emperor, but they betrayed and killed him. What does it come to?

I do not know if Master K'ung was right about men being mostly good, but I am certain of one thing: the Legalists are wrong. If you push men down hard enough, they are sure to rise.

Our lamp is dimming; the air is getting cold. My grandson pulled a lever that filled our passage into this small room below the First Emperor's burial chamber with dirt. Now we and our histories are sealed in and the tales of my friends of the Jade Room, as well as my own writings, are safely hidden until you come. I hope.

We lie down together; my grandson rests his head on my right shoulder.

When you come, I expect we will be here. I pray that the Great Royal Library at Hsienyang, the last repository of so many ancient documents, will not be destroyed. But I don't think my prayer will have a good answer.

— Ssu-ma Ch'ien, Grand Historian

The Nomad Girl*

On clear nights I see the moon rising
through a small window in my room,
but it is the Chinese pillow moon,

not the hunting moon of the Hsiung-nu,
the lean mountain moon that runs free
on the high peaks of the K'unlun.

Here they build high walls—as if
it is bad luck to see the horizon.
They are frightened of wind!

My brother can shoot a flying bird
riding at full gallop,
and reach it as it hits the ground.

Our father treated both of us the same.
He never told me, "You can't do this,
your feet too small, your arms too weak."

These cripple women are soft!
They put shiny things in their hair.
They whisper, "My lover is this—he is that..."

My father will send me secret wings some day
and then my song will be no songbird's fluting
but the scream of the hawk, that loves what it kills.

---

* This poem reverses the famous legend in China about a Chinese noble
lady who is taken by barbarians and goes to live with them. She marries a
chieftain, has children, and grows old. When, many years later, she is released
and returns to China, she finds to her sorrow that she is no longer at home
in either place.

The Journey of Baroness Hsu

When his state was destroyed
the Duke of Wei lamented.
His sister, the Baroness Hsu,
came far to console him.

Traveling east, she saw
the five-star dragon, its mouth
red Antares, breathe fire
into the summer night.

Stopping by rivers at dusk
she gave bread to the river lords
and listened to the *hoong*,
sad song of mulberry leaves.

The Herd Boy and Weaver Maid
kept her company on the journey,
one riding north, one south
of the River of Silver.

Once a year the two lovers meet
on a bridge magpies make for them,
all night they run to each other
until the soft dawn rises.

She brought Wei a cup of water
from the Lady of the River Hsi,
twigs of plum blossoms
gathered on South Mountain
...and told him of all these things.

Hills Rising above Clouds

Down there are dragons
curled like flags on a still day.
And dancers, barefoot on wet streets.
Down there the high official, the low
beggar, sleep on two sides of a moon gate.
Freed of broom and whip,
a concubine and a daughter-in-law
lie hip to hip whispering stories.
West Lake fairies drift like dragonflies
over the deepest places...no one
can guess what they will do next.
On the hill road above the city
a crazy man is walking in white air.
Every joint in his body aches
with loneliness, but he is happy;
very soon the Immortals will appear
and bring him to the Isle.

AFTERWORDS

Chronology of the Reign of Ch'in Shih-Huang-Ti, First Emperor*

258 B.C. Ying Cheng, the future First Emperor, is born

250 B.C. Lu Pu-wei, the merchant, is made Prime Minister of Ch'in

245 B.C. On the death of his father, Cheng becomes King of Ch'in

245 B.C. Lu Pu-wei names himself Regent for the boy-king

238 B.C. Lao Ai rebels against King Cheng and is killed

237 B.C. Lu Pu-wei is exiled to Shu in the south, later commits suicide

227 B.C. Assassin Ching K'o attempts to kill King Cheng

221 B.C. Ch'i, the last feudal state, surrenders without a battle

221 B.C. King Cheng becomes Ch'in Shih-huang-ti, First Emperor

219 B.C. Li Ssu becomes Grand Counselor of Ch'in

219 B.C. First Emperor begins fruitless search for Elixir of Immortality

214 B.C. General Meng T'ien is building the Great Wall

213 B.C. The ancient *Thirteen Classics* are almost all burned

212 B.C. First Emperor murders over four hundred scholars

212 B.C. First Emperor banishes eldest son, Crown Prince Fu-su, to the Great Wall

212 B.C. Work begins on the huge Epang Palace

210 B.C. During royal tour in the south, First Emperor dies

210 B.C. Chao Kao, Chief Eunuch, and Li Ssu, Grand Counselor, join forces, plot suicides of Fu-su and Meng T'ien, put First Emperor's younger son, Hu-hai, on the throne; Hui-hai becomes Second Emperor

209 B.C. Popular uprisings everywhere

208 B.C. Chao Kao dominates empire, Li Ssu is killed

207 B.C.   Hu-hai, Second Emperor, commits suicide and
            nephew Tzu-ying becomes Third Emperor

207 B.C.   Chao Kao killed by Third Emperor

206 B.C.   Third Emperor submits to rebels and is killed

206 B.C.   Rebels burn Ch'in capital, Hsienyang, and loot
            Mount Li, tomb of First Emperor

206 B.C.   Empire divided up by rival generals, who then
            fall out

202 B.C.   Liu Pang, the peasant, becomes emperor, founds
            Han Dynasty, which will last more than four
            hundred years with one brief break

---

* This time-line is largely based on Sir Arthur Cotterell's chronology in his
excellent book, *The First Emperor of China: The Greatest Archeological Find of
Our Time*, published in 1981 by Holt, Rinehart and Winston. Must reading
for anyone interested in this pivotal period in the history of China and the
world.

The Real Life of Ssu-Ma Ch'ien, the Grand Historian

At the end of *First Emperor: Tales from the Jade Room*, some of the fictional Ssu-ma Ch'ien's last thoughts were of the royal library at Hsienyang, the only place in which the precious art of lore and learning of previous ages, and his own, were left. As he feared, that library was indeed burned, and many masterworks were lost.

But across the vast realm of the Ch'in Empire, bits and pieces of nearly all the ancient writings had been kept in secret, at great risk, by people who believed in learning and followed the old ways, especially Confucianism. Thanks to these brave souls, when the Ch'in was succeeded by the dynasty known as Former Han (forerunner of the historic Han Dynasty) from 206 B.C., much of the ancient learning was recovered and, where necessary, pieced together.

The famous leader of this work of reclamation was the real Ssu-ma Ch'ien, the Grand Historian, who served Han Emperor Wu, a hundred years after Ch'in's downfall. Ssu-ma Ch'ien wrote a history of the blackhairs, as the Han Chinese called themselves. His book—also in part his father's book—titled *Shih Chi*, or *Records of the Grand Historian*, is regarded by the Chinese as their most important historical work, ancient or modern. It is one of the world's great histories.

Ssu-ma Ch'ien's birth and death dates are uncertain, but the great translator Burton Watson, in his book, *Records of the Grand Historian (Ch'in Dynasty)*, published by Columbia University Press, 1991, suggests the years 145 to 89 B.C., with question marks.

In one disastrous year, Ssu-ma Ch'ien sent a memorandum to Emperor Wu in defense of a Han general, Li Ling, who had to surrender to a much larger force of barbarians in China's north, the Hsiung-nu. For speaking out, Ssu-ma Ch'ien was sentenced to choose castration or suicide. Quoting the famous scholar Burton Watson, "...he chose to suffer the shame of mutilation in order that he might finish the writing of his history... This...assured him a place of honor among the world's great historians."

While gathering material for this fictional history of the First Emperor, I was of course reading Ssu-ma Ch'ien, who with a successor, Pan Ku, provided virtually our only written sources of near-contemporary information about the First Emperor. I was engaged by Ssu-ma Ch'ien's fine writing, ever-enquiring mind, unwavering sense of honor, and perhaps most of all, his choice to live with castration so he could go on with his writing.

I had already created a group of high-ranking imperial servants, all fictional, and employed them to tell the stories of the First Emperor's life. Now, I thought, why not bring Ssu-ma Ch'ien back in time and make him the eunuch storytellers' Recording Secretary! So that's how Ssu-ma Ch'ien got into this book.

For Further Reading

If you want to steep yourself in the fascinating prehistory and history of ancient China, here are books I read in the course of writing this novel. Every one was rewarding, most were invaluable, some crucial. This is not a complete list of the relevant books in English; I read for pleasure and not in an organized way. Also, since my reading took place over roughly thirty-three years, I can't guarantee you will find all the books listed here. Whatever in my book is not pure imagination came from one or another or several of these books. I take full responsibility for whether or not I understood what I was reading, and for all mistakes, misjudgments and misunderstandings in this book.

BOOKS ABOUT ANCIENT CHINA, ESPECIALLY THE CH'IN EMPIRE

Clements, Jonathan, *The First Emperor of China*, Sutton Publishing Limited, 2006 (brief summary of the life of the emperor)

Cotterell, Sir Arthur, *The First Emperor of China: The Greatest Archeological Find of Our Time*, Holt, Rinehart & Winston, 1981 (superb study, must reading)

Debaine-Francfort, Corinne, *The Search for Ancient China*, Harry N. Abrams, 1999 (brief, excellent pictorial summary, focused on archeology)

Levi, Jean, *The Chinese Emperor: A Novel*, Harcourt Brace Jovanovitch (novel by a master)

Murowchik, Robert E., General Editor, Cradles of Civilization, University of Oklahoma Press, 1994

Pan Ku, *The History of the Former Han Dynasty*, Two Volumes, The American Council of Learned Societies, Third Printing, 1960 (background on the succession of the Han Dynasty after the decimation of the Ch'in)

Ssu-ma Ch'ien, Burton Watson, Translator, *Records of the Grand Historian: The Ch'in Dynasty*, Columbia University Press, 1993

Yuan Yang and Xiao Ding, *Tales of Emperor Qin Shihuang*, Foreign Languages Press, Beijing, 1999

BOOKS FOCUSING ON ARCHAEOLOGY

Chang, Kwang-Chih, *The Archaeology of Ancient China*, Third Edition, Yale University Press, 1977 (excellent survey of archeological findings up to 221 B.C. by a pre-eminent scholar)

Chang, Kwang-Chih, *The Formation of Chinese Civilization: An Archaeological Perspective*, Yale University Press, 2005 (the best, most thorough collection of its kind, a breakthrough book)

Chang, Kwang-Chih, Editor, *The Formation of Chinese Civilization: An Archaeological Perspective*, Yale University Press, 2005 (published twenty-five years after the earlier volume, it is amazing to see what has been learned and what is surmised today! Among other things, the book celebrates the introduction of Western scholarship in collaboration with Eastern science and non-Marxist ideas presented alongside Marxist ideas)

Murowchick, General Editor, *Cradles of Civilization: China, Ancient Culture, Modern Land*, University of Oklahoma Press, 1994

Rawson, Jessica, *Ancient China: Art and Archaeology*, Harper & Row, 1980

BOOKS FOCUSING ON HISTORY

Blunden, Caroline and Elvin, Mark, *Cultural Atlas of China*, Revised Edition, Checkmark Books (a Division of Facts on File), 1998 (a beautiful, fascinating book)

Cotterell, Sir Arthur, *China: A Cultural History*, Meridian, 1988

Fairbank, John King and Goldman, Merle, *China: A New History*, Enlarged Edition, Belknap Press of Harvard University Press, 1998 (You cannot improve on this book for lucid explanation and sensible theorizing)

Fitzgerald, C.P., China: *A Short Cultural History*, Barrie & Jenkins, 1935

Gernet, Jacques, *A History of Chinese Civilization*, Cambridge University Press, 1982

Granet, Marcel, *Chinese Civilization*, Meridian Books, 1958

Hucker, Charles O., *China's Imperial Past: An Introduction to Chinese History and Culture*, Stanford University Press, 1975

Latourette, Kenneth Scott, *A Short History of the Far East*, Fourth Edition, The Macmillan Company, 1964

Spence, Jonathan D., *Emperor of China: Self-Portrait of Kang-Hsi*, Alfred A. Knopf, 1975

Wu, K.C., *The Chinese Heritage*, Crown Publishers, 1982

BOOKS ON RELIGION, LITERATURE, PHILOSOPHY

Bynner, Witter, Translator, *The Way of Life According to Lao Tzu*, The Berkeley Publishing Group, 1972

Chang, K.C., *Art, Myth, and Ritual: The Path to Political Authority in Ancient China*, Harvard University Press, 1983

Denma Translation Group, Translators, *Sun Tzu's The Art of War*, Shambala Publications, Inc. 2001

Fingarette, Herbert, *Confucius—The Secular as Sacred*, Harper & Row, 1972

Legge, James, Translator, *The I Ching: The Book of Changes*, Dover Edition, 1965 (there are many editions but this is the original one)

Waley, Arthur, Translator, *The Analects of Confucius*, Vintage Books, 1938

Watson, Burton, *Chuang Tzu: Basic Writings*, Columbia University Press, 1964

Watson, Burton, *Han Fei Tzu: Basic Writings*, Columbia University Press, 1964

Wing-Tsit, Chan, *A Source Book in Chinese Philosophy*, Princeton University Press, 1963

BOOKS OF CHINESE STORIES
100 Pearls of Chinese Wisdom, Sinolingua, 1999

The Traditional Chinese Festivals and Tales, Chongqing Publishing House, 2001

Birch, Cyril, Editor, *Anthology of Chinese Literature, from early times to the fourteenth century*, Grove Press, 1965

Birrell, Anne, Translator, *The Classic of Mountains and Seas*, Penguin Books, 1999

Birrell, Anne, *Chinese Myths*, British Museum Press/The University of Texas Press, 2000

Carpenter, Frances, *Tales of a Chinese Grandmother*, Tuttle Publishing, 1973

Roberts, Moss, Translator/Editor, *Chinese Fairy Tales & Fantasies*, Pantheon Books, 1975

Spence, Jonathan, *The Death of Woman Wang*, Penguin, 1978

Walls, Jan and Yvonnie, Translators, *West Lake: A Collection of Folktales*, Joint Publishing, 1980

Werner, E.T.C., *Myths & Legends of China*, Dover Publications, 1994

Zhang, Fang, *Animal Symbolism of the Chinese Zodiac*, Foreign Languages Press, 1999

GENERAL REFERENCE BOOKS
China: 7000 Years of Discovery, China's Ancient Technology, China Books & Periodicals, 1983

Aero, Rita, *Things Chinese*, Dolphin Books, 1980

Barraclough, Geoffrey, Editor, *The Times Atlas of World History*, Hammond, 1980 (super collection of maps and data)

Bloodworth, Dennis, *The Chinese Looking Glass*, Revised & Expanded, Farrar Strauss & Giroux, 1980

Blunden, Caroline and Elvin, Mark, *Cultural Atlas of China*, Revised Edition, Checkmark Books, 1998

Clayre, Alasdair, *The Heart of the Dragon*, Dragonbook, 1985

Perkins, Dorothy, *Encyclopedia of China*, Checkmark Books, 1999

Temple, Robert, *The Genius of China*, Prion Books Limited, 1998

SPECIALIZED STUDIES
Bodde, Dirk, *Festivals in Classical China*, Princeton University Press, 1973

Chung, Chih, *An Outline of Chinese Geography*, Foreign Languages Press, 1973

Creel, Herrlee, *The Origins of Statecraft in China*, Vol. One, The University of Chicago Press, 1970

Pruit, Ida, *A Daughter of Han: The Autobiography of a Chinese Working Woman*, Stanford University Press, 1945

Puett, Michael J., *To Become a God: Cosmology, Sacrifice, and Self-Divinization in Early China*, Harvard-Yenching Institute, 2002

Scholz, Piotr O., *Eunuchs and Castrati: A Cultural History*, Markus Wiener, Publishers, 2001

Yang, Martin C., *A Chinese Village*, Columbia University Press, 1945

BOOKS OF CHINESE POETRY IN TRANSLATION
Birrell, Anne, Translator, *New Songs from a Jade Terrace*, Penguin Books, 1986

Graham, A.C., Translator, *Poems of the Late T'ang*, Penguin Books, 1965

Hinton, David, Translator, *The Selected Poems of Po Chu-I*, New Directions, 1999

Hinton, David, Translator, *The Selected Poems of Tu Fu*, New Directions, 1989

Kwock, C.H., McHugh, Vincent, Translators, *Old Friend from Far Away*, North Point Press, 1990

Liu, James J.Y., *The Art of Chinese Poetry*, Midway Reprint, 1983

Liu, Wu-chi, Yucheng Lo, Iving, Editors, *Sunflower Splendor*, Anchor Press, 1975

Morris, Ivan, Editor, *Madly Singing in the Mountains*, Creative Arts Book Company, 1981

Red Pine, Translator, *Poems of the Masters: China's Classic Anthology of T'ang and Sung Dynasty Verse*, Copper Canyon Press, 2003

Rexroth, Kenneth, Translator, *Love and the Turning Year: One Hundred More Poems from the Chinese*, New Directions Press, 1970 (one of the greatest translators)

Rexroth, Kenneth, Translator, *Women Poets of China*, New Directions Press, 1972

Rorex, Robert and Fong, Wen, Translators, *Eighteen Songs of a Nomad Flute: The Story of Lady Wen–Chi*, The Metropolitan Museum of Art, 1974

Waley, Arthur, Translator, *The Book of Songs*, Grove Press, 1960 (classic anthology of the earliest Chinese poems)

Waley, Arthur, Translator, *Translations from the Chinese*, Alfred A. Knopf, 1941 (the masterpiece of the translator's art)

Yushu, Wang, Translator, *Selected Poems and Pictures of the T'ang Dynasty*, China Intercontinental Press, 2006

Watson, Burton, Translator, *Chinese Lyricism from the Second to the Twelfth Century*, Columbia University Press, 1971

Watson, Burton, Translator, *The Columbia Book of Chinese Poetry: From Early Times to the Twelfth Century*, Columbia University Press, 1994

Watson, Burton, Translator, *Su Tung-P'o: Selections from a Sung Dynasty Poet*, Columbia University Press, 1965

Weinberger, Eliot, Editor, *The New Directions Anthology of Classical Chinese Poetry*, New Directions, 2003

Yuanchung, Xu, *Selected Poems and Pictures of the Song Dynasty*, China Intercontinental Press, 2006

Yin-nan, Chan and Walmsley, Lewis C., *Poems by Wang Wei*, Charles E. Tuttle Company, 1958

Young, David, Translator, *Wang Wei, Li Po, Tu Fu, Li Ho*, Field Translation Series, 1980

TRAVEL GUIDES TO CHINA

Brown, J. D., *China: The 5 Most Memorable Trips*, Frommer's, 2003 (great armchair book when you're getting ready to go)

Thompson, Hugh, and Lane, Kathryn, Project Editors, *Eyewitness Travel Guides: China*, Dorling Kindersley Travel Guide, 2005 (ditto and great pictures!)

A Note to the Reader

I am not an old China hand; in fact, I first visited China in the fall of 2006 on an Elderhostel tour. Most of what I know about China came from books. If that surprises you—I hope it does—I think you may be interested in my tale.

China entered my heart through three passageways more than thirty years ago. The first opened when my friend from work, Kipp Cantor, visited me in a hospital, where I lay in traction resting a bad back. Since I could not read extended material, she brought me a very beautiful book of Arthur Waley's translations of Chinese poems. Of all the poetry I have read, I love them and their authors best. The second passage presented itself during a 1976 visit I made to the Metropolitan Museum in New York City, when I turned a gallery corner and saw a group of life-size terracotta warriors—a fragment of the army the First Emperor created to guard himself in the afterlife. The third passage, at that same exhibition, lit up with the immortal Shang Dynasty bronzes, for me the most beautiful of all human-made objects.

My interest and imagination thus fired up, I searched and found more Chinese poetry in translation, and also began to read every book I could find on ancient Chinese history. The rest is history—a semi-historical novel, at any rate, because it rests on fancy more than fact.

I am grateful to the authors of all the books I have read, but I want to single out two books in particular for their excellence. The first is *The First Emperor of China: The Greatest Archeological Find of Our Time*, by Arthur Cotterell, published by Holt, Rinehart and Winston in 1981. Sir Arthur has been my trustworthy guide to a time, place and man largely crusted over with legend. His book is thorough, lucid and persuasively argued. The second is *Chinese Myths*, by Anne Birrell, published cooperatively by the

British Museum Press and the University of Texas Press in 2000. This lively study by a noted scholar was written for general readers. She offers a superb selection of Chinese myths, vivid, fascinating and imaginative. If you read no other books in the preceding "For Further Reading" section, read these two!

I would like to thank Anne Walker Thoits Squires, who was present when this book began and encouraged my work on it with kindness and unflagging interest.

I am grateful to Anthony Skey, Dick Cluster, David Doneval, Matt Fusco, Ruth Ide, Bonnie Bishop, Andrea Walker Squires, Courtney Walsh and many other readers for their invaluable guidance and suggestions. I am tremendously in their debt, especially to Anthony* who has, at short notice, delivered me this review impression:

"Fantasy, legend, romance, humor, cruelty...all skillfully interwoven by Squires. His deep interest in China's ancient, mysterious civilization lights every page. Many scenes are cinematic in their sweep and grandeur. These imaginative, yet believable "tales from the jade room" will surely inspire a host of readers to study this fascinating culture, so different from that of the West."

I would like to thank a fine writer and teacher of creative writing, Erika Dreifus, who in her course on writing historical novels at the Harvard Extension School, said magic words to me: "How about turning in your first chapter next Tuesday?"

I am deeply grateful to my editors at Marshall Cavendish. Lee Mei Lin and See Phui Yee, who has edited the manuscript honestly, patiently, and with wonderful humor, are pearls of great worth. Thanks to Phui Yee in particular, I now understand the potential of the editor/author relationship to be collaborative rather than combative. Again and again, she has

---

* Anthony Skey, Lieutenant Colonel, U,S. Air Force (retired)

found potentially embarrassing mistakes and lapses in structure and gently called attention to them, making it not a chore but a considerable pleasure to set about correcting them. Thank you, Phui Yee!

I am most deeply indebted of all to my late mother, the painter Mac Squires, who taught me to want to be an artist and never stopped believing that I would achieve something worthwhile one day. She is my past, just as my wife, Bonnie Bishop, and my daughter, Andrea Walker Squires, are my present and future. I love you all and I dedicate this book to you.

Conrad Squires
Nahant, MA
December, 2008

About the Author

Conrad Squires is a writer and poet who lives halfway up a hill that overlooks Short Beach and the Boston Ships' Channel in Nahant, Massachusetts, just north of Boston. He is retired, having owned and managed a successful direct mail fundraising firm for over twenty-five years.

The greatest benefit of retirement is that it has given Conrad time to finish *First Emperor: Tales from the Jade Room*, an excursion into the life of China's greatest warrior, the man who essentially created modern China two hundred years before Christ.

Conrad is also the author of a chapbook of poems, *Dancing with the Switchman* (Puddinghouse Press, 2001) and a textbook, *Teach Yourself to Write Irresistible Fundraising Letters* (Bonus Books, 1993)